SEALS

SUB RESCUE

OPERATION ENDURANCE

S.M. GUNN

AVON BOOKS
An Imprint of HarperCollins*Publishers*

This is a work of fiction. Names, characters, places, and incidents are products of the author's imagination or are used fictitiously and are not to be construed as real. Any resemblance to actual events, locales, organizations, or persons, living or dead, is entirely coincidental.

AVON BOOKS
An Imprint of HarperCollins*Publishers*
10 East 53rd Street
New York, New York 10022-5299

Copyright © 2002 by Bill Fawcett & Associates
ISBN: 0-380-80829-3
www.avonbooks.com

First Avon Books paperback printing: March 2002

Avon Trademark Reg. U.S. Pat. Off. and in Other Countries, Marca Registrada, Hecho en U.S.A.
HarperCollins® is a trademark of HarperCollins Publishers Inc.

Printed in the U.S.A.

10 9 8 7 6 5 4 3 2 1

"SIR, ARE WE EXPECTED TO MAKE A SHIP TAKEDOWN ON A CIVILIAN CRAFT IN INTERNATIONAL WATERS?"

"No," Danzig said with some small amount of irritation. "Your target will be in the water."

"In the water?"

"Yes, Lieutenant," Danzig said. "For reasons we do not have to go into here, it is necessary for the target to appear to his guards to have been killed. The intent is for him to go over the side of the ship at a predetermined point. A team of you SEALs will be there to recover him."

Muttering among the SEALs could be heard in the room.

"The method of defection is a very unusual one," the CIA man said, "but it was suggested by the target. For reasons yet to be fully known, the man insists that the Soviets must think he's dead." Danzig paused briefly, then continued. "This man is one of the highest placed officials in the Soviet biological weapons program who has ever tried to defect to the West. The fact that he insists on such a risky defection has something to do with the information he's bringing out with him. Apparently, if they think he's alive, they will change or hide some portion of the program.

"I cannot emphasize this enough," Danzig said with feeling. "Getting this man out alive has *top priority* back in the States."

PROLOGUE

Late 1980s
Aralsk-7 Scientific Headquarters
Renaissance Island, Aral Sea
Kazakhstan/Uzbekistan
Union of Soviet Socialist Republics

The Aral Sea is brackish saltwater, with the area around it mostly arid desert or mountains. And those portions of land that are only semidesert are at most sparsely populated. An expanse of desolate, barren land: excellent for security purposes. Anyone entering who didn't belong would stand out immediately. Tourism was not a trade encouraged on the shores of the Aral Sea by its Soviet controllers.

The Aral Sea has been receding. The small town of Aralsk, on its northern shore, was once on the water but is now sixty miles from it. In the community, The Soviet Army's Fifteenth Directorate maintained facilities and housing for up to a thousand troops and personnel. It was the military command post for the facilities on Renaissance Island, the southernmost island within the Soviet Union.

Since 1954, the Soviet Union had been testing biological weapons on the island. Renaissance Island, the southernmost island within Soviet territory. Being completely surrounded by water, the officially named Scientific Field Testing Laboratory was secure from prying eyes.

The settlement at Aralsk-7 was located on the northern portion of the island, a ninety minute plane ride from Aralsk, on the mainland. It consisted of bar-

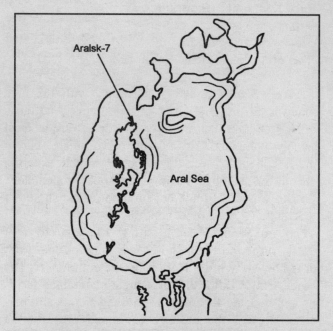

Aralsk-7

Aral Sea

Aerial view of Aral Sea

racks and residential houses for the officers and men of the military detachment responsible for the maintenance and functioning of the island's facilities. There was also a special group of several hundred soldiers trained in chemical and biological warfare techniques, Military Unit 25484, who worked directly with the weapons being tested. In addition, up to 150 scientists and special technicians would swell the small population of Aralsk-7 during testing periods. They would also stay in the barracks and other housing during the long, hot testing season running from May through September.

Warehouses, maintenance shops, a canteen, power station, and little else made up the balance of the living area at Aralsk-7. Resources were slim; even the drinking water had to be brought in by tanker. The structures were all stark, functional Soviet construction, concrete and block, or rough wood. Sufficient, but not very comfortable. Hot during the day and cold at night, Aralsk-7 was considered a hardship post in a country with a history of very hard living conditions.

Military flights from nearby Barkhan Airport were the only ones allowed to come or go from the island. The small seaport at Udobnaya Bay had an equally severe position. Supplies and materials came and went by water, but the bay also held the small fleet of fast patrol boats that guarded the waters around the island. The boats were armed, and their crews experienced in using their weapons.

For the scientists, staff, and soldiers of the facility, the main entertainment consisted of seeing whose batch of vodka or other locally brewed alcohol could dull the feelings of isolation the fastest.

The working compound was about a mile from the living area. High chain-link fences, topped with coils of sharp barbed wire, surrounded the compound. The fence lines ran in two parallel rows, separated by a ten-meter-wide strip of sand. At other military installations, the strip between the fences would ordinarily be patrolled by attack dogs. But using dogs would create the possibility of disease transmission at this particular site. Besides, dogs wouldn't subsist well on the rough diet of fatty sausages, vegetables, and black bread given to the scientists, technical personnel, and soldiers alike.

The substantial concrete buildings of the general laboratories, workshops, and vehicle bays were at one end of the rectangular compound. In the center area, surrounded by more fencing and overlooked by armed guards in towers, were the secure biological laboratories and animal buildings.

The test subject animals were in their own buildings inside this laboratory complex. These structures were well-insulated and -ventilated to keep the environment inside healthful for the hundreds of rodents, sheep, monkeys, and other livestock. The food for the animals, especially fresh fruit for the primates, was secured and regulated closely, for the animals had to be kept in prime condition for their lethal tests. Pilfering of their valuable food by the less well-fed staff was discouraged.

The tightest security of all was in the biological weapons labs themselves. Both biological and military security was ensured by using a three-zone system of barriers and filtration. The outer zone, Zone 1, which ran around the outside wall of the laboratory, contained the general offices, shops, and minor preparation labs. Zone 2 in the interior of the building, separated from Zone 1 by sealed walls and airlock-like doors. Zone 2 contained live bacteriological specimens, and the lab facilities necessary to work with and examine them. The zone had the aspect of a separate building surrounded by an outer shell.

The central zone, Zone 3, was the hot zone, sealed from almost all outside contact. Air entering and exiting the Zone 3 labs was filtered and scrubbed, doubly so before being exhausted to the outside. Beyond the air, very little left the zone's sealed interior. Technicians worked in pressurized plastic suits to protect them from the deadly disease organisms they worked with daily. These organisms had been worked with and modified into effective, predictable, weapons of mass destruction. And to make sure nothing untoward happened to the contents of the labs, it was required that two people at a time—a scientist and a technician—be present whenever work was done. This was required not only for safety reasons, but so they could watch each other for security purposes.

The weapons bunkers were at the southern end of the compound, separated from the laboratory complex by another row of fencing. In two rows of four low, earth-covered bunkers, the weapons themselves were stored. Behind thick concrete and steel doors were stacks of munitions in carefully sealed cases—munitions filled with some of the deadliest diseases on earth, which were scheduled for open-air testing on the range facilities to the south.

The prevailing winds around Renaissance Island blew to the south. It was one reason for placing the huge open-air testing site on the island's southern end. The eighty square miles of the testing range was covered with sandy soil, with only sparse patches of grass as ground cover. Summer heat could bake the ground, raising the temperature of the sand to 140 degrees Fahrenheit. This helped reduce the possible spread of leftover microorganisms after a test. The lack of animals, and even low numbers of insects, helped contain the unintentional spread of a biological weapon.

Bright sunlight was detrimental to the biological weapons being tested. So, to keep the summer sun from unbalancing a test, weapons were fired at night. The darkness not only protected the weapons from the sterilizing effects of the sun, but kept their secrets safe from observation by overhead satellites.

Despite its importance, the appearance of the test site was nondescript. Black wooden poles were spaced out at one-kilometer intervals. Each pole held detection devices for tests, or to give out a warning. These were the largest objects standing up from the plain. From the weapons themselves, there were no craters, blast sites, or rubble.

The huge area of the testing site had seen air-burst bombs and artillery shells, sprays from planes and other aircraft, and missile warhead testing. What all of the ordnance had in common was the deadly nature of the fillings used. Plague, brucellosis, tularemia, and anthrax had all been released, contaminating the soil for years to come. There were no towns, villages, or other settlements nearby. Only the flat dull expanse of the dusty plain, and the death it contained.

CHAPTER 1

0700 ZULU
Aralsk-7 Test Site
Renaissance Island, Aral Sea
Kazakhstan/Uzbekistan
Union of Soviet Socialist Republics

Nothing grew across the wide expanse of dull, tan soil. The sparse, thin grass had been burned by early summer heat to little more than a brown memory. Whatever moisture might be blown across the large teardrop-shaped island came from the surrounding waters of the Aral Sea, whose water was among the most polluted in the world.

Once the fourth largest inland body of water on earth, poor management and the increasing demands of ever-more desperate "five-year" plans had wreaked havoc with the fragile local ecology. Increasing requirements for more and more water to irrigate failing croplands had cut off the Aral Sea's feeder rivers. Now it was the world's sixth largest inland body of water, well on its way to shrinking down to seventh and less.

But in spite of the desertlike appearance of the island, and the inhospitable environment that surrounded it, it still held life, or at least it would for a while.

In the darkness of the night, at a south-central site on the island, well away from where any prying eyes could have been, a peculiar design was drawn out with objects on the plain. Spreading like the spokes of a wheel, animals in cages were in line from a central point in the sand. At varying distances along the "spokes," more cages curved in arcs of concentric circles.

The grunting coughs and screams of the dozens of primate occupants of the cages, could be heard over the light sighs of the soft night breeze. Most of the cages held Hamadryas baboons, thousands of miles from the African jungles where they were born. These apes did not appear badly treated. They were healthy, well-fed, clean, and had been cared for. But many of them were terrified. The fearful screams came from those animals reaching up and jerking at their imprisoning cages. Others, who had already succumbed to their terror, sat huddled in their cages, their long arms wrapped around themselves.

The cause of the animal's fear was not immediately apparent. At the center of the radiating spokes was a simple post with what looked like nothing more than a melon-sized metal sphere with a few wires leading from it, down the post, and off into the distance. But there was a primitive feeling of death in the air, and this was what raised the fears of the cages' occupants.

The fitful breeze died away. Then, suddenly, the metal ball exploded.

The noise the baboons had made earlier was soft music compared to the cacophony of screams and screeches that came from their throats now. Those that sat huddled in their cages either jumped up with fright themselves, or hugged themselves all the harder and settled down on their sides in a fetal position.

One particular baboon had stood up in his cage and grabbed the bars solidly. In his panic-driven rage, he jerked at the bars on one side of the cage. These cages had been used numerous times before. They had taken abuse from the animals they held and had been repeatedly repaired. One of these repairs finally bent, gave way, and broke, leaving a thin point of wire sticking out, a wire tipped with a razor edge.

The reaction of the occupants of many of the cages seemed disproportionate to the blast they were exposed to. The ball's explosion was very slight for its size. There was little in the way of metal fragments, and no crater at all; even most of the post was still standing. All that could be seen was a smoky cloud of fine mist, or dust, spreading from where the ball had been. The smoke drifted out, encompassing the surrounding cages. The slight smoke and disturbance in the air went away after a few minutes. The apes in the cages eventually settled down, the terrified ones finally unwrapping themselves and looking around.

What the baboons saw after a short time was the bouncing lights of approaching, dull-painted vehicles. The vehicles stopped, their lights shining across the area, and then figures walked up to the cages in a clumsy waddle. Now, the baboons could see the figures as people, completely covered in plastic or rubber suits.

The swollen faces with huge cheeks were in fact respirators. Some of the people, holding flashlights, had boxes hanging down from their shoulders by straps. Others wore tanklike backpacks with handles and hoses leading from them. Those wearing backpacks were accompanied by others in the same protective suits, but not carrying any other obvious equipment.

"Come on, Mikhail," one of the men called out, his voice rendered tinny and distorted by the speech diaphragm of his protective mask. "The sooner we get this done, the faster we can get out of these suits."

Mikhail had a Model RDP-4V decontamination backpack on, and he was spraying down the cages, over the protests of the occupants. Working the pump handle of the backpack up and down with his left hand, he loosely scrubbed the outside of the cage with the brush on the end of a spray pipe in his right hand. A lamp strapped to his head illuminated the strange scene.

"Don't let the sergeant hear you, Sergei," Mikhail replied, continuing to spray. "He's sweating just as hard as we are. But if we mess up this job, the academicians will complain to the officers, and the shit won't stop rolling downhill until it lands on us."

As Sergei and another man picked up the sprayed cage by its handles, Mikhail sprayed the bottom, engendering another burst of outrage from the inhabitants. "Shut up you miserable beast," one of the men holding the cage said. "You eat better than we do."

"Yeah," Mikhail said, "but we're going to live a lot longer."

"I wonder what they're testing now?" the other cage carrier said.

"You're better off not knowing," Sergei said, "and a hell of a lot better off not even asking. If the sergeant heard you, or worse still, that *zampolit*, we'd all be pulling duty for the rest of the year." He was referring to the political officer.

The sergeant the men were so afraid of was a short distance away, working at the ground, the box of his KPO-1 sampling kit open at his waist. With a special probe, he was picking up a soil sample and placing it into a jar racked within the kit. As he stood up and saw the men with the cage, he growled over to them, "Speed it up over there, you men. I want to be done with this job before I melt!"

The heavy protective suits the men all wore were made of cloth covered with a thick coat of rubber, with integral boots, gloves, and a hood. The suits prevented the men from coming in contact with whatever had been released from the bomb, but they also made working even in the cooler evening environment very difficult. As the men continued to work, decontaminating and picking up the cages, the heat inside their protective coverings grew. And with the increased strain, the chances of a mistake increased.

The cages were being stacked in trailers as they were hosed off. The animals inside still loudly protested their situation, but the men were quickly tiring and just wanted to get the job done. They still had to unload the cages at the laboratory buildings and then decontaminate their vehicles, equipment, and themselves.

"Last one, Mikhail," Sergei called out. "Get out of that thing and come on."

Mikhail was becoming exhausted by the hot work. The poor diet and long hours the men were accustomed to didn't allow for even a young man to have a large reserve of strength. But stoicism in the face of adversity is a Russian trait, and the young soldier wasn't about to let his comrades down. However, his concentration wasn't what it had been just an hour earlier. The amount of time the man spent encased in the heavy protective suits was limited. But the site had to be completely cleaned well before daylight, and this evening wasn't a very cool one. The poor job he was doing scrubbing and decontaminating the last few cages went unnoticed by Mikhail and the rest of his squad, especially the corners and edges he missed on the last cage of the day.

As the men loaded the last cage onto the trailer, none of them saw the sharp shard of wire sticking from one corner of the cage. The baboon inside had finally quieted down. Either his fear had tired him out or whatever had been in the bomb had already started affecting him.

As Mikhail came up to the trailer, he was struggling to get out of the harness to his decontamination sprayer. As one of his squad mates helped him take off the backpack, Mikhail slipped and fell back against the trailer. In his exhaustion, the young man could neither feel nor care much about doing anything more than getting out of the field.

"Come, Mikhail," Sergei said. "This job will be over soon. One of the senior privates has promised me some of the real vodka he brought back from Aralsk. None of that local swill for us tonight. Maybe one of the lady technicians will even see fit to join us."

"Not much chance of that," Mikhail replied with a thin smile, invisible under his protective mask. And as he climbed into the back of the UAZ-469B vehicle towing the trailer, he never noticed the small puncture a sharp piece of wire had made in the back of his suit and into his skin.

1300 ZULU
Aralsk-7 Canteen
Renaissance Island, Aral Sea
Kazakhstan/Uzbekistan
Union of Soviet Socialist Republics

Almost a caricature of a Great Russian bear, Dr. Joseph Ivanovich Kashnavili could make himself immediately known to all just by entering a room. Tall and broad, with a booming voice, full black beard, and a thick thatch of unruly black hair, Joseph was almost always seen with a wide smile showing under twinkling eyes. Today, as Kashnavili entered the canteen, was something of an exception. The smile was there, but the eyes were drawn and the face under the beard haggard.

A much different man, Aleksandr Kondrachev was almost the exact physical opposite of the big man entering the room. Of medium height, sandy hair, and a slight build, Kondrachev's light complexion was topped off by his usual thoughtful expression as he sat reading at a table by himself. As the senior supervisor in the room, he was kept at a respectful distance by the others in the canteen. As Aleksandr looked up and saw his friend advancing on him like an avalanche—the big man almost couldn't move any other way—a smile crossed his face.

"Welcome once again to a fine evening at Tmu Tarakan, eh, Aleksi?" Joseph boomed out.

"The Kingdom of the Cockroaches indeed, my shy, retiring Joseph," Aleksandr shot back.

"I see you're being your usual self, eh, Aleksi?" Joseph intoned.

The other patrons of the canteen were more than familiar with the big doctor. They all worked at Aralsk-7, developing and testing biological weapons for the Greater Soviet, their Rodina, or motherland. The kind of work they did, and especially the environment at Renaissance Island, could depress almost anyone. The work was hard, the environment harsh, and the *zampolit* were always ready to note down any complaint as a sign of unreliability.

Alcohol and assignations were the normal way of alleviating the boredom and stress for many of the technicians and scientists. The overwhelming good humor of the large Russian doctor was always a welcome respite from the strains of the day.

"So your latest witch's brew is not quite as tasty as you had hoped, Aleksi?"

"Please, Joseph, don't broadcast it so loudly. Not everyone here works on the same part of the program."

"Ha! The story of whether a test worked or not, and if we'll go home early, spreads through here faster than gossip among the babushkas on the streets of Moskva."

Most of the other patrons of the canteen silently agreed with the pronouncement from the big man. But they still started to get up and leave in order to give the two men room to talk in private. Unofficially, they might know more than they were supposed to, but experience and observation had built caution into each of them.

The bearded Russian went over to a large stainless steel urn and drew two cups of hot tea. As he returned to his friend's table, he noticed that the population of the room had dropped considerably. "You really must work on your people skills, Aleksi," Joseph said as he sat down at the table. "Your moping around can empty a room faster than a dropped flask in a lab."

"A broken flask of our latest test material might not cause everyone to move so quickly," Alek said moodily.

"L4-836 not everything you expected it to be?"

"Not yet, at any rate. You would think that a strain of anthrax found among the rats in the sewers of Kirov would be the nastiest thing on the planet. But the field testing just isn't proving that out. The symptoms shown by the apes are slight at best. Only about thirty percent are having the disease bloom out and cause them to crash.

"When a disease like this anthrax strain builds up in

an infected organism, it will either overwhelm the body's immune system and cause a sudden crash and death, or the body will fight it off." Alek was as security conscious as any person at Aralsk-7, but as he warmed up to his subject, he spoke more openly to his friend. "This strain actually seems less lethal than the norm. It showed every indication of being what we had been looking for, but it's just not meeting the test requirements."

"A thirty percent lethality rate within forty-eight hours of the test seems positive," Joseph commented.

"Yes, it's fast in about a third of the subjects, but it's less lethal than normal pulmonary anthrax. That takes several days, but can be ninety percent lethal when untreated. This is puzzling me."

As Alek stopped and took a drink of his tea, he finally noticed his friend's haggard appearance. "You look pretty tired, Joseph. All this fast living around here finally slowing you down?"

"Not hardly, my friend," Joseph said with a loud grunt and a heavy rolling of his shoulders. "It would take a lot more than can possibly be found around here to slow down a true Georgian. We have a lust for life and live it well, you know."

"So I have heard you mention once or twice," Alek said with a smile.

"No, it was just that they were shorthanded in the infirmary again," Joseph continued, ignoring Alek's comment. "Another of the doctors was ordered to report to the Army's Fifteenth Directorate headquarters in Aralsk. Since my project isn't moving right now, I volunteered my services to fill in. It's good to be just a simple doctor for a while, even for some of these blockheaded young conscript soldiers they send here now.

"Just as I went on duty yesterday morning, a young private from the chemical company showed up. This youngster couldn't have been more than a year away from his mother's apron strings, but he had to show he could play with the big boys. He had tied one on late the night before and stumbled into his barracks, falling down the stairs in the process. It was hard enough to tell which was hurting him more—the wound on his head or the pounding that was going on inside of it. Treatment was simple enough, a few stitches, a compress, aspirin, and a day's observation for a concussion."

"Any complications?" Alek asked.

"Outside of a good case of boils freshening on his back—hardly unusual in this environment—no. Though he did start off my rounds well."

"How's that?"

"When I sat him up after my usual magnificent job of stitchery, he thanked me profusely by proceeding to vomit all over me. You'd think one of these technicians could make up something a little better than that lamp oil they pass off as vodka around here. But there's little enough to do for entertainment, I suppose," Joseph said with a big sigh. "It's not like we'll do much better."

"You shouldn't push yourself so hard, Joseph," Alek said, with no little concern in his voice. "Even if the infirmary is shorthanded, you need to take at least some time to rest."

"Bah!" Joseph snorted. "There's plenty of time for sleep in the grave. Life is for living. Something you could do a little more of, my diminutive friend of the great brain."

"I have my enjoyments."

"Oh yes, as if you could exercise your penchant for swimming in these poor waters around us. All I need is some good wine, the company of some fine women, and maybe a bit of song." With that statement, Joseph leaned back in his chair, stretched, and yawned prodigiously, looking for all the world like a black bear getting ready to swallow the overhead light fixture.

"But maybe, just maybe," he continued, "you're a bit right tonight. I may just dream about my loves. Another day done in the service of the Rodina, eh, Aleksi? No, tonight I think I'll stay away from any liquid escape. It just may be what's been making me feel poorly recently. Either that or it's that old age thing everyone says sneaks up on you when you're not looking. But some entertainment might not be out of order. Maybe tonight they'll show one of those decadent Western films instead of another rousing example of Soviet might during the Great Patriotic War."

"Hah!" Aleksandr exclaimed. "You might as well wish for fresh sturgeon from out of the Aral. There would be a greater chance of finding that than of our getting a decent film. But maybe you'd just better get some sleep, you look even more exhausted than when you first came in."

"I'm . . ." Joseph began, his face suddenly flushed red, and the rest of his words never came out. With the first passing of the red flush, Kashnavili's face became dark, turning blue around the lips with cyanosis. As he clawed at his throat, a violent fit of coughing overtook the large man. He fell forward over the table, then overturned the tea glasses in his struggle. As Alek looked on with shock, his friend slumped over backward in his chair and crashed to the floor.

"Joseph!" Alek shouted, shaking off his paralysis as he jumped up from the table. Even as his friend toppled from his chair, Alex could see it was too late. As he rushed to Joseph's side, he recognized what was killing him—correction, had killed him, the scientist in Alek coldly observed. Joseph Ivanovich Kashnavili would no longer laugh at the world, or observe its foibles from his vantage point. He had crashed out from anthrax.

The few others who were still in the canteen stood or sat frozen for a moment before they pulled even farther away from the stricken body on the floor. Fear showed starkly on their faces as they all began a rush for the exits. This was what many of them feared the most. One of the horrible demons they worked with daily had walked in among them . . . and had taken one of their own.

The death of a single researcher does not bring the Soviet biological weapons program to a halt. Within a few months of his death at Aralsk-7, Joseph Kashnavili's widow and two children had left their apartment in Kirov, where he had been stationed at the Institute of Microbiology, and returned to their native Georgia in the Ukraine.

But Kashnavili was not going to be allowed to rest easily, no matter what might have been done to take care of his family. He was not only the victim of one of the weapons he had been working on, his body was also being held hostage to a quirk of biology. An unusual aspect of laboratory-grown or purified biological cultures is that some become much more virulent and deadly after passing through a human incubator. Dr. Joseph Kashnavili had been just such an involuntary incubator. During the autopsy that followed his death, a new biological culture was grown from the organs harvested from his body. His lungs especially turned out to be teeming with a new, and much more lethal, strain of anthrax bacilli.

Known as "Variant K," after the man who had created it, the new anthrax was examined closely by Soviet bioweapons technologists. In the investigation that followed Kashnavili's death, it was determined that the source for his infection had been the injured young soldier who had gone to the infirmary that fateful morning. The soldier was found to have a case of subcutaneous anthrax. It was never fully explained just how he had come by the initial infection. Normally not a contagious disease, Kashnavili had been so thoroughly contaminated by the young soldier, who showed almost no symptoms himself, that he had come down with the disease. The young soldier even recovered from his infection after a short hospital stay and a course of antibiotic treatment.

But the new Variant K strain could not be treated easily with antibiotics. Testing found Variant K to be highly resistant to most forms of antibiotic therapy used in the normal courses of treatment for anthrax. Variant K would also grow well in laboratory media, and even flourished in bulk production. The new anthrax could be weaponized as easily as earlier strains, reduced to a fine, dry, gray-brown powder with the consistency of almost microscopic dust. But even when dried and reduced to micron-sized spore particles, Variant K lost none of its original lethality. A spot of the dust the size of a sharp pencil point could be enough to infect anyone who breathed it in.

And the disease that grew from inhaling that fine dust caused the deadliest form of anthrax infection, pulmonary anthrax, which invaded a victim's lungs. After an incubation period that could be measured in hours rather than days, Variant K would suddenly bloom throughout the victim's body, first cutting off the person's air supply.

From showing symptoms that at most resemble a mild case of the flu or a chest cold, Variant K would suddenly grow and savage its host, killing over ninety-five percent of its victims. Except for not being easily contagious between victims and those unexposed around them, Variant K was very close to being a perfect biological weapon. Ten grams of the Variant K powder, an amount that would fill only half a small tea cup, had the potential to be deadlier than a metric ton of nerve gas. And unlike nerve gas, which could dissipate in hours, the spores could remain a deadly source of infection in the environment for decades.

Since his friend's death, Aleksandr Kondrachev had worked long, hard hours in the field and back at his office and laboratory in the Kirov Institute of Microbiology. It was as if he was seeking to expunge some personal guilt by burying himself in his work. And his work centered on the very thing that had taken his friend's life.

The new anthrax strain fit many of the requirements Alek had been given for a new weapon. Further tests at the Aralsk-7 site and in the laboratory had proved the new strain's potency. Culture media and growing techniques improved on and perfected by Alek made the production of the new strain in quantity a much more efficient process than earlier methods. In a macabre twist of fate, his friend's legacy would be one of the greatest defenses the Rodina would own.

With the weaponized anthrax available in bulk, new means of applying the weapon were completed. The massive SS-18 intercontinental ballistic missiles, with a range of over 11,000 kilometers, were armed with warheads holding the Kondrachev-developed anthrax submunition. His design could now be filled with a potent weapon, the only thing that had kept it from being fielded before. Each of the ten independent reentry vehicles in an SS-18 warhead could release a swarm of spherical bomblets over a populated target. Each sphere had the capability of infecting and killing tens of thousands of people. Men, women, and children were now the targets of Soviet contagion rather than the flash, burn, and blast of a thermonuclear detonation.

Aleksandr was noticed by the higher commands and was nominated for an award, a medal for his contribution to the defense of the homeland. But all he could see was the death of his friend in front of him: Joseph Kashnavili, who so loved life and being able to help people that he had volunteered his extra time in a clinic he didn't have to be in. It was work that had cost him everything. Any accolades coming to Kondrachev seemed to him like the dust of Renaissance Island, dry and empty of life.

Many of those in positions of authority and power attributed the reports they heard of Kondrachev's depression to his tremendous work load. The man didn't drink often, worked tirelessly, and had no family to be concerned with. And his results made his superiors look very good to their own superiors.

Kondrachev was ordered to report to the headquarters of the Biopreparat organization. The supposedly civilian organization's headquarters were located in a nineteenth century, Russian-style yellow brick mansion. Surrounded by a concrete wall, it sat on the narrow Samokatanya Street in the old German Quarter of Moscow. In fact, Biopreparat oversaw the vast majority of the Soviet biological weapons development program. And it ran a cooperative effort with other organizations in the greater Soviet sphere.

The 150 administration workers and office staff at the Samokatanya Street headquarters worked under the supervision of Major General Yuri Korvin, late of the Soviet Army's Technical troops. A tall, thin vulture of a man, a resemblance made stronger by his balding head and long, thin nose, Korvin was a fierce proponent of the biological weapons program. He was also a political animal, ambitious and jealous of his power and station. Anything that could add to his personal prestige or that of his organization was something to be cultivated. He recognized the importance of some of his people, and the results that they delivered, to the furthering of his own ambitions. He would promote people who showed their worth, and then await the proper gratitude for his action.

0500 ZULU
Biopreparat Administrative Headquarters
Samokatanya Street
Moscow

As he arrived in the second floor office of his superior, Kondrachev looked at the high ceiling of the room and the Russian antique furniture that furnished it. Korvin, sitting behind his desk, had been reading papers as Alek was ushered in by a senior secretary. After a moment, Korvin looked up, smiled thinly, and indicated that Kondrachev should take a seat. Settling into the high-backed, plush old chair, Kondrachev felt much less comfortable than he may have looked.

"Your new developments have drawn attention in high places," Korvin said dryly.

"I'm flattered," Alek said in a nervous but offhand manner.

"As well you should be, Kondrachev," Korvin snapped. "Your work has been outstanding of late. But reports of your attitude speak in less glowing terms. They indicate a certain lack of respect. You may think that you are indispensable to this organization, but I assure you that you are not!"

"My apologies, Comrade General," Alek said in a submissive tone. "I meant no disrespect. I have just been concentrating on my project. The pressure of my work, you understand . . ." He let his words trail off.

Somewhat placated after having cracked the whip over his underling, Korvin went on in a milder tone: "Of course, of course. And your work has been excellent. The procedures you developed and put in place at Aralsk-7 and the Kirov facility are both ingenious and useful. They will add to the overall safety and efficiency of our programs. In light of this, you are being promoted and transferred here to Moscow. You will become one of my deputies, the Inspector of Bacteriological Safety and Production for the whole of Biopreparat."

"Sir," Alek said, stunned, "I don't know what to say."

"There is nothing to say," Korvin replied. "You have established yourself as both an able researcher and a good manager of the people and resources under your responsibility. Though you've spent most of your recent time in the laboratory, you have maintained a good working relationship with the rest of your colleagues. This ability has been noticed, as well as your scientific accomplishments.

"You will have an office and modest staff at one of the Biopreparat facilities here in Moscow. There will be a laboratory for your use in continuing your own lines of research. But your primary duties will be to oversee all of the safety and testing procedures in both our laboratories and production facilities. You will also conduct liaison duties between Biopreparat and other ministries and departments as may be required."

Settling back in his chair, Korvin enjoyed the look of astonishment on Kondrachev's face. Using first the stick and then the carrot on the people working under him was one of his enjoyments in life. "Relax and enjoy yourself a bit, Alek."

Kondrachev was startled at Korvin's use of his first name.

"This is a big jump in your career," Korvin continued. "I expect you to do well in this new assignment. It will be a very visible post. A number of important people will get to know you and recognize your name."

"I will do my best sir," Alek said truthfully.

"Excellent," Korvin said with a thin smile. "I would expect nothing less from you. My secretary will assist you in getting moved and settled in. You will see that there are definite benefits to your new position to go along with the responsibilities. As a single man, you may find that the prospect of being stationed in Moscow has additional points in its favor."

The supposedly sly wink Korvin used to deliver his last line seemed to Alek forced and grotesque. As

Korvin stood and came around his desk, Alek came immediately to his own feet.

"Thank you sir," Alek said as he accepted a soft, dry handshake from Korvin.

Nodding his head, still smiling thinly, Korvin indicated the door and turned back to his desk.

CHAPTER 2

"**G**ood afternoon, Chief," the tanned and fit-looking young officer said as he walked into the platoon room.

"Afternoon, sir," Senior Chief Boatswain's Mate Frank Monday replied from behind the desk. "There's some fresh coffee in the pot."

"Great," Lieutenant Greg Rockham said as he stepped over to the small table behind the desk. Drawing a steaming cup of coffee from the spigot of the old-style, battered green thirty-cup percolator, the lieutenant commented, "A fresh pot, huh? You're not planning on making a late night of it, are you, Chief?"

"No, boss. Chief Mackenzie from Second Platoon has the duty this weekend, and I said he could use my pot. Everything's pretty much squared away as far as the platoon goes."

Balancing the heavy porcelain Navy-issue coffee

mug in his hand, Rockham sat down on the corner of the desk and looked over the chief's shoulder at the sheaf of papers he had in his hand. "So we're good to go?"

"Everything's fine, boss. The platoon has shaped up nicely. They're with the yeoman now, going over records. No one wants to have any problems on deployment. We've got a good mix of seasoned operators, and they balance out the young lions well. Some of those new guys have brought some real skills in with them. Mr. Daugherty is still leery of Ferber, though."

"Hell, that's funny, Chief. After all, it wasn't that long ago that Mike Ferber was Shaun's first phase instructor. There isn't any real problem, though, is there? I thought they'd gotten past all of that weeks ago."

"No problems at all, really. It's just funny sometimes. You'd swear that if Ferber shouted 'Drop,' the next sound you'd hear would be the air sucking in behind Daugherty as he hit the deck and started pumping them out."

"Probably," Rockham said with a laugh, "but they've worked well enough together during training. Besides, Mike's going to be with my squad, Red's going to be with you in Second. Hell, he was an ensign just a few weeks ago. Now be nice to him, Chief. I remember being in awe of all you chiefs for years."

"As is only proper, sir," Chief Monday answered in his most solemn tone. "But I shall raise him with the proper respect for true Navy traditions."

"Right," Rockham said with a big grin. "So do try not to strip him of his entire paycheck in the poker game." Then the grin faded and he became serious. "But what about Bryant? Still have any questions about him?"

"Well, he's young and enthusiastic, but he's a hard worker and willing to learn. I think he's got the makings of a real operator. The only reason he didn't stay over at SDVT2 was that he wanted to get out and see some more action. That, and the big sonofabitch didn't fit in the eight-boats all that well."

"But you answered that question you had about him maybe being clausty, didn't you?"

"Yeah, he hasn't got any problem with claustrophobia that I can see," the tall chief said as he leaned back in his chair. "I had Wilkes assigned as his swim buddy on the last few night dives. He says the boy's a natural in the water. And for Wilkes to say that is no small thing—he's part dolphin himself. No, Bryant just needs a little more seasoning is all."

"Great," Rockham said as he stood up from the desk. Moving over to the wall behind the chief, he looked over the platoon roster listing all of the men's squad assignments and their positions in the squad. The fourteen enlisted men and two officers broke down into two squads of eight men each.

Fourth Platoon, SEAL Team 2

	1st Squad	*2nd Squad*
OIC-	Lt Greg Rockham	Ltjg Shaun Daugherty
AOIC-	IS1 Mike Ferber	SCBM Frank Monday
Point-	BM3 Ryan Marks	BM3 Mike Bryant
AW-	EN2 Dan Able	MM2 Roger Kurkowski
RO-	AO2 John Sukov	RM3 Henry Lutz
Grenadier-	GMM3 Ken Fleming	SK2 Pete Wilkes
Corpsman-	HM1 Jack Tinsley	HM2 Henry Limbaugh
AW-	EM3 Wayne Alexander	GMG2 Larry Stadt

"With the shortage of corpsmen in the Teams, I can't believe they let us have two," Monday said, turning from his desk to face the lieutenant. "Between Limbaugh and Tinsley, we could damned near open our own hospital."

"Hopefully, neither one will have the chance to play doctor on this deployment," Rockham commented. "But Tinsley has some great experience in cold-weather ops. That's going to be nice to have available once we're in Norway."

"Limbaugh is also up to speed on all of the newest bells and whistles from out of the schoolhouse," Monday said. "He was in first phase with Ferber at BUD/S, and Mike says he really knows his stuff. Apparently, they had a foreign exchange officer from the Thai navy in one class who was a real hard case."

"What do you mean?" Rockham asked, puzzled at the odd information.

"The guy wouldn't stop at all. But he just wasn't built for the weather in Coronado. It was a winter class, and during Hell Week the guy hyped out three times."

"Hypothermia?" Rockham said incredulously. "And he went through it three times?"

"That's what Mike said. Limbaugh worked on the guy every time, and they brought him back without a problem. He just wanted to go back out with his class, but he physically couldn't take the cold. They finally had to roll him back to a summer class on a medical, otherwise he would have killed himself trying."

The conversation was interrupted by a knock at the

door. As the two men looked over, the door opened. First Class Intelligence Specialist Mike Ferber, the leading petty officer of Fourth Platoon, said, "This a closed meeting or can anyone attend?"

"Oh, I guess just about anyone can wander in," the chief said. "What's up, Mike?"

"Paperwork's all done, the t's dotted and the i's crossed," Mike replied as he entered. "The rest of the guys were just behind me. They should be coming in any minute now."

"All the departments set?" Monday asked.

"All done," Ferber answered. "Able and Kurkowski were just finishing packing up down at Ordnance a while ago. The boxes are sealed and the manifests completed. Tinsley was doing some last minute scrounging down at Supply, but everything's set now."

As the men were talking, the rest of the platoon started to come into the room. The platoon's other officer, Lt. (jg) Shaun Daugherty, had come up to the coffeepot and was drawing himself a cup. The young-looking officer's red hair stood out no matter where he was in the room. The rest of the SEALs took seats or leaned up against the green-painted concrete block walls. Fourth Platoon had been working together for weeks during their predeployment training, and the men had settled into a well-coordinated, cohesive group.

Predeployment training had been constant drills and classes, as each of the men learned about his new Teammates and the position he would be expected to fill in the platoon and in his squad. Long hours had been spent in the field on exercises as well as in the classroom, and everyone knew what was expected of him, as well as what each man had to contribute. They had learned not only their own job and position, but cross-training had seen to it that each man could competently fill any position in a squad.

Each man's strengths had been added to the whole, balancing out or eliminating any possible weaknesses. Like a line of thoroughbred racehorses, each man was in the peak of condition, ready and looking forward to the upcoming challenge.

Both the old hands and the newest men in the platoon were enthusiastic about their upcoming deployment. They just wanted to "go there and do that." To be in the action. That was the reason most of them had volunteered to join the Teams in the first place.

"Okay," Chief Monday said, and the talk immediately faded away. "All of the departments have checked in and are done. The platoon boxes packed and all your own gear squared away?"

A chorus of agreements came from the men. "Okay, that pretty much makes it complete. Any comments, Mr. Rockham?" Monday said as he turned to the officer.

"Thanks, Chief." Turning to the men, Rockham said, "I just wanted to tell you men that both the chief and I are in agreement that Fourth Platoon looks outstanding. There isn't much of a question in our minds that this will be a great deployment. As all of you know, we're going to be cross-training with our NATO counterparts in the Norwegian forces. That means we're going to be operating with their Marinejagerslag doing some real cold-weather training, SEAL style. We're also going to get in some high-speed work with their Beredskapstropper counterterrorist unit. And don't worry, I'm sure the names will get easier to pronounce once we get used to them."

A chuckle ran through the men as the lieutenant pointed out the tongue-twisting names.

"Our cold-weather training has been a little limited here in Virginia over the summer." That comment drew another chuckle, as the men were reminded of the sweltering heat and humidity of a southern Virginian summer. But I'm sure our hosts will find a glacier or two to help cool us off. To get us started right, I've already got the first keg on ice over at my place. Chief, they're all yours."

"Okay, I expect to see you all here Monday at 0400 hours. That's in the A.M., gentlemen. Liberty is down, and I'll see you all at Mr. Rockham's."

0400 ZULU
14033 Princess Drive
Virginia Beach
Virginia

Anticipating the inevitable noise and revelry at their ranch-style house in Virginia Beach, Sharon Rockham had taken their young son Matt with her as she went to visit her friends for the evening. This would not be the first SEAL party she had seen, and she hardly expected it to be the last.

It was still a pretty mild affair by SEAL standards. While most of the platoon looked on, in the backyard, Shaun refereed a push-up match between Ryan Marks and Wayne Alexander. Second Class Boatswain's Mate Ryan Marks was a huge black man, muscular even in comparison to his Teammates, who were all in excellent physical condition. At first glance Marks appeared to be as wide at the shoulders as he was tall. And the large round bulges of his shoulders looked like he was using bowling balls for shoulder pads. He was the point man of first squad, and in spite of his size, could move silently and slowly through any terrain.

The other man in the competition was Engineman Third Class Wayne Alexander, also of first squad. At five-foot-three, he was the shortest man in the platoon, but it would be hard to consider him small. Built like a fireplug, Alexander looked like a brown-haired bulldog, a resemblance only broken by his bushy mustache. His arms were thicker than an average man's legs, and there was almost no apparent taper from his barrel chest down to his waist.

Having instigated the competition, Machinist's Mate Second Class Roger Kurkowski, one of the automatic weapons men of second squad, was egging on the two competitors to beat the other man out. Since the two men were so strong, and the night could only last so long, Kurkowski had "evened out" the competition by placing a full keg of beer squarely on the back of each of the men on the ground.

Most of the platoon stood around voicing encouragement, opinions, and general comments on the situation at hand. Marks was given points for speed, but Alexander continued to pump himself up and down with the regularity of a machine.

Lieutenant Rockham stood to the side and watched the proceedings with an increasingly glazed look, Senior Chief Monday next to him. "So, Chief, how does this compare to the deployment parties back in your Vietnam days?" Rockham asked.

"Couldn't get Bam-me-Bah beer in kegs," Monday answered from around the unlit cigar he held between his teeth. "Outside of that, things haven't changed much."

A roar went up from the onlookers as the keg slipped off Marks' back. With Daugherty declaring Alexander the winner, a loud discussion regarding the details of the competition began among the onlookers. Alexander just looked up from where he was on the ground, the heavy keg still on his back, and asked, "Can I drink it now?"

"Sounds good to me," Marks answered, then he reached down and lifted the keg off his Teammate's back.

"Chow's on!" Third Class Gunner's Mate (Missiles) Ken Fleming shouted as he pushed his way out of the side door of the house. Placing a big iron pot down on a folding table, Fleming wiped the sweat from his bald head. "Come and get it before I throw it to the Marines."

"I would have thought sandwiches and munchies would have been enough for this mob," Second Class Storekeeper Pete Wilkes said as he walked over to the table.

As he drew another mug of beer from the keg sitting in a tub of ice next to the food table, Second Class Gunner's Mate (Guns) Larry Stadt said, "Hey, you should always eat when you're drinking, that way you can drink more."

"Who said that?" someone asked.

"My eighty-three-year old German grandfather," Stadt replied. "And he should know, he's still doing both."

"I hope the Norwegians don't decide to withdraw from NATO after this group shows up," Rock commented as men began to fill dishes with the fragrant, steaming contents of Fleming's pot.

"Hoo yah!" Alexander bellowed as he lifted a full aluminum beer keg over his head and began doing knee bends while holding it up. Marks was holding a mug of beer to his Teammates lips, so he could swallow at least some of the spilling brew on the upstroke of his exercise.

"Um, yeah," was Senior Chief Monday's only comment.

1200 ZULU
Paskaderian's Café
Tchaikovsky Street
Moscow

First Captain Gregoriy Rostov was a careful, methodical man. Which did not mean he was someone who lived in particular fear of anything. But in his years in the Spetsnaz and as a GRU Intelligence officer, his own experiences and training in tradecraft had taught him to never take anything for granted.

A glance at the tall, slender man, the firm-visaged, hawk-nosed face, and the athletic manner with which he carried himself would not have given anyone the impression that this was a man who feared anything. Instead, the quick way his eyes took in and made note of everything around him indicated confidence as well as an alert mind.

That afternoon, Rostov had been given an invitation to an "informal" meeting by a trusted friend. The invitation was a simple one, suggesting that Rostov come to a café at a given time and accept a drink from someone who wished to meet him face-to-face. Bored with what was otherwise a wasteful visit to higher command in Moscow, Rostov found the invitation intriguing enough to follow through on it.

Arriving at the designated location at the proper time, Rostov found what appeared to be just an old-style Russian café. The weight of the very small, flat 5.45mm PSM automatic in his coat pocket had a reassuring feel to it. Such a small caliber weapon was intended for concealment and special penetration power. The small high-density bullet could penetrate normal body armor and still kill. And the weapon wouldn't make a noticeable bulge in a coat, or even a trouser pocket. Rostov knew you had to be very accurate with such a weapon. But marksmanship with personal weapons was a skill he had mastered long ago.

Pushing open the heavy wooden door, Rostov was

only faintly surprised to see a huge man sitting at a table near the door, a man whose appearance fairly shouted "KGB bodyguard" to Rostov's senses.

It wasn't that the man appeared threatening. There was just something subtle about his posture, the way he wore his coat, that told Rostov he was a security operative of some kind. In any jungle, a predator recognizes another predator.

The big man sat at a small table, a glass of tea and a folded newspaper in front of him. Rostov would not have been surprised if a weapon was concealed by the paper. And the table was so small it could be tossed out of the way in an instant. There was no obvious threat, but the man had the same tension-filled air about him that a bomb preparing to explode would have.

Rostov looked at him and the man calmly gazed back. In that short glance, volumes of information were exchanged. Two killers recognized and acknowledged each other, the KGB man deferring to Rostov. But deferring only in a limited way.

The air crackled about the two men for an instant, then the moment was dissolved by the appearance of a waiter. Rostov allowed himself to be led through the almost empty dark interior of the café to a small alcove in the back.

There, another big man was sitting, but in a more relaxed pose. But still, the man radiated a sense of power; power held in check. Rostov looked into two dark eyes that fairly shone with intelligence as the man gestured to a seat facing him in the small alcove.

"Please sit, Comrade Captain Rostov," the big man said with a slight smile.

"Thank you, Comrade General," Rostov replied as he took the proffered seat.

The small smile remained on the older man's face as he watched Rostov sit. The waiter returned with a tray a moment later. He set down a glass of vodka in front of each of the men, placed a small platter of coarse black bread, hard cheese, and pickles on the table, then withdrew without having spoken.

"So you recognize me, Rostov?" the older man asked, breaking the silence.

"It was suggested that I come to a small café that is just a short distance from the corner of Kalinin Prospekt and Tchaikovsky Street. Near that intersection is the SEV building, holding a number of major KGB offices," Rostov said. "So I thought it might prove prudent to familiarize myself with some of the people who might be in that building. When I came to the café, of course I noticed that Lieutenant General Leonid Stankevich, head of Department Fourteen of the First Chief Directorate, was sitting in it. As a master technician in the tools of espionage, and especially the, ah . . . more subtle ways of eliminating the enemies of the Rodina, your reputation precedes you."

"Bravo, Captain," Stankevich said. "I see your own reputation for thoroughness does you justice, though I dislike the fact that you might be able to access a dossier on me. I will have to speak to the proper persons about the laxities at the KGB files. I trust that the balance of your reputation might not be embellished?"

"The GRU has a sufficiency of its own files," Rostov said mildly. "They usually do not find it necessary to bother their brother service for information. But, you said 'the balance' of my reputation?"

"I was also the head of Laboratory Twelve earlier in my career," Stankevich said cryptically.

This was something Rostov hadn't known. Laboratory 12 was where some of the most lethal devices used by the KGB, and occasionally the GRU, had come from. Poisons, drugs, disguised weapons, and more had come from practitioners of the arcane arts at 12. It was no surprise that the director of such a place would later become the head of the KGB department devoted to the development of espionage hardware and lethal devices.

This train of thought raced through Rostov's mind without him showing any exterior sign of his surprise. "An interesting assignment, General," Rostov said. "But I'm afraid that would have little to do with a simple sailor such as myself."

"A simple sailor?" Stankevich said with a snort. "Comrade Rostov . . . Gregoriy, if I may?"

He was answered with a simple nod from Rostov.

"I think anyone with your career accomplishments can be considered as more than a simple sailor," Stankevich stated. "Don't you agree? Only a few years ago, while already a senior officer, you led a number of operations in Afghanistan. That was as the head of the only Naval Spetsnaz component to operate in Afghanistan, as I recall."

"It was simply that I thought some direct combat experience would do my men good," Rostov said stiffly.

The hardness that came over Rostov at the mention of Afghanistan did not go unnoticed by Stankevich. He decided to press the point.

"Well, your combat record is considered excellent in a number of high-ranking military and political circles. And yours is still one of the most decorated special units to have operated in Afghanistan. You did lose some people on one operation I noted. And a number of your superiors have held that point against you."

"The Afghan mujahideen is a much more skilled and resourceful fighter than some would believe here in Moskva," Rostov said icily. "And you cannot gather quality combat experience without a cost. Some in higher command feel that they should not risk their skills or persons in such endeavors."

His last words were so cold, they would have formed frost from the air had they been solid.

"Perhaps so," Stankevich said in a more conciliatory tone. "Or you simply had the bad luck to work under cowards. Well-connected cowards with people in high places looking out for them. No, you have always been more of a man of action than of politics. Even as a young officer, a senior lieutenant, you showed a flair for direct action. It was during an assignment to a residency in Vienna that you experienced your first active combat, I believe."

"It was hardly combat," Rostov said in a self-deprecating manner. "One of the political tools used by the local apparatchik had become . . . excessive. He had to be put down. The same as you would with any out of control rabid dog."

"You volunteered to eliminate an individual the West considered a major terrorist," Stankevich said plainly. "And you did so single-handedly . . . and in such a way that it appeared to be the results of an internal power struggle within his own group. That shows not only skill, but a certain elegance of thought and plan."

"All of this remembrance is interesting," Rostov said, with mild irritation. "But what does it have to do with my meeting you here under these circumstances?"

"The point then is this," Stankevich said firmly, leaning forward in his seat. "There is a large group of military and political leaders who feel that perestroika and all of these other accommodations with the West are a serious threat to the security of the Greater Soviet. These actions will only serve to damage our standing with the peoples of the world. And it will seriously weaken our resolve to protect the Rodina."

"Such things have been discussed before," Rostov said quietly. "But never openly."

"No," Stankevich agreed. "But the ideas have been put forward by some who have spoken in the wrong place and time. They were derided and put down as reactionaries. And their careers came to an abrupt end. I am part of a group that feels we need to be able to speak openly, but only from a position of strength. To meet that end, we have decided to unofficially divert some of our more classified resources to a more, um, flexible location under our direct control."

"Nuclear weapons!" Rostov said in a deceptively mild tone. "You are speaking of treason."

"No, no, not at all," Stankevich said heatedly, "and we are not speaking of something so crude as nuclear weapons. Such a thing would be useless to us. We could not use them without risking retaliation from the West. And we are not in a position strong enough to resist such retaliation.

"We are speaking of a more subtle weapon, though one just as destructive. And all we wish to do is to take control of such a weapon to increase the strength of our hands. The hands of men willing to use such force. And we can protect ourselves from outside interference. We have subtle ways to accomplish such protection, as I am sure you understand."

The thinly veiled threat was not lost on Rostov. The bodyguard between him and the outside door wasn't a real concern to the Spetsnaz officer. But the much more dangerous threat personified by the man sitting across from him was quite a different matter. He controlled various forms of assassination that could not be easily protected against.

But this situation might not be a threat to him personally, Rostov thought. Much of the general philosophy being spoken of at the table was something Rostov found he could agree with. Maybe even turn it to his own ends.

"And what would you have me do to further your plans, Comrade General?" Rostov asked.

Leonid Stankevich had thoroughly investigated the man sitting across from him. Well before the suggestion was made, Stankevich suspected that agreement would be the eventual result. The sly old warrior was satisfied with the results of the meeting so far.

"Arrangements are being made for an open-air test of a biological weapon. I think you will agree that it would be a much more subtle weapon than the sledge-hammer approach of a nuclear device?" Stankevich said in a conspiratorial tone. "And such a weapon has a certain amount of fear that comes just by its mere existence."

Rostov didn't say a word. But his heart rate jumped at the thought of using a biological weapon. Based on lethal diseases, such things would give any sane man a shiver of primal fear.

Taking his silence as agreement, Stankevich continued. "The testing site has been chosen. It is a small island in the White Sea. That is inside your area of primary operations, I believe?"

"As you well know, I lead the Northern Fleet's Spetsnaz brigade out of Penchenga," Rostov said sharply. "The whole of the White Sea is in our operational area."

"Excellent," Stankevich said with a smile. "And you have complete freedom to plan and conduct training operations for your unit. You have the autonomy and authority to obtain support, transportation, and reliable manpower?"

Rostov nodded, beginning to see where the general was going.

"Well," Stankevich continued, "with you and your men's training in chemical and biological operations, we think you are perfect for the job."

Though he suspected he already knew the answer, Rostov asked the obvious question. "What job?"

"Why, to steal the weapons, of course," Stankevich stated plainly.

Even with his expectation, the reality of it shocked the Spetsnaz officer. It would put a weapon of mass destruction in private Soviet hands. Such a thing was deadly dangerous to even contemplate. Anyone caught conducting such an operation wouldn't even see the inside of the worst of the gulags. They would be drained of information like a glass emptied of water. And Rostov knew that Moscow had people who could break absolutely anyone. A quick, shallow grave would be the end result. But only if they were caught.

In spite of himself, Rostov was surprised at just how easily he accepted the thought and logic of such an operation. And the warrior in him was already considering options and selecting his team. But there still were questions.

"Just who is in this operation besides yourself?" Rostov asked bluntly.

"That isn't something you need to know, Captain," Stankevich said, the general in him emerging.

"But the committing of such an audacious action would cause an immediate investigation," Rostov said.

"True," Stankevich agreed. "But we already have a cutout in place. There is a KGB Border Guards maritime officer—more of a blunt thug, really—who is disposable. He is completely corrupt, and that makes him an excellent tool. As long as he is kept in the dark about the true situation, any blame can be laid at his doorstep. The financial value of such a weapon would be more than enough enticement for him. Besides, resting the blame for such an action on this individual would be a service to the Greater Soviet."

Rostov was intrigued. He picked up the glass of vodka, now beaded with condensation from the air, and held it up. "Leonid," he said.

Lifting his own glass, Stankevich touched it to Rostov's. "Gregoriy," he said.

And the two men drank.

1625 ZULU
68° 28' North, 16° 53' East
Ofot Fjord
Norway

Located on the most northern point of Europe, Norway holds a significant strategic position for the defense of NATO, Western Europe, and even the North Atlantic. To reach the Atlantic, Soviet ships and submarines leaving from their northern Russian ports had to pass within a relatively short distance of Norwegian shores to reach the Atlantic. Norway recognized the need for a significant naval defense soon after the end of the Nazi occupation during World War II. To build part of this defense, the Norwegian military established in 1953 their equivalent of the U.S. Navy Underwater Demolition Teams.

The Navy UDTs helped train their Norwegian counterparts soon after the creation of the new unit. As the threat from the Soviet Warsaw Pact grew, so did the need for specialized NATO units. By 1968 the Norwegian forces recognized a need for additional skills and missions to be assigned to their frogmen. In that year, the Norwegian frogmen were divided into two units. One unit was assigned the Navy's explosive ordnance disposal task. The other was considered to be pure commando. The new unit, the Marinejaegerkommandos (MJK), or Navy Hunter Commando Team, was the Norwegian equivalent of the U.S. Navy SEALs.

The U.S. Navy SEALs soon established close ties with the MJK, and were cross-training with them from early on. Due to their training in a very rugged environment, the MJK were thought to be some of the finest woodsmen and outdoor survivalists in the free world. SEAL platoons conducted winter training and exercises with the MJK and considered the effort time well spent. The SEALs brought home skills in winter warfare they might not otherwise have been able to learn. And the Norwegians learned some of the newest technology and combat tricks from the U.S. masters of the craft.

Cooperation became so close between the two units that the SEALs helped in the training of Norwegian military candidates for the MJK. A five-level course for the MJK had been established at the Norwegian diver school, the Dykker-og froskemannsskolen, at the Haakonsvern Naval Base outside of Bergen. The first level of MJK training consisted of basic selection,

underwater swimming instruction, parachuting, pa-
trolling, survival, and navigation courses. The second
level of training took place at and around the Ramsund
Naval Base in northern Norway, almost 120 kilometers
north of the Arctic circle. It was here that the MJK
training became even harder, and the U.S. Navy
SEALs assisted in adding to that level of difficulty.

The entire SEAL platoon was involved in the operation. The SEALs were playing the part of the aggressor
forces in this exercise, with the MJK candidates expected to track and eventually ambush the SEAL platoon. But the SEALs didn't see the scenario going
quite that way. Instead, Fourth Platoon was going to
turn the tables on the candidates.

Having observed and tracked the Marinejaegerkommando candidates for the better part of the day, the
SEALs knew the path they were taking and just how
they were traveling it. Having gathered this intelligence, the SEALs carefully chose their killing ground.

In the Teams, there was never any problem with an
officer or other leader accepting advice from any of his
men. And Lieutenant Greg Rockham was no exception
to that long-accepted procedure. Through the recommendations of his platoon chief, Rockham could see
that the upcoming ambush was going to hold a few sur-
prises for the MJK candidates.

Senior Chief Frank Monday had been in the Teams
since the early 1970s. He had been on deployments
with some of the last SEAL units sent to Vietnam and

had seen active combat. This experience was getting to be a rarity in the Teams by the late 1980s, as men retired or reached a rank where they just couldn't man a gun and go out into the field as much as they might have liked. Even Monday was going to go up for master chief soon, a rank that would make him too valuable to just run a platoon in the field. Rockham had a tremendous resource in the knowledge and experience held by the chief, and he wasn't going to waste it.

The men from Fourth Platoon had been carefully situated and concealed at the ambush site. This care didn't take any conscious effort on the part of the platoon leadership. The men were thoroughly trained and knew what was expected of them. The location of the ambush site was Rockham's decision. The rest of the action was just standard operating procedures for a point ambush. On this particular ambush, there was an additional twist added by Rockham and Monday; now it was a reverse L-shaped ambush.

Men were hidden away next to bushes, rocks, or whatever cover they preferred. Camouflage was provided by the mottled woodland pattern of greens and browns on their Gore-Tex trousers. Over the same pattern Gore-Tex jackets, they wore hooded overwhite parka covers. The mixed white and green camouflage patterns had proven very effective in locations such as this, near the top of the treeline.

Most of the SEALs were armed with Colt M16A2 Model 727 carbines, still called the CAR-15 by a lot of the operators in the Teams in spite of their fourteen-inch barrels. A number of the carbines had M203 40mm grenade launchers mounted underneath the barrels. The balance of the platoon, the automatic weapons men, held M60E3 light machine guns.

Since it was a training exercise, the muzzles of the weapons were covered with blanks adapters. The 5.56mm and 7.62mm blanks would make noise and flash, but little else would come out of the muzzles. The grenade launchers were loaded with M583 white star parachute flares. The flare in Ken Fleming's launcher had been slightly modified for the ambush. The plastic cap of the round had been removed and the cloth parachute taken off the flare. With the plastic cap pressed back on, the flare would function normally, but quickly fall to the ground while burning.

Several of the SEALs had other modified grenades. Two of the men had canister-type grenades that had chunks of evergreen branches tied to them. The tree branches seemed to be excessive camouflage, and would make the grenades difficult to throw.

In carefully selected locations in front of the line of

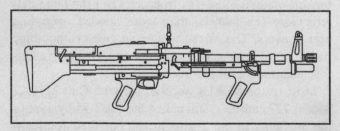

M60E3

SEALs were M112 demolition charges buried in the snow. The 1.25 pound blocks of C-4 plastic explosive were primed with a pair of M6 electrical blasting caps to ensure their detonation on command. In addition to the explosives, the SEALs on the flanks of the position had flash-crash grenades at the ready. The flash-crash grenades were simply modified M116A1 hand grenade simulators with the burning safety-fuse igniters removed and replaced with M201A1 delay fuzes, such as those found on standard M18-series smoke grenades.

The 1.3 ounces of photoflash powder in the cardboard bodies of the M116A1 simulators would make a brilliant flash of light and a thunderclap of noise when they went off. But there would be little in the way of fragmentation from the thick cardboard body of the munition.

The Norwegian instructors wanted the Level 2 training to be an additional weeding-out process. Part of the curriculum included training in basic demolitions. It would be a bad idea to allow men who were otherwise competent, but had an innate fear of explosions, to handle explosives. It was thought that a violent series of unexpected explosions, flashes, and cracks of noise would go a long way toward locating those candidates who couldn't make the grade. So the SEALs were going to do their best in aiding in the weeding-out process.

Since all of the men were training north of the Arctic circle by almost seventy-five miles, the early fall days were short. By mid-afternoon the sun was already dipping below the horizon, but the SEALs were all in their positions. The area they were settled in had a gorgeous view of the mountains. It also overlooked the dark, cold waters of the fjord stretched out in the distance. The place seemed almost too beautiful for the violence that sat waiting to be unleashed. But in the gathering darkness and the dying light of the Arctic sun, Fourth Platoon of SEAL Team 2 patiently waited in the snow.

With a sliver of sun still over the horizon, the MJK candidate platoon entered the SEALs kill zone. The group of over fifteen candidates was larger than the usual MJK twelve-man unit, but they were moving well, following the track the SEALs had laid out for them. Scout skiers had been sent out ahead of the main body by the candidate leaders. These point men weren't far enough forward, however, to find the spot where the SEALs had hooked back to overlook their own trail. By the time the scouts discovered the ruse, it would be too late to warn their fellow candidates.

As the lead skiers of the main body of the group entered the kill zone, Rockham prepared to fire the demolition charges. The detonation would be the signal to initiate the ambush. After following their set SOP, the men would withdraw and fall back to a previously determined rallying point.

Rockham flipped back the d-ring safety bails on the Mark 1 miniature blasting machine he held in his hand. With the bails moved, the handles of the machine were free to spring out. Watching carefully to make sure no candidates were too close to where the charges were planted, he waited for the main body to reach the center of the kill zone.

Several rapid squeezes of his hand built up a charge in the generator of the blasting machine. When the charge had built up enough strength, the circuitry switched and sent the firing impulse down through the wires.

The electrical impulse flashed through the wires, reaching the M6 blasting caps wired together in series. The electricity heated the bridge wire in the center of the caps to incandescence. That heat fired the easily lit ignition charge of barium styphnate and barium chromate. That flash in turn set off the lead azide intermediate charge. The shock of the intermediate charge initiated the base charge of RDX. That explosion, taking place buried deep inside the C-4 of the M112 block, detonated the main charge.

The complex sequence of events for the firing process took only a few microseconds from squeeze to explosion. The widely spaced 1.25 pound blocks of plastic explosive detonated in a single shattering roar. Their detonation simulated the firing of four M18A1 claymore mines, which would have been used in a real combat situation.

Just as the detonation of a line of claymore mines would have initiated a live-fire ambush, the M112 blocks signaled the beginning of the SEALs' ambush. The Fourth Platoon ambushers opened fire on the startled MJK candidates.

Several of the SEAL 40mm grenadiers fired their parachute flares into the air. The thump of the launchers was followed a moment later by a faint pop as the flares ejected from their tubes almost six hundred feet in the air. As the burning magnesium flares descended slowly on their small parachutes, the brilliant light cast a wavering illumination over a scene of building confusion on the part of the candidates.

The 40mm flare that had its parachute removed was fired over the candidates heads toward a safe zone some distance behind them. When that flare popped, its burning magnesium candle fell to earth and back-lit the candidates, silhouetting them for the SEALs' fire.

With their flares launched, the M203 gunners lowered their weapons and switched to firing their carbines. The din of their 5.56mm blanks was added to the overwhelming fire of eight automatic weapons. The heavier roar of the 7.62mm M60E3s sounded out loudly over the lighter rips of the 5.56mm carbines.

The platoon SOP was for each weapon to fire two full thirty-round magazines. The belt-fed M60E3 machine guns would each fire a single hundred-round belt. The two flankers on either end of the SEAL formation would first fire a single magazine from their weapons, then toss a grenade. Since they were conducting a training op, the grenades were the flash-crashes, and they were intentionally thrown into a safe area.

As the candidates responded to the sudden ambush, the roar and flash of the two grenades startled them further. But these were not just green troops. They had already been through the first part of the selection process and had all served for at least a year in the regular armed forces. In what was very good time, the MJK candidates organized themselves and responded to the SEALs' ambush in the only proper way open to them: they charged the guns.

This was expected by the SEALs when they had originally laid out their reverse L-shaped ambush. The men with the canister grenades pulled the pins and tossed the cans out in front of the formation. The wind was coming in from the east, to the left of the SEALs' position. The light breeze helped the spread of the violet and green smoke as the grenades burned in the snow.

The use of the evergreen branches tied to the grenades was clear now. Since the metal bodies of the canister-type M18 smoke grenades heated up as they burned, the bulky branches slowed the grenades sinking into the snow. Staying on the surface longer, the grenades were able to put out large clouds of colored smoke.

The smoke helped obscure the SEALs' withdrawal from their positions. But the candidates could see through the smoke well enough to make out the SEALs and give chase. As the candidates stormed forward, they met the other item the colored smoke was obscuring.

Two M7A3 CS tear gas grenades had been tossed out with the smoke canisters. The faint white clouds of tear gas had been completely hidden by the colored smoke. Now the candidates were no longer seeing as well as they had been. The CS gas seared the linings of their noses, mouths, and lungs, in addition to the tearing and great pain in their eyes. But in spite of this, the candidates were still game. They continued giving chase, which was when they ran into the SEALs' last surprise.

In a normal L-shaped ambush the long arm of the L is made up of the ambush attack force. The short leg of the L is usually situated to cut off the forward movement of the target forces. This allows the blocking group to fire down the length of the target force, as well as hold them in the killing zone for as long as possible.

For the SEALs' reverse L-shaped ambush, Rockham had followed Chief Monday's advice and put the second squad in line squared off from the first squad. Now, as the SEALs of the first squad withdrew, they drew the candidates force into the killing zone of the second squad.

As the candidates came into the second killing zone, the hidden SEALs opened fire. No C-4 detonated on the second ambush. But the rain of additional flash-crash grenades supplied sufficient explosive thunder.

The candidates could still see, through streaming eyes, the backs of the withdrawing SEALs. But now there was an entirely new group firing on them. Then the withdrawing SEALs stopped and turned on their pursuers. They added their firepower to what was already being put out by their Teammates in the second squad.

In the noise, flash, and smoke, some of the candidates became seriously confused. Instead of properly responding to the threat, a number of the candidates milled about badly or went off in the wrong direction.

The SEALs had taught the young men a serious lesson about the fog of war and the deadly confusion of combat.

CHAPTER 3

Within a week of his first meeting with Korvin, Aleksandr Kondrachev again found himself being called to the building on Samokatanya Street. But this time, instead of going to Korvin's office, Alek was directed to another office room. When he arrived at the door and knocked, he was immediately greeted with a gruff, "Enter!"

The room had been set up for conferences, with a long, heavy, dark-wood table in the center. Surrounding the table were tall-backed chairs of the same vintage as the main table. Seated in the room was Yuri Korvin and a man Alek had never seen before. Since he had been in Moscow such a short time, meeting a complete stranger was hardly a surprise for the young scientist.

What was strange was the level of deference Korvin showed to the other man as he introduced Alek. The big man was wearing a dark suit of severe cut, which wrapped around his frame and gave him the appearance of being a large barrel with a head on it. His heavy, gruff appearance blended in well with many of the higher-ranking political commissars Alek had seen on the state-run news programs and in the paper. Introduced as Lieutenant General Leonid Stankevich, he remained seated and merely nodded curtly at the introduction.

With little preamble, General Stankevich asked Alek a series of questions about tac testing of Variant K, what the environment had been, and if the material had actually showed the virulence that had been reported in the documentation. It was obvious to Alek that the general knew exactly what he was talking about and had been fully briefed on Variant K. He answered all of the questions as truthfully and completely as he could. But one question troubled him greatly.

"And you witnessed the death of Academician Kashnavili directly, I understand?" Stankevich asked.

"He was a fully accredited doctor of medicine," Alek said, bristling.

It was obvious that Stankevich was not used to being corrected in even a minor way by an underling. But the raising of a heavy black eyebrow was all that showed of his displeasure.

"Kondrachev, you forget yourself!" Korvin said sharply. "You will have to excuse Comrade Kondrachev, General. I understand that he was close friends with Comrade Kashnavili."

A heavy grunt was all that was forthcoming from the general.

"My apologies, sir," Alek continued. "But to answer your question, yes, he succumbed to the infection right in front of me."

"And there was no prior warning?" Stankevich asked.

"Outside of some minor fatigue that could be attributed at the time to long working hours, no sir," Alek answered.

"That is of note," General Stankevich continued. "We are going to arrange a series of tests for both Variant K and your new aerosol delivery system. You will arrange the safe transport of a number of your filled munitions to the naval base at Arkhangelsk. We will give you a timetable for later in the year, when the test site is prepared and the conditions correct for our study."

"May I ask where the test will take place, General?" Alek asked, receiving a sharp look from Korvin. "So that the materials may be properly packaged and prepared for your test series," he quickly added.

"Very well," the general replied. "We shall be conducting our tests in a cold maritime environment on the island of Morzhovets at the mouth of Mezenskaya Bay in the White Sea. It is a very isolated area with no population centers of any note for dozens of miles in any direction."

"Yes sir, and your test target?"

"That is something we shall supply ourselves and is not of your immediate concern. I have been told that you are not only the developer of this new battle strain, but that you are also Biopreparat's new deputy of safety?"

"Yes, General. But it is a post I have only recently been placed in."

"No matter, I am sure you will serve well in it. Your concerns do you justice. But these tests are matters which do not concern you directly. You will be told what you need to know in a timely manner for you to do your job."

"Thank you, sir."

Getting up from his seat, General Stankevich responded to Alek's comment with a curt wave. Alek had remained standing through the bizarre meeting, but Korvin quickly stood when the general came out of his seat.

"Think nothing of it," Stankevich said. "I am sure that you and Comrade Korvin have things to talk about. I can find my own way out. I shall be in touch." And with that, General Stankevich moved out of the room.

After following him to the door and saying his good-byes, Korvin turned back to Alek. "You young fool," he spat. "You have no idea who you were just talking to, do you?"

"No sir, I—"

"You will very quickly have to learn how to keep your place," Korvin said, interrupting. "That was Lieutenant General Leonid Stankevich, of the KGB's First Directorate!"

"The KGB," Alek said, blanching, "but what would they want with me?"

"With you, nothing. They are interested in the results of your work, nothing more, I'm sure."

"But the KGB?"

"You have not yet heard of Department Fourteen of the First Chief Directorate?"

"Only in passing, when they came to Kirov asking for some samples a few years back."

"Well, General Stankevich was the head of Laboratory Twelve up to a few years ago. And they have been able to ask anyone for anything."

Alek had heard of the infamous Laboratory 12. It was where exotic hardware was developed for the Soviet's intelligence services. And the materials developed were usually of a very lethal nature. Rumors had abounded of how some of the developments of Biopreparat and others had been used to eliminate enemies of the state. And their interest in his own work meant that his development of a defense for his beloved Russia was now going to be corrupted—into covert weapons for assassination and terrorism.

These thoughts flashed through Alek's mind as he stood there, only half hearing Korvin. He could now well imagine the course "additional tests" might center on, and just what they would be supplying in the way of their own targets. The KGB also ran the gulag prison system in the Soviet Union. And a large number of work camps surrounded the White Sea area.

"I will tell you this, to warn you as to just how dangerous the bear was you just poked at so disrespectfully. Have you ever heard of the Flute program?" Korvin asked.

"No, what is that?" Alek responded.

"It is the development of biological weapons for

specific applications by the KGB," Korvin said in a low voice. "They have always been interested in our work here at Biopreparat. Sometimes, I think they stir up some of the conflict between ourselves and the Army's Fifteenth Directorate just to keep the both of us off balance. And now they are interested in you, Alek. This could mean great things for your career, as long as you remain careful."

The smile on Korvin's face as he said the last few lines could have been compared to the toothy leer of a bare skull, had Alek noticed such things. But then, Korvin had not noticed the deep ideological struggle that was taking place not three feet from where he was standing. Rather, he thought he had put a proper amount of fear into his underling to keep him in line in the future.

The reality was going to prove very different.

0947 ZULU
1425 Vilnius Place, Apartment 412
Fili, suburbs of Moscow

Kondrachev tried again to bury himself in his work, but he could no longer develop the passion he once held for it. The images of the Russia he had striven to help defend for so long were blurring. In the People's Paradise he had thought Russia could be, there wasn't much room for the kind of leaders he had been meeting. During some of his inspection tours, he had been offered all types of bribes and inducements to look the other way.

Men in control of some of the most lethal materials ever conceived of were incompetents solely concerned with protecting their bit of turf. And in Moscow the situation was much worse. The people around him were more concerned with protecting their own status and position, and retaining the privileges that status brought, than the results of the jobs they did.

Perestroika was new, and it was the buzzword on everyone's lips. Soviet Party Chairman Gorbachev wanted new accommodations to be made with the West. Changes were being tried in the Soviet economy, and these frightened a lot of the people. Both the people in charge and the average Muscovite wondered what would happen next.

As far as his own work went, Korvin was well-satisfied with the results Alek was producing. Procedures were being streamlined at some of the plants of Biopreparat, efficiency was up, and Korvin's own world looked stable. Anything that worked for Kondrachev also made Korvin look good.

Rarely did a meeting go by where Korvin didn't make sure Alek knew just where his new position had come from, in spite of Alek's work, and who he owed it to. Ability counted toward the advancement of a person's career, in Korvin's opinion, but not nearly as much as obedience and loyalty did. And as Aleksandr's work drew more attention from those placed above Korvin, the more concerned he became that his new "protégé" not become too popular.

For Aleksandr the world had become a dark place. The new testing of Variant K had undermined his confidence in his country's leadership. And with his faith in his country's political system shaken, came questions about just what he had been doing at Biopreparat.

The Biopreparat program had been started back in the early 1970s in response to the U.S. government putting forward the convention against the use, storage, and production of biological weapons. The Soviet leadership had been convinced that if the U.S. wanted the rest of the world to cease investigating these weapons, there must be a discovery in the field that the Americans had made and wanted no one else to share.

This had been the situation back during the Great Patriotic War when the United States had supposedly been a Soviet ally in the fight against the Axis powers. But at that time, the Americans had developed atomic weapons in secret. The Soviets had to steal the secrets of the bomb in order to build their own. If the Americans had learned from their mistakes then, what could they have under wraps now?

So the Soviet Union went forward with the greatest biological weapons development and production program the world had ever seen. And Alek knew he had made his contribution to that program. But what if the Americans had been telling the truth all along? That biological weapons were just too dangerous to be produced, let alone ever used. Even now the Americans were suspicious of the Soviets, believing they had been secretly conducting just such a program, as they indeed had been in Biopreparat.

As he sat in his apartment deep in thought, an insistent buzzing sound finally penetrated Alek's concentration. He looked to the window of his apartment, and saw a small fly buzzing at the glass. It was still relatively warm outside and the sun was shining, so the fly was bumping into a barrier it couldn't see, a barrier keeping it from the light. As Alek watched, the fly moved along the glass and became caught in a small web in the corner of the window. Even though there wasn't a spider in sight, Alek could see that the small insect was enmeshed in the strands. With each struggle, it was held all the more firmly.

Alek didn't like flies; they were a vector for the transmission of disease. They could spread some nasty infections, unintentionally, of course. But the work he had done was to create infections that would be spread intentionally. So the fly seemed to him higher up on the moral ladder than he felt at that moment.

He got up from his chair and moved to the window, reached down and gently pulled the fly from the web it was caught in. Opening the window, he released the fly into the outside air. Even with the cold of winter coming on, the fly would have a better chance in the freedom of the outside world than wrapped in a web.

Alek had made his decision. He had to get out of Biopreparat and the Soviet Union. He would defect to the West.

With the big hurdle of that decision, he knew he needed to find a way out. His life as a scientist had not prepared him for how to take such an action. He needed help, but just asking for such a thing was out of the question. Even during these enlightened times of perestroika, the prisons and mental hospitals were ready and waiting to accept more inmates who had attempted just what he was considering.

He had been out of the Soviet Union before, on trips to Europe, to attend medical and scientific conferences. During such meetings he had gained valuable information whose originators would have been shocked to see the use to which their knowledge was being put. But those trips had helped his work, not the kind of problem that was facing him now.

He had relatively few friends, none whom he could think of who might be trusted to help him. His old friend Joseph would have known better what to do. Even what he was planning now wouldn't have shocked the big Georgian. But Joseph might still be able to help him, he thought. His friend had spoken often about a brother in Georgia who was in some form of import-export business. The black market was simply a way of life in the Soviet Union. Many things were "imported" either from the West or from local suppliers to feed the needs of the consumer economy.

Joseph had always mentioned his brother's business with a twinkle in his eye and a broad wink. It embarrassed his wife Sonja, and she would protest that Joseph shouldn't speak of such things. Then he would just laugh with that big, booming voice of his and say that there was no need for her to worry.

The Kashnavili household had always had enough of the necessities of life, and more than a few of the luxuries. Many of the goods were things not easily available to Soviet citizens. Never anything serious, just a radio, or music tapes that weren't on the official imports list, even clothes.

Alek decided that Joseph's brother, Dmitri, would be his first contact. He would plan a visit to Joseph's widow and their two children. Sonja had moved her family back to the Kashnavili family farm near Sukhumi on the shores of the Black Sea. There, he could find Dmitri.

When Alek approached Korvin with the request for a few days holiday, he was surprised at the man's reaction. Korvin was more than happy to let him have the time he needed to see his friend's family and assure himself of their situation. No doubt believing that it was Kondrachev's concern for the well-being of his friend's family that had increased his melancholy of late, a visit could be just the thing to lift the man's spirits.

"That sounds like an excellent idea, my dear Aleksandr," Korvin said. "I know you have been concerned with your friend's family and their well-being. You have seemed a bit preoccupied lately and not concentrating on your work as well as you could. A visit to the Black Sea may be just the tonic you need.

"I want you back here fresh and sharp for an upcoming trip. Valentin Sarkisov, the head of the Second Main Directorate of Health, has requested a man from Biopreparat to accompany him to a conference in Helsinki. I want you to be the man to represent us."

"But sir—" Alek tried to protest.

Korvin would not hear of it. With a wave of his hand

he dismissed Alek's concerns, saying, "As I understand it, the trip will be a long one. Sarkisov does not like to travel by air, and as a Hero of the Soviet Union, he is indulged in this. The conference staff will travel to Helsinki by ship and leave out of Tallinn in Estonia. It will be a short crossing of the Gulf of Finland, and that should be no hardship for you.

"You will be the Biopreparat representative aboard that ship, Alek," Korvin said firmly. "And I expect you to comport yourself in the proper manner."

He continued in a more relaxed tone, "And you needn't worry about your work. I understand that the only major upcoming project are the tests requested by General Stankevich?"

"Yes sir," Alek replied. He could hardly have forgotten them.

"And you have now satisfied yourself about the tests?" Korvin asked with a raised eyebrow.

"Yes sir," Alex answered. "The general's office sent over all the materials I needed regarding the safety of the test site, including the prevailing winds and tides in that area. They will have to make allowances for any changes in the weather, but they have a time window that will allow for that. Other than that, my schedule is clear."

"Then you should be on your way. You may use my name in making your arrangements for the trip. The change of scenery will be good for you. And I expect you to return here all the better for it."

Aleksandr thanked his superior and said he was looking forward to the visit. In his own thoughts, he also agreed with Korvin that the change would be good for him. But it was going to be the beginning of a much bigger change than Korvin could have suspected.

1230 ZULU
68° 34' North, 16° 15' East
North of Evenes
Norway

The whole world had gone white.

It was more than just an absence of color. There wasn't even much in the way of dark. Mostly, there were just different grades of white. The dim sun in the hazy sky cast little in the way of shadows, so all that could be seen was white on white with different shades of white in between.

There was a moving spot on the plain of snow, sliding along on two skies in ruts that could barely be seen. "Join the Navy, travel, see colorful places," the skiing man said to himself. "The only damn bit of color in this whole place is my number."

The tips of his cross-country skis slipped into the edge of his field of vision as the man pushed himself along. Over his mottled camouflage Gore-Tex jacket and dark pants, he wore the parka from a set of over-whites, a thin white snow camouflage. On his chest and back was a yellow rectangle with the number 19 printed on it in black. Across his back was slung a heavy M14 rifle with a folding metal stock. The brown wood and black metal parts of the rifle had been covered with white tape. The tape aided in camouflaging the weapon in the winter environment.

"Lead from the front, in the Teams you always lead from the front," the man said to himself as if repeating a mantra. "Well, how in the hell do you lead anyone when there's no one in sight?"

In spite of his mutterings, it was obvious to anyone who might be watching that the man was pushing himself very hard through the snow on his short cross-country skis. As his ski went forward on one side, his opposite arm reached ahead with his ski pole. As the forward ski slipped back, the pole was shoved hard into the snow, driving himself forward. Then the trailing ski was pulled forward and he continued a long, sliding in a stridelike motion with his feet.

Finally, up ahead on the track the man was following, a thin line of sticks appeared. One hundred meters in front of the sticks, he could see a line of square targets, their dark centers standing out against the white background. A few other figures stood near the line of poles.

"Come on, boss," some of the men cheered, "push it!"

As the skier approached the firing line on what was now obviously a firing range, he stabbed his poles into the snow. Unslinging the rifle from his back, he went into a standing firing position.

Larry Stadt and Henry Lutz both quit their yells of encouragement as Lieutenant Rockham settled into his firing position. Neither of the two SEALs were running the modified military biathlon course, so they had waited at the last of four shooting stations. Rockham would be the last SEAL to fire, and was the last man in the competition.

The Norwegian official standing nearby was simply holding his clipboard and watching Rockham and his targets. If the man approved or disapproved of the two SEALs showing their enthusiasm for a Teammate, he showed little outward sign. His blue eyes simply watched the events with glacial patience. In his country, the biathlon was a very serious event. The combination of cross-country skiing combined with precision shooting had been a primary military skill in the Scandinavian countries. And nowhere was the event taken more seriously than in the Norwegian military.

For twenty kilometers, a seven-man SEAL unit had been competing with a number of equal-size Norwegian teams along the grueling course. Each man operated as an individual, but their combination scores, measured as the time they took to complete the course, was what mattered. This was different from many other courses of the same event. In the Olympics, they competed with .22 target rifles. This biathlon was being run with full-size battle rifles.

At four firing stations, each competitor had seven rounds to hit five targets. The ranges had been at 250, 200, 150, and now finally 100 meters. The first three long ranges had been fired from the much more stable prone position. Each firer had lain down in the snow and dropped the black targets off their white backgrounds. Now, after skiing cross-country for sixteen kilometers, at close to the most exhausted point, the shooters had to fire at the closest targets from the hardest, least stable, firing position.

As he stood at the firing line, Greg Rockham wrenched down on himself. The iron-hard will that had helped make him a SEAL was now at work controlling his body. His breathing slowed, and even his rapid heartbeat calmed a bit. Nothing of the outside world existed for the moment but the black spot a hundred meters away. The world simply slowed and went away as Rockham surrounded himself with a bubble of concentration. Through the rear peep sight of his rifle, he centered on the first of his targets.

With the front blade of the rifle sight now rising up and down with his every breath, Rockham reached his point of firing. As the front blade lowered on an exhalation, he stopped for a moment and held his breath. The rifle held steady, firm up against his shoulder, his cheek welded to the stock as he took his shot.

With the front blade centered in the rear peep and frozen on the target, he began his trigger pull. The index finger on his right hand first took up the slack in the M14's two-stage trigger. Then as he added pressure steadily with his finger, the sear suddenly released. The big rifle bucked as it recoiled and the shot roared out.

Immediately moving his sights on to the next target, Rockham knew it would be faster to just continue shooting in a smooth motion rather than stay and check each target on the follow-through after a shot. Even as his rifle was coming down from the recoil of the first shot, it was lining up on the second target. With a

smooth consistency, the SEAL officer put out his first
five rounds. There would be no need to manually reload his additional rounds of ammunition; each of his
shots had struck their marks. With the sound of his last
shot still echoing across the snow, Rockham double-
checked his targets as he reslung his weapon across his
back. Grabbing up his ski poles, he pushed off for the
last leg of the cross-country run.

The biathlon was a timed event. The cross-country
skiing took the most time, of course. But each missed
target in the shooting portion added two full minutes to
the total time for completing the course. SEALs love a
good competition, and Rockham was no different. And
no matter what the event, they would give it their all,
especially when their other Teammates depended on
them to help them all win. Rockham had been pacing
himself for his last big cross-country push. And now he
raised the final rate of that pace.

Nothing mattered in the white world surrounding
him then but the constant slide and drag of his skis.
With each movement of the skis came an equal pushing with his arms and the ski poles he held. No more
kidding thoughts crossed the SEAL lieutenant's mind.
His entire concentration was centered on what he had
to do. As hard as he had focused on his accuracy in
shooting, he focused doubly hard now against the twin
enemies he was facing—distance and time.

With each of the men in a team running individually,
there was no way to see just who might be ahead, so
the effort of each man had to be an all-out affair. And
that was something the SEALs could do very well.

Almost before he realized it, the finish line appeared in the distance ahead. As Rockham approached the end of the course, he could hear his Teammates well before he could make out their individual features.

Roger Kurkowski's bellow, *"Hoo yah, Rock!"* could be heard echoing out above all the other yells. As Rockham approached, his men along the finish line shouted out their support. Even he was surprised at the level of their enthusiasm. And as he slid across the finish line, pandemonium erupted among the American SEALs. Even some of the more stoic Norwegians had broad smiles on their faces.

Rockham slid to a stop and bent over to try and catch his breath. His men gathered around him as he straightened, and then he immediately bent over again from the force of the congratulatory blows on his back and shoulders. He barely managed to ask "How'd we do?" between thumps.

The red-topped face of Shaun Daugherty came up from the crowd in front of Rockham. His young-looking face was split in a wide grin as he shouted over the din, "We came in second! Just behind the Marine-jaegerkommando team. They won, but we made them work for it!"

For a visiting military group, even one as accomplished and athletic as the SEALs, just placing in a biathlon event was considered a big deal. Coming in second, in front of a number of experienced Scandinavian military biathlon teams, was unheard of. The SEALs had done extremely well in what was practically a Norwegian national sport. It was as if a European soccer team had come to the U.S. and fought an NFL football team to a standstill.

"Shit, no kidding," Rockham said as he heard the news. "How'd the others do?"

"Ferber hauls ass on the skis, but he missed two targets on the first range and two more on the last," Shaun said. "But Marks comes on like a black avalanche, and he nails everything with the first shot."

Fourth Platoon's leading petty officer, Mike Ferber, was going to catch some good-natured ribbing about his shooting ability. But that same ribbing would have been much worse for Marks, the platoon's qualified sniper. If Marks had missed the same targets, he would have caught hell from his Teammates for days, in spite of his impressive size.

The celebrations that would go on that evening would be long, loud, and hearty. The SEALs had been training with their Norwegian Marinejaegerkommando counterparts for months now. And good strong friendships had been forged from mutual respect on both sides.

In the Teams, it was a long held tradition that if you worked hard, you were entitled to play hard. And as good Navy sailors, the SEALs tried to uphold that tradition, as they worked very hard indeed. But even a good tradition can sneak up on a man when he isn't looking.

"Oh damn," Rockham croaked from his bed as he failed to pry open his gummed-together eyelids. "Who's shelling the building?"

Staying in the same room with Rockham at the Ramsund Naval Base's bachelor officers' quarters, Shaun Daugherty was already up and using the head facilities as he heard his roommate awaken. As Rockham slowly slipped off the covers and sat at the edge of his bed, Shaun came back into the room.

"Man, Rock," Shaun said with a wide grin. "If you feel as bad as you look, maybe I should just call for a body bag now and save time."

"So that isn't artillery fire," Rockham said with a wince as his voice gathered strength. "It's just my head throbbing. What in the hell did we do last night?"

"Last night?" Shaun said in a puzzled tone. "I don't know what you're talking about. We've been here in Denmark for the last three days."

"Denmark!" Rockham practically shouted. As the pain knifed through his head like a dull explosion, he noticed the wide grin pasted across Shaun's face.

"Fuck you," Rockham said with quiet venom. As the tone of threatened mayhem and death in his voice increased, he added, "And the horse you rode in on, and your immediate family, aunts, uncles, cousins, and all of the other Daughertys back to the beginning of time."

Rockham ran a hand across his face and peered out of bloodshot eyes as Shaun stepped over to a nearby counter. Returning to the bed his platoon leader remained planted on, Daugherty held out a steaming hot cup of coffee in one hand and a bottle of aspirin in the other.

Taking the proffered items in both hands, Rockham first sipped the coffee.

It was a good cup of strong black, Norwegian style coffee. The Norwegians did love their coffee, and were the largest individual consumers of the drink in Europe. And right then, strong black coffee was something the SEAL lieutenant looked on with real favor.

"Bless you, my wayward son," he said. "All is forgiven. But you've been hanging around Kurkowski way too long. His peculiar sense of humor is starting to rub off on you, and that could be an ugly thing."

As he swallowed some aspirin and chased it down with the coffee, Rockham grimaced. "Ugh," he said. "Just what the hell was it that we drank last night?"

"Something our hosts brought out," Shaun said. "All I remember about it was that it was clear. I think they called it aquavit, or something like that. Somebody told me it was potato whiskey. After the first belt, I could feel it start to etch the enamel off my teeth. So I went back to drinking that Pils brand beer. You know, for a basically puritanical bunch, these Norwegians really know how to throw a party. That is, if you actually like pickled fish."

"If you dare to mention food again," Rockham said in a soft growl, "I guarantee you will regret it. Did anything happen I should know about now?"

"I'm not completely sure about that myself," Shaun answered. "There haven't been any explosions or other unexplained noises during the night. Things got a little blurry for me too as the festivities went on. There was something starting up when Stadt climbed up on a table and was shouting about Odin and Valhalla. I'm not sure if he wanted us to go there or send someone there. The guy looks so Nordic to begin with, with those blue eyes and blond hair, I think some of our hosts were comparing him favorably to some old Viking leader. Personally, I was hoping things would calm down before the horned helmets and battle-axes started coming out."

There was a knock on the door. Rockham stepped into the head as Shaun answered it. A moment later Shaun entered as Rockham was standing at the sink, looking into the mirror and wondering if brushing his teeth would be worth the horrible noise it would make. Sceing the look on the younger officer's face, Rockham became all business.

"What is it?" he asked, his hangover forgotten.

"That was Sukov. He had the duty and pulled commo watch last night," Shaun answered. "We're being recalled immediately. We are officially on alert as of the receipt of these orders."

Holding out a sheaf of papers in their envelope to Rockham, Shaun stood by as the lieutenant quickly shuffled through them. "Sitrep?" he asked.

"Nothing to report on the situation yet," Shaun answered. "You know as much as I do. The chief is already turning out the men. Transport is being sent to us. The Navy wants us at Holy Loch in Scotland soonest. The men are already putting together the platoon boxes."

Hangovers or not, when the game bell rings, the SEALs are ready. Within hours the men of Fourth Platoon had packed and sealed up their platoon boxes. They barely had time to say good-bye to their Norwegian hosts before a C-130 Hercules cargo transport plane had arrived for them at the nearby airfield.

Like the men who fought on the sharp edge of things all over the world, their hosts knew better than to ask anything of their SEAL brothers in arms. The men of the Team quickly loaded and secured their equipment containers. As soon as the packing had been checked and secured by the aircraft crew's loadmaster, they were climbing aboard themselves. A quick refueling and the blocky aircraft was climbing back into the air.

The SEALs were on their way on the 1,200 mile flight to the western side of Scotland and the U.S. Navy submarine base at Holy Loch.

CHAPTER 4

1335 ZULU
U.S. Navy Support Activity
Holy Loch, Dunoon
Scotland

After only a flight of about four hours, the C-130 carrying Fourth Platoon and their equipment landed at the Glasgow Airport. As the aircraft taxied away from the terminals to the hangar area, the SEALs were wondering about the next stage of their trip. As the plane came to a stop and the rear ramp came down, their answer was standing there in the form of a civilian bus and truck.

The only information the driver of either vehicle had was that they were to pick up the SEALs and their gear and take them to the U.S. Navy base at Holy Loch, which they already knew. There was little enough reason for the men to further question a driver who had no information to give them. With their platoon boxes loaded aboard the truck, and Mike Ferber riding shotgun on their gear, the SEALs boarded the bus and were on their way.

Even in the Teams, they often enough followed the military tradition of "hurry up and wait." The ride across western Scotland was pretty enough, but the men were getting tired of scenery. Finally arriving on the Cowal Peninsula, the men had their first view of the waters of Holy Loch.

The rolling green hills of Scotland and the Cowal Peninsula framed the blue waters of the loch. A scattering of civilian craft could be seen at different points on the water, but the eyes of the SEALs were drawn to the gray ships of the U.S. Navy offshore. Submarine tender ships were afloat around the area, and a huge craft floated in the center.

The craft, a dry dock, looked like a, rectangular office building set on its side in the water. Its gray color added to the concrete-looking appearance. The massive ship had an open central well deck as well as an open bow and stern. Though it didn't show, the thick sides of the dry dock held tanks that could be flooded to lower the craft into the water. A ship could then go up into the central well. Pumping out the ballast tanks would raise the dry dock, taking whatever ship was in the well up along with it. A large Navy ship could be engulfed by the dry dock and lifted clear of the water.

Next to several of the submarine tender ships could be seen the low, black shapes of submarines. Originally, during the days of diesel submarines, a group of half a dozen subs might be moored next to a tender. The image of a mother pig and her suckling piglets gave the nickname "pigboats" to the early subs. But these new hunters of the deep were large and looked more like all-black killer whales or some other ocean-going predator. None had names or even identification numbers visible from the moving bus. Boomer boats, the ballistic missile submarines, were based out of Holy Loch, but none could be identified by name as the SEALs finally arrived at the base itself.

The land facilities of the base were something of a surprise to the SEALs. Instead of a formal Navy base, the structures in the town of Dunoon itself were used. The Holy Loch base had been used by submarines since the Second World War. But it was in 1960, with the advent of the boomer boats and the Cold War, that the decision was made to turn over the old Royal Navy base to the U.S. Navy. Submarine tender ships, floating dry docks, and other repair and support facilities had been added to the base since that time. But such facilities were either aboard ships offshore or in leased buildings in town.

SEAL detachments had operated from some of those submarines in the loch, especially in the 1980s, with the increase of the Teams' capabilities. And now the SEALs were back.

Their arrival was less than exciting. The bus driver passed through Dunoon and down to the waterfront, stopping at a civilian building near the water. A Navy officer was on hand to meet the bus, and the SEALs hoped he had some information for them. As the bus pulled to a stop, the side door opened and the officer stepped aboard.

"Lieutenant Rockham?" he said.

"That's me," Rockham answered.

"Could I see some ID, please?"

This seemed a little odd and excessively formal for Rockham, but he had been an ensign once himself. When you were the most junior officer around, it paid to be careful. Dutifully, he pulled out his wallet and showed the man his military ID card.

"Thank you, sir," the ensign said after quickly studying the card. "These orders are for you."

He handed over a sealed manila envelope to Rockham. The SEAL officer quickly opened the envelope and scanned the few pages it contained.

"I'm Ensign Larry Bagwell," the officer said, "and I've been assigned to be the liaison for you and your men while you're here at Holy Loch. My orders are to take your men and their equipment to the berthing facilities arranged for you. They are at the home here. There are secure storage facilities available for your equipment in an attached garage. I'm afraid this isn't much more than a converted warehouse, the beds are mostly cots in several smaller rooms. But I was told size and security were paramount."

"That's fine Mr. Bagwell," Rockham answered. "We've stayed in considerably worse."

Chief Monday left the bus and went over to Ferber, who was waiting in the truck. After telling Ferber what was going on, Ferber had the driver take the truck up to the big overhead doors at the side of the building. As soon as it pulled inside, Monday and Ferber had the men unloading equipment boxes and checking locks and seals.

"Do you wish to go to the BOQ now, sir?" Bagwell

asked. "We have rooms for yourself and Mr. Daugherty at the local hotel."

The young officer had a lot to learn yet, and Rockham saw no reason to chew on him. When on alert, and especially when they were in isolation, the officers of a platoon ate, slept, and lived alongside their men. That was how it had always been in the Teams.

"Lieutenant Daugherty and myself will be staying with our men," Rockham said firmly. "Have mess facilities been laid on?"

"You can eat in that restaurant right over there," Bagwell said, pointing to a low building not a hundred feet away. "Outside of that, I haven't been told what other facilities are available to you and your men, sir."

As the two officers were speaking, Mike Ferber had climbed down from the cab of the truck and walked over to the bus door.

"Thank you, then, Mr. Bagwell," Rockham said.

The flustered young officer left the bus as Rockham turned to face Chief Monday, who had come back out from the garage.

"Not bad, Skipper," Monday said. "There's head facilities, showers, and more than enough racks for all of us. But I have to say, this is the damnedest Navy base I have ever been to."

"Okay, Chief," Rockham said with a laugh. "Have everyone grab a rack. Come on Shaun, we'll see what luxurious accommodations have been assigned to us."

A few of the men within earshot laughed at that last remark. It was common for the SEALs to be treated as not completely welcome visitors to some of the Navy bases they were sent to. The nature of their operations made them closemouthed to outsiders, even those in their own service. And since little information would get out about these known warriors, scuttlebutt usually filled the information vacuum. That, combined with the SEALs' reputation as hard partyers, tended to make Regular Navy base commanders not always the most hospitable.

But the warehouse looked clean and comfortable. The men could take care of the rest of their needs themselves if they had to. There was obviously more the SEALs wanted to ask, but that wasn't something they were going to do with outsiders looking on.

Later, in one of the smaller rooms they had appropriated for themselves, the two platoon officers had a meeting with Chief Monday and Mike Ferber. Rockham had taken the time to carefully read the orders he'd received, and there wasn't much more there than he had read on the bus.

"Okay, we've been put on alert and are in isolation as of now," he said bluntly.

Being on alert meant something might be coming down and the men were going to see some action. But being in isolation also meant they couldn't leave their area. There would be no interaction between the SEALs and anyone else, other than ordering food nearby. This was normally the time they would be briefed on whatever op they were to prepare for. And in the privacy and security of isolation, the platoon could plan their actions and even practice what they might do on the op. But this wasn't going to be that kind of isolation.

"All the orders say are that we are to stand ready to receive further orders," Rockham said, some irritation in his voice. "There are no details given at all."

"Okay," Chief Monday said. "That just means some rack time for the guys. I'm sure Mike and I can run them through enough PT to keep their edges from getting too dull."

Ferber, who had been a first phase BUD/S instructor shortly before transferring into Team 2 and Fourth Platoon, grinned widely at the chief's suggestion.

"Anything on how long we might be waiting?" Shaun asked.

"Nothing at all," Rockham answered.

"These things can sometimes just dissolve and go away," Chief Monday said to Daugherty. "It doesn't do you any good to get excited about what might be coming. You can't be sure you're on an op until the plane lifts off, and sometimes not even then."

Chief Monday had long years of experience in the Teams, and his advice was based on that experience. "I'll get the men fed and then start them out checking over the gear, Skipper," he said. "We left Norway in a hurry, and I want to make sure everything is ship-shape."

Considering that the chief had supervised the packing and loading of the Team's gear, Rockham had little doubt that everything would be found in good condition. But the work would keep the platoon from thinking about what might be coming.

"Sounds good, Chief," Rockham said with a smile. "I could use a bite myself now."

"Feeling better now, are we?" Shaun said innocently.

The next day brought little in the way of answers for
the men of Fourth Platoon. But the second day brought
considerably more questions, with the arrival of a
number of trucks and more SEALs.

The vehicles consisted of two vans and a semi truck.
Each of the nondescript commercial vans were towing
a trailer, with the contents covered from casual view.
But the men of SEAL Team 2 had seen those trailers
and their contents numerous times. Looking more like
a large covered propane gas tank than a watercraft,
each of the trailers carried a Mark VIII SDV—a SEAL
Delivery Vehicle.

The SDVs, more commonly called "eight-boats,"
were small submersibles that were intended to transport
four SEALs and their gear over long distances underwater. The boats were operated by a pilot and a navigator—an enlisted man and an officer, respectively. The
nineteen-foot-long, black fiberglass eight-boats had no
viewing ports, just two sliding hatches at the bow and
after compartments on each side of the hull.

The eight-boats were wet-type free-flooding submersibles; they didn't remain dry inside while under
way. Which meant that each one of the crew and passengers had to wear breathing gear or use regulators
hooked up to air tanks in the boat.

The other vehicle was a forty-foot flatbed trailer,
with the huge contents of the bed covered with a big
tarp over a framework. The outline of whatever was

under the tarp was well-hidden, but the low springs on the flatbed trailer indicated more than a little weight.

When the two vans stopped, their doors opened and eight SEALs climbed out. The three officers came over to where Rockham and Daugherty were standing in the raised overhead door of the warehouse. The first man to get to the door—Lieutenant Fisher, according to the name tag on his uniform—stuck out his hand.

"Fellow lost travelers, I presume?" Fisher said with a grin as he shook hands with Rock and Shaun in turn.

"Welcome to the land of the lost," Rockham said with a laugh, realizing that Fisher had a sense of humor about everything.

"May I introduce the rest of my flock?" Fisher continued. Without waiting for an answer, he indicated the officer standing next to him. "And this Joe Average–appearing individual is Ensign Sam Paulson."

"Hi," Paulson said sheepishly as he shook hands.

"Along with him we have Lieutenant William 'Mr. Bill' Rogers," and Fisher indicated the lean, brown-haired man standing on the other side of him.

"Welcome aboard," Rockham said as he shook hands all around.

"Thanks," Rogers said. "Glad to finally be here."

"Finally?" Shaun asked with a questioning look.

"This time yesterday, we were all back at SDV Team at Little Creek," Fisher explained. "We received orders to get two SDV crews together as well as a DDS and a support crew. A C-5A was waiting for us when we arrived at the air station, and we haven't stopped moving until we got here."

"You fly in to Glasgow?" Rockham asked.

"We should have been so lucky," Paulson said.

"They flew us in to Machrihanish," Fisher explained. "After putting us aboard some ferry in Campbeltown, we crossed the bay and unloaded at Ardrossan. We've been trucking the rest of the way through some nice countryside."

Machrihanish was a huge military airfield to the southwest of Holy Loch. Boasting one of the longest runways in the world, the airfield would have easily been able to accept the giant C-5A aircraft.

"You bring that big mother with you on board the aircraft?" Rockham said, indicating the covered flatbed.

Dry Deck Shelter

"That's the new transporter for a Dry Deck Shelter," Rogers said. "I think this is her first official deployment outside of CONUS," by which he meant the continental United States.

"Official?" Shaun said. "So you have some orders for us?"

"No," Fisher said, puzzled. "We were told that orders would be waiting for us here. You don't have them?"

"Nope," Rockham said. "We're regular mushrooms here."

"Kept in the dark and fed horseshit?" Paulson interjected.

"You've got that right," Rockham said with a laugh. "The only thing we've been given is mostly dark. No shit of any kind, really."

"Damn," Fisher said with feeling.

Ensign Bagwell came up, looking as harried as always. As far as the SEALs could tell, that was the junior officer's permanent expression.

"Sorry gentlemen," Bagwell said. "They just told me you had arrived."

"Gentlemen," Rockham said with a little humor, "may I introduce our liaison with the base, Ensign Bagwell. If anyone has information for us, it will be the good ensign."

"I'm sorry, sir," Bagwell said apologetically, "but I've only been told where you can secure that large flatbed under guard. It will be taken out to the *Los Alamos* as soon as possible. As far as anything else goes—"

"We know," Rock interrupted. "We're under isolation."

"Aw, nuts," Paulson said with some feeling.

"And just where is the *Los Alamos*?" Fisher asked.

"She's the big floating dry dock out in the loch," Bagwell said.

"Okay," Fisher drawled as he looked out at the huge, floating gray-colored structure the SEALs had come upon earlier. Over a hundred meters long, the *Los Alamos* was shaped like a huge shoebox with thick walls and open ends. An entire nuclear submarine was now within the two walls of the dry dock. Right now the dry dock looked to be preparing to sink into the water. Men were busy all about her removing equipment that had been used to work on the submarine up in the cradle within the structure. Moving something so massive had always fascinated the engineer in Fisher. And he was looking forward to seeing this operation take place.

Later in the warehouse, the officers and the leading petty officers of their detachments were relaxing and enjoying a few beers. Ensign Bagwell had made certain that the Base Exchange had some of the better local brew sent over. The enlisted men were also relaxing in their open area, swapping stories. Bryant had recognized a few of the guys he had served with at SDV Team 2 and was introducing them around. Back in another area, the officers were trying to decide just what their next move might be.

"I don't know what we're going to be doing," Fisher

said. "They didn't give me any mission parameters at all. We've got a DDS with us and an SDV to put in her. Even a spare boat and crew. But no submarine."

"What do you mean?" Shaun asked.

"Well, the SDV can be launched off anything that can pick her up," Paulson said. "But the DDS can only be mated to the deck of a converted submarine."

"And there's damned few of those available," Rogers said. "There's the *Cavalla*. She was the first sub converted to take a DDS. But the last I heard, she was at Pearl and operating in the Pacific. There are some Sturgeon class boats converted or being planned to. The *Tunny* is undergoing refit, so she isn't available, which is too bad. I've worked off her and she's a great boat. The *Archerfish* is on a Med cruise. And I don't know which other boats might be available."

"So here we are with a zillion dollars worth of equipment, manpower, and training," Rockham said, "and we don't know what we're supposed to do with it?"

"That seems to be about the size of it," Fisher agreed.

"Even for the Regular Navy," Rogers said, "that seems a little screwed up."

Chief Monday and several of the others nodded in agreement.

"I wonder why they didn't pull the detachment out of Machrihanish for this operation?" Shaun wondered out loud.

The Teams maintained Naval Special Warfare Units (NSWU) in several locations around the world. These

Command & Control elements were intended to support Naval Special Warfare detachments operating in their areas. NSWU-2 was manned with SEALs from SEAL Team 2 and based at the Machrihanish airfield.

"I don't know," Fisher answered. "But we were told we wouldn't be having any contact with them when we arrived at Machrihanish."

"Curiouser and curiouser," Rockham said.

"Well, I hope they don't take too long to tell us what's going on," Rogers said. "It will take us at least a day or so to mate up that DDS with whatever boat they bring in. This whole system is still being developed."

"Any problems?" Shaun asked.

"Just the usual teething ones," Rogers said. "The same as you would get with any new system. Procedures are still being developed, and there could be a bug hiding somewhere for us to find."

As the SEALs sat discussing past actions and theories about their possible future one, Ensign Bagwell came into the warehouse. Knocking on the door frame—the door to Rock's room was open—Bagwell got the attention of everyone in the room.

"Yes, Mr. Bagwell," Rockham said. "Any news for us?"

"Yes sir, there is," the ensign said.

Suddenly, everyone in the room was giving Ensign Bagwell their undivided attention.

"I have a bus and driver outside for your convenience," Bagwell said, pleased to have good news. "The *Archerfish* has arrived and is tied up to the tender *Hunley* right now. She's going to be taken in to the *Los*

Alamos soon. There are several civilians who have also just come in. I have been asked to bring you and your men to the headquarters building for a briefing."

"Outstanding, Mr. Bagwell," Rockham said, with additional sounds of agreement coming from the others in the room. "We shall be more than happy to accompany you. Looks like it's going to be the *Archerfish*, Mr. Bill," Rock said as an aside to Lieutenant Rogers.

"As long as she's here," Rogers said, to the mutual agreement of everyone.

1420 ZULU
SubRon 14 Headquarters
U.S. Navy Support Activity
Dunoon
Scotland

It was a short trip to the headquarters building of Submarine Squadron 14. In keeping with the intent of the Navy to blend in with the local surroundings, the HQ was located in a civilian building, a converted, large private house. Whether this was the normal headquarters or just something being used temporarily, the SEALs had no idea. And they were too intent on following Ensign Bagwell and getting more information about their mission to think of asking.

Whether the building had been a mansion, a manor, or some kind of schoolhouse didn't matter to the SEALs. What mattered was the information they were going to receive there. As the men were ushered into a large windowless hall, they took note of the portable chalkboards at the front of the room on either side of a wooden podium. Each of the chalkboards were covered with a sheet to conceal what was on it.

Rows of chairs were set facing the podium, and the SEALs didn't need to be told that the seats were for them. As the men milled about for a moment choosing seats, the sounds of an argument could be heard coming from somewhere close by. Ensign Bagwell looked considerably less than comfortable, which was pretty much the standard expression for ensigns.

The sound of a door closing hard came ahead of footsteps coming up to the door of the hall. A Navy commander stood framed in the doorway for a moment, glowering at the SEALs.

"Nothing but a bunch of glorified, knife-carrying killers," he said with contempt. Before anyone in the room could say anything, the officer turned on his heel and stormed away.

Having been met with scorn from the men of the Regular Navy before, this was nothing new to the men of the Teams. But they were surprised nevertheless, and were silent for a moment.

"Yeah," Kurkowski said, breaking the silence, "but it's not always a big knife."

The tension broken, a chuckle flowed through the room as the men went back to taking their seats. "Just who was that masked man, Sheriff?" someone said.

"That was Captain Warrick," Ensign Bagwell volunteered. In the Navy, any commander of a ship, no matter what his standing rank, was always referred to as Captain. "It was his sub that was bumped in rotation to get the *Archerfish* into dry dock. He's not very happy with the delay."

"Really?" someone said.

As the comment initiated another round of soft laughter, Chief Monday growled, "Belay that!"

As the men settled down, Ensign Bagwell stood up and shouted, "Attention on deck!"

All of the SEALs snapped to, coming to their feet at a position of attention as a group of people entered the room. The leading man of the group—a Navy captain, by the rank on his uniform—stated loudly, "Take your seats," as he went up to the podium.

Four Navy officers and two civilians entered the room. The officers were a captain, a commander, and two lieutenant commanders, the gold dolphins on their uniforms indicating they were all of the submarine service. This was something the SEALs had all seen before. The officers could be involved with some part of the briefing, support, or just be some kind of qualified onlookers.

But one of the others entering the room was definitely not what the SEALs were used to seeing on a naval installation. To say that the woman walking up to the front of the room was easy to look at would have been an understatement. She was striking. There was a very trim figure under the tailored business suit, with a nicely filled out jacket as well. The nylon-encased legs extending out from the knees down from the skirt were very much worthy of attention as well.

But it was her face, framed in thick honey-blond hair, that seized the attention of a number of the men in the room; it was drawn back in a bun clipped to the back of her neck. And the green eyes that flashed at the men spoke of intelligence, as well as a no-nonsense attitude.

With their size and general fitness level, the SEALs in the room resembled a professional football team. And like many fit and confident men, most of the SEALs had good-sized libidos as well. It was with a disdaining look at the reactions of some of the men in the room that the woman sat down on one of the four chairs at the side of the podium.

The last person to enter appeared to be a bureaucratic type in a good suit. He was tall and had the look of a desk-bound warrior, something the SEALs had seen too much of. The carefully trimmed hair, graying at the temples, and impeccable suit labeled the man as an "Intel weenie" to a number of the more experienced SEALs.

None of the SEALs noticed the intent look that Chief Monday gave the suited newcomer. It was a look of both recognition and immediate dislike. But the chief had been in the Teams far too long to let anything like that show on his face for very long. The look was there, and then it passed, noticed only by the man to whom it was directed.

"Take your seats!" the captain said as he walked up to the podium. The men sat down, eager to find out just why they had been gathered in Scotland.

"I am Captain Edward Kane," the officer continued,

"the commanding officer of SubRon Fourteen and this base. All of you men have been brought here for a specific mission, which I have no direct knowledge of. Mr. Danzig here," Captain Kane indicated the man in the suit, "will fully brief you.

"This other officer here," Captain Kane said, as he turned to the lieutenant commander standing just to his side, "is my operations officer, Commander Walters."

Commander Walters nodded to the SEALs sitting in front of him.

"Ops will be available to assist you in any way that we can here," Captain Kane continued. "If you have any specific needs, please feel free to come to him.

"Men, I will leave you to Mr. Danzig," Kane said as he stepped away from the podium. "Ensign Bagwell, if you will accompany us, please. Men, keep your seats."

With that, the captain followed by his ops officer and the harried Ensign Bagwell, left the room.

Stepping up to the podium, Danzig began to speak. "I'm Peter Danzig, an assistant DDO"—Deputy Director for Operations—"and I have been sent here to brief you men on an upcoming operation." The SEALs stirred at this announcement. Any form of DDO giving them their briefing meant that this was an Agency-inspired operation. Though the Teams had worked with the CIA since the days of the UDTs, there was little love lost between the two organizations. To the SEALs, an Agency spook was someone who could barely be trusted. To the CIA career man, the SEALs were a tool to be used as required.

"Everything you hear in this room is classified Top

Secret. You men have been brought here to conduct a clandestine recovery of a foreign national at sea," Danzig said as he walked over to one of the covered blackboards. Flipping back the cloth, Danzig exposed a detailed chart of the Gulf of Finland.

"The man you are to recover is a high-ranking Soviet official. He is part of a special Soviet delegation on biological warfare that will be attending a conference in Helsinki in ten days." Danzig pointed at the general location of Helsinki.

"The individual is an early middle-age male," Danzig continued, "reported to be in excellent health and condition. His hobby is skin-diving and he has spent a number of hours skin and scuba diving around the Soviet Union.

"The delegation will be crossing the Gulf of Finland from Tallinn, almost directly across the gulf from Helsinki. They will be traveling on a large commercial ferry run by the Silja Lines, the *Finnjet*." With that, Danzig turned to the other blackboard and uncovered a number of smaller charts and photographs. At the center of the display was a photo of a large white ship with blue trim. A handsome craft, the upper deck of the ship in the shot was crowded with people.

"The *Finnjet* is a passenger and vehicle ferry with a length of 212.8 meters, a beam of 24.4 meters, and a draft of 7.2 meters. She can carry up to 1,790 passengers and 374 cars. She is powered by twin screws that push her at a top speed of 18.5 knots in the winter."

"That's all very good sir," Lieutenant Rockham

stated as he lifted his hand. "But are we expected to make a ship takedown on a civilian craft in international waters?"

"No," Danzig said with some irritation. "If that were the case, we would have gone to another SEAL Team more specialized in that work. Your target will be in the water."

"In the water?"

"Yes, Lieutenant," Danzig said. "For reasons we do not have to go into here, it is necessary for the target to appear to his Soviet guards to have been killed. The intent is for him to go over the side of the ship at a predetermined point. A team of you SEALs will be there to recover him."

As muttering among the SEALs could be heard in the room, Danzig continued.

"The method of defection is a very unusual one . . ." the CIA man said.

"That's for sure," muttered one of the SEALs. He was immediately silenced by a look from Chief Monday.

". . . but it was suggested by the target. For reasons yet to be fully known, the man insists that the Soviets must think he's dead. This man is one of the highest placed officials in the Soviet biological weapons program who has ever tried to defect to the West. The fact that he insists on such a risky defection has something to do with the information he's bringing out with him. Apparently, if they think he's alive and has defected, they will change or hide some portion of the program.

"I cannot emphasize this enough: getting this man

out alive has top priority back in the States," Danzig said with feeling. "Now if your question has been answered, I'll get back to the overview of the mission."

Lieutenant Rockham sat back in his seat. But he wasn't going to easily forget the slam he just received from a civilian right in front of his men. Looking to his right, he could see that Chief Monday was sitting with the muscles of his jaw clenched. Something was bothering the chief, and it seemed to be more than just the insult to his platoon leader.

"The *Finnjet* makes the crossing from Tallinn to Helsinki in about four hours. The distance between the two cities is only some eighty kilometers across the gulf. There is a navigation buoy to the southwest of Helsinki where the ship has to slow prior to lining up to enter the Helsinki harbor. It is at this buoy that the target intends entering the water. The target will be wearing a wet suit underneath his clothing. We understand that it's a relatively lightweight one worn in cooler waters. His own experience in scuba diving will help you at this point."

Danzig paused. Looking over all of the SEALs, he continued, "The plan is for the target to appear to be drowning to the passengers of the ship. Your team is to come up underwater and help him get away. If the target goes under the surface, his watchers will assume that he has drowned.

"What we plan is that your men hide underwater and recover the target. You will have breathing equipment available for him and he simply will not surface again. Since speed is of the essence in this cold water, you will be transported by SDV to the buoy. The *Archerfish* will be the parent submarine for this operation. Captain North," Danzig nodded to the Navy officer still sitting next to the blonde, "and his executive officer have assured me that they can get you to the target area in time.

"The waters in the area of the buoy are too shallow for the *Archerfish* to enter," Danzig explained, pointing to a larger scale chart of the gulf off Helsinki. "But the charts indicate deep water within only a few kilometers of the target area.

"The *Archerfish* is presently going in to the covered dry dock. There she will be fitted with the DDS some of you men brought with you from Little Creek. You have five days from today to get the DDS ready and to practice for your mission.

"Dr. Sharon Taylor," Danzig indicated the woman, "and myself will accompany you on board the *Archerfish*."

At the thought of a woman coming with them, there was another round of muttering among the SEALs. As Dr. Taylor sat stony-faced, Danzig headed off any protests.

"Dr. Taylor is a fully qualified intelligence analyst with my organization. Her job will be to immediately begin the debriefing of the subject once he is on board the submarine. The importance of the information he delivers will be quickly determined by Dr. Taylor and myself."

"Or what?" Kurkowski said in a not so quiet voice. "We throw him back for a bigger one?"

Another chuckle went through the SEALs in the

room, breaking the tension that had been building during Danzig's lecture. Dr. Taylor immediately stood up and faced the men.

"You sailors may know it or not even care," she said heatedly, "but this is a chance to get some information on the most secret program the Soviets have. They have consistently been lying about their biological weapons program since they signed the Biological Weapons Convention back in 1972. That convention was supposed to eliminate these weapons from research, production, and stockpiling.

"We have evidence," the doctor continued, "that there was a major biological weapons accident in the Soviet Union back in 1979 at Sverdlovsk. That there was an outbreak of anthrax is well known and has been documented in the world press. What hasn't been told was that the 'outbreak' wasn't due to tainted meat, as the Soviets have told the world. Instead, there was an accidental spill of a biological weapon that was being produced in bulk.

"Classified estimates put the number of dead in the hundreds. The Soviets themselves admit to sixty-four dead because of the so-called outbreak. That outbreak was caused by a weapon of war, of mass destruction, one the Soviets have fielded. They've reportedly equipped some of their ballistic missiles with biological warheads, warheads that could wipe out whole cities without any other damage. We have no other hard information on the weapons they have developed, or how they intend them to be employed. This is our best chance to get some of that information."

The obvious passion the doctor had for her subject impressed the SEALs. They were men who worked with deadly weapons and explosives on a constant basis. Even their basic operational environment, under the sea, was full of dangers that could kill them because of a single mistake. The SEALs faced those dangers without a qualm. The idea of weapons based on diseases, killer bugs—that thought could frighten the strongest of them.

"Dr. Taylor," Danzig interjected, "has doctorates in both Microbiology and Genetics as well as her M.D. She reports directly to the Deputy Director of Science and Technology. If she feels that the information this defector might deliver is important, that was good enough for the United States to stage this operation."

"Okay, Doctor," Lieutenant Rockham said quietly. "You've convinced us. If it's humanly possible, we will get your man out. But Mr. Danzig, why us? Why Fourth Platoon in particular?"

"It is going to be a cold water operation. Your command back at Group Two," Danzig said, referring to Naval Special Warfare Group 2, which directed the operations of all the SEAL Teams at Little Creek, "said that your men would already be acclimatized to a cold operation because of your recent training in Norway.

"If there are no other questions, we will leave you to discuss the details of the plan among yourselves. All of your officers will receive an information packet with everything we have available on the operation. Captain North and his XO have said that they will be available at your convenience."

Gulf of Finland

* * *

Much later, the two SEAL officers from Fourth Platoon were in their room back at the warehouse. Shaun Daugherty was sitting on the edge of one of the bunks, while Rockham sat at a small table against one wall. On the table were spread a number of charts, photographs, and all of the other papers that had been in the large envelope he'd received from Danzig.

Tossing down his pencil, Rockham ran his fingers through his hair as he gazed down at the sheaf of notes he had written. "Geez, this thing has to go down fast," the SEAL said bitterly. "Not only does this op take place right in the Soviets front yard, we have to penetrate the waters of a friendly country to boot.

"According to Captain North, of the *Archerfish*," he continued, "the Soviet Navy considers the Baltic Sea and especially the Gulf of Finland to be their own private bathtub. They've even put naval Spetsnaz teams into the waters of Sweden and Finland. They have subs working these waters all of the time. Including some with minisubs aboard, a lot like our SDV. If we ended up facing the naval Spetsnaz, we'd be going up against the Soviet version of the SEALs. This thing could go hot in a heartbeat."

"Well, we've never said no to a hot op before," Daugherty said, leaning forward and resting his elbows on his knees. "I don't see why we should start now."

"Because some operations aren't planned out well enough, were impossible to begin with, or are just too stupid to do," Rockham said plainly. "There have been plenty of times an operation was brought forward where it just shouldn't be done. And it took a hard decision to turn it down. But this doesn't look like one of those times."

"So we're going ahead with it?" Shaun asked.

"Yup."

"What's the plan?"

"According to the charts and what Captain North told me," Rockham explained, "he expects to be able to get to within two kilometers of that navigation buoy before he feels the water gets too shallow for the safety of the boat. This is all based on the accuracy of the charts Danzig brought and the information the captain had aboard the *Archerfish*. Personally, I'm planning for us having to make at least a one kilometer longer run."

"What's going on with the *Archerfish* being in dry dock anyway?" Shaun asked. "Is there something wrong with the boat?"

"It's just for security, according to Captain North," Rockham said, leaning back in his chair. "Danzig doesn't want anyone to be able to see the crew putting the DDS on her back. He's even had tarps drawn over the top of the hull to block any Soviet satellite views."

"Rogers see any problems with getting the DDS mounted in time?" Shaun asked as he reached for one of the photos on the table.

"None that he can see," Rockham said. He stood up and stretched. "In fact, he said it will take less time to get the DDS mounted, secured, and tested than it will to get the *Archerfish* up in the dry dock and back out again."

"So what are they going to do to cut back on that time?" Shaun said as he reached for another photo.

"Not raise the dry dock enough to have the sub clear the water," Rockham said. "Apparently, the only problem with the whole operation is that they haven't done it here before. But Rogers has his crew doing all of the mounting work. The *Los Alamos* crew is really just running the crane and watching the show."

There was a knock on the door.

"Enter," Rockham said, almost without thinking.

Lieutenant Fisher came into the room, wiping his hands on a rag. "Okay, the eight-boats came through the trip just fine. We'll be able to launch them first thing in the morning."

"Great," Rockham said. "Where's Paulson?"

"He's still in the garage," Fisher said. "He's double-checking the battery hookup and the local power supply. There's no problem, he just wants to make sure the batteries are fully charged for tomorrow."

"Any problem with the local power supply?" Rockham asked.

"Nope." Fisher glanced at a chart on the table. "It almost wouldn't matter if there was. Paulson brought enough spares from the Creek to practically build a whole extra boat."

"Thorough in his job, is he?" Shaun asked as he put the pictures to the side.

"Oh, the guy is a godsend to the program," Fisher said emphatically. "He's got his Marine Engineering degree from the University of Michigan. Then he decided to join the Navy and go through BUD/S in order to work underwater as much as he liked. The guy doesn't look it, but you couldn't stop him with an anchor once he sets his mind on doing something. He'd just beat the anchor into a boat and keep on going."

"Sounds like a good operator," Rockham commented.

"He is," Fisher agreed, "and he's a great team player. But he does love his machinery."

Getting up from the bunk, Shaun asked, "So, what's the plan of the day for tomorrow?"

"I've got the chief getting the men up and putting the platoon through PT early. You're invited," Rockham said to Fisher.

"Oh gee, sounds like fun," the SEAL officer said with a grimace.

"If you like that, you'll like this even better." Rockham smiled broadly. "Then we're going to spend the day running practice pickups in the Loch. I want the SDVs to each take out two swimmer pairs. The other element from the squad will supply the targets. Once they do a pickup and return, the SDV will run a two kilometer course and then they'll do it again."

"But you can't get five people in the back of an eight-boat," Fisher said.

"That's why being the first pair back to the boat with your target will be such a good thing," Rockham answered, a wide smile breaking out across his face. "They get to go for the ride. The other pair gets to tread water until the SDV gets back. Then they switch and do the whole thing again."

"It pays to be a winner," Shaun said from the door.

"Hoo yah!" Fisher and Rockham said with a grin.

"But what about second squad?" Shaun wondered. As the assistant platoon leader, he led the second squad.

"You'll be going over the plan and doing drills here in the garage," Rockham said. "You get your chance to get wet tomorrow afternoon."

"Open circuit rigs?" Shaun asked, referring to the breathing equipment the men would use during the evolution.

"Yeah," Rockham said, frowning. "According to Danzig, this target has had underwater experience. Apparently he's been a scuba diver for a number of years, just sporting, though. I figured the easiest way to pick him up and cut down on any problems would be to run open circuit and have an octopus rig on every swimmer."

"That should be good enough," Fisher said thoughtfully, "as long as this guy can clear a mask. Once you get him into the SDV, he can breathe off the boat air."

"Given the situation, I figure we'll let him breathe down the rig his swimmer has on. If the tank runs dry, he can switch over to boat air," Rockham said considering the situation. "It would be best to keep things as simple as possible."

"I agree with that," Shaun said. "Now I'm going to hit the head and then the rack, in that order."

"Oh," Fisher said with a grin. "Thanks for sharing that."

"Okay, set up for another run," Chief Monday said.

Lieutenant Rockham and Chief Monday were suited up, and each man was sitting on one of the two safety boats. Sitting at the stern of the sixteen-foot Boston Whaler boats were Ryan Marks and Dan Able, both men in full wet suits with what was now completely soaked clothing over their suits. Floating in the water some two hundred yards away were two swim pairs of SEALs. John Sukov and Ken Fleming made up one pair, and Jack Tinsley and Wayne Alexander made up the other. Observing the whole thing were the men from the second squad.

"Chief," Rockham called out, "belay that last. Send everyone in."

"You heard the skipper," Monday called out loudly. "Everyone out of the water and in to shore."

The wet and cold SEALs gratefully climbed out of the water. But even though they had the chance now to grab some chow and dry off, none of the men were satisfied with their performance that morning. The waters of Holy Loch were a pretty dark blue in the midday sunshine, but underneath the surface they were dark and cold. Visibility was measured in feet.

The SEALs had been trying all morning to have the swimmer pairs come up to the targets. The men who were dressed over their wet suits went into the water. And as soon as the "targets" had rolled off the back of the boats, the swimmer pairs had struck out toward them.

Each man of the swimmer pair was wearing a twin set of aluminum air tanks and an octopus regulator. The octopus rig had a complete second mouthpiece, allowing two men to easily breathe from the same set of tanks. Slipped up on their left arms, each of the swimmers also had a spare dive mask. The idea had been for the swimmer pairs to get up to the men in the water as quickly as possible, without having to surface. Once they got to the floating men, they had to draw the men down, put a regulator in their mouths, and finally give each man a dive mask.

Problems with the procedures had cropped up immediately. Spotting the men in the water was easy; getting to them without surfacing to take an additional direction sight had proven almost impossible. In seven tries, the swimmers had located the men only twice. In addition, the men in their wet suits had proven very hard to keep under the surface. Even Marks, who was so big and muscular his body fat was around one percent and he normally sank anyway, couldn't be pulled easily under the surface. The SEALs were cold, tired, and very frustrated.

The first two feelings were ones they could simply ignore. Frustration in not being able to complete a job was not something they were used to.

Back at the warehouse, the SEALs were less than their usual joking selves. In spite of being able to peel out of their exposure suits, they only felt slight relief. With the normal postdive aroma in the air, consisting of the smells of seawater, sweat, neoprene, and rubber—what had been described as "undersea and underwear"—the SEALs cleaned and stowed their gear. That done, they were ready for a hot shower and some lunch.

Back in their room, Rockham and Daugherty had shed the balance of their equipment, put it away, and were now drying off. Both officers had been in and out of the water all morning with their own swimmer pairs as the squads switched off running the pickup drills.

"Skipper," Chief Monday said as he stood at the open door. "The men are ready. I'm going to release them for chow."

"Great, Chief," Rockham said. "Make sure the bottles are charged this afternoon. I want us to be back in the water by 1400 hours."

"Aye, Skipper." And the chief headed back to the garage.

"And another fun afternoon chasing a drowning rat," Shaun said disgustedly.

"I don't think Marks would take too kindly to being described as a drowning rat," Rockham said with a chuckle.

"Well, maybe not a rat," Shaun said, backtracking when he thought about the huge SEAL. "But you know what I mean."

"I sure as hell do," Rockham agreed. "But I just can't figure out how we can come up to the guy in the water without surfacing. It would be okay if we had the time to do a sweep of the area. But the time is short because of his exposure to the cold."

"According to Tinsley and Limbaugh," Shaun said, "we have, what, twenty to thirty minutes max from the time he hits the water to get him back to the sub?"

Thinking about the level of cold water experience between the platoon's two SEAL corpsmen, Rockham had decided to go with their recommendations above those of anyone else.

"About that," Rockham said as he sat on his bunk and began drying his feet. "Limbaugh treated a lot of hypothermia cases during his tour at BUD/S. Tinsley agrees with him that the sooner we can get the target out of the water, the better."

"There's no way for us to get around the cold problem while still in the water?" Shaun wondered aloud.

"Hell, if there was any way to heat the inside of those miserable SDVs," Rockham said with feeling, "someone would have come up with it years ago. Those things are a long, cold, dark ride. The first guy to come up with an efficient SDV heater will have a lot of thankful SEALs on his side, as well as a bucketful of money."

Still thinking about the problems with their pickups, the two SEAL officers headed off for chow. At the restaurant, Chief Monday was nowhere to be seen. Not giving any thought to their missing chief, the two officers picked out a hearty meal and set to the food with gusto. Though the fare was plain, it was good and hot and there was plenty of it. A long swim in cold water burns up a lot of fuel, and the SEALs were refilling their tanks.

Back at the warehouse later, the platoon came upon

the sight of Chief Monday sitting in the garage. At the chief's feet was a large gray-painted cubical box, almost two feet on a side. Flipping through a manual while sitting on the box, Monday looked up as the platoon filed in.

"Watcha got there, Chief?" Mike Ferber asked.

"A little something I remembered from the old days of the Teams," Monday said with a grin. "I thought of it this morning and went to check it out with some of the other chiefs. Found one over on the *Simon Lake*."

"Found one what?" Rockham asked as the platoon was gathering around their chief.

"An old piece of technology from the early sixties," Monday said as he got up. Bending over the box, he flipped the two latches and opened the lid. Nestled inside the fitted compartments was what looked like a large yellow bowl with handles, and various knobs and protrusions hanging about it.

Pulling the dish from the box, the rest of the platoon could see it had an open mouth with a metal X over it. In the center of the opening, sticking up from the bottom of the bowl, was a black metal rod.

"Okay," Kurkowski said. "I've got it. It's a prehistoric microwave."

"Not quite," Monday said as he put on his best lecture voice. "This device is the AN/PQS-1B handheld sonar. It has an adjustable range of twenty, sixty, and 120 yards. The device will detect metallic or other objects within the set range, announcing the echo returned through the headset in the case there. The

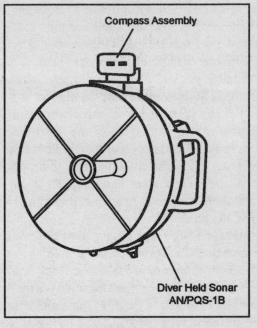

Compass Assembly

**Diver Held Sonar
AN/PQS-1B**

AN/PQS-1B Sonar

operator manually aims the dish with the use of these convenient handles. Once the target is located, the bearing can be taken from the magnetic compass mounted on the top of the dish. It's old technology but it still works."

"Well I'll be damned," Rockham said fervently. "This thing will spot our target while still underwater."

"Such is its intended function sir," Monday said formally.

"And there isn't any chance you've been checked

out on this thing, have you, Chief?" Rockham said as he raised one eyebrow and looked at the chief.

"It just so happens that I remember a few hours spent with one of these little wonders back in my youth as a frogman, yes sir," Monday said, and laughed.

"Truth is, Skipper," Monday continued in a relaxed vein, "I didn't know if any of these were still about. I went and checked with some of the other chiefs. One of them remembered they had this on board the tender *Simon Lake*. They use it to find things dropped overboard in the loch. I went and checked it out. Works fine, and there are plenty of spares, including fresh batteries, in the box."

Lieutenant Fisher and Ensign Paulson walked into the garage then and approached the men.

"The eight-boats are in the water, Rockham," Fisher said. "They're all set for this afternoon's runs."

"Just what the hell is that?" Fisher said, spotting the device in the chief's hands. "You trying to put up a satellite dish?"

"It just may be the answer to our location problem," Rockham said. "It's a handheld sonar rig that a swimmer could use from the back of the SDV."

"Cool," Paulson said, eliciting a pained look of strained patience from Fisher. As he looked further at the device, Paulson said incredulously, "This thing is using tube technology!"

"If you ask the chief nicely, Mr. Paulson, sir," Kurkowski said in a serious voice, "he just might tell you what it was like to serve aboard the *Hunley* during the Civil War."

The reference to the Civil War era submarine was lost on several of the SEALs, though Ensign Paulson looked up with a sheepish grin.

"You know," Paulson said, "this just might work."

"And our master engineer has spoken," Fisher said sternly. "Thus let it be so."

"You know, Skipper," Mike Bryant said, "I had an idea that might help locate the target faster, as well."

"Let's hear it, Mike," Rockham replied.

"Two things really, sir," Bryant said, a little self-consciously. "If we come up from underneath the target, he'll be silhouetted against the surface. Our bubbles will be impossible for anyone to spot from that big ship, but with them coming up around the target, they'll at least warn him we're below."

"Not bad, Mike," Chief Monday said.

"What's the second part?" Daugherty asked.

"We could run a line between the swimmer pairs," Bryant continued, warming up to his idea. "Like the buddy lines we used at BUD/S. It doesn't have to be anything more than a thin line. But with it stretched between two swimmers, if they miss the target but pass on either side of him, they'll hit him with the line."

"That increases the chances of finding him, all right," Rockham agreed. "We'll give it a try this afternoon. Prep the gear, Chief, and show me your new toy."

"Aye, Skipper," Monday said.

Putting on the cold, wet, and clammy equipment was just one of those things SEALs endured. But this time the men had more enthusiasm with the idea that they might start hitting their target better. Possible success was always a good morale booster.

Using the SDVs that afternoon added a new dimension to the SEALs' operation. Now the swimmers launched from the eight-boat when they were tapped on the shoulder by the spotter at the surface. Coming up from underneath the target, the SEALs found they could even do the approach in the SDV. Coming up from underneath while running at a shallow depth of about ten feet, they could easily spot the target and get to him quickly.

Bryant proved out another of his ideas in handling a buoyant target. He strapped on several weight belts to overload himself. By inflating his life jacket, he could swim well enough and not bob to the surface. As soon as he grabbed the legs of the target, he released the air in his life jacket. The extra weight belts helped pull both Bryant and his target down into the eight-boat.

Bryant's swim buddy would put the mouthpiece of his octopus rig right up into the target's face and push the purge button. Air would be bubbling out of the mouthpiece, and the target had a much easier time getting a breath and securing the mouthpiece. Slipping the mask over the target's head was the next question. But that one was only going to be answered once they were on the mission. The target could either clear his mask or not, they didn't have any kind of helmet they could put over his head instead.

It was soon discovered that no one in the platoon

could pick up on using the handheld sonar rig better than Chief Monday. On several runs, they found that the chief could direct the SDV from the rear compartment, using the eight-boat's internal intercom system. All the chief had to do was plug into the system with his throat mike and headset. Then he could guide the SDV from the open rear compartment by just lifting up the sonar set.

The SDV had its own sonar system, but the handheld AN/PQS-1B was much more flexible and could even be pointed up from the rear compartment. The system appeared to work. Out of six dives that afternoon, the SEALs hit the target all six times, each time finding and recovering the target within ten minutes of launch.

It was a much happier platoon that left the loch and went in for a well-deserved dinner that evening. There was just one more thing Rockham wanted to try that night: a target pickup in the dark.

For the test that evening, Fisher was the navigator of the eight-boat and Lopez was the pilot. The cocky little SEAL pilot had a quick grin and ready laugh. And he had little trouble driving the boat, his skills learned from long hours of drill. Bryant had known Lopez back at SDVT-2 and said the little Latino was a natural in the water.

The swimmer pair on the night op was going to be Lieutenant Rockham and Mike Bryant. Chief Monday was going to run the sonar and be the signal man on the surface. The SEALs had decided that there wasn't any way to run two swimmer pairs from the SDV on the pickup. There was only room in the rear compartment for four men and their gear. With only three swimmers, the fourth space would be taken up by their target.

The SDV wallowed badly in the water as the SEALs going on the practice run climbed aboard. Helping the men from the Boston Whaler were Mike Ferber and Roger Kurkowski. Instead of Ryan Marks being the target, Henry Lutz had been "volunteered" by the chief. Lutz was much closer to an average build and height, so getting him on board the SDV would be at least closer to the real target.

"Mike," Kurkowski called over from his position at the bow of the boat.

"What?" Ferber said from the middle of the boat where the coxswain sat.

"If this is a dry run, why does everyone have to get so wet?" Kurkowski asked with a serious expression.

As he watched the SDV move away from the whaler, Ferber thought for a moment. "That was big of you, Roger," he said as he looked up at Kurkowski. "The chief will be glad to know you volunteered to be the target for the rest of the week."

Aboard the SDV there was little humor, only concentration on the job at hand. Chief Monday stood at the stern of the craft, his head just above water. The AN/PQS-1B was down in the rear compartment of the SDV, along with Rockham and Bryant. The two SEALs in the open compartment sat facing aft, their backs to the forward bulkhead. That way they were able to help hold Chief Monday stable.

The other Boston Whaler was over five hundred yards from where the SDV was barely moving just below the surface. As soon as Lutz went over the stern, Monday ducked down under the water.

"Target in the water," he said over the intercom. "Compass bearing zero one seven degrees."

"Zero one seven degrees, aye," Fisher repeated.

Lopez reached up with his left hand and turned the bezel on his compass to read 017 degrees. Then he turned the throttle up and the SDV was moving off.

There was little enough to see as the eight-boat moved through the dark waters of Holy Loch. The overcast night sky prevented even the moon from putting any light down and under the surface. This would be a real test of the chief's sonar rig, Rockham thought as the small craft moved through the water.

They were only at a depth of ten feet, but the water was cold, and the cramped quarters kept the men from moving around to warm themselves up. Chief Monday had set the range selector of the sonar rig to 120 yards. There was no return echo yet and wouldn't be for some time, but the chief still diligently swept the sonar dish back and forth, in spite of the heavy current forcing him back.

Lopez noticed the drag of the chief sticking the sonar dish out into the slipstream of the SDV. The eight-boat was moving at just over five knots, so the chief had to be working to hang onto his gear. Working the pedals with his feet, Lopez made a small adjustment to the rudder of the SDV, bringing the glowing indicator of the compass back in line with the setting on the bezel.

Fisher also worked with his own Doppler sonar rig, an integral part of the SDV's instruments. But it had been decided that they would not use the more powerful sonar of the SDV on the real operation, or wouldn't if the handheld system worked. The more powerful sonar put out a lot of noise when used in the active, searching setting. And that could draw unwanted attention while they were at sea.

The system the chief was using was much lower in power. If it was overheard by a possible Soviet submarine, or even a Finnish patrol boat, it could easily be mistaken for a commercial fish locator. The pinging tones of the AN/PQS-1B couldn't be consciously heard by any of the SEALs, but a good electronics system would be a completely different story.

So the SDV sped through the dark. There was no phosphorescence in the waters of the loch to even brighten up the area. Though it seemed much longer in the pitch-black water, within three minutes the SDV was in range of the target. Now Chief Monday was getting echo returns on his headset. The fuzzy-sounding echoes indicated that he was centered on a soft target rather than a hard one such as a boat hull.

As the SDV approached the target, the echoes went from very high-pitched to lower. Reading off the compass heading from the top of the dish, Monday corrected the path of the SDV. As the target got closer, the chief had to switch the range setting on the sonar, going from 120 yards down to sixty, and then finally to twenty yards. The SDV had reached the target within four minutes. This was even better time than they had originally thought.

Now it was up to the swimmers.

Leaving the compartment, Rockham and Bryant separated out to eight feet, the maximum extent of their buddy line. The two SEALs swam forward and up, trying to see the target but having no luck in the black water. All they had to go by was the last compass heading Chief Monday had announced over the intercom before telling the SDV to stop. Now, as the two SEALs swam forward and up, they kept a close eye on their depth gauge and wrist compass.

Then the buddy line hit something in the water. The drag on the line automatically turned the two SEALs in toward the center and whatever the line had hit. In what seemed to be very long seconds, Rockham's hands touched a kicking leg, one that was fully clothed and wasn't wearing a swim fin.

Grabbing hold of the legs, Rockham felt Bryant grasp his arm to tell him that he was there too. With the signal from Bryant, Rockham reached up and opened the valve on his life vest with one hand. Immediately, the gas blew out and Rockham sank, drawing the target down with him.

Bryant had the job of getting the air to the target, so he swam to Lutz's face and pushed out the extra regulator mouthpiece on his octopus. Once Lutz had air, it was a simple matter to hand him the dive mask.

Now Bryant also took hold of the target, and both SEALs swam back in the direction of the SDV. With

Chief Monday's guidance, the SDV came up closer to the SEALs. Monday had activated a chem light. The soft green glow of the stick showed the two SEALs where the rear compartment was in the dark. Now they were able to settle in with their charge, and Monday gave the go-ahead to Fisher and Lopez.

Swinging the SDV around, Fisher directed Lopez according to the back azimuth of the direction they had come from. Setting his compass to 193 degrees, Lopez drove the SDV back to the waiting boat. When they would be rendezvousing with the *Archerfish*, the SDV would use its Burnett 512 pinger system to let the sub know they were coming. Then the sub could put out a low-power homing signal that Fisher could follow on his instruments.

The homing technique had been practiced by the SDV crewmen until they could do it in their sleep. But with the *Archerfish* not yet out of dry dock, they had to settle for using the sonar system held by Chief Monday to get back to the whaler they had started out from. The system worked, and the SDV arrived back at the whaler with the target intact. The total elapsed time for the operation had only been eleven minutes. It could be done.

0918 ZULU
Holy Loch
Scotland

After just a few celebratory beers the night before, the SEALs were back up the next morning ready to try the system again. This time Rockham wanted the target drop-off boat to be moving at ten knots, slightly more than the speed Danzig said the *Finnjet* would be making at the navigation buoy.

Again it was Rockham and Bryant as the swimmer pair and Chief Monday as the sonar man. Fisher and Lopez were back in the cockpit. Most of the second squad were working with Lieutenant Daugherty, examining all of the platoon's diving equipment and giving everything a full maintenance check.

The speed run worked, adding only four minutes to the overall time from target in the water to the SDV's return to the boat. But Rockham was still not satisfied. He pulled the crew out of the water, leaving the SDV to be checked over by Ensign Paulson and Steve Handel. As the five men from the SDV sat on the shore discussing the situation, Bill Rogers walked up.

"The DDS is mounted and checked out," Rogers announced. "The *Archerfish* should be back in the water by 1600. It took most of the night, but we just finished our double check."

"Great," Rockham said. "We can do a practice run from the DDS tomorrow, if Captain North will cooperate."

"You shouldn't have any trouble at all with North," Rogers said as he crouched down next to the SEALs. "He had his crew helping us all they could. They're gung-ho for this operation. Though I think he believes it will be a hairy one."

"That's normal enough for a sub skipper," Fisher commented. "On this op, we're going to be in shallow water a lot. That makes sub drivers nervous. They're only happy with a couple thousand feet of water under their keel. Gives them someplace to hide if the bad guys come looking for trouble."

"Speaking of trouble," Rockham said, changing the subject, "I'm not happy with how fast the SDV is getting in and out of the area. Isn't there any way we can speed her up?"

"Well," Fisher said thoughtfully, "she's pretty much going all-out now. It's the drag of the chief and his rig that's slowing us down some. But I don't see any way we can change that. Since the run is really not much over a kilometer or so, we could change the screw from the power one to the speed one." He meant the propeller.

"Speed one?" Rockham asked.

"Yes," Fisher answered. "There's two different screws available, one for maximum power, the other for speed. We've been running with the power screw, since Danzig hasn't been able to give me any information on the currents we'll be facing. It also meant that we could put up with the drag from the rear compartment being open and the chief hanging out.

"But since the run is really only over a fraction of the SDV's range, we could change over the screws. The speed screw will suck up more battery power to overcome the drag, but it will give us a knot or two more speed."

"Sounds great," Rockham said enthusiastically. "Have Paulson do the switch over immediately."

"No problem," Fisher answered.

"Speaking of Danzig," Chief Monday said, "I wonder where he and that doctor got off to."

"Just off doing spook stuff, I imagine," Rockham said. "You don't like him very much, do you, Chief?"

"We have a little history together," the chief said grimly, and volunteered nothing more.

Privacy was something that had to be respected in the Teams. The men had to work so closely together all of the time that it was only inside his own head that a man could really have any privacy at all. So Rockham left the chief to his own council.

Later that afternoon the trials of the SDV with the speed screw worked out to Rockham's satisfaction. As the men were squaring away the gear and recharging batteries from the day's evolution, Rockham went aboard the *Archerfish* to speak to Captain North.

In his stateroom on the upper deck of the *Archerfish*, Captain North was in the middle of a discussion with his executive officer regarding Danzig. Even though the captain had the most spacious quarters on the ship, the compartment was all of ten by eight feet. And much of the available space was filled with the furnishings, which included a safe, a combination desk/closet unit, and a number of consoles and instruments hanging from the walls.

When he was invited into the captain's quarters, Rockham had been surprised to find out that Danzig had refused to let the *Archerfish* take part in the practice runs. In fact, Danzig didn't want the ship to leave the cover of the *Los Alamos* until the last moment. And even then, he preferred the sub move out under the cover of darkness.

"This is outrageous," Captain North said bitterly. "The people of Dunoon and Holy Loch have worked with the U.S. Navy for years. There have been hundreds of boomers that began and ended their patrols from these waters. And that Agency officer thinks these people will report a sub with a hump on her back?"

"So no practice with the DDS wet, sir?" Rockham asked.

"More than that, Lieutenant," Captain North continued in the same tone of voice. "Danzig wants your men and their equipment aboard at the earliest opportunity. It may be that the timetable is moving up."

"That shouldn't be a problem sir," Rockham said. "My men are almost all packed to begin with. The SDV can be brought over this evening and lifted aboard under cover. That should satisfy Mr. Danzig's security requirements."

"Apparently, we will be going directly back to the States after the mission is completed," Lieutenant Commander Beam said.

"So it would be best that your men bring everything they have aboard," Captain North added. "We've removed a number of torpedoes and left them here in the Holy Loch stores. There's more than enough room for all of your men and their gear in the torpedo room."

"Thank you, sir," Rockham said sincerely. "I'll get back to our quarters and have the men get ready."

"Very well, Lieutenant." Captain North rose from his chair, put out his hand, and shook Rockham's hand with a firm grip. "I'm sure we'll have an good voyage,

Lieutenant. I liked the way your men were working today. You have a good crew."

"Thank you sir," Rockham said with some small surprise. "We will get the job done."

The next day, the SEALs from all three detachments were hard at work moving gear and stowing it away on board the *Archerfish*. Rockham spent some time in his room in the warehouse going over his selection of who would be going on the actual SDV run. It had been a hard selection process, but he was using his last moments of relative privacy to finalize his choices.

Chief Monday would be in the SDV. He had well proved himself the best with the handheld sonar rig. So would Rockham himself. As the officer in charge of the operation, it would be his ass on the line if anything went wrong, and the best way to control the situation was to be on the spot. Besides, in the Teams, you always led from the front. Long hours in BUD/S had been spent with the instructors hammering that fact home.

The next selection was a bit more difficult. Bryant had proved himself a very able swimmer and was very good on the pickup. But Limbaugh was the most experienced corpsman on hypothermia. Their target wouldn't be very valuable if he died on the pickup. The SEALs had done everything they could to make sure the target wouldn't drown, but the cold was another question.

As Monday went past his door, Rockham called out, "Chief!"

"Yes, Skipper?" Monday said as he came to the door.

"Could you please have Limbaugh and Bryant report to me here as soon as they can?"

"They're both in the garage," Monday said. "I'll have them here in a moment."

"Thanks, Chief," and Rockham turned back to his paperwork.

Within minutes the two SEALs Rockham had asked for were at his door. "Come on in and take a seat," he said.

As the two settled in, Bryant looking much less than comfortable, Rockham explained his situation.

"Henry, Mike," Rockham started, "I had to make a hard decision, and it involves both of you. There are damn few hot ops going on in the world, which may be a good thing. But that means there are few opportunities for you men to really see if all of your training is worthwhile.

"The op we have coming up is going to be an important one, but the space in the SDV is very small and we'll only have one in the DDS. I can only choose one other man to go in the boat.

"The package we're going to pick up is an important one. You both were at the briefing and you know how much is riding on getting this man back alive. I don't know just what it is he's bringing with him that's so important. In fact, I'm not sure I care. He is a defector, and that means he's turning his back on his mother country, for whatever reason. Normally, you'd look on a guy like this as a traitor, no matter what. But this particular individual is risking his life big-time to get over to us. Rockham took a breath and shifted gears. "We've all been cold," he said. "A bunch of us have faced hypothermia, and you both know how painful that can be."

Bryant and Limbaugh could only nod at that statement.

"So it's important that we give this guy every chance we can. To do that, I want Limbaugh in the boat with the pickup crew. If he feels we have to surface or whatever to keep the package alive, well, I want that information right at hand.

"Mike, I'm sorry," Rockham said sincerely. "But that's the way it's going to be. I expect you to do everything you can for the mission, you are a very valuable part of it. It was your suggestion that helped make it possible."

"Thank you, sir," Bryant said. "I'd better get back to work. Our own gear is just about set, and I was giving the SDV people a hand."

Rockham got to his feet. As he shook Bryant's hand, he said, simply, "Thank you."

"You're welcome, Skipper," Bryant said, and left the room.

"Limbaugh," Rockham said, turning to the corpsman. "I want you to give some thought to keeping this individual we're going to get from hyping out. Whatever you think you need, speak out and let someone know. If it's around, we'll get it for you."

"Aye, Skipper," Limbaugh said with a tight smile, "I'll work on it immediately, sir."

* * *

As Bryant walked back to the garage, he thought about what the skipper had said. It was straight up of the boss to tell him why he wasn't going on the op. And he would be a liar if he said he wasn't disappointed. But his disappointment was nothing to what this Russian was going to face. Everyone in the SEALs had been cold. And they all had their memories of it.

CHAPTER 5

January 1987
Hell Week
Class 142
Naval Special Warfare Training Command
Coronado
California

The noise, wet clothes, misery, and general confusion of the large group of students was something the veteran SEAL instructors had grown used to in their constant effort to maintain the quality of the men who entered the Teams. The large number of students in a pre–Hell Week class was something the instructors could deal with handily. But there was something they never grew used to—the smell.

You put a large number of sweating, saltwater-soaked, shivering examples of humanity in an enclosed room, and the temperature went up as the oxygen level went down. And rising above it all was a miasma, a stench, a reek that would be banned as a chemical weapon in modern warfare.

The smell was something that had to be experienced to be believed. Some instructors swore you could cut a chunk out of the air those students were in, walk outside of the room with it, and watch it melt in the sun. The atmosphere in that classroom had taken on a life of its own, and some of that life came from the anxiety felt by all those students.

The students never noticed the smell, or if they did, they were too miserable to comment on it. They had all volunteered for Basic Underwater Demolition/SEAL training. BUD/S was considered one of the most physically and mentally demanding courses offered in the U.S. military. All the students knew that they could make it through, the instructors weren't allowed to kill you. But the conviction about that rule was beginning to waver in some of their young minds.

This was going to be their last motivational speech before the class entered Hell Week, one of the traditional turning points during BUD/S. Since the beginnings of World War Two, that one week accounted for the most trainees dropping from the course. The Teams, as the men who served in them called them, were strictly voluntary. You volunteered into the Teams, and you could volunteer out.

All of the young men standing in that room knew that just a few steps outside the door was hanging a polished brass bell. Ringing that bell got you out of training immediately, and out of the compound within hours.

But not one of those young men in that room that day had any intention of adding their headgear to the growing line of helmets underneath the bell. Mute testimony of the earlier classmates who didn't have what it took.

The command master chief entered the room at the right of the stage in front of the students. He walked in like a Titan missile, broad-shouldered, narrow-waisted, a tall, powerful man. Supremely fit and confident in his own abilities. His khaki dress uniform was spotless over gleaming black shoes. At his right breast were rows of ribbons that the students knew he had earned in many of the world's hot spots, most of which the public would never know about. And above his ribbons gleamed a polished gold Trident, the Naval Special Warfare Insignia, something every young man in the room hoped to pin on his own chest someday.

The piercing black eyes of the command master chief immediately zeroed in on the class leader, the highest ranking officer among the students.

As the class leader first saw the command master chief enter the room, he called out loudly: "Master Chief Coogan!"

"Hoo yah, Master Chief Coogan!" the class shouted out with one voice.

"Take your seats," the impressive man in the khaki uniform called out from the stage. When the class sat down, the command master chief went into his speech to help convince the students that each and every one of them could make it through the upcoming week. All it would take is for each man to reach down deep inside himself and find more there than he ever thought he had. And even with that, it would take the teamwork of all his classmates working together to get them through.

In spite of the intense nature of the speech the command master chief was giving, the warmth of the room and the closeness of the air combined to make some of the students sleepy. One of these young men was Michael Bryant, who had already spent one enlistment in the Army before learning about the SEALs. This was where Mike wanted to be, and he knew he would either make it through to graduation or they would have to carry him off the beach.

In spite of his concentration, the words of the master chief slipped into a kind of drone as Bryant and many of the other students became semihypnotized. When the command master chief bellowed out, *"On your feet!"* the lecture was over. The students were quickly hustled out of the room to continue with their training.

It was late Sunday, the day before Hell Week was to begin, when the students had to lay in their bunks and think about what was coming on. Six days with almost no sleep. Six days of maximum output. Six days in which to learn that a man was capable of ten times the physical endurance that he originally thought possible of himself. And how many of his classmates would still be there one week from today?

Suddenly, chaos erupted.

In spite of their concerns, most of the members of Class 142 had fallen asleep. The week began at 0001 hours Monday morning, and the instructors were not wasting one moment of that time.

Doors crashed open and large explosions rang out as

firecrackers were tossed into waste baskets. Instructors were screaming unintelligible orders, strange sounding commands to fall out onto the grinder wearing one left boot, a right swim fin, shirts untucked, and a soft cap.

But a student never questions the orders of an instructor, not even when two of them are shouting commands that contradict each other. Out on the grinder, the central exercise yard of the compound, other instructors were also yelling commands, while training fire hoses on the students, firing M60 machine guns loaded with blanks into the air, and making sure the wafting colored smoke from the burning smoke grenades didn't thin out too much.

More orders were shouted at the students. The group was dropped for exercises while the noise continued all around them. The only illumination on the area was the sickly green light of activated chem lights strung up all around the compound. But this fitful light was more than enough for the instructors. They could easily see that all of the students were dressed wrong.

The students were to have fallen out wearing a right running shoe, a left boot, shirts tucked in, and their helmet liners. "Couldn't they follow simple instructions?" was shouted at them. After another set of violent exercises, back into the barracks they ran, bumping into other classmates either running to or from the grinder. Within a half hour the students were all thoroughly confused, uncomfortable, and wide awake. What they didn't realize was that every piece of clothing they owned was also cold, wet, and sandy. The organized chaos conducted by the instructors had a plan behind it. And the students wouldn't have the chance to get into clean, dry, and warm clothes for the rest of the week.

Hell Week was vicious, Hell Week was brutal, and Hell Week was meticulously planned and choreographed. The next week would bring the students as close as possible to the level of exhaustion, confusion, and pain of combat without their having directly experienced it.

But even with the violent beginning, Hell Week had much harder training exercises—or "evolutions" as they were called—that had to be completed. Each boat crew of six men—five enlisted and an officer, preferably— had to continue at a grueling pace to move about the compound and the area surrounding it, all while carrying their equipment and heavy rubber boat. The instructors were pleased: they had their first dropout within two hours of Hell Week starting.

Everyone in the Teams believes that anyone who would quit during training, and especially Hell Week, would quit during combat. Whether this is true cannot be proven. What has been proven is that the men who complete this course of training, and that never-to-be-forgotten week, would not quit, ever.

But it wasn't the lack of sleep, the constant movement, and the heavy physical output that most graduates of BUD/S remember—it was the cold. The permeating, will-sapping cold of the Pacific waters.

Mike Bryant remembered hypothermia, and the level of pain you felt as it came on. Every graduating member of Class 142 would always remember those bone-chilling days during Hell Week when they all swam in the Pacific during the second week of January 1987.

Even under a sunny sky, the water was chilling. Under a leaden gray layer of low dark clouds, it was positively forbidding. As the surf crunched into the shoreline, the students knew it would only be a matter of time before they were in its icy grip again. In spite of the area being in "sunny southern California," the offshore waters were fed by the California current, an ocean river of cold water running down from the Alaska coast. In spite of the sun, the California current keeps the offshore waters at an average of 55 degrees throughout the year.

The instructors would carefully time the students' exposure to the water. But it wasn't just the getting wet that caused you to "hype out." The water could easily be warmer than the air, especially when you considered the wind chill effect. Once the water had actually warmed the body up, the students were again stood up in the cold air. But exposure to the cold was measured by the instructors, and they had time and temperature charts that had to be strictly followed. Hypothermia could quickly kill, and they wouldn't allow that to happen. The instructors kept a careful watch for any of the danger signs. The students wouldn't be allowed to die—just to feel the misery of a cold close to death.

Shivering took on a whole new meaning to the students of BUD/S. This was a cold that penetrated all the way to the core of a man. All the muscles of the body tried to warm the blood by moving involuntarily. Instead of the normal shivering everyone had felt in the winter, this deep muscular contraction was painful in itself. The heavy hip flexor muscles felt as if they wanted to pull themselves free of the bone. It was a fight to open a hand, bend an arm, or even to walk. Speaking was hard at best, standing still impossible.

But even with being dipped into and out of the cold waters of the Pacific, the instructors still had another level of misery they could graduate the class to: the steel pier.

If a student felt a fear of the cold, the steel pier could build up that fear to almost panic level. Made up of pierced steel planking used to quickly lay out runways during wartime, the steel pier could literally suck the heat out of a man, especially an exhausted man who was stripped down to his underwear and wetted down with a hose.

Bryant still could only just remember the steel pier during Hell Week. After a short time, most of the details of that week became a blur. It was a time to endure, to continue, to gut it out and succeed. But he remembered that the steel pier had almost broken him.

With the instructors baiting them on, it was a dark, windy Monday night of Hell Week when Class 142 climbed out onto the steel pier and stripped down to their skivvies, as ordered. With cold seawater spraying down on them from a fire hose, the men would exercise on the pierced steel planking, or worse, be forced to lay still.

The cold was brutal. It felt as if the life was being sucked right out of you. And then after eternity had gone by and was up for its second go-round, the instructors ordered you on your feet and moving for more exercises. Evolutions followed: clothes on, clothes off, run, carry your rubber boats on top of your heads, lift the boat up, hold it up with your shivering arms extended, put it down. And then it would be a return to the steel pier. Strong men broke and quit rather than face that freezing metal again.

Hypothermia first caused deep pain as the body shook almost to the level of convulsing to try and keep itself warm. Wherever you were, your body didn't want you to be there. The mind had to overcome the desires of the body. The body's survival reflexes would kick in involuntarily, and blood would be drawn from the extremities to keep the heart, organs, and brain as warm as possible. And if the downward spiral of cold continued, then the mind started to slip.

First, the student would become what the SEALs call "a little dingy," as thought became harder. Confusion would start to fill his mind. Bryant barely remembered the Navy doctor at BUD/S telling him to say "bell, boat, and oar." And the concerned man would not move on until the words had been said, or the student removed from training. You might get rolled back to another class to try again, or shown the door out and back to the regular Navy.

Mike Bryant concentrated and spoke. The words came out a little slurred from his shivering, but he continued on.

The waters at BUD/S were normally chilling. In the winter, they could become life-threatening, but the students' exposure to the cold was lessened accordingly. If the body's core temperature drops from the normal 98.6 degrees to around 93 degrees, the mind becomes sluggish and speech slurs."

When the body's core reaches 91 degrees, the slurring is very noticeable, thought becomes difficult, and the person is clumsy as their brain tries to direct their muscles. At a core temperature of around 89 degrees, the person becomes drifty, stuporous, and semiconscious. This is a dangerous and health-threatening stage. With a core temperature of around 87 degrees, the person is barely conscious and even the body's shivering has stopped. At this point a person's heart slows and could easily cease. Brain damage and death are a very real threat here.

The main lesson at BUD/S was based on the premise that the human body was capable of ten times the output and endurance normally considered possible. Completing BUD/S proved that to each man who made it through.

Having faced this threat—that incredible feeling of cold—added to the spice of being one of the few people graduating from BUD/S that warm spring day in May. From over a hundred men who started, only a handful remained. Mike Bryant would always remember that day. And now he also remembered the cold of training. And realized the man they were tasked with recovering faced a very real and painful death from a cold he would be just barely protected against. This guy had to have balls—great big brass ones.

CHAPTER 6

0600 ZULU
U.S. Naval Support Facility
Holy Loch
Scotland

On the west side of Scotland a cold fog was moving up from the south, following the Firth of Clyde. It rolled along the water, going past Dunoon and filling Holy Loch. The clammy, gray mist covered both the water and the land, rolling up the hills until it was finally held down by its own weight. The mournful hoot of foghorns announced the arrival of a long, gray day. Normally, a U.S. nuclear submarine has little concern for fog or other weather on the surface. But with the subs tied up to tenders, docks, or slipped into dry docks, they were in the world that weather affected. And the fog was a blanket that hid everything from view.

In the wardroom of the *Archerfish*, Captain North, Lieutenant Commander Beam, Lieutenant Rockham, and several of the submarine's department heads were sitting over coffee, discussing the upcoming operation. Practice runs had continued with the extra eight-boat. The other craft, being slated for the operation, was now secured inside the DDS bolted to the submarine's deck. The balance of the SEAL platoon's equipment and munitions had been stowed away aboard the *Archerfish*, and the men were now staying aboard the sub.

There was little to do but wait for the final orders. As the officers sat at the table in quiet conversation, Lieutenant Jack Carter, the operations officer for the sub, entered the compartment with a message from the radio room.

"Captain," Carter said as North took the message held on a clipboard. "Mr. Danzig and Dr. Taylor have come aboard. COB"—the chief of the boat—"has put them up as you had directed."

"Excellent, Lieutenant Carter," North said as he held the clipboard. "Carry on."

Lieutenant Carter returned to his duties, and the others in the room looked on as Captain North lifted the cover sheet from the message and began to read. When he was finished, he looked up at the men seated around him. "Gentlemen," he said quietly, "we have received our final authorization, the mission is on. If everything is a go from all of the departments, I would like us to be under way as soon as possible. There's a fog rolling in, and I would like us to take advantage of its cover."

A chorus of "Aye aye, sir" came from the other men in the room. As the CO got up from his chair, all of the men in the room rose. Within a short time the level of activity substantially aboard the boat increased. As the *Archerfish* made ready for sea, a subdued excitement could be felt by both the SEALs and the sub's crew alike.

When dusk had blanketed the area in darkness, tugs helped move the *Archerfish* away from her protected position at the base. The *Los Alamos* had been held partially submerged, but still holding the *Archerfish* in her screened well deck. Now the concealing tarps were removed and the *Archerfish* began to move under her own power.

The captain, pilot, several officers, and crewmen manned the small bridge at the top of the sail. The plexiglass windscreen did little to keep out the chilling cold of the wet fog, but it did give a convenient point for the marking down of headings and courses with a black grease pencil. Everyone kept a close watch on the dark waters.

Two men even stood as lookouts out on the fairwater planes on either side of the sail. Each man wore insulated, bright red coveralls as well as a life jacket. The men on the rounded deck of the hull had safety lines hooked to their waists and slipped into grooves running along the deck. But little could be seen by the men on the deck and bridge. The real eyes of the submarine was now the extended mast of the BPS-14 surface search and navigation radar, standing up on top of the sail, behind the bridge.

In the gloom, the large submarine moved away from Holy Loch like a giant sea creature pulling away from shore. She was going to the deeps, the environment attack submarines were designed for. In shallow water and near the shore, the great nuclear ship moved clumsily, a bit like a grounded whale. But in the depths of the sea she would become the great steel predator she was intended to be.

As the sub moved down the loch, the fog made her little more than a dim silhouette, just a darker gray shape in the mist moving across the blue-gray water. Small running lights on her sail and hull were lit, but only for a short time, while she was in civilian waters. The large bulge of the DDS bolted to her back behind the sail was hidden to even the sharpest eyes on shore by the enveloping fog.

But the only eyes watching the ship's passage were the dark windows of the stone church steeple and the swaying branches of the trees on the hills. The beginning of a covert operation required a covert departure. And nature had assisted on this one.

With the submarine under way, the SEALs quickly settled into a quiet routine. Their quarters were in the torpedo room several decks directly below where the DDS was bolted to the hull. The entrance to the DDS was through the weapons shipping hatch where the torpedoes and other ordnance were moved into and out of the sub.

Normally, the weapons shipping hatch was only used to load Mark 48 Advanced Capability torpedoes, SUBROC UUM-44A nuclear antisubmarine missiles, or sub-Harpoon UGM-84A antiship missiles. But no submarine weapons would be moving through that hatch again until the present mission was long over.

There were no stairs, doors, ceilings, or walls aboard a Navy ship, only ladders, hatches, overheads, and bulkheads. The toilet was called a head. But the showers retained their landlubber name, though some of the veteran chiefs referred to them as "rain lockers." Individual rooms were now compartments, a term also used to refer to major sections of the boat.

The ladder leading to the weapons loading hatch and the DDS was mounted to the bulkhead just outside the commanding officers' stateroom on the top, control room, deck. So the SEALs would have to move through all three of the decks in the operations compartment in order to do any work in the DDS on their gear or eight-boat contained inside.

The interior central, operations, compartment of a submarine was organized something like a three-story house; a long, narrow, and extremely crowded house. The main, top, deck held the control room, attack center, computer room, and other major nerve centers of the ship, along with the CO's and XO's staterooms and other compartments. On the second deck were the crew's living spaces, the three separate officers' staterooms, the officers' wardroom, and the crew's mess room along with the pantry and galley. The bottom, third deck held additional crew living spaces but was mostly filled with machinery and storage compartments. The third deck was dominated by the central torpedo room and its stowage areas, the biggest area in the front of the ship.

Accommodations for the SEALs had been easy to arrange without any loss to the normal crews' berthing.

No nuclear weapons were aboard, so there were no SUBROCs to remove. A number of the several Mark 48 ADCAP torpedoes had been removed from the nineteen aboard and left behind at Holy Loch in order to give the SEAL platoon and the two additional SEAL detachments berthing space in the torpedo room.

The huge, 3,500-pound torpedoes were twenty-one-inches in diameter and over nineteen feet long. Removal of twelve of the underwater weapons, over half her load, left the *Archerfish* with sufficient ordnance to defend herself, while making plenty of room for all of the SEALs. Blue-striped bunk pads placed on the torpedo racks gave the Team operators a reasonable level of comfort.

The fact that the SEALs were bunking with racks of torpedoes, each with a 650-pound high explosive warhead, did not affect the men in the slightest. These were operators who worked with explosives on an almost daily basis. The long, sleek, green-painted cylinders of the torpedoes, each with a bright blue plastic nose cap, were just machines to them. Terribly destructive machines, but with no mystery about them to bother the SEALs' sleep.

The four complex breeches of the Mark 63 torpedo tubes at the front of the compartment, each angling off toward the bow of the submarine, held ominous placards hanging from their controls, cards that read, WARNING in bright red, and further, in black print— WARSHOT LOADED. These caused a slight pause for each SEAL who saw it. This was a real mission, a hot op. And such a thing didn't come along in the Teams

every day. There were SEALs who had spent years
training for just such an occasion, and it had never
come to them. Now, for Fourth Platoon, it was game
day.

Making up the berthing arrangements for the SEALs
on the mission was normal in the routine of the *Archerfish*. With her modifications to accept the DDS also
came the requirement to carry the SEALs or other specialized personnel. The two officers from the CIA were
another matter.

Peter Danzig was simply moved in with the other officers to share a three-person stateroom. Dr. Taylor was
a different situation. Nuclear submarines do not normally have any kind of guest quarters, and a woman
aboard a sub made the situation even more unusual.

The XO ended up giving up his stateroom to afford
Dr. Taylor some semblance of privacy. Captain North
gave her permission to use his private head and shower
facilities, located between his and the XO's staterooms
on the main deck. Lieutenant Commander Beam in
turn moved in with some of his fellow senior officers,
and ended up sharing the same stateroom as Peter
Danzig.

The bumping of berths continued on down the line
of officers. Finally, several of the lowest ranking young
ensigns and lieutenant j.g.'s aboard ended up "hot-
bunking," with five of them assigned to a single stateroom.

Hot-bunking was a longtime tradition in the submarine service. With space at a premium, men on different watch schedules would often find themselves

sharing sleeping space. As one man came off watch to get a meal and some sleep, another would be getting up from his rack to go on duty. When the other man finally crawled into his bunk, it could still be warm from the last person who used it.

Prior to the beginning of the next day's morning watch, Lieutenant Rockham came across Lieutenant Commander Beam in the central corridor of the second deck near the wardroom. The XO was coming off watch, having been the command duty officer during the night. The XO still had a watch shift to stand before he could get any sleep. But a meal in the wardroom appealed to both men.

The wardroom was a reasonably attractive compartment for a warship. The long table with its red tablecloth and white china place settings was lined with a dozen steel office-type armchairs with green padding. Along the walls were mementos of the *Archerfish*—her christening ceremony, plaques, photographs, and even some items from her WWII namesake, the SS-311 *Archerfish*, a Balao-class diesel-electric sub.

One item standing out among the WWII memorabilia was the Presidential Unit Citation awarded the SS-311 for sinking the aircraft carrier *Shinano*, the largest Japanese man-o'-war sunk by a U.S. sub during the war.

A large brass ship's clock kept meticulous time from its position on the wardroom bulkhead. And the crowded but cozy atmosphere of the room was only marred by the electronics and communications consoles on the bulkhead. Even at meals, the CO was not out of immediate contact with his crew. A microphone was clipped to the underside of the wardroom table at the head where the captain always sat.

As the two men entered the wardroom, they saw Captain North already seated at the table, drinking coffee. The CO had been up late into the night the evening before, overseeing the maneuvering of his command ship down the Firth of Clyde, through the North Channel between Scotland and Ireland, and into the North Atlantic. It wasn't until after his craft moved out under the blanketing waters of the Atlantic that the CO had retired for the night.

"Skipper," Beam said, with some small worry in his voice. "You're up early. Anything wrong?"

"No, XO," North said with a shake of his head. "I just thought I would get an early start on the usual sleep deprivation of a cruise. Nothing you aren't used to, eh, Mr. Rockham?"

Remembering long nights spent in the Teams, and that long week without any sleep at all during BUD/S training, Rockham smiled. "Nothing we haven't experienced before, sir."

"Well," the CO said with a sigh, "there is something a bit new to get used to. I thought I would give Dr. Taylor a chance to get in an early shower today. First time I've had to knock to enter my own head. And how are things working out with her boss, Mr. Danzig?"

"I don't think he's very pleased with his boat ride, as he calls it," Beam said with a smile. "I had to explain to him just how a shipboard shower works and how quickly he was expected to finish. He somehow didn't seem satisfied to learn about fresh-water rationing."

"He'll get used to it fast," North said with a wide grin splitting his face. "After all, he hasn't much of an option. And how are your men settling in, Mr. Rockham?" North said, turning to the young SEAL as he was sitting down at the table.

"Couldn't be better, sir," Rockham said as he sat. "Outside of some routine work with our gear and the eight-boat, we have little in the way of watches to stand. The men are building up some sack time."

Accepting a cup of coffee from the wardroom steward, Rockham continued, "Not that I'm too worried that they'll get completely out of shape from all of the enforced inactivity, but how long do you think it will take us to arrive on-station, sir?"

"That's something that will be decided shortly, Lieutenant," North said in a disapproving tone. "Mr. Danzig has informed me of our expected rendezvous time with the target. He received the final information from Langley last evening. As of now, I have a window of only a few days to get us to the Gulf of Finland.

"The choke point," North continued, "will be the straits around Denmark. That's where we will have to reduce speed considerably to get through without being detected. The waters there are shallow and busy enough that I'm already very unhappy about taking this boat through them. But they shouldn't be a major problem. I intend to continue running at flank speed for the next eight hours or so to get us to the mouth of the straits as quickly as possible.

"It will take us the best part of a full day or more to get through those waters around Denmark and then into the Baltic Sea proper. We will have to slow considerably to remain undetected from any passing ships. From there it will be less than two days to the gulf waters off Helsinki. So about four days or less to your little swim, Mr. Rockham.

"And with that, gentlemen, I leave you to your meal." Standing up, North waved to the men to remain in their seats, took a final swallow of his coffee, set the cup down and left the wardroom.

The two officers were soon joined by several others either coming off watch or preparing to go on. China plates were filled with food by the stewards and placed in front of the officers. Conversations were momentarily stopped as the hungry men began to eat.

Dr. Taylor and Peter Danzig entered the wardroom a few moments after the occupants of the room had begun to eat. At the disdainful "Please, don't" from Dr. Taylor, the men who had been getting up from their seats as the woman entered the compartment settled back into their seats.

Dressed in a smaller set of the standard dark blue coveralls many of the crew wore, Dr. Taylor still cut a striking figure in the unflattering clothes. Her thick gold hair was tied back in a ponytail and covered with a blue ship's baseball cap. Like all of the other caps worn by the crew, this one had the words USS ARCHERFISH and SSN 678 stitched in gold thread above and below the silver twin dolphins symbol of the submarine service. Peter Danzig was also wearing the same type of coveralls, less the cap. But the eyes of the officers in the room were not on him.

A number of the ship's officers were on watch or otherwise occupied, so there were plenty of seats at the wardroom table for the two newcomers. As a chorus of "Good mornings" went about the table, Dr. Taylor and Peter Danzig took seats to join the men at their meal. After sipping from his cup, Danzig remarked, "Outstanding coffee. It's good to see that the stories about the coffee in the submarine service being the best in the Navy are true."

"Well, Mr. Danzig," Lieutenant Commander Beam stated with a smile, "when you can't tell whether it's day or night topside, a good cup of coffee can be a necessity. All the efforts of the supply department and the cooks go into serving the best food and drink they can. Good food helps make for good morale."

As a full breakfast plate was set down in front of each of the CIA officers, Dr. Taylor arched an eyebrow at the food being served. The scrambled eggs on the plate in front of her were fluffy, the bacon crisp, and the bread obviously freshly baked. "I must say that the food on board is excellent," she said. "It's hard to see how your men can eat like this and still remain fit for the military. Exercise can only do so much, and that kitchen of yours seems to run constantly."

"We call it a galley in the Navy, ma'am," Beam replied. "And the cook pretty much does run it like a twenty-four-hour restaurant. Not only do the off-watch men drop by sometimes for a snack or just to hang out, he also serves five full meals a day."

"Five meals," Dr. Taylor exclaimed with surprise. "But why so many?"

"You may not have noticed it yet," the XO said, "but we don't run a normal twenty-four-hour schedule on board a sub. As soon as we were under way, the boat went over to a six-hour watch schedule."

"Six hours?" Taylor said with a puzzled frown. "But that's not even a normal working day."

A chuckle went around the table as the Navy men responded to the doctor's remark. The frown on Dr. Taylor's face deepened as she thought she was being made the butt of a joke. "No, ma'am," Beam said with a disarming grin. "You don't understand. The men stand a duty watch of six hours. Then they go off-watch and pull another six-hour shift.

"Each individual performs maintenance on the boat and all of this machinery around us. Or they run drills, do studies, take tests, or any other duties that might be assigned to them. It's only after a full twelve-hour day that a man can crawl into his rack and grab six hours of sleep."

"An eighteen-hour workday!" Dr. Taylor exclaimed. "But you must lose complete track of time running on a schedule like that."

"It has been known that the odd man may end up a little short of sleep now and then, ma'am," Beam replied wryly. Another round of light chuckles went around the table. "But you get used to it," he continued. "There really isn't any night or day down here. Sometimes, you can only tell what part of the day it is by what's being served from the galley."

"But last night," Danzig interjected, "the lights in the control room were switched over to red. We only used to do that kind of thing years ago to get your eyes accustomed to the dark. That, and so you could see without wrecking your night vision."

"Same reason as today, Mr. Danzig," Beam answered. "We rig out for red light at night in case anyone in the control room has to make a periscope sighting or the ship has to surface. We're going to have to be particularly careful on this cruise that we don't break the surface or have a run-in with any surface contacts. A lot of our course is going to be in pretty shallow water for a nuke sub. The Soviets consider the Baltic to be their own private bathtub, no matter what the Finns or the Swedes say. Everyone aboard is going to have to stay very sharp from the beginning to the end of this mission."

"Hopefully that won't be any kind of problem," Danzig said. "This boat was chosen partially because she spent a lot of time under the ice and has done a number of operations in shallow water."

"True enough, sir," Beam replied, "but no submariner is ever happy without a lot of open water under his keel for him to hide in."

"Well, your captain was another reason this ship and crew were picked for this operation. Your CO has a lot of shallow water experience under his belt and has proven himself well under pressure."

"Oh," Beam said mildly as he leaned back in his chair. Some of the other officers in the room looked oddly at their XO. His reaction to Danzig's comment seemed out of place.

As he raised his coffee cup to his lips, Beam said innocently enough, "You must be talking about the skipper's experience with Ivy Bells."

The comment could have been a bomb dropped on the wardroom table, given Danzig's startled reaction. As Beam took another sip of his coffee, Danzig first looked shocked and then angry. "You know about Ivy Bells—" Danzig began angrily.

Beam cut Danzig's reply off with a sharp, "Of course I do. It's not like it's much of a secret anymore. Not with that traitor Pelton having told the Soviets about it. He blew the whistle on that and a whole bunch of other intelligence operations before being stopped." The venom and revulsion in Beam's voice were obvious to everyone in the room. His feelings were strong regarding a traitor to the country he served so diligently.

As Danzig glared at the Navy officer, sputtering with the beginnings of some kind of retort, Lieutenant Rockham decided to verbally step between the two men.

"Ivy Bells?" he asked, leaving the question hanging in the air.

"Well," Danzig said, as the anger slipped away from him somewhat. "Since it has already come out in the public arena, you could find out about it easily enough. Ivy Bells was the code name for an intelligence operation conducted by the Navy against the Soviets. The operation continued through the whole of the 1970s and resulted in some very valuable information.

"The short version of the story is that a Navy submarine went into the Sea of Okhotsk, between Japan and the Soviet Union. They tapped into a phone cable running southwest along the sea floor between the Kamchatka Peninsula and the Soviet mainland. The sub attached a pod containing a phone tap and recording device to the underwater cable without being detected."

Now Danzig had the undivided attention of everyone in the wardroom. Food was left cooling on plates as the occupants listened to the CIA case officer.

"The nuclear submarine *Halibut* originally put the recording pod in place on the cable. She would go into the area and exchange the full tapes in the pod for fresh ones on a pretty regular schedule. A lot of classified information went along that cable from the Soviet bases on Kamchatka to the mainland and their big naval base in Vladivostok.

"The Soviets never suspected that the cable could even be tapped. It just never occurred to them. So the information running along the line wasn't even encrypted most of the time. The whole operation was a real gold mine of information. The operation went on so long that the *Halibut* had to be replaced. In 1976 the *Parche* took over the tape exchange mission."

"So what happened to the operation?" Rockham asked. "And how does Captain North fit into the picture?"

"North wasn't a commander then," Danzig answered. "He was the operations officer on the *Parche* during her last runs on the tap."

"Last runs?" Rockham asked.

"Yes," Danzig said with bitterness. "Ron Pelton was an intelligence analyst with the NSA in the seventies and into the eighties. He sold out the U.S. for Soviet dollars. For fourteen years he sold secrets to the Soviets. We finally nailed the bastard in August 1985 when a KGB defector mentioned meeting with an NSA man years earlier. With his report as a starting point, the FBI finally tracked Pelton down and busted his ass. He was convicted of espionage in 1986 and will spend the rest of his days rotting in a federal prison."

"But what happened to the cable tap?" Rockham asked.

"Satellite photos taken in 1981 showed a group of Soviet ships working over the location of the tap. When the *Parche* went in later to exchange the tapes, the whole pod was missing. That sub almost didn't get out of there. The Soviets were on guard and had set a pair of their hunter-killer subs to cruise the area. The *Parche* just barely slipped past those boats and got out of there with her hull in one piece."

"And your skipper was in on that?" Rockham asked Beam.

"Yes, and it must have been a hairy one," Beam answered gravely. "The old man doesn't talk about it much. He'll mention the operation and what they did on the earlier trips. But he never talks about getting away from the two Alfa-class subs the Soviets had guard-dogging the site.

"But I'll tell you what," Beam continued, heat rising

in his voice. "Our skipper could slip this boat into the Kremlin's bathtub and steal Gorbachev's rubber duck if he had a mind to. And there isn't a man aboard who wouldn't go there and back with him."

With the thoughts of the captain's experiences and Beam's comment still on everyone's mind, conversation died off in the wardroom for a moment. Only the constant hum of machinery and the rattle of pans and crockery in the galley could be heard. The relative quiet was disrupted a moment later as a harried-looking young ensign noisily entered the compartment.

As the obviously rushed young officer sat down and started to gulp his coffee, he looked up at everyone around the table. A look of stern admonition was in the XO's eyes and he seemed about to speak. But then he stopped in amused silence as the young officer's eyes locked on the attractive woman sitting at the table.

"Yes?" Dr. Taylor finally said as the young man continued to stare.

That broke the spell of the moment as the suddenly flustered young man tried to speak. "Uh, um," he stuttered, "ah, nothing, ma'am."

Several of the other men at the table had a hard time hiding their amusement at the young ensign's consternation at seeing a woman at the wardroom table. The XO came to everyone's rescue when he spoke out with a gruff, "And how was your watch, Mr. George?"

"Um, fine, sir," the embarrassed young man answered.

"I think you're free to continue with your duties as soon as your finished," Beam continued in the same tone.

"Yes sir," the young man said. And he virtually attacked his food a moment later. As soon as he was finished bolting down his meal, the young ensign muttered his excuses to everyone in the room. His almost running from the compartment looked like more of an escape than anything else.

Laughter quickly broke out among several of the officers after the ensign had left. Even Dr. Taylor had a hard time suppressing a smile at the young man's discomfiture. "God, were we ever that young?" Lieutenant Ed Tullerbee, the weapons officer, said between chuckles.

That comment brought out a new round of laughs in the wardroom. "But why did you call him Mr. George?" Dr. Taylor asked. "The name tag on his uniform said Bell."

"Another tradition of the Service, ma'am," Beam said with a smile still on his face. "Ensign Bell is the most junior officer on board. Tradition dictates he is George, as in let George do it, until a more junior man is assigned to the crew. He is given just about every scut duty officer assignment available."

"That's right, ma'am," Carter, the operations officer, said. "We've all been through the same thing. The Service has changed a lot, and he won't get some of the same harassment some of us went through on our first cruises. But he's going to be kept busy the next few weeks, that's for sure."

"It still seems cruel to haze someone like that unnecessarily in today's military," Dr. Taylor said disapprovingly.

"Not at all, ma'am," Beam replied. "It isn't hazing at all. The skipper wouldn't stand for that. It's just a traditional way to get a young officer his sea legs fast. He'll pick up everything he needs to know quickly and be very familiar with the layout of the boat. On top of that, he will learn how to think on his feet.

"Everyone here, especially the skipper and the chief of the boat, will see to it that he has all the help he can take. But if he can't handle the stress, it's a lot better to find it out now rather than later, when men's lives might be at stake."

All of the officers, Rockham included, nodded at the XO's last remark. The meal was concluded soon after Mr. George's abrupt departure, and everyone left the wardroom. After the relative calm of the meal, and the ensign's unwitting comic relief, the raised level of tension that ran through the ship could again be felt.

CHAPTER 7

Well before the SEALs could even begin to perform their operation, they had to get to the Gulf of Finland. The gulf was an arm of the Baltic Sea, and the Baltic was almost completely surrounded by land. To the north and east was Finland; to the west, Sweden; to the southwest, West Germany; and then East Germany, the Soviet Union, and Poland made up the balance of the shoreline. Two NATO allies, two neutral countries, and the enemy surrounded the Baltic.

Only a small, fairly narrow passage existed between the Baltic and the North Sea. It was a six-hundred-kilometer V-shaped connection that went past Denmark, Norway, Sweden, and Germany.

With the DDS secured to her back like a remora on a shark, the *Archerfish* stood out even among military ships. It would be obvious to any observer that there was something special about the craft and her mission. This obvious sign of her nature prevented the ship from being able to use the Kiel Canal through part of Germany.

Transiting the canal would have shaved over half the

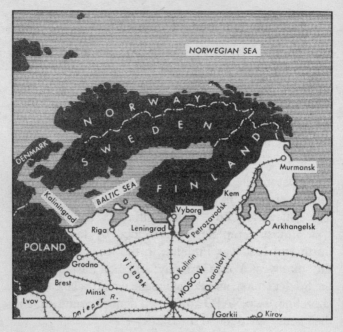

Russian Defense

distance of her trip into the Baltic. But it would have also exposed her to the many prying eyes lining the canal. The Soviet navy would have quickly put out a greeting party from their forces at Leningrad on the far corner of the Gulf of Finland.

The covert needs of the mission overrode any other considerations. The *Archerfish* was going to have to do a quiet transit of international waters. And no craft, military or civilian, would be allowed to know that a huge nuclear submarine was passing by beneath them.

2115 ZULU
55° 18' North, 10° 56' East
Control Room
USS *Archerfish*
Store Baelt Channel
Between Fyn and Sjaelland Islands
Denmark

Soon after leaving the North Channel between Ireland and Scotland, the *Archerfish* entered the deeper waters of the Atlantic. Once given the room to maneuver, the captain ordered the normal "angles and dangles" diving exercises. The series of steep dives and equally steep up angles were intended to find out if anything was improperly stowed aboard the boat. Outside of a few minor items shifting about, and Ensign Paulson clucking over the eight-boat in the DDS, everything on the ship was secure.

The two civilian passengers were not quite as sure everything was all right when the maneuvers took place. Even with the captain's announcement of diving exercises over the 1-MC address system, they were caught unawares of just what was coming.

Master Chief John Richards, the chief of the boat, was the highest ranking enlisted member of the *Archerfish*'s crew. Because of his knowledge and experience, he was deferred to by everyone aboard, including the officers and the captain. As an old hand, he had gone through many dive exercises, some considerably worse than what they had just done. He was proud of his ability to walk along a steeply angled deck and drink a full cup of coffee without spilling a drop.

Of course, if the COB did spill some coffee on his uniform, it was a poorly informed crewman who pointed it out. Richards was of medium height but with a very heavy, powerful build. Though an easygoing sailor with twenty-two years of experience behind him, spilling his coffee could seriously irritate the senior NCO.

But when the COB met up with a very irate, and attractive, blond doctor, who was wearing what appeared to have been a full cup of tea on her coveralls, his experience did not cover the situation. Failing to calm the good doctor down, the COB abandoned the area and retreated to the relative safety of the control room and a duty station he was long used to.

The officer of the deck of a submarine has a duty station at the front center of the control room. It is there that the OOD "has the conn." From that position, he can direct the maneuvers and operation of the craft as it slips through the water. The position of the OOD rotates through the watches among a number of qualified officers in the crew of a submarine. This is also the central position often taken by the captain. And as the *Archerfish* entered the tight, restrictive waters off Denmark, the captain was at the conn.

Captain North sat forward on his seat, looking over to his left toward the helm where the two seamen steering his boat sat at their controls. The helmsman on the right of the pair used his aircraftlike wheel to move the ship's rudder and maintain her course. The planesman to the left operated the ship's dive planes, moving the craft up and down in the water. The console with the telegraph control that ordered the speed of the boat was between the two men.

When the officer of the deck—in this case the captain—ordered a change in speed, the telegraph would be used to send the command to the engine room. An answering call would come immediately back to announce receipt of the command. Back behind the center console sat the diving officer. The three men were seated in comfortable bucket seats, complete with seat belts, so they couldn't be thrown from their controls by a violent maneuver. Standing to the left of all of these positions was the chief of the watch, who oversaw his men.

The panels in front of the men held a bewildering array of dials, screens, and switches. But the practiced eyes of the chief of the watch and the diving officer scanned them all with ease. The captain could sit comfortably with full confidence in his crew and their leaders. In this close situation, the COB was holding the position of chief of the watch, and the XO took the position of dive officer.

As always on an underway submarine, sound was at a minimum. The "acoustic advantage" was when one submarine could hear the other before being heard herself. This advantage was one jealously held through design and training. The ship had been carefully silenced as she was being built: machinery, pipes, and conduits were insulated from the hull. In an underwater world, the first one to hear the other side was usually the winner. To help keep sound waves from bouncing off the steel hull of the ship, resilient-compound blocks had been attached to her hull as an anechoic coating.

The crew also followed noise discipline as a matter of habit. Hatches and other covers were closed easily and never slammed, items were rarely dropped, and even if they were, they hit a linoleum-covered deck. Tools were not struck against machinery as work was done. And voices were kept low; orders were spoken, not shouted. The living spaces aboard the boat were quieter than most libraries. In all, the interior of the submarine was a calm, controlled environment surrounded by a cold, unforgiving sea.

And as the ship entered the waters around Denmark, the sea about her was becoming crowded. To maintain security, the submarine would not traverse the waters on the surface. And there wasn't an escort ship to take her through. The *Archerfish* was on her own, being directed underwater by her competent crew and their experienced captain.

Aft of the control room, on the starboard, or right, side of the craft, was the sonar control room. Sonar was the ears, and underwater, even the eyes, of the boat. Running in the passive mode, the BQQ-5 sonar suite could listen to all of the various sounds in the water. The noises picked up by the sensitive instruments of the bow-mounted BQS-6 spherical sonar array, the hull-mounted sensors, or towed array that could be pulled behind the submarine on a cable, went through the computer processors of the BQQ-5.

In spite of the advanced computer-driven processors

of the BQQ-5 system, men had to be in the analysis loop. The digital computer of the BQQ-5 reduced the number of watch standers who had to listen through earphones and watch the screens as information was discovered and displayed. But the computers could only identify what they had already known. New contacts had to be discerned by human ears.

The sonarmen aboard a submarine conduct their duties as half science and half art. It took experience and competence to make a good sonarman. One of the sonarmen aboard the *Archerfish* was ST First Class Randy Peters, a red-haired young man who had come up in the ranks quickly due to his ability with the sonar system and the ease with which he worked with others. His last aspect could be even more important than the first, given the crowded conditions and long hours aboard a nuclear submarine.

Peters had the watch on sonar as the *Archerfish* entered the Kattegat. In the passive mode, the sensors of the BQQ-5 simply listened and analyzed the sounds they picked up. In the active mode, the huge spherical BQS-6 sphere in the nose of the boat could almost boil the water next to the hull with the sound energy it could put out. That sound would come back as echoes from whatever target the submarine was trying to locate. And those same sounds would show where the submarine was located to any other ships that might be listening.

So the *Archerfish* crept along at fifteen knots, half her top speed, listening carefully all the while. It took a long eight hours to traverse the Kattegat, and now the sub was between the Danish islands of Fyn and Sjaelland, the Danish capital of Copenhagen on the shore opposite Sjaelland. They were in the Store Baelt Channel, and the heavy shipping normally found on her waters were relatively light during the late evening hours.

But the *Archerfish* had been ducking various commercial craft all day as she had traversed first the Skagerak and then the Kattegat, while moving from the North Sea into the Baltic. There were three hundred kilometers between her and the much more open waters of the Baltic. Now she was in one of the narrowest points she would have to pass, a channel only fifteen kilometers wide between the two main islands of Denmark.

The captain had been holding his position in the control room for hours. A watch change had put some of his best people at their posts for this very tight maneuvering spot. It wasn't that the channel was too narrow for the submarine, but the waters were shallow. By almost scraping the bottom, her sail remained underwater, but she was still at periscope depth. This was not a comfortable position for a ship that normally hid by going deep.

As the BQQ-5 computer announced the acquisition of a signal, Peters immediately centered his console on the sound. The other sailor on watch in the sonar control room, as well as Lieutenant Tullerbee, the weapons officer, were tuned out and ignored as Peters listened to his headphones. Reaching over to the 1-MC, he made his announcement to the conn.

"Conn, Sonar," Peters said quickly, "I have a new contact bearing one eight zero, designated contact number Sierra two-seven."

Reaching up to the 1-MC, Captain North held the transmit switch open. "Captain aye. What have you got, Peters?"

"I don't know, sir, it's a close contact dead ahead on the surface. There's almost no machinery noise sir, and I swear I heard music."

"Okay, start your track," the captain said as he released the transmit switch.

"Sonar aye," Peters replied.

Peters reached over and flipped a switch on the large reel-to-reel tape recorder net to his console. As the reels began slowly turning, the computer in the BQQ-5 also began further analyzing the sounds being recorded.

In the control room, Captain North now had another of many surface contacts to deal with. It couldn't be too close, as sonar had only just picked it up. But a visual examination of the situation was called for.

"Well, this trip just keeps getting better and better," North said under his breath as he moved to the periscopes in the center of the compartment.

The *Archerfish* had two periscopes, as did most nuclear submarines. The larger scope to the rear was the search periscope that had range-finding ability, night vision, a camera, and other electronics and optical capabilities. To contain all of this capability, the search scope was thick through the mast and made a more noticeable track through the water when it was raised. The periscope mast was covered with a mottled rubber coating to minimize sound and radar reflection and camouflage it against the surface. But it was still big.

The forward attack periscope was a much simpler optical instrument, with some magnification ability and not much more. But it was also more slender and difficult to see. The mast was also covered in a mottled gray rubber coating, but since it made such a small wake in the water, it was used for the plotting of a torpedo attack.

As he turned and walked around the railing that guarded the periscope position, Captain North called out, "Up scope."

"Up scope aye," Master Chief Richards said as the COB pulled down the control that hydraulically raised the periscope.

Bending down, Captain North had his eye to the rubber cap over the lens of the periscope as the device rose from the deck. As he rose with the periscope, he rotated it so he was looking forward of the submarine. He stopped and just looked through the glass for a moment in surprise.

"Helm, all stop," Captain North ordered.

"All stop aye," Seaman Darryl Hackett called out from his position as the helmsman.

"Answers to all stop, sir," Hackett said as the telegraph rang back from the engine room.

As the big undersea craft started to slow, the captain called out to his chief of the watch. "COB," he said quietly, "hand me that copy of *Jane's*, please."

Taking the large blue-covered book from the small

bookcase next to the plotting tables aft of the periscopes, the COB handed it to the captain. Quickly scan-
ning through the pages, the captain stopped and began
examining the book more closely. As he ran his finger
down the page, he spoke out loud, "White hull, three
masts, uh-huh," North said, almost to himself. Then he
closed the book and addressed the control room.

"Okay, gentlemen, let's take this one easy. There's a
tall ship, a three-masted schooner, not five hundred
meters off our bow. Now, since my name isn't Nemo
and this ship isn't the *Nautilus*, what say we try not to
ram and sink the royal yacht of Denmark. Helm, all
ahead slow."

"All ahead slow aye," Hackett said.

"Answers all ahead slow, sir," came the confirmation
announcement.

"Guide starboard two degrees," North ordered as he
handed the big *Jane's* back to the COB.

"Two degrees starboard aye," Hackett said as he
turned his control wheel slightly.

The submarine returned to a five-knot forward
speed. Even such a slow speed built up a lot of inertia
in the 4,700-ton craft. As the ship moved, Captain
North turned back to the periscope.

"Damn," he said loudly. "There was another sailing
ship behind her. And it's cutting right toward us. Helm,
hard right rudder. Down scope!"

"Hard right rudder aye," Hackett said as he turned
the wheel.

As the COB pushed on the control to the periscope,

it seemed that the slim metal shaft would take forever to lower into its seat. The tip of the periscope sank beneath the water as the schooner headed directly toward it.

As the big craft moved to get out of the way of the unsuspecting sailing ship, she turned out of the central shipping channel. In spite of all of the information the *Archerfish* had in her own charts, and the details Danzig had brought with him, there were changes in the sea floor that were not shown on the charts.

As the schooner slipped past just overhead, it had no knowledge that the keel of its hull had just missed the sail of the submarine, passing not three feet over the periscope as it lowered. But to the side of dredged shipping channel, the currents had moved and adjusted the sea floor. Now, a small sandbar loomed just ahead of the *Archerfish*. As the big craft turned, the bottom of its hull impacted with the sand.

The two Fourth Platoon officers were sitting in the wardroom enjoying a cup of coffee when Lieutenant Fisher walked in.

"Hello, Matt," Rockham said. "Draw yourself a cup and pull up a chair."

"Thanks," Fisher replied. "That's just what I came down here for."

"Where's Paulson?" Rockham asked as Fisher was drawing himself a cup of coffee. "I haven't seen him for a while."

"He went up into the DDS with Lopez and Handel," Fisher said as he walked back to the table, gazing at the materials hanging on the bulkheads of the wardroom. "He wanted to do a once-over before we get to the target area. The up and down maneuvers the captain ordered made him nervous about the boat. I swear, the man dearly loves the SDVs. It's not like I don't think a bunch of them myself, but he wants them to shine. He feels this will be the first combat use of the eight-boat ever."

Having walked halfway around the table gazing at the bulkheads, Fisher drew out a seat opposite Rockham. As the SDV officer sat down with a full cup of coffee, he raised it to his nose and inhaled deeply. Exhaling with a sigh, he sipped his cup with obvious pleasure.

"Like the stuff, do you?" Shaun Daugherty said with a grin.

"The drink of life," Fisher replied. "And the best in the Navy is on board the subs."

"I dunno," Rockham said, "you should try some of the brew that Ken Fleming turns out."

"Who?" Fisher asked.

"Ken Fleming," Rockham replied. "He's in first squad. The guy's a gourmet cook, would you believe. Does it as a hobby. On deployments, I've seen him take—"

The conversation came to an abrupt end as the deck tilted and a shock ran through the sub. Fisher, who had been sitting with his back to the forward bulkhead, flipped over, slamming into the side of the compartment and spilling his coffee all over his shirt front.

Rockham, who was facing forward, managed to keep his seat, but only because his chest was stopped by the edge of the table. Shaun tilted sideways, but grabbing the edge of the table kept him from going any farther.

The cries of startled men and the crash of loose gear sounded throughout the boat as the big submarine struck and ground over something yielding. The boat groaned deeply, like a living thing, as she bounced and lifted. The 1-MC overhead sounded out over everything else: "This is the captain. We have struck a sandbar. All damage control parties report."

"What the hell—" Rockham started to say. But Fisher was rushing out of the compartment.

"Shit!" Shaun shouted. "There's men in the DDS!"

Working in the hangar chamber of the DDS was like being inside a horizontal gas tank. The metal walls were lined with reinforcing ribs, and the metal radiated cold, as it was at the temperature of the water that surrounded it. There was also a clammy wet smell of the sea in the chamber, not at all like the clean ocean smell of the seashore.

For all of its size, the hangar could only hold a single SDV. The small craft sat on a rolling cradle that would be pushed out the outer hangar door by the DDS crew during launch. There were some tools and materials kept in the DDS, but most of the materials were brought up from stores when there was work to be done inside the chamber. Electrical power and compressed air and gas connections to the *Archerfish* also helped men inside the DDS conduct maintenance on the SDV.

In spite of the conditions, Paulson couldn't have been happier. Though he looked like just an average person on the street you wouldn't look twice at, Paulson had an iron will. That will had gotten him through the University of Michigan's Marine Engineering program in just under three years. It was also what got him to give up the possible financial gains he could have received in the outside world and led him to join the Navy, where he received his commission. And it was most of all responsible for helping to bring the physically slight man through the rigors of BUD/S.

Though he never ran at the front of the pack, and he wasn't the leader during PT or sports, the men of the platoon and the SEALs who knew him respected Paulson for always pulling through. It didn't matter if you were in the middle, it mattered if you finished.

And what helped set Paulson's mind toward entering the SEALs was his passion for the sea and the underwater world. Specifically, he loved the machines that could take men through the water and into the deeps. So his involvement with the SDVs was a natural evolution of his career in the Teams.

But right then, Ed Lopez and Steve Handel could have done without some of Ensign Paulson's passion. They had been going over all of the components of the eight-boat ever since chow. Though the SEALs knew full well the importance of maintenance—their lives and those of their Teammates depended on it—there was such a thing as being obsessive about it.

As Lopez checked the rear control surfaces of the

eight-boat, Paulson operated the controls from inside the cockpit. Handel was coiling up the cables that had been used to top up the charge on the batteries.

"Right full rudder," Paulson called out from the cockpit.

Though the voice sounded dull and odd in the confines of the hangar, Lopez had no trouble hearing the officer. He reached through the rear of the SDV, past the rudder and above the five-bladed screw, to grab hold of the push-pull rod sticking out from the hull of the boat. The rod moved the rudder from side to side, according to how the pilot pressed the pedals in the cockpit.

"Left full rudder aye," he called back out.

"No no!" Paulson shouted. "Right full rudder!"

"Ayee, ayee, right full rudder aye," Lopez said with a grin to Handel. And he yanked on the push-pull rod to be certain it didn't have excessive slack.

As Handel opened his mouth to speak, the *Archerfish* struck the sandbar.

Lopez was knocked forward and off of his feet. With his hand still tangled with the control surfaces of the SDV, Lopez had his full weight go across his right forearm. As his hand braced against the vertical rudder surface, and the back of his arm was stopped by one of the blades of the screw, the bones of his forearm snapped audibly, the ragged end of one tearing through the skin.

Handel flew forward and landed heavily on his right side near the inner door of the hangar. Smashing down on his shoulder, he could feel something in his upper chest pop. And then the pain started.

Inside the cockpit of the SDV, Paulson had been just sitting back down on the flat deck of the boat when the blow came. He bent forward, smashing the right side of his face into the instrument panel. The heavy Plexiglas covers of the instrument containers absorbed the blow without any trouble, but Paulson's face was another matter. As the pain and white lights exploded behind his eyes, Paulson slumped down, unconscious. His last thought was for the well-being of the men he had brought into the DDS.

Handel dragged himself up from the deck, pain spearing through his chest and down his arm. But the SEAL could see his Teammate, Lopez, lying on the deck with a bleeding arm. Going over to the stricken Lopez, Handel saw the jagged end of a bone sticking through the skin of the Latino's arm. The bleeding SEAL was going ashen-gray with shock.

Seeing that his Teammate was in far worse shape than he was, Handel grabbed at his uniform belt and quickly undid the buckle. The swinging of his right arm caused so much pain to lance through the SEAL's chest that his skull felt like it exploded. As red and yellow lights flashed behind his eyelids, the SEAL fought to stay conscious. The nausea that raised the gorge in his throat was bad, but puking on his Teammate was far less hazardous to his health than just letting him lay there and bleed.

Choking back his bile, Handel slipped the hand of

his useless right arm into his trousers. Pulling off his belt, he quickly slipped it around Lopez's upper arm. Cinching down on the tag end of the belt, Handel drew the makeshift tourniquet tight. Normally, he would have put pressure on a wound to stop the bleeding. But the razor-edged end of the bone sticking up prevented that.

Staggering over to the inner door of the hangar, Handel picked up the mike that was hooked into the 1-MC of the ship.

"Corpsman to the DDS," he croaked. "Corpsman to the DDS!"

Dropping the microphone, he heard footsteps coming up the ladder leading down from the access sphere into the submarine. As the SEAL turned to the bow of the SDV, Lieutenant Fisher pulled open the inner door to the hangar.

"Lopez, he's bleeding," Handel croaked as relief flooded through him. And with the relief came the beginning of what could be life-threatening shock. Powerful arms grabbed the SEAL and lowered him to the floor. Handel looked up into the eyes of Greg Rockham as Rockham and Shaun Daugherty controlled his fall.

"Mr. Paulson," Handel gasped as he fought to stay conscious, "inside the SDV . . ."

Closer to the vehicle than Rockham, Daugherty pulled back the cover of the cockpit that had slid forward in the crash. Reaching inside, he felt for a pulse on the side of Paulson's neck.

"He's alive," Shaun shouted.

As the two SEAL corpsmen came into the hangar, Handel lost the fight and slipped into soft, warm darkness.

The next thing Handel remembered was looking up into the face of an angel. Golden hair surrounded by a white glow framed green eyes looking down at him. The lips of the angel pursed as if to give him a kiss, and then a brilliant white light hit his eyes.

Dr. Sharon Taylor hadn't practiced medicine in years, but the level of injuries in the SEALs who had been in the DDS demanded that she offer her help. The table in the officers' wardroom turned out to be quickly convertible into an examination and treatment table. Several of the cabinets around the room held a tremendous variety of medical supplies. Though the submarine didn't have a formal sick bay, the wardroom was intended to be a rapid substitute.

Dr. Taylor bent over the still unconscious SEAL on the table and tightened her mouth in concern as she pulled up one of the man's eyelids. The four square yellow battle lanterns on the ceiling—overhead, she corrected herself irritably—flooded the area with light. Shining the beam of a penlight into the SEAL's eye, she tested for neurological damage. The pupil contracted correctly as the man groaned and moved his head.

"Relax sailor," she said in a soft, soothing voice, "you're all right, you're in sick bay."

"How . . . how's Lopez and Mr. Paulson?" Handel croaked through a dry throat.

Astonished that the man's first thought would be for his fellow SEALs, Dr. Taylor said, "They're fine. You did okay with that first aid, Lopez will be fine and so is Paulson. You've been unconscious the longest."

The injured SEAL's head slipped back and his eyes closed. But this time he was simply asleep and not unconscious. Tinsley and Limbaugh, the two SEAL corpsmen, along with Ron Edgars, the corpsman for the *Archerfish*, were standing around the table, looking at her.

"He'll be fine," Dr. Taylor said. "He's just going to sleep for a bit. When he is awake, we'll have to strap in that shoulder of his."

"Yes, ma'am," Limbaugh said. "Fractured clavicle?"

"It looks like," Dr. Taylor said with an odd look. The SEAL corpsmen were competent, to say the least, as was the ship's corpsman. But this Limbaugh seemed a competent doctor. There was more to this man than she could see on the surface.

"We'll take over for now, ma'am," Tinsley said. "You've been a big help. Thank you."

As she stepped out of the wardroom, Taylor was only slightly surprised to see almost half of the SEALs lining the passageway. The big joker—Kurkowski was his name, wasn't it?—was standing closest to the door and spoke to her as she came out.

"Ma'am," the big SEAL said, with surprising shyness. "Will he be all right?"

"Yes, he'll be fine," Taylor replied. The tenderness and concern she heard in the big man's voice also surprised her. "All three of them will be fine."

"Okay, you heard the doctor," the loud voice of Chief Monday sounded out. "Now break up this party. These submariners have work to do and you clowns are in their way."

As the crowd of SEALs started moving away, the big, quiet chief stood there for a moment. "Thank you, Doctor," he said, and then moved down the passageway.

Going down to the crew's mess, Taylor decided a cup of coffee was what she needed rather than tea. She wanted to be awake for a while, in case there were complications with any of the injured SEALs. The crew's mess was a much larger compartment than the wardroom. Tables much like picnic tables with built-in benches lined the floor. Sitting at one bench, she saw three of the SEAL officers. The officers were given a respectful space by the rest of the men in the mess.

Drawing a cup of coffee from a huge urn, she turned and walked over to the SEALs' table. As they began to rise at her approach she said, "Please, I appreciate the thought, but I think we're all too tired for the formalities."

When she sat down, Lieutenant Fisher was the first to speak, as Rockham and Daugherty looked on.

"How are my men, Doctor?" he asked.

"They could be a lot worse," Taylor said honestly. "I don't know that Handel saved the life of Lopez with that tourniquet of his, but I do know it helped slow the bleeding a lot until we could get him treated."

"And how is he, ma'am?" Rockham asked.

"Look, I'm getting a little tired of the 'ma'am' bit all

of the time," Taylor said irritably. "My name is Sharon, or Dr. Taylor if you want to be formal."

"Yes, ma—Dr. Taylor," Rockham said with a quiet smile.

"As to your question, Handel will be fine. He has a broken right collarbone and a really amazing bruise that's developing on his right shoulder. He's not going to have much use of that arm for a while. But he's past the danger from shock.

"Lopez has a worse injury," Taylor continued. "He has a compound fracture of the right wrist. It's been set and splinted, but he's going to need some serious recuperation to recover from that break.

"Lieutenant Paulson probably has the most painful injury, or at least it's going to be the worst-looking for some while. He broke the left zygomatic arch and maxilla of his face."

"Pardon me, Doctor," Fisher said with concern, "he did what?"

"He broke his left cheekbone and upper jaw," Taylor said simply. "The blood that covered his face was mostly from his bleeding sinuses. I want to observe him for a possible concussion, but he's going to be hurting with that face for a while. And the bruising is going to look like he went into a prize fight with a grizzly."

The SEALs at the table raised their opinion of the doctor a notch with her attempt at a joke.

"So obviously none of these men are going to be able to dive for a while?" Rockham asked.

"The broken bones are obvious," Taylor said tiredly.

"And Lopez won't even be taking a shower for months. I'm not sure Paulson could even put on a face mask without passing out. And even if he did, his sinuses could start bleeding and he could drown in his own blood before he could surface. No, I'm afraid none of these men will be in the water for some time."

"So," Fisher said, "that's it, then?"

"What do you mean?" Sharon asked.

"Lopez and Handel were the pilot and backup pilot for the SDV," Fisher said with a sigh. "We don't have anyone else to drive the boat."

"Yes we do," Rockham said. "Mike Bryant was in SDVs not six months ago. He was a pilot, wasn't he?"

"Yes he was," Shaun said excitedly.

"And that means?" Sharon said.

"We're still in the game, Doctor," Rockham said as he got up from the table. "If you will excuse me, I have some planning to do."

All the SEALs got up and left the mess quickly. As Dr. Taylor sat at the table by herself, she said quietly, "I never had that effect on men before."

CHAPTER 8

1020 ZULU
Officers' Club
Northern Fleet Naval Infantry Brigade Base
Penchenga
Kola Peninsula
Union of Soviet Socialist Republics

Captain Lieutenant Vasili Rutil sat across the table from his old Spetsnaz unit commander. The officers' club had a number of quiet alcoves where old comrades could sit and swap tales of past deeds and times gone by. For the lieutenant and Captain Rostov, some of the deeds they were speaking of had yet to be done.

"So, Vasili," Rostov said as he reached across the table and poured a drink. "You have done very well in pulling the old squad together."

"It wasn't very hard, sir," Rutil responded. "As soon as they heard you had a mission, you couldn't keep them away. Frolik would have gone AWOL from his command if that transfer hadn't gone through."

"Frolik is about as dependable and steadfast as the

mountains themselves," Rostov said with a chuckle.

"Only to you, sir," Rutil continued as he picked up his glass. "To everyone else, he's about as dependable as a bear with a toothache. About the same size as one too, come to think of it. You were the one who led that rescue mission against the mujahideen. Those Afghan women who staked him out wouldn't have left anything recognizable as human."

"I was just sorry we couldn't have gotten all of the men out," Rostov said regretfully.

"That was the general's problem," Vasili said bitterly. "Him, and those damned politicians."

A long silence settled over the two men as they thought of the men they had left behind in the mountains of Afghanistan. The war had been a long and bloody one for both sides. After a few early successes, the Soviet Union had quickly found itself bogged down in a guerrilla war reminiscent of the U.S. involvement in Vietnam.

"Well, we're going to have the last word over those people who sold this country out," Rostov said, anger rising in his voice. "Those old women in the Politburo and the pet dogs they raised in rank in the military have no idea what it means to be a fighter in the front ranks."

"But are you sure this General Stankevich is the one you want to follow?" Vasili said in a low voice.

"He will be as deeply involved as we are Vasili," Rostov said in a conspiratorial tone. "The only difference between us is that we shall be the ones in direct possession of the weapons and not him. I never intended to turn all of them over to him. If it comes down to a betrayal by anyone, we will still hold the upper hand. We can show these dogs what it means to have a will of iron, and a hand of one to match."

"But what of this KGB border officer he has put on to us?" Vasili asked.

"He is exactly as Stankevich said he was—a thug and nothing more. He has been a blot on the record of all good Soviets for long enough," Rostov said in disgust. "At least when we get rid of him, it will do some direct good. He will cover our involvement in the operation as a cutout. He doesn't know exactly what the operation is or who we are, only that he is expecting a large reward for the theft of government supplies. And that is something he has done over and over again on his own.

"Simply put, he will appear to have taken the items himself. And by eliminating him, that will be one less parasite in the world."

"I just don't know, Captain," Vasili said in a concerned tone. "To have risked so much and come so far in the service, only to risk everything now . . ." he trailed off.

"The way our government is running things now, Vasili," Rostov said, "there will be little enough to support a soldier later on. They are giving the house away to the West for vague promises. The people will not continue to stand for what has been going on. Something will happen, and it will happen soon. We have to be prepared to make the best of it, and doing that from a position of strength will be best.

"Vasili," Rostov continued in a much softer voice, "I

have known you since you were a junior lieutenant in the navy. The first time I saw you, you were leaning over the rail and thought you were going to die. I told you that you would live, and you have, and done well besides. There is no other person I would rather have at my side on this operation than you. We will take the risks, but this time we will have the rewards as well."

"Every man in your unit feels the same way about you, Gregoriy," Vasili said, in a rare use of Rostov's first name. "The problem wasn't finding the men that could be trusted to make up your squad. It was choosing just which ones to take along.

"I have put together the unit you asked for," Vasili continued. "No one of lower rank than sergeant, and every man served under you in combat. The two youngest men, Adamenko and Nosenko, are reconnaissance trained. They can track a cat across a dry rock and survive in areas where a goat would starve. But that kind of work is really a young man's game.

"Frolik is the lead NCO. Given that the man is more of a force of nature than a soldier, that's probably the safest place to put him anyway. Zabotin is the other master sergeant, but he will lead the demolition team. Sergei Nemec is his backup. And Kerenski is a backup sniper to Frolik. And Ivan Tsinev is the communications officer.

"From the most junior enlisted man on up through the officers, each of them jumped at the chance to serve directly with you again. You are still a legend among these men."

"Well," Rostov said, trying not to show the emotion he felt, "this time there will be more for these men to have afterward than just a few pieces of metal and ribbon pinned on their chests. Those others who have never faced death have only experienced a weak form of life. We have taken its full measure, haven't we, Vasili?"

The two officers quietly laughed together. Then Rostov continued in a more serious tone.

"You have until the end of the week to get all of the men together. Our transport is being laid on, and I want us to be under way by next week. I am willing to use this Belik character, but I do not completely trust his abilities. I want us to have at least two days' flexibility in our schedule. The operation is listed as simply a field exercise, but I want no last minute complications to draw attention.

"It shall be as you order, sir," Vasili said crisply.

"Then let us finish this fair vodka and get into some good food here, eh, Vasili?" Rostov said with a smile.

"That too," Vasili said as he lifted his glass, "as you command."

0710 ZULU
55° 5' North, 13° 36' East
Torpedo Room
USS *Archerfish*
Baltic Sea

"Attention on deck," Mike Ferber said loudly. "Woman entering the compartment."

"Must you do that?" Dr. Taylor said as she entered the torpedo room.

"Why yes, ma'am," Ferber said, puzzled. "That isn't for you, ma'am. That's for the men. The same thing would have happened a couple of times if you came down the forward ladder—that one goes through the crew's living spaces."

"Very well," Dr. Taylor said in an exasperated tone. "I suppose it prevents me from seeing any of your men running about in their underwear."

"Better than you know, ma'am," Ferber said with a grin. "Most SEALs don't wear underwear."

"I don't even want to know," Taylor said, flushing pink. "Please just take me to Ensign Paulson."

"His rack is right over here, ma'am," Ferber said, all business at the mention of the injured SEAL. "Lopez and Handel are right next to him."

The center of the large compartment was taken up by a huge, multitiered rack over twenty feet long holding layers of torpedoes in their cradles. On either side of the compartment were additional smaller racks which also held torpedoes. Dr. Taylor could see a bewildering array of pipes, conduits, and additional machinery at the far, front end of the compartment. Though she had almost no knowledge of submarines, she surmised that the conglomeration of machinery was the working end of the torpedo tubes.

A number of the torpedoes had been removed and their spaces filled with mattresses and bedding. These had to be the "racks" petty officer Ferber had been speaking of. Few of the beds had bodies in them. The SEALs were mostly sitting about the compartment, several of them having been interrupted at a card game, by the looks of the playing cards scattered on a makeshift table of metal boxes.

As she followed Ferber down the side of the compartment, Dr. Taylor was very conscious of the eyes of the men watching her. But she focused her attention on the several injured SEALs lying on the bunks.

Lopez had a soft cast on his arm, and the wide grin he gave the doctor either showed his constant good spirits, or the pain medications she had given him were working very well. Both he and Handel were on bunks across from where Ensign Paulson lay. The multiple layers of torpedo racks kept any of the men from sitting up or on the edges of the racks. It looked like the last thing Paulson wanted to do was get up.

As she approached the injured officer, she could see that her original estimation had been conservative at best. The whole of Paulson's face was swollen, the worst of it being on the right side, where the broken bones were. A variety of colors had flooded the ensign's face, blue being predominate. It almost looked as if the man's face was a sculpture made from a blue balloon.

A dark-haired SEAL with a chest like a barrel came up next to Ensign Paulson's rack carrying a steel box. It was Kurkowski, as his name tag said, and he set the obviously heavy container on the floor with apparent ease.

"A seat for you, ma'am," he said politely.

Thanking the man for his courtesy, Dr. Taylor sat and looked to her patient.

"Feeling better, Ensign?" she asked in a soft voice.

His right eye was surrounded by tissue so swollen, she could barely make it out. What she could see was so bloodshot as to appear to be almost a red ball. But the other eye was alert and looking at her clearly.

"Yes, ma'am," Paulson barely said in a mumbled voice.

"Don't try to speak," Taylor said. "You've badly hurt your face, but it looks like everything will be fine. Have you been able to eat anything?"

"The cook brought down some soup for him earlier, ma'am," Corpsman Tinsley volunteered as he walked up. "He got some down. One of our men is up in the galley making something up for him."

"Well, it will be better if he can eat something," Taylor said. "Otherwise the drugs could start irritating his stomach. You SEALs even take a cook with you on these trips?"

"Not quite, ma'am," Ferber said with a small laugh.

"You know, Team One had a senior chief who had started in the Navy as a cook," Kurkowski said nearby.

"Well, we don't quite have that," Ferber continued, "but one of our men likes to work in the galley when he can."

Just then, the subject of their discussion, Ken Fleming, walked into the compartment from the rear hatch.

"Would you believe this tub has a cook who doesn't know how to make a fucking custard?" Fleming said as he entered the compartment carrying a tray. "Works from a mix! What a cheating bastard. At least he had the ingredients I needed. Hey, Enswine, got some chow for you."

Then the tall SEAL saw the doctor sitting next to Paulson's bunk. The man flushed all the way to the top of his bald head as the woman looked up at him with amusement in her eyes.

"Oh," the SEAL said, flustered. "Excuse me, ma'am. I didn't see you there."

"That's quite all right," Taylor said with only a small smile. "I was just checking up on my patient. Obviously, he's in good hands. I'll leave him to your care."

As the doctor got up to leave, she saw Kurkowski coming up to the bunk with a number of pillows. The corpsman and several of the SEALs were helping Paulson sit up enough to eat. The woman was astonished at the tenderness she saw the powerful men show their injured comrade.

"You'll like this one, sir," Fleming said as he put the tray down on the box. "The glass has got a shake in it I warmed up before bringing it down. I figured cold wouldn't exactly be what you wanted right now."

"At least you'll have some kind of skill to serve you when the Navy finally tosses your skinny ass out of here," Kurkowski said.

"I seem to remember you eating everything but the pot at the last platoon party," Fleming retorted.

The other injured SEALs seemed to be fine. And both of the men were watching the exchange between Kurkowski and Fleming. Taylor decided they were in good hands with the SEAL corpsmen there, and she removed herself from the compartment before the two men came to blows.

"Are they always like that?" she asked Ferber, who had gone with her to the hatch.

"Yeah, pretty much," he said with a laugh. "But they're just joking around. If they weren't, I'd be a lot more worried.

"Doctor," Ferber said seriously. "I just wanted to say thanks, for what you did for my Teammates."

"Your own corpsmen did more than I did, Ferber," Taylor said sincerely. "They are more than competent."

"Thanks, ma'am, I'll tell them you said so," Ferber said in a quiet voice. "Just for your information, Limbaugh was most of the way through medical school before he enlisted."

"Well, I hope at some point that he decides to finish," Taylor said. "He has some real skill."

"And my name's Mike, ma'am," Ferber said with a wide smile.

"Mine's Sharon, Mike," Taylor said with a smile of her own.

As she started up the ladder at the end of the passage, Dr. Taylor could hear some catcalls coming from the torpedo room as Ferber reentered the compartment. Some of the men must have seen their short exchange outside of the hatchway. His voice was starting to rise in a growl as she went up to the second deck. She shook her head at the very mixed and contrary nature of the men she had just been with.

When Dr. Taylor entered the wardroom, all of the other SEAL officers, as well as Peter Danzig and Captain

North, were sitting around the table. Papers, charts, and manuals were scattered across the top of the table, some held down with coffee cups.

"Doctor," Lieutenant Fisher said, looking up. "How are my men?"

"There's some improvement," Taylor said, sitting down at the table, "but nothing major. I expect the swelling in Ensign Paulson's face to go down fairly soon, and he's in no real danger. But there is absolutely no question that none of those men will be going in the water anytime soon."

"Outside of a few sailors with bumps and bruises, they were the worst injured of any of the crew," Captain North said. "The ship is fine, damages were minimal at most. We've already made up the time we lost. And you gentlemen say the operation will still go through?"

"It must go through," Danzig said heatedly. "At this late stage we have no way to make contact with the target."

"The operation will go through, Mr. Danzig," Rockham said with a grim expression. Turning to Lieutenant Rogers, he said, "Bill, you're sure none of your men can pilot the eight-boat?"

"Everyone has time on her, sure," Rogers said, leaning forward and resting his arms on the table. "But I need them to operate the DDS during the launch and recovery cycle. Even as it is, the recovery of the SDV is going to take some time to cycle through."

"I just don't see any other way around it," Rockham said. "It looks like Bryant is the only way to go."

"I watched him go over the boat after the accident," Lieutenant Fisher said. "He knows his way around the craft. When I questioned him on it, he sounded like a good, solid operator."

"Okay then, Matt," Rockham said finally. "He's going to be with you in the cockpit. Anything goes wrong, you'll be able to either talk him through it or take over. Limbaugh and the chief will be in the back with me.

"What does our time to the target area look like, Captain?" Rockham said looking to Captain North.

"Right now we're about twenty-five miles off Ystad, on just about the southernmost point of Sweden," the captain responded after a moment's thought. "From here it's about 560 statute miles, or nine hundred kilometers, to Helsinki.

"What I'm planning to do is head toward Helsinki on the normal shipping route. Helsinki is the second largest port in Scandinavia. They run nine million passengers and ten million tons of cargo through her harbors every year. I expect we'll have a nice, fat civilian cargo ship or liner come along this route. When we come across one, I can tuck the *Archerfish* in close and run at the same speed as the surface ship. That will hide us in the ship's shadow."

"Shadow, Captain?" Sharon asked as she took the cup of coffee Rockham offered her.

"An acoustic shadow, Doctor," Captain North answered. "What we really would be doing is using the noise of the ship to mask ourselves. We could then run much faster without having to dash and listen.

"To answer your question before you ask it, Doctor," Captain North said before Taylor spoke, "a submarine sees with its ears. Our sonar hears best when we're moving slow. The first sub to hear another is considered to have the acoustical advantage, so it's not something we like to give up easily. When we have to cover a lot of territory, we tend to move in fast dashes, and then slow to listen. With something to hide behind, we can move as fast as it does. And merchant ships from any country like to get their cargoes in port as quickly as possible."

"But why all of the concern about other submarines?" Dr. Taylor asked. "Surely we're the only one around here."

"Not hardly, Sharon," Danzig said. "The Soviets have craft all through these waters. They've run submarines right up to the Swedish coast, even landed men on Swedish soil, according to reports. Even though we're legally in international waters, if the Soviets found us here, they would dog our tracks closely with any available naval forces. We would lose our target for sure."

"Captain to the conn," the 1-MC overhead called out.

"That, gentlemen and lady, is probably our escort," Captain North stated as he got to his feet. "I left word in the conn to notify me if anything appropriate came up on sonar. If you will excuse me . . ."

What sonar had spotted was indeed a ship heading toward Finland. With a careful look through the periscope, Captain North confirmed they had a large icebreaker in sight, one that was flying the Finnish flag. A quick examination of their reference collection confirmed that the ship was the *Kontio*, a Karhu-2 class icebreaker controlled by the Finnish Board of Navigation. With a top speed of 18.5 knots, the *Kontio* posed no problems for the *Archerfish*. Tucking in fairly close to the heavy craft, the *Archerfish* steamed on toward Helsinki. In a little more than a day the *Archerfish* found herself off the coast of Finland.

Almost a full day ahead of schedule, the *Archerfish* sank into the deeps off Helsinki. The hundred meters of water within a few hours of the Finnish shore was a restful depth for the big submarine. Enough modifications had been done to the seawater inlets and vents along the hull of the *Archerfish* to allow her to bottom—actually rest her hull on the sea floor—and still run her critical machinery.

So the submarine waited on the bottom of the Gulf of Finland. Her antenna buoy was easily able to reach the surface, so Peter Danzig was able to stay in contact with his superiors back in Washington. The next morning, confirmation came over the radio link that the *Finnjet* had left Tallinn.

CHAPTER 9

Two KGB men accompanying Sarkisov's delegation were standing in the passageway outside the main cabin area for the Soviets about an hour after the ferry had left the Reisisadam Ferry Terminal in Tallinn. The ferry *Finnjet* used by the Silja Line for the Tallinn-Helsinki run was more than comfortable. The 210-meter-long ship had a capacity for 1,790 passengers, and had a bunk available for each one. For a cruise that normally took only four hours, this was an excessive level of luxury to the two KGB men. But the fact that each of the people they were assigned to watch had their own cabins did make the KGB men's work easier.

Not an active part of the Soviet delegation to the Helsinki Conference, the two KGB men were still kept constantly busy. Their job was to nursemaid the members of the delegation while outside of the Soviet

Union. The *nyanki*, or nursemaids, as they were called, made certain nothing happened to their charges, both from outside actions and especially from inside plots. If any one of the several *nyanki* with the delegation saw something they considered suspicious, they were authorized to act immediately. Any one of the delegation could suddenly find themselves on their way back to Mother Russia and a disciplinary action if they committed an action the *nyanki* considered wrong.

Some of the additional KGB personnel assigned to the delegation had much the same job. But these men were called "shepherds" and were much more of the strong-arm type. Their job was to make sure that no outsiders brought their decadent Western influences too close to the delegates.

All of these KGB men took their jobs very seriously. If any of the delegation members defected, the KGB man responsible for the individual could find himself on a fast trip home. On their return, the *nyanki* or shepherds who had failed in their mission would receive a long stay at a prison or gulag at best, a firing squad at worst.

Aboard the *Finnjet* was the last time the KGB guards would have the delegation in an isolated environment. Defecting from a ship at sea would be next to impossible. So even though they remained alert at all times, this was their last chance to relax, at least a little bit.

"Oleg," the smaller, more innocuous KGB *nyanki* said, "did you notice how fast Minister Sarkisov headed for his first-class cabin?"

"They call them 'commodore class' aboard this floating hotel," Oleg, the big KGB shepherd answered with a disapproving frown. "And yes, I did notice. He must have had a good stock of vodka already on ice in it before he arrived."

"Ha," Arkadi exclaimed quietly. "It's not like he needed it. He certainly put enough away just this morning before sailing."

"I saw a bit of that drinking myself," Oleg said. "Not bad for an over-seventy-year-old Hero of the Soviet Union. But he was hardly the only one fortifying himself. Even that little academician—what's his name, Kondrachev?—was putting it away early. I thought he didn't drink much."

"These bookish types," Arkadi said knowingly, "you'll get used to them after a few more trips. Once they get away from their laboratories, they just don't know how to contain themselves. It's usually nothing. They drink and carouse a bit, and then pay the price in the morning."

"Well," Oleg considered, "I still think he may need a little closer attention. His dossier says he's single with few things back home to help keep him in line. That makes him a more likely target for the Western agencies. Besides, we wouldn't want him to blurt out the wrong thing to the wrong ears."

"Certainly not at all," Arkadi agreed as he looked to a list of names and cabins in his hand. "He's in number 213, tourist class. He must be a mid-level academician at least, to rate one of the smaller private cabins. I'll tell Vasili to keep a close check on him."

* * *

The *Archerfish* stirred from where she rested on the bottom. The Westinghouse S5W reactor in her reactor compartment responded to commands for more power. As control rods withdrew from the reactor core, the nuclear reaction taking place inside increased in temperature. The increase in temperature boiled more water in the steam generator, and her steam turbines spun faster, pouring 15,000 shaft horsepower into the single propeller shaft. As the huge multibladed screw began turning, the *Archerfish* moved forward.

"Make turns for five knots," Lieutenant Commander Beam ordered.

"Making turns for five knots aye," the diving officer repeated as he adjusted the speed control in front of him.

"Helm, set course three-five-zero," Beam ordered.

"Course three-five-zero aye," Seaman Hackett responded from his position in front of the controls.

Captain North walked into the control room with a cup of coffee in his hand.

"Captain in the conn," Lieutenant Commander Beam said loudly.

"Carry on, XO," Captain North said calmly. "Take her in."

The big submarine moved forward, gradually picking up speed.

"Take her to periscope depth," Beam ordered.

"Periscope depth aye," the diving officer repeated. "Planesman, up bubble."

"Up bubble aye," George Kahuna Weaver, the big Hawaiian sitting at the planes control, reported. As he drew the wheel back toward himself, the nose of the submarine lifted and she headed toward the surface to level off at sixty feet.

In the torpedo room, the SEALs were making their last minute arrangements. The DDS crew under Lieutenant Rogers were already up in the DDS, preparing it for operation. Matt Fisher and Mike Bryant were checking out their breathing rigs. Since the two SDV crewmen would not be leaving the craft during the dive, they decided to go with their normal Mark 15 breathing rigs—or lungs, as they were called—rather than using an open circuit scuba rig.

The Mark 15 underwater breathing apparatus was a closed-circuit system that used sophisticated electronics to maintain a proper percentage of oxygen in the breathing circuit. The large, heavy system fit inside a rigid backpack with various controls and indicators that attached to the operator's wrist on a small console.

The efficiency of the Mark 15 system would allow the SDV operators to spend an extended length of time underwater without ill effects. And, if the SDV had to remain on-station during some kind of delay or emergency, Bryant and Fisher would be able to leave the tanks of boat air for the SEALs, and maybe their passenger, in the rear compartment.

The rest of the SEALs would be wearing normal air scuba rigs, with twin aluminum cylinders, each holding eighty cubic feet of air under 3,000 psi pressure. The double-stage regulators each SEAL was using allowed them to breathe the tank air, adjusted to the ambient pressure of the water surrounding them. In addition, a complete second mouthpiece and second-stage regulator was attached as an octopus to their rigs. The second regulator would be used by the target when they picked him up. Or took him down, depending on how you looked at it.

The main problem all of the SEALs were facing was the exposure to the cold water. For protection, they were each wearing an acrylic pile undersuit that covered each man from his feet to his wrists and neck. Over the pile suit went a special thin-composition dry suit. The dry suit would keep the water from reaching the operator's skin and draining the heat away from him quickly. The acrylic pile undersuit maintained a layer of air between the operator and the dry suit, air that insulated him from the frigid cold of the water.

A tight rubber collar and cuffs sealed off the neck and hands of the SEALs. For additional protection, hoods were pulled over their heads and thick, foam neoprene three-fingered mittens went on their hands. Over all of this went a Mark 4 life preserver and an extra-heavy lead weight belt.

There was a minimum amount of special equipment going with the men. Each SEAL had an MX-300 transceiver in a waterproof bag. The submarine was going to maintain a radio watch with its antenna just at the surface. Only Chief Monday was assigned to be in contact with the submarine, but the additional radios would act as a backup.

Chief Monday also had his AN/PQS-1B handheld sonar rig with him. But Lieutenant Rockham watched Limbaugh stuff some odd-looking plastic bags into a satchel and had no idea what the corpsman was doing.

"Just what are those things, Limbaugh?" Rockham asked.

"Kind of an emergency insurance, Skipper," Limbaugh said as he handed one to Rockham.

It was a thick, clear plastic bag, about a foot long and half that wide, over an inch thick, and full of some kind of smoky gel. Just visible at the center of the gel was a metal disk or clip of some kind. "And this is a what, Limbaugh?" Rockham asked.

"Well, sir, they call them a baby bun warmer in the hospital where I picked them up."

As Rockham stared at his corpsman, Limbaugh quickly explained. "They're an emergency medical heating unit, sir. They use them in the neonatal care unit to help keep babies warm. You snap that metal disk in the center of the bag and it starts a chemical reaction. The bag warms up to about fifty degrees centigrade. Not enough to burn, but plenty warm. It would be kind of a last ditch measure, sir. But if we're looking at losing the target, I figured it wouldn't do any harm to give them a try."

"How?" Rockham asked.

"Unzip the guy's suit and slip a couple of them up against his chest," Limbaugh explained. "It should at least help a little to keep his core temperature up. I'd consider packing some up against his head as well. The trouble is, exposing him to the cold like that could shock the hell out of him, maybe even stop his heart. Also, these things don't get that hot, but he'll feel like we're pressed branding irons against him. So I'm only planning to use them if I have to."

"Great thinking, Limbaugh," Rockham said, impressed. "Baby bun warmers, no shit." The SEAL officer just shook his head.

Then it was time to make the long climb to the DDS. With the assistance of their Teammates, the heavily laden SEALs went up the ladders to the central passageway on the top deck, just outside the captain's stateroom. There, the men found Captain North waiting for them.

"Good luck, SEALs," North said. "We'll be waiting for your return."

With that, there was really nothing else to say. Each of the men climbed up the ladder that led up through the weapon's loading hatch and into the access sphere of the DDS. Lieutenant Rockham was the last man to go up the ladder. As he peered back down into the submarine, he received a final thumbs-up from his Teammates on the deck below. Then the hatch to the DDS was closed and sealed.

Considerably more complicated than backing the family car out of a garage, the launching of an SDV from a DDS attached to a submarine that's under way was a dangerous, complicated ballet. Instead of simply moving front, back, and sideways, the launching also had the added dimension of up and down and the pressure of the water flowing by. And the first step of the whole procedure was the flooding of the hangar.

Passing up their breathing rigs and then climbing onto the central access sphere of the DDS had only been the first step. Now the SEALs had to work in the cramped enclosure of the hangar bay. The curved walls of the tanklike hangar kept any of the men from walking upright. Only Ed Waterstone of the DDS crew was short enough to move almost easily through the hangar. The big SDV sitting on its cradle took up most of the interior space. With difficulty, the men first put their breathing rigs inside the eight-boat, and then climbed in themselves.

The *Archerfish* had slowed considerably for the launching procedure. Barely making headway, the huge craft slipped slowly through the water, stabilized by her fairwater planes. Lieutenant Rogers and his DDS crew maintained constant contact with the conn of the submarine through the intercom in the DDS. When all of the final preparations had been made, Lieutenant Rogers announced that they were flooding the hangar.

Flooding the hangar chamber of the DDS changed the buoyancy of the *Archerfish* by several tons. So the announcement to the conn was a lot more than a courtesy, as the submarine had her trim changed noticeably. But the men in the DDS, and especially the SDV, did not notice the submarine adjusting herself below their feet. Instead, they were concentrating completely on the cold waters of the Gulf of Finland now swirling about their feet.

As the cold water rose, the men felt it clamp down on their legs. The initial cold quickly penetrated their protective clothing underneath their dry suits. The DDS crew would be able to move about and help warm themselves up that way. This was not the case for the SEALs in the SDV.

Inside the black fiberglass hull of the eight-boat, the SEALs had to sit and accept the water rising about them. Bryant and Lieutenant Fisher on the front compartment were sitting side by side and going through the preoperation checklist for the boat. The full face masks they wore made it easy for them to communicate with each other over the eight-boat's intercom system.

In the rear compartment of the eight-boat, Rockham and Limbaugh were sitting facing the stern, their backs up against the front bulkhead. Between the two SEALs there was a canvas carryall hanging strapped to the tubular framework of the SDV. The carryall had a number of pockets and pouches for holding equipment, and Limbaugh placed his warming pouches in one of the largest.

On the aft side of the compartment, his back to the big metal sphere that contained the SDV's twenty-four-volt DC electric motor, sat Chief Monday. His AN/PQS-1B sonar rig held in his lap, the chief had plugged into the intercom system that allowed the crew and passengers of the SDV to communicate with one another.

The communications intercom centered around a bone-conduction earphone that the SEALs could slip under their hood, and a special microphone. The microphones were Type M-3 models and were part of the regulators attached to the SDVs life support system. The mouthpiece of the regulators had been replaced with N-3E oral cavity models, which allowed the wearer to speak normally with little distortion.

Use of this system allowed the passengers to communicate with each other and the crew. A special underwater telephone system, the DV-811W UQC, also allowed the crew in the cockpit to communicate with the same microphones and earphones, with either the DDS crew or the submarine itself. Depending on conditions, the SDV could communicate with the *Archerfish* from almost a full kilometer away.

To allow for him to get out of the SDV and remain in communication with the boat, Chief Monday had his regulator set up with the same equipment as the one in the SDV. With a long coil of cable at hand, the chief could move away from the SDV and still call in securely along the wire. But at that moment none of the SEALs wanted to talk to anyone.

The temperature of the water rising about them was painfully cold, especially around the face, crotch, and hands. The cold was so intense it felt almost as if the skin was burning. But the only thing the SEALs could do was a limited range of isometric exercises to try and help warm them. As they worked their muscles, stressing each against the other, the DDS crew continued the launching procedure. The cold was simply something the SEALs had to endure.

When the hangar was fully flooded, the large door across the rear began to open. The nine-foot-wide round door completely closed off the rear end of the hangar compartment from the sea. As it slowly opened, the blue-green glow of the water beyond started to show. When the door was fully open and locked into place, the men of the DDS crew went behind the SDV and started to draw out the track framework the cradle would move on. This framework extended out of the DDS more than the length of the SDV. At the far end was a small winch with a cable running up to the SDV cradle.

Now, with everything set, Chief Sam Casey of the DDS crew went back and started winding the winch back. With the submarine dead still in the water, the bubbles from the SEALs breathing rigs rose almost straight up to the surface. As the cable tightened, the SDV finally began to back out of the DDS.

To help move the SDV along, John Grant, an American Indian, and probably the strongest member of the DDS crew, began pushing back on the cradle assembly. As the SDV emerged from the open end of the DDS, Grant finally had to stop pushing, since he could no longer brace himself against the deck. Grant and Waterstone went to the sides of the SDV near the bow and attached the bow planes. Now the SDV had control surfaces at the bow and stern of the craft. ·

All through the launching procedure, Lieutenant Rogers was in constant contact with the crew aboard the eight-boat. As Bryant and Fisher made ready to get under way, their three passengers in the rear compartment could overhear every comment and report. Rogers gave Fisher, the navigator of the eight-boat, the final navigational information he received from the quartermaster in the control room of the *Archerfish*. With the starting position locked into the inertial navigation system of the eight-boat, their trip was ready to begin.

The sliding covers over the two compartments were closed and sealed, and the DDS crew released the tie-downs that secured the SDV to the DDS cradle. As Bryant blew a small amount of air into the eight-boat's buoyancy tank, the craft started to rise above its cradle, away from the deck of the *Archerfish*. Now even Chief Monday was certain that the operation was under way.

The SDV sailed on through the dark water at a depth of only twenty feet. The computerized Doppler navigation system displayed information on the screens in front of Lieutenant Fisher, keeping him updated on their location. The *Archerfish* had released them only a few kilometers from their target, the ship channel navigation buoy. At a modest four knots, to conserve battery power, the SDV was going to take over a quarter of an hour to cover the two kilometers.

To conserve the air in their breathing rigs, Monday, Rockham, and Limbaugh had switched from their regulators to ones attached to the eight-boat's life support system. There were hundreds of cubic feet of compressed air in the air tanks of the eight-boat, more than enough to keep the three men breathing for hours. They also had the twin eighty-cubic-foot air tanks on their backs as additional breathing gas. But for now the four air manifolds on either corner of the rear compartment, each with its own double-stage regulator attached, were convenient.

The long minutes passed as the SDV silently glided through the water. Bryant kept careful note of the time, according to the elapsed time clock to the lower left of his control panel. Next to the clock was the magnetic compass he had set as they left the *Archerfish* and moved out on course. Even though Fisher would be the navigator, Bryant would be able to keep the SDV on course and follow the reverse course back to where they had left the submarine.

The bulk of the instrumentation for the eight-boat was contained in heavy waterproof metal cylinders in the bow of the craft. Three thick Plexiglas covers were over the ends of the cylinders where they came through the instrument panel. It was through these covers, and the switches and knobs protruding from them, that the pilot and navigator controlled and guided the SDV. The men sat flat on a metal deck, just as their passengers did in the rear compartment. A joysticklike control came up between Bryant's legs to allow him to adjust the bow and stern planes of the SDV. Pedals down under his feet adjusted the rudder at the stern.

As Bryant drove the SDV, Fisher maintained a close watch on the obstacle avoidance sonar. When the sonar signaled something ahead of the SDV, Fisher quickly checked his other instruments and his notes, written on waterproof paper. They should be approaching the navigation buoy, and the sonar agreed. Through the fiberglass hull of the SDV the men could now hear a muffled ringing sound as a bell tolled.

Telling the men in the rear compartment just what was going on, Fisher had Bryant slow the SDV as it approached the buoy. The big floating steel structure was attached to the sea floor by a heavy chain and concrete block.

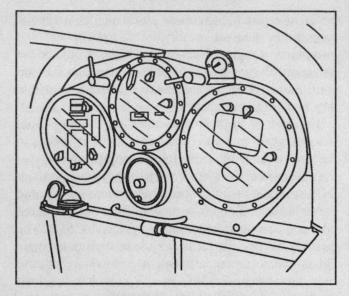

Eight-Boat Control Panel

The long black shape of the eight-boat slipped silently up to the heavy mooring chain of the buoy. Even if they hadn't had the sonar equipment, locating the buoy wouldn't have been a problem. The ringing sound they had heard, the bell of the navigation buoy, carried for long distances underwater, even farther than it could have been heard in the air.

The round buoy marked the side of the navigation channel approaching the Helsinki harbor. Here, the *Finnjet* would have to slow down and align itself to the main channel for the last leg of her journey. And now the SEALs had to determine just which side of the channel they were on.

Bryant and Fisher slid back the covers of their compartment as they approached the buoy. Bryant blew out a little more ballast and pulled the stick back to send the SDV toward the surface. The speed of the craft slowed as power to the motor was reduced. At a very slow crawl, the SDV came up the last few feet to the buoy.

Chief Monday slid back the starboard cover of the rear compartment. A long coil of communication wire was in the pocket of the hold-all at the front of the compartment. As he switched regulators to go from boat air to his own tanks, Monday could see Rockham doing the same thing. Rockham stood up in the compartment and reached for the heavy mooring chain, a length of light rope in his hand. As the SDV slowly came up to the chain, Rockham securely tied the line to the chain and the pad eye on the rear side of the compartment. Now the SDV could hang on the line and not drift as Chief Monday headed for the surface.

The SDV was secured at a depth of about fifteen feet, just a few feet below the bottom of the buoy. A quick slash of a SEAL's knife and the SDV would immediately be freed. The water had a particularly murky green tint to it as Monday carefully went up to the surface. The light was enough for him to see the sides of the buoy, and the shells and marine concretions, the barnacles, whelks, and limpets that grew on its sides. He was careful not to brush against the growths; the shells could have razor-sharp edges.

Just below the surface, Monday paused and placed his hands against the buoy. Holding his breath, he listened.

Aside from the deafening ring of the bell, he could hear no engine sounds. Slowly and carefully he let his head just break the surface of the water. As he looked about, a sudden loud bark erupted not two feet above his head.

It startled him. Had he been able to, Chief Monday would have jumped several feet in the air. Looking up, he saw the face of a Greenland seal that had been sunning itself on top of the buoy. As he cursed at his unit's namesake, the seal uttered another loud bark and jumped from the buoy. The sleek black form of the marine mammal flashed past the SDV, also getting a rise from the men still aboard her. Then, with a easy flip of its fins, the seal rolled over and sped away.

"You guys get that?" Monday said through his throat mike.

"Roger that, Chief," Fisher said back. "You check if he had a girlfriend?"

"Funny sailor," Monday continued. "We're at the right buoy. This is the red one. I can just see the green one about half a klick away."

The old sailor's memory note, red-right-returning, told the chief that the red buoy they were moored to would be on the right, starboard, side of the *Finnjet* as it passed between the buoys. As he floated there in the water, Monday wondered if there were any more Greenland seals about. It wasn't that he was afraid of the creatures, though they had a nasty bite. But their alarm at his presence could warn someone else watching that something was amiss.

But no more sleek heads peeped over the edge of the buoy. Chief Monday had the watch, as the SDV had intentionally arrived ahead of schedule to ensure they wouldn't miss the *Finnjet*. He took hold of a small flange sticking out from the side of the buoy and just ignored the cold on his face. Ice formed on his face mask and he pushed it up on his forehead. There wasn't anything else to do but wait. If their target failed to make his jump from the ship, they would have to return to the *Archerfish* and wait another week. Then a second attempt could be made as the ferry left Helsinki.

CHAPTER 10

Alek Kondrachev had no way of knowing all of the mechanisms he had set into motion once he had decided to defect to the West. The fact that a number of SEALs were waiting in the freezing water would have concerned him. The idea that an entire nuclear submarine had been sent to get him would have absolutely astonished him.

Instead of thinking about all of the things that might be happening, he sat in his stateroom and contemplated his last hours as a Soviet. The country of his birth was changing, and he would not be there to see it. In fact, if anything went wrong in the next hour or so, he wouldn't be around to see much of anything.

He looked about his stateroom in a distracted manner. The world had taken on an unreal aspect. No matter what happened, he knew his life was going to change drastically. He had made his plans, and the contact that had reached him through Joseph's brother seemed to take his plan seriously. Now there was no more time to question things. Now it was time to act.

He had spent the morning trying to appear anything but the nervous wreck he was inside. At Minister Sarkisov's party that morning, he had tried to appear jovial and even a heavy drinker. If he did show any unusual signs, perhaps the KGB *nyanki* would simply attribute it to his being drunk. At least no one had taken a sip from his glass and noticed it was nothing but mineral water.

His preparations for his escape, which is how he saw his defection, were completed. Underneath his clothes, he was wearing his 3mm-thick neoprene wet suit. It would be at least some protection in the icy waters of the Baltic. He also had a length of nylon line coiled up beneath his coat. The plan he had considered was to slip a loop of the rope over a deck fitting, then lower himself into the water. Once in, he only had to let go one end of the rope and it would slip back around the fitting and into the water. Then he could yell for help and draw the attention of someone on deck.

His contact had told him that divers would take him under the water. It was a frightening thought, but he had been skin and scuba diving enough to believe he could handle the situation.

But the constant appearance of one of the KGB *nyanki* had given him second thoughts about his original plan. He had to get out onto the deck and reach the stern. Maybe he could still do it. But as he left his cabin, he could see the *nyanki* watching from the end of the corridor. As he turned and walked to the rear of the ship, the unsteadiness in his legs wasn't completely due to his still pretending to be drunk.

Vasily watched one of his charges walk away down the passage. It was the academician, Kondrachev. The exaggerated way the man tried to walk straight made him look all the more drunk. There wasn't any place he could really go on the ferry, but it wouldn't do for the damned fool to fall down a flight of stairs and break his neck. Then he would be filling out the paperwork for a month.

Alek walked to the rear of the big ship. It was sunny outside, so a number of people were out on deck. But most were still inside their cabins or in the protected parts of the ship. It was the upper deck that was the most crowded; at least part of the stern seemed to be open to the air.

As he walked to the rear of the ship, it seemed to Alek that someone else was stepping in his shoes. It wasn't him walking, it wasn't his eyes looking over the rail. He could see the big red buoy just coming up to the rear of the ship. The bell from the buoy rang out with an odd, muffled sound to his ears. The whole thing seemed unreal and foggy, as if viewed through rippled glass. Then things came into focus in a hurry as the KGB man who had been watching him came out onto the stern of the ship.

Vasily came out onto the open rear deck with some dislike. It was nice and warm inside the ship. Why did

the academician have to come out here into the open?
Then he saw the reason. The academician was leaning
over the rail near the corner of the deck. The poor fool
had probably drunk too much, and the little movement
of the ship had been more than enough to make him
sick. He was vomiting over the rail.

The academician turned away from the rail and saw
him standing there, exactly as the KGB man intended.
The expression of shock on his face told Vasily that he
might not be done leaning over the rail yet. The slim
man turned and bolted to the left rail again. Slammed
into it and flipped over the side!

The astonished KGB man simply stood there for a
moment. Then he bounded to the rail, shouting, "Man
Overboard!"

He got to the rail in time to see Kondrachev roll over
in the water, rear back and wave his arms weakly. The
man wasn't dead from the impact, but the cold water
and his soaked clothes would drag him down in moments. Snatching at one of the red life rings hanging
from the rail at regular intervals, Vasily heaved it over
the side. As he did, he heard the sound of voices and
running feet coming up behind him. And the shrill
hoots of an alarm were sounding from somewhere on
the top deck.

The over seven-meter fall to the water took Alek by
surprise. But not as much as he'd been surprised when
he turned and saw the KGB man. It might be a moot
point if he'd intended to go over the side or had actually fallen. But the shock of hitting the hard, cold water
stunned him.

For a moment all he could see was green water. Flailing about, he finally managed to break the surface. He was far enough back from the stern of the ship that he didn't feel he had to worry about the screw pulling him in. As he twisted about, he saw the stern of the ship pulling away from him and people starting to line the rear deck. He raised his arms and tried to wave, but the weight of his arms sticking up drove his head underwater. As he thrashed his way to the surface again, a separate, analytical part of his mind observed his situation.

Wouldn't it be funny, he thought, if he really did drown rather than defect?

Chief Monday saw the ship coming up to the channel. If he wondered for a moment if it was the right ship, that question was answered as soon as he saw the side of the hull. The white paint job was looking smart, with a bright blue line of trim the length of the hull. And right in the middle of the hull were the words FINNJET SILJA LINE in huge blue letters.

"In sight, in sight, in sight," Monday repeated for his Teammates down in the SDV. They could no doubt hear the big ship, if the bell on the big lighted buoy hadn't deafened everyone yet. He pulled up his waterproof binoculars and peeled off the plastic bag he had put them in for additional waterproofing. It paid to give attention to the little details.

As he watched the big ship, it came alongside the buoy and passed it, not three hundred meters away, and continued on its way. Where the hell was this guy? Monday wondered. Had they been brought out here for some kind of sucker play? If Danzig had been fucking with his men for some goddamned reason of his own, he would—

Then Monday saw a body go over the starboard side of the ship and impact in the water. The body was tumbling and not in control when it hit the water. Monday took a moment to make a sighting along his compass on whoever had fallen off the ship. As he did so, he saw the arms rise up and wave. It would take several miles for the big ship to slow and turn, and by the time it got back to them, the mission would be over.

Dropping his binoculars, Monday let them dangle by the strap he had put around his neck. Pulling the Motorola MX-300 radio up, he ripped the plastic bag off it and keyed the transmit switch.

"Fish! Fish! Fish!" he said three times distinctly.

It was the signal to the submarine, which should have been listening. It also told his Teammates at the other end of his communications cord that the target was in sight. As Monday reached up to pull his face mask down, fate decided he had pushed his luck hard enough over the years.

Monday hadn't noticed the wake of the big ship as it passed. He was so busy doing everything that he was supposed to, he just hadn't paid attention to it. The bow wave wasn't big, as such things go, but then a single man in the water isn't very big to even a mild exercise of the ocean's power.

With his hand no longer holding onto the side of the buoy, Monday was picked up by the wave and slammed against the side of the steel structure. The flange that he had held to keep himself steady now smashed into his side. As he felt the snapping of his ribs, Monday slid along the side of the buoy. The shells and rust he had noticed before tore at his suit, slicing through the gray material along his right side and back.

Everything that had happened on the surface took only a few seconds. The men below never knew the wave had driven Monday up against the buoy. Instead, they had gotten ready to pull away from their mooring and proceed with the mission. Rockham stood and cut the line securing them with a quick slash of his knife. Then he saw Chief Monday coming down from the surface. The chief was swimming stiffly, but Rockham resumed he might have iced over a bit while he was up on the surface.

When Rockham reached out to the chief, he was waved away. Monday climbed back into the rear compartment and called out a compass bearing to Bryant. Full power was fed into the electric motor and the SDV surged ahead.

Now Chief Monday was holding up his AN/PQS-1B sonar dish and aiming it up and forward. It was only a minute before he picked up something on the extreme range of the sonar. As they approached the target, the chief had Bryant slow the SDV so they wouldn't pass under the man in the water. The chief clicked the range switch over to sixty yards. Then he clicked it again to twenty yards. Now Rockham could actually see the silhouette of someone on the surface. The man was kicking, but it was obvious he was struggling with his waterlogged clothes.

They were only thirty feet away from the man when Rockham and Limbaugh left the rear compartment of the SDV. They swam up to the surface slowly, each man pulling up his octopus regulator. As they approached from underneath, each SEAL hit the purge button on his octopus regulator. Air begin surging from the regulator, bubbling up to the surface.

In spite of the fact that the *Finnjet* was almost a kilometer away now, the SEALs realized there was always the chance someone would have some binoculars or a camera on the man in the water. So they both were careful not to break the surface. As Rockham reached around behind Alek to get a secure hold on him, Limbaugh went around to his front and held up the regulator.

On the surface, Alek was tiring fast. The buoyancy of his wet suit was not enough to make up for the drag of his clothes. He gave a sudden start as the water started bubbling violently in front of him. Then he could see a dark shape. Sudden fear flushed through the scientist. He knew it was unreasoned fear, but it was very real in spite of that. He swallowed his fear, and a bit of seawater, and ducked his head under the surface.

Limbaugh saw the man duck down, and he shoved the regulator out toward him. He was relieved to see the man put it in his mouth and blow out any remaining water before taking a breath. The man's eyes grew wide as Rockham held him around the waist. He struggled for an instant and then relaxed. Now Limbaugh could strip off the extra mask he had around his arm and slip it over the man's head.

Rockham saw Limbaugh give the man his octopus rig and was glad to see that the guy at least knew how to take a breath without choking. At Limbaugh's nod, Rockham got a good grip around the man's waist. Now that he had the big silver mouthpiece of the octopus rig in his mouth, it wouldn't do to let the guy surface. As Rockham began to bleed air from his Mark 4 life jacket, he saw Limbaugh hand the Russian his extra mask.

Alek tasted the fresh, cold air as it rushed into his lungs. Even the roar of the bubbles exhaling past his ear had a good sound to it. He felt someone grab him around the waist and assumed the diver in front of him must have a partner behind him. Through the distortion of the water, he saw the diver in front of him holding out a face mask. Alek let the man put the mask over his head, then he reached up and settled it properly into place.

Pressing on the top of the mask, Alek blew air out his nose. The air bubbled to the top of the mask and displaced the water out of the bottom. When all of the water had been cleared from his mask, he settled it back down over his face. Now he could breathe and see.

By now they had sunk several meters below the surface. Alek's ears began to hurt, and he pushed the bottom of the mask up against his nose and blew through his nose. He felt his ears pop and the pain go away as the pressure on his eardrums equalized against the water. He saw the diver in front of him give him a thumbs-up sign. Alek repeated the gesture back.

Limbaugh watched the Russian clear his mask easily and then equalize the pressure in his ears. It looked like they just might be able to pull this one off, if the guy was as competent in the water as he appeared at first glance. But the big danger was still from the cold. They had to get back to the *Archerfish* quickly.

Limbaugh signaled Rockham, and the two SEALs got on either side of their charge and pulled him down to the SDV. The small craft had been moving slowly underneath the SEALs as they recovered the target. Bryant and Fisher had both slid the covers back from the cockpit and were looking up as the two SEALs brought the Russian down. There was a moment's rocking and movement of the SDV as the SEALs first put the Russian aboard and returned to the rear compartment themselves. Monday called out "All secure" over the intercom, and the SDV turned back the way it had come.

Fisher guided the SDV back along the course his instruments told him. Bryant followed the lieutenant's directions, and kept an eye on the compass on the instrument panel to his left. He had set the indicator line—what was called the "lubber line"—on his compass to the heading they had followed out to the buoy. The fact that they had hit the buoy on their first pass was great. Now they had to do the much more important action of hitting the sub as quickly as possible.

In the rear compartment, Chief Monday was sitting and trying to ignore the pain in his side. What helped cut back on the pain was the numbing sensation of water seeping into his dry suit. A dry suit wasn't much more than a rubber bag when it sprang a leak, with about as much insulating properties as a thin bag. But there wasn't anything the SEALs could do for him. Besides, the target they had picked up looked to need help a lot more than Monday did.

Fifteen minutes had passed since the SEALs had gotten the Russian into the SDV. If there were very many more minutes in front of them, all they would get back to the sub with was a very cold corpse. Limbaugh could feel the Russian start to shake as the hard shivering hit him. The SEAL reached around the Russian and started to rub him violently to try and build up even a minute portion of heat.

Rockham saw what his corpsman was doing and immediately leaned forward and rubbed the Russian's legs. Limbaugh had put his arms around the Russian and was pulling him close, anything to try and get some heat into the man. Rockham scooted across the compartment and did the same thing from the other side. Chief Monday was rubbing the Russian's legs now, neither of the other two SEALs noticing in the dark compartment how the chief's motions were becoming more and more irregular.

Limbaugh finally made his decision when he felt the Russian's shivering start to subside. It wasn't that the man was warming up; instead, his body was starting to shut down from hypothermia. Reaching into the carryall on the bulkhead, Limbaugh pulled out several of his baby bun warmers. Snapping the metal disk caused the reaction to start inside the bags. Limbaugh couldn't feel the heat of the reaction through his thick gloves, but he knew it was there. Reaching over in front of the Russian, he tore open his shirt front and quickly unzipped his wet suit.

The shock of the colder water hitting his bare chest caused Alek to gasp. He no longer knew exactly where he was or what he was doing. But whatever it was, he knew he didn't like it. Then the shovel full of red hot coals landed on his chest and he screamed.

Both Limbaugh and Rockham heard the thin scream come out of the Russian as the heating pads went under his wet suit. Limbaugh quickly zipped up the suit to conserve the heat. Then he went back to holding the Russian as closely as he could, to also insulate the man from the cold with his own body.

In the cockpit of the SDV, Fisher started picking up the sonar signature of the submarine on his obstacle avoidance system. He called out over the DV-811W UQC underwater telephone. Within moments he heard the voice of Lieutenant Rogers come back over the same system. Moments after that, the Burnett 512 pinger on the outside of the DDS started sending out a low-power signal for the SDV to home in on. The range and azimuth indicator in the instrument package told the SEAL officer that the SDV was within six minutes of reaching the submarine.

When he called back to the rear compartment, neither of the SEALs in the stern responded to his call. Fisher finally banged on the bulkhead to get the SEALs attention.

Limbaugh dropped his regulator mouthpiece and slipped the boat air one over his face. The N-3E oral-cavity mouthpiece of the boat regulator had a Type M-3 microphone in it, which let the SEAL talk into the intercom system. Limbaugh slipped the bone-conduction earphone under his tight-fitting hood.

As soon as he was in contact with the cockpit, Fisher told Limbaugh that they would be docking with the submarine within ten minutes. They were already past the thirty minute time limit they had figured the Russian could survive in his inadequate exposure suit. Besides just reaching the submarine, they also had to dock and recover the SDV. Once in its launching cradle, the entire launch procedure would have to be run in reverse. By the time it was done, the Russian would be long dead.

"Tell the sub to prepare the forward escape trunk," Limbaugh said.

Without asking any questions, Fisher relayed the message as Bryant began his approach run to the *Archerfish*.

On board the submarine, Captain North had the message relayed to him from sonar. Reaching up to the 1-MC, he made a shipwide announcement.

"Make ready to recover divers. Corpsmen to the forward escape trunk."

Jack Tinsley put down the hand of cards he had been holding and bolted from the torpedo room, pausing only long enough to grab up his medical pouch. Elsewhere in the submarine, Ron Edgars, the ship's corpsman chief, also moved forward, to below the escape trunk.

The escape trunk of the submarine was intended to allow men to enter or leave the sub while underwater. The trunk was in the shape of a large steel sphere with a hatch on the bottom and another on the side. A ladder led from under the lower hatch to the deck in the forward crew's living space, just off the chief petty officer's quarters.

The sphere could be flooded with water and a hatch opened in her side. Being below the top of the sphere, the side hatch allowed a bubble of air to be trapped above the hatch. This permitted people to enter the sphere with the side hatch open. Then they could speak to the submarine with their heads in the bubble of air. Once the outside hatch was secured, air could be let into the escape trunk, forcing the water out. Then it would be a simple matter of opening the lower hatch and entering the submarine.

The escape trunk was small, cramped, and difficult to work in. But it could be entered and blown clear in under a minute if the situation warranted. And right now the situation was very dire.

As the SDV approached the submarine, Bryant came in over the stern to come up on the DDS cradle. The DDS crew had already extended the rack and pushed out the cradle. Now they had deployed a line tethered to a float. By grabbing the front of the SDV, one of the DDS crew could hook a short line from the SDV to the tethered line. Then, with the SDV at a dead stop, it would be a simple matter to flood its buoyancy tank and slowly settle the craft on its cradle. But for this recovery, the SEALs in the rear compartment had no time to waste.

As soon as the SDV slowed over the deck of the submarine, Rockham and Limbaugh slid back the cover over the rear compartment. Chief Monday fumbled at trying to help the two SEALs with the Russian, who was almost comatose. But again, neither SEAL noticed that the chief had trouble coordinating his movements. As Limbaugh left the compartment with the Russian, Rockham reached back to assist Chief Monday on getting out of the SDV. All of the SEALs were cold and stiff, so Rockham didn't think anything of Monday's slow movement.

When Rockham looked Monday in the eye through his face mask, he gave him the circled thumb and forefinger question for "Are you okay?"

Monday responded with a thumbs-up, which was not quite the right signal. It should have been a return of the same signal Rockham had given. So Rockham pushed the chief up ahead of him as both swimmers headed for the forward escape trunk.

The DDS crewmen watched the SEALs leave the SDV and start swimming forward. The four men didn't seem to be in distress, and the crew continued with the recovery of the SDV.

With one arm around the Russian, Limbaugh kicked with his fins and pulled himself along the outside hull of the *Archerfish*. A grooved track in the deck, normally used a safety line anchor for anyone outside the sub while it was on the surface, ran up and past the forward trunk hatch. Limbaugh grabbed this track with his free hand and pulled both of them in toward the hatch.

Rockham came up close behind Limbaugh and the Russian, making sure that Chief Monday stayed ahead of him. Reaching the escape trunk, Rockham moved forward and signaled the sub by knocking on the trunk hatch. Then he turned the controls that began flooding the trunk.

If the submarine had not unlocked the controls, Rockham would not have been able to flood the trunk. As soon as the pressure inside the trunk equalized and the water had risen above the hatch, Rockham was able to spin the wheel and unlock the hatch.

Pushing the limp Russian ahead of him, Limbaugh went into the escape trunk. Rockham signaled Chief Monday to go into the trunk ahead of him, and the chief slowly did so. Normally, the steel sphere of the escape trunk was too small for more than three divers, especially with their breathing gear. So Rockham shed his air tanks, took a last deep breath, and slipped the straps around the underwater log—a speed sensor sticking up from the deck in front of the escape trunk hatch.

On his single breath of air, Rockham ducked down into the crowded escape trunk and pulled the hatch shut behind him. Once in the trunk, Rockham was able to lift his head up into the bubble of air and gasp in a deep lungful of freezing cold, moist air.

Getting to the controls, Rockham picked up the intercom and notified the submarine that there were men in the trunk. Then he operated the valves and released compressed air into the sphere. As the water lowered, he was able to reach over and help Limbaugh pull the mask off the Russian's face. The man was breathing, but it was short and labored breaths. His skin was white and pallid in the light of the single battle lantern inside the escape trunk.

When the water had left the trunk, Rockham bent over and spun the central locking wheel on the lower hatch. Force from below lifted the hatch as soon as he had it unlocked and a warm gush of air came up into the trunk, along with the concerned face of Tinsley.

It was only a few moments for the SEALs to lower the unconscious Russian to the deck of the submarine. Limbaugh almost slid down the ladder to be next to the man he had worked so hard to keep alive.

The CPO's washroom was only steps away for the men. They picked up the Russian and bodily carried him into the washroom and one of the shower stalls inside. With the water turned on to just warm, the corpsmen quickly stripped the Russian, ripping the thin wet suit off with their hands.

The corpsmen worked on the Russian in the stream of water until he finally twisted weakly in their hands and gasped. He was alive. Standing in the washroom door, Rockham looked over at Chief Monday as he watched what the men were doing.

"All right, Chief," Rockham said. "I was worried about you."

As Rockham slapped Chief Monday on his back, the dry suit the chief was wearing made a squelching sound. The chief made a grunting kind of gasp through clenched teeth. Then he collapsed. Now everyone could see the torn part of his suit that had been hidden under his arm. And the pink-stained water that was leaking out from the cuts in the material.

CHAPTER 11

1545 ZULU
55° 54' North, 15° 24' East
Chief Petty Officer's Living Space
USS *Archerfish*
South of Karlskrona
Baltic Sea

Chief Monday awoke to find himself looking up at a perforated, off-white acoustic ceiling not two feet over his head. About a foot away to one side was a wall of the same perforated material, while on the other side he saw a half-open set of heavy maroon curtains. Sitting on a padded chair just visible through the opened curtains was a very large man reading a book.

"Where in the hell am I?" Monday asked as he tried to sit up. He felt weak as a kitten and ached everywhere. The sudden stabbing pain in his side made him lay back down quickly, a small groan escaping him in the process.

"You're here in the goat locker aboard the *Archer-*

fish, Senior Chief," John Richards said as he got up from his chair. Putting his book down, the big man stepped over to the bunk space that held the SEAL chief.

"The goat locker?" Monday said weakly. "What am I doing in the chief's quarters? I should be down in the torpedo room with my men."

"When they brought you in here, you weren't exactly in a position to argue," Richards said quietly. "The corpsman wanted you dried off and bundled up in a bunk as quickly as possible. So they just brought you in here. They had you in the chief's shower for so long warming you up, I thought you were going to wrinkle up and go down the drain."

"Jesus," Monday said, settling back into the pillows. "I feel like shit, Master Chief."

"Funny you should say that," Richards said with a smile. "From what I understand, you weren't a whole hell of a long way away from meeting Jesus on a face-to-face basis. You were well beyond being drifty; working on dead, as a matter of fact."

"Damn I feel like a fool," Monday growled. "A chief's supposed to set an example to his men, and here I go hyping out like some young squid fresh out of boot. I cannot remember a damned thing of what happened on the op."

"Let's see," Richards said, as he leaned against the rack of bunks and began ticking off points on his fingers. "You busted two ribs and tore open a suit in water that was cold enough to kill an unprotected man in about fifteen minutes. Then you completed your mission, including locating a single man floating in a couple of square miles of water with a thirty-year-old sonar rig. Helped keep the guy alive while getting back to an underway submarine. And then locked in through the escape trunks."

"Oh," Richards continued, "and you did all of this while gutting out the cold along with injuries your corpsman said came pretty close to punching a hole in your lung. And they say there's a slash in your side that makes it look like you were the loser in a backwoods bar fight. Yeah, I can see how a man who did that might feel he hadn't set a good enough example for his men. You want a cup of coffee?"

"Thanks, Master Chief, I wouldn't mind one," Monday said sheepishly. "Man, I do feel like I've got the worst case of flu. A couple of aspirin wouldn't hurt either."

"That's the aftereffects of hypothermia," Richards said. "You'll be fine in a while. That little Russian feels about the same way. He's a tough boy himself. I'll see what I can do about the aspirin. Your corpsman and lieutenant wanted to know when you'd come around, so I guess I'd better go tell them."

"Wait a second, Master Chief," Monday said. "How is that Russian? And just how long have I been here?"

"The Russian?" Richards said as he leaned back against the bulkhead. "He's fine. Like I said, he's a tough one too. He's been talking his head off about something. I'm just the chief of the boat here, they don't necessarily tell me everything, you know."

Both Richards and Monday had a laugh over that. The day that a senior chief petty officer in the U.S. Navy couldn't find out what he wanted to know would be the day ships no longer floated.

"As far as how long you've been here," Richards continued, "you've been out of it a little over a day."

"Over a day!" Monday said. "I've got to get back to my platoon."

As Monday again tried to rise, the pain in his ribs hit him hard. He settled back down into his bunk before he started coughing and really tore something loose.

"I think maybe you'd better listen to what your body is telling you," Richards said simply. "I'll tell your officer and corpsman that you're up. Mostly."

"Thanks, Master Chief," Monday said with a tired smile.

"Think nothing of it, Senior Chief," Richards said easily. "And as long as you're hanging out in my chief's quarters, my name's John."

"I'm Frank, John," Monday said, holding out his hand.

"Hey, nice to meet you," Richards said as he shook his hand.

"Conn, this is Sonar. I have a contact Sierra seven-fiver, bearing zero-seven-zero. She's less than two thousand meters away sir."

"This is the conn," Lieutenant Commander Beam, the OOD of the watch, said into the 1-MC. "What have you got, Sonar?"

"It sounds like a Soviet Whiskey-class boat," Peters said. "She must have been right on the bottom to just appear like that. Right now she's running pretty much a parallel track to us, Conn."

"Roger that, Sonar, begin your track." As Beam reached across the panel of the 1-MC, he switched the control to reach just the captain's stateroom. Captain North had been up for almost thirty hours, and had finally gone to his stateroom to catch a few hours sleep. But he had left orders to be wakened if they made any Soviet contacts.

"Captain, this is the conn," Beam said.

Within a few seconds the speaker of the 1-MC sounded with Captain North's voice. "North here, Conn," the captain said as he forced sleep from his voice. "What have you got, Beam?"

"Sonar has a contact, Captain," Beam said. "Peters thinks it's a Soviet Whiskey class, sir, and it's very close by on a parallel track."

Within a very few minutes, Captain North had left his stateroom and was heading into the control room. Master Chief John Richards was standing by the passageway and handing the captain a full cup of coffee as he came through the hatch.

"Thanks, COB," North said as he moved to the front of the control room. Approaching his XO, he asked, "What have you got, Beam?"

"Things are pretty much as I told you, Captain. We have what Peters has now confirmed is a Soviet Whiskey-class submarine holding a parallel course to our own."

"Any aggressive moves?" Captain North asked as he took a sip of his coffee.

"None whatsoever, Captain," Beam said. "If she knows we're here, she doesn't show it."

"What do you think?" North asked.

Walking over to the plotting board, Beam looked down at the well-lit surface of the table, with a large chart of the southern section of the Baltic Sea spread out on it. The quartermaster had begun making notations showing the Soviet submarine running alongside the track of the *Archerfish* as soon as the data had come in from sonar. Pointing at the track, Beam followed along it with his finger.

"I think what we have here is one of the Soviet incursions into Swedish national waters," he said. "If you follow the extrapolated line of their course, it takes you very close to the Swedish navy base at Karlskrona. The Soviets have run more than one espionage trip into those waters over the last ten years."

"I agree," Captain North said as he examined the chart. "Pass the word, I want the ship on ultra quiet. Make us a hole in the water, XO."

Rather than going out on the 1-MC, the announcement would be passed down to maintain a very high level of silence throughout the ship. Even what little extraneous noise had been made before would be eliminated. Men would only speak when necessary, and even then in a whisper.

"We'll just sneak on by, Tom," North said in a low voice. "It could be they're on their own version of our mission. There have been a number of landings of Soviet naval Spetsnaz teams on Swedish territory. And I don't think they're going in at this time of the year to spot blondes on the beaches. Have Peters tag this one on his track record. Maybe we can give him a hard time by sending this out to the Swedes at some point."

"Just as long as they can't figure out who made it or where it came from," Beam said.

"Oh, I think that's going to be arranged," North said with a smile.

The two Navy officers stood in the control room watching the crew operate the ship. Not a mile away was a Soviet submarine that had no idea it had been detected. The two silent steel whales quietly moved through the water, each keeping to their own counsel.

"Skipper," Sukov said from the hatchway at the rear of the torpedo room. "I think you'd better come up to the wardroom."

"What's going on, John?" Rockham said as he walked over to the hatch. "I thought you were helping the doctor and Mr. Danzig?"

John Sukov spoke Russian fluently. Both he and Lieutenant Daugherty, who spoke Russian like a native, thanks to his maternal grandmother, had been assisting the two CIA people in debriefing their Russian guest. Both SEALs held Top Secret security clearances. Even though the Russian spoke English, the two SEALs had been of help during the debrief.

"There's some stuff going on that you'd better know

about, Skipper," Sukov said quietly. "Danzig is the one who sent me to get you. There may be another mission coming up, sir."

Puzzled, Rockham told Mike Ferber where he was going. Then the SEAL officer followed his man up the ladders to the officers' wardroom. There, he found a very serious-faced Peter Danzig and Sharon Taylor sitting on either side of the Russian defector. Sukov had told Rockham that the Russian's name was Alek, and that was about all.

"Lieutenant Rockham," Danzig said as Rockham came into the room, "this is Dr. Aleksandr Kondrachev."

The Russian was sitting at the far end of the wardroom table, the blue Navy coveralls he was wearing a bit baggy on his slight body. In front of the man was a steaming glass of tea. The Russian's face was drawn and there were dark circles under his eyes. But the eyes themselves were animated, and they lit up even brighter as he looked at Rockham.

"Lieutenant Rockham," Alek said in his accented English as he started to get up from the table.

"Woah, wait a second there, sport," Rockham said as he stepped forward.

The Russian was still pretty unsteady on his feet and had almost fallen over in getting up to greet the SEAL. Catching him, Rockham helped him back into his seat.

"Thank you, sir," Alek said as he sat back down. "Perhaps I'm still a little tireds from my swim."

Rockham smiled at the Russian's odd choice of word. Then he reached out and shook the man's hand.

"I can see how that little dip in the water might make you tired," Rockham said. "It got my chief down a little bit as well."

"Chief?" Alek said.

Daugherty rattled off a phrase in Russian that caused Alek to nod in understanding.

"Oh, yes," Alek continued. "I hope your chief is doing well? I understand you were the one who pulled me into the submarine."

"Myself and a number of others," Rockham said simply. "We're glad to get you out."

"As am I to be out," Alek said. "And I assure you, sir, it was very important that I tell you all what is happening. It was worth the risk to myself and your people."

Rockham didn't know what to say to that, so he sat down at the wardroom table. The top of the table was covered in charts and handwritten papers, and there were two tape recorders running.

"Just what is it that's so important that you have to say it to me?" Rock asked.

"It was a decision made by your intelligence operative here," Alek said, indicating Danzig. "It is very important that we get to the test site while there is still time."

"Uh, wait just a minute there," Rockham said. "This is just a little beyond me here. What test site? What do you mean, 'still time'?"

"Perhaps I should give you some background," Alek said.

"Oh, that would be nice," Rockham said, a bit sarcastically.

Just as Danzig began a sharp retort he saw Captain North come into the wardroom. North, seeing the people sitting around the table, figured the debriefing was still going on and turned to leave. "No, Captain, don't go," Danzig said. "Please join us. This is going to involve you and your ship soon enough."

Still tired, Captain North sat down at his customary spot at the head of the table. Frowning, he looked at Danzig and simply waited.

Alek Kondrachev began his story, with Sukov and Daugherty helping to translate when necessary.

"It was back during the Great Patriotic War, what you people in the West call World War Two, that the Soviet military first used biological weapons in combat. When the Germans were storming through our country in 1942, tularemia broke out among their ranks. In the late summer of 1942, the great Nazi war machine had ground to a halt on many fronts.

"The Nazi's weren't destroyed by the disease, far from it. But their troops suffered greatly from pain, a bad cough, and just general illness. That little germ, *Pasturella tularensis*, delayed the Nazi advance, and that delay gave the Greater Soviet time it so desperately needed to evacuate factories and set up war production in more protected areas. That disease may have changed the course of the war for us and maybe for the whole world.

"But it was a two-edged sword that cut through the German ranks that year. In the years before and after 1942, there are maybe ten thousand cases of tularemia in the whole of the Soviet Union. But late that summer in 1942, there were over a hundred thousand known cases among the Soviet people alone. We never did learn just how many cases of the disease swept through the Nazi ranks.

"In 1972, when your President Nixon put forward to the world his treaty to ban all biological weapons, the Soviet leadership knew he had to be hiding an even greater weapon than your atomic arsenal. So they increased their concentration on biological weapons research and production.

"Earlier, the Soviet Army had their Fifteenth Directorate be responsible for military biological weapons development. They had been in existence since 1945. But in 1973, a secret Kremlin decree created Biopreparat to develop biological weapons.

"Biopreparat worked hand in glove with the army's Fifteenth Directorate for years. Most of our original personnel came directly from the army's laboratories. We also ran vaccine development, biological antipest measures, and general biological and genetic research facilities throughout the Soviet Union. That way we could share information and even gather germ cultures from around the world without rising suspicions. Some of our weapons came directly from cultures we acquired openly from your Centers for Disease Control in Atlanta.

"But what we did at Biopreparat was develop weapons for the mass destruction of whole populations. Make no error, that was our mission. We even developed and tested long range warheads loaded with biological weapons to mount on our SS-18 strategic missiles. We could easily have laid waste to vast areas of your United States and the rest of the Western countries."

Dr. Taylor looked stunned. When the Russian stopped for a moment to catch his breath, she said, "So they've actually done it," anger rising in her voice. "They've put bio warheads on missiles—ICBMs, at that. And they actually used biological weapons in combat before."

"Make no mistake, Doctor," Alek continued. "The people in charge of production at Biopreparat care little that they're making weapons. They haven't seen the results of what they do. Almost no one has. We've only had tests conducted on animals. What is coming up now is far worse."

"Worse?" Rockham asked.

"Oh yes," Alek said gravely, nodding. "It was the final reason for my getting out. They are going to be conducting human tests, in the open, with a weapon I helped develop."

The Russian scientist dropped his eyes and stared at the tabletop with his last statement.

"Human testing!" Taylor said, shocked.

"I don't see why that should surprise you, Doctor," Danzig said. "We've suspected all of this for some time. This is simply the first real confirmation we've had."

"But we have a chance to recover the weapon!" Alek said excitedly, looking up. "This will be the first time they have used a northern test site in decades. If you can just get a group of your men in there, they can bring back a sample."

"A sample of what, Dr. Kondrachev?" Danzig asked.

"Variant K," Alek said quietly. "It is a particularly virulent strain of anthrax. It is resistant to all the antibiotics we tested it with. And it has an almost hundred percent lethality. But with a sample," he said more excitedly, "your people could make a vaccine. That would greatly reduce the value of Variant K as a weapon."

"And you say this weapon is going to be used in an open air test?" Rockham asked.

"Yes," Alek said, facing the SEAL. "I was brought in to check the test sites. They are on a small island in the Beloye More."

"The White Sea," Sukov translated.

"And you want us to go on that island and bring back a sample of a disease?" Rockham said, astonishment in his voice.

"It looks like that's about the size of it, Lieutenant," Captain North said.

1843 ZULU
58° 20' North, 6° 12' East
USS _Archerfish_
The Skagerrak
East of the North Sea

It was some thirty hours since Alek Kondrachev had made his suggestion that the SEALs land on Soviet territory. In that time, the _Archerfish_ had traversed the channels of Denmark, avoiding both the royal yacht and any random sandbars. She was some fifty kilometers off the coast of Norway in the Skagerrak, the waters between the North Sea and the Danish waters of the Kattegat.

With five hundred meters of water available for his ship to maneuver in, Captain North was considerably happier than he had been for days. He had also managed to catch up on some badly needed sleep. During this time, he had been examining the waters surrounding the target suggested by Alek Kondrachev. The situation was not helping to maintain his happy mood.

Peter Danzig had been using the radio to inform Washington, the intelligence community, and the SEALs' own command as to just what had been suggested. Downloads of satellite transmissions had also given Danzig some badly needed information regarding the waters they would have to cross.

As far as communications with the SEALs' command had gone, Danzig was less than satisfied. The decision to accept and conduct the operation had been placed squarely on the shoulders of Lieutenant Rockham. It didn't matter how important the intelligence community thought the operation might be. Rockham was the officer on the scene, and the decision to go ahead would be his alone.

Before he would make his final decision, Rockham wanted a full briefing held for all of his men. Even his injured ones. Ensign Paulson's injuries had started to subside, but now there was a mixture of blue, red, yellows, and a kind of green scattered across the injured side of the SEAL's face. But both of the young man's eyes were open and he was alert, though the injuries did prevent him from talking much.

Chief Monday had recovered quickly. His flulike symptoms from his bout with hypothermia were almost completely gone. Dr. Taylor was almost amazed at the rapid progress all of the men made. Even the broken bones of Lopez and Handel didn't keep them from the briefing. Mike Ferber had told her that in the Teams, everyone's opinion was valued. And from what the doctor could see, this wasn't just lip service.

The officers' wardroom was too small by far to accept the crowd that had to attend the briefing, so the crew's mess, the single largest open space on board the submarine, was placed off limits to the general crew and taken over for the time being. All twenty-two SEALs on board were now in the compartment, as well as the two CIA officers, Dr. Kondrachev, Captain North, and Lieutenant Commander Beam. The arrival of Ops Lieutenant Jack Carter with a number of charts under his arm indicated the briefing was about to begin.

Placing the charts up on the wall where movies were normally shown, Lieutenant Carter faced his audience. Carter was a career Navy officer and had given briefings on subjects from personal hygiene to a nuclear missile launch. But this would be the first time he would be giving a briefing where men's lives could hang in the balance. Men whose eyes he could look into across the compartment. And he could feel the pressure from the minds behind those eyes.

"Gentlemen, he began, "and lady," he added quickly. "I have been tasked with giving you this briefing. If there are any questions, please feel free to ask them at any time."

Turning to the first chart, which showed a large section of the Arctic leading up to the northwestern shore of NATO and the Soviet Union, Carter lifted a long ruler. Pointing to a spot on the chart, he began.

"The target for this operation is a small island inside the mouth of the White Sea. If this place looks like it might be right in the Russians' backyard, well, you're close. This place isn't in the Soviet's backyard. It's more like parked in their driveway right outside the garage door.

"This will be a cold water operation, to be sure. The White Sea is much like a huge bay, indented deeply into northern Russia. Almost completely surrounded by land, the White Sea has western Russia to the south, west, and east, and the Kola Peninsula to the north. It is a relatively shallow sea, averaging two hundred feet in depth, down to over 1,100 feet on its western side.

"The approximately 35,000 square miles of the White Sea is connected to the Barents Sea by the Gorlo Strait. The Gorlo Strait is shaped something like a reversed letter C, as you can see here, with the opening facing to the west. It is bordered by the Kola Peninsula to the west, northern Russia to the east, and the Kanin Peninsula to the north.

"It is below the Kanin Peninsula, at the narrow

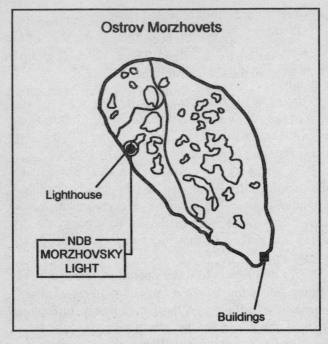

Ostrov Morzhovets

Lighthouse

NDB
MORZHOVSKY
LIGHT

Buildings

Morzhovets Island

mouth of the strait itself, that Morzhovets Island lies. That island is the target, right smack in the middle of Russian territorial waters.

"Roughly oval in shape, Morzhovets Island is oriented on a northwest to southeast axis. It's all of fifteen kilometers long and seven kilometers wide, giving it an area of over seventy square kilometers. Largely a rocky island, Morzhovets had just about all of the arctic land features—rocks, hills, tundra, trees, and snow. Between the rocky areas are mixed areas of forest and marsh.

"There has apparently been little in the way of human habitation on the island. There is a small group of buildings on the southeastern point."

Moving to a large printout of a satellite photograph, Carter continued. "Satellite imagery shows us at least half a dozen rough buildings. There are signs of additional construction and digging in the area of the buildings but nothing substantial has been put up. They may be prepared tent sites.

"There is a large boat dock area and a small motor pool parking area to the west of the buildings. The motor pool holds half a dozen vehicles ranging from jeeps to trucks. All of them are soft-skinned and there are no signs of any kind of armored vehicles being supported.

"There is a very simple system of two dirt roads on the island. The longest is about twelve kilometers long and stretches from near the dock through the thickest portion of the island and ends on the upper north shore. A second, shorter road is only about five kilometers long and goes from near the westernmost shore to join the other road on the upper west half of the island. According to Dr. Kondrachev, there are test sites prepared both to the north and south of the crossroads.

"An unmanned, automatic lighthouse is on the western shore of the island, just to the south of the branch road. Another dock structure is near the lighthouse."

Turning away from his maps and photos, Carter faced his audience. "The only personnel on the island in the past have been hunters and loggers. With the es-

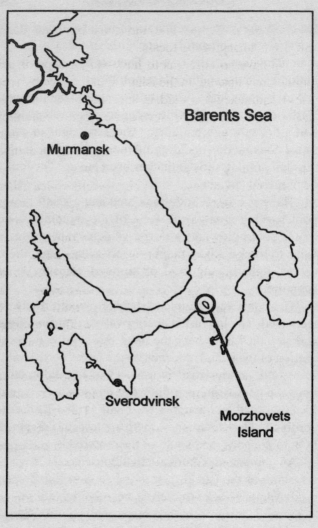

Barents Sea

Murmansk

Sverodvinsk

Morzhovets
Island

White Sea

tablishment of the test site, the island has been placed off limits to any of the locals.

"We have no count as to how many troops or personnel may now be on the island. But if we go by what Dr. Kondrachev has said is standard procedure, you can expect there to be several platoons of chemical troops to support the test site. When the estimated hundred prisoners are brought in, there should be another twenty to thirty guards along with them.

"So what you have is a military controlled island more than twenty kilometers offshore of the nearest mainland, which is directly to the south. There are at least two test sites that Dr. Kondrachev knows of, both of which are reached by the single service road.

"To make the situation a little more interesting, the Kola Peninsula is only sixty kilometers away to the west, across the mouth of the Gorlo Strait. The Kola is probably one of the most militarily important chunks of Soviet real estate there is outside of Moscow itself.

"Murmansk, one of the bigger Soviet ports, is about 450 kilometers to the northwest of Morzhovets Island, on the northern coast of the Kola. The bulk of the Northern Fleet is based out of Severomorsk, about sixteen kilometers northeast of Murmansk, on the upper northeastern edge of the peninsula.

"Just to the north of Murmansk is Polyarnny, the major base for the bulk of the Northern Fleet's submarine forces. This is where the Soviets are keeping a large number of their Typhoon-class boomers, along with a bunch of their attack subs to help protect them.

"Scattered throughout the Kola are some forty Soviet air bases as well as two army motorized rifle divisions and the Northern Fleet's naval infantry brigade. That's all along the top of the White Sea. Near the bottom of the White Sea are the major ports of Arkhangelsk and Sverodvinsk.

"Arkhangelsk is a major seaport, running almost year round except for during the very worst of the winter. Heavy use of icebreakers helps keep the port open and the sea lanes clear. Sverodvinsk is a major industrial and ship-building center. The Number 402 shipyard at Sverodvinsk is the world's largest submarine building center. The bulk of the Soviet navy's nuclear submarine fleet came out of this one yard.

"During World War Two, the Allies ran convoys to both Murmansk and Arkhangelsk for several years. We have an intelligence dump on all of the charts and information on the waters of the White Sea from those convoys. In addition to that information, NATO has had ships off the Kola for years pulling 'gatekeeping' duties. They've kept an eye out for the Soviet boats coming out of Murmansk and Sverodvinsk. A lot of the newest Soviet sub classes have been identified this way. Some of that data is in our sonar library to help us ID a contact.

"But these gatekeeping ships also did a lot of mapping of the sea floor during their time on-station. That's what's going to help us now.

"The last of the warm waters of the Gulf Stream pass around Norway and into the Barents Sea right along the north coast of the Kola. This makes for a number of thermal layers that we can use to get us in close to where we want to go. The White Sea is situated on a continental shelf, part of what's called the Baltic Shield, which doesn't slope off until it's well past the Gorlo Strait. But the soundings from the Arkhangelsk convoys and the gatekeepers have found a fairly deep trench, what's called a 'tongue of the ocean.' That, we can follow up to within striking distance of the island. There's still going to be some shallow water we have to cross, but it's going to be a hell of a lot deeper than what we went through getting into the Baltic. Probably damned few sailing ships as well."

A chuckle made the rounds of the SEALs at that last comment. Even Paulson managed a lopsided smile.

"What all of that means is that we can get you in close. The captain is certain he can get us close enough that your SDV can make the run and back on a single battery charge. The water flow through the Gorlo Strait has put a sandy bottom on the rock floor around the island. That means the *Archerfish* can lay up on the bottom and wait. Our DDS acceptance modifications included moving some of the hull fittings so the boat can bottom and still run her critical machinery.

"There is no way for us to find out which test site is going to be used when. The Keyhole satellites aren't of much use to us at this time of year. Cloud cover is pretty much constant at these latitudes in the early winter. We have gotten some good shots of the island. The photos we have," and Carter turned back to a large printout of the island, "show several streams emptying into the sea. One of these streams is on the westernmost point of the island and is moving fairly quickly, fast enough that it hasn't frozen over. Open water has been confirmed at the mouth of that stream. If you went in underwater, you could get out onto the land."

"What is the estimated current at that location?" Lieutenant Fisher asked.

"She's moving pretty fast upstream," Carter answered. "But the water spreads out quickly once it enters the White Sea proper. You couldn't take an SDV up into the stream itself—estimates put the flow at over eight knots. But you will be able to secure her to the bottom and move in to the mouth of the stream underwater.

"You would have to get on the island and set up an observation post overlooking the crossroads to confirm which site was going to be used. Once the site is used, all we would need is a sample of the snow or soil from several spots downwind of the test. Dr. Taylor tells us that even a small sample will be enough to grow a culture from, identify the disease, and develop a vaccine.

"Weather changes pretty fast in these parts. The Russians are working under the same weather constraints as we are, and they need fairly good weather, no snow and little wind, for their test. According to the latest meteorological information, they are going to have that weather early on. From what we've been able to learn, the test site will be set up and then the gulag prisoners brought in. They'll never know it's a weapons test, they'll probably be told they're on some work detail.

"We've got a window of about twenty-four hours to get to the island before the scheduled test.

"If there are no further questions?" Carter looked about the serious faces in front of him. These men had absorbed every word of what he'd said. But their discussion, and their decision, was something they wanted privacy for.

"Thank you," Carter finished. "Lieutenant Rockham, I will leave these materials for you."

With that, Lieutenant Carter left the compartment. Captain North stood and faced the men.

"Men," he said very seriously, "the *Archerfish* will get you in. What happens on that island, only you will be able to know. But my ship and her crew are at your disposal. We will get you in, and we will get you out. XO?"

As Lieutenant Commander Beam shook his head, Captain North again looked at the SEALs. "Good day, gentlemen."

As he turned and left the compartment, Chief Monday got to his feet. "Attention on deck!" he said loudly.

All of the SEALs immediately got to their feet, including Ensign Paulson. They stood there at attention while Captain North and Lieutenant Commander Beam left the compartment.

Turning to Peter Danzig and Dr. Taylor, Lieutenant Rockham said, "Would you excuse us, please."

Danzig opened his mouth as if to say something, then thought better of it, got up and left. Dr. Taylor looked around the room for a moment, and then she too left. Now the SEALs were alone to make their decision. As the men sat down, conversation picked up after a moment's silence.

"So, who gets to go to Moe?" Kurkowski asked, coining a name for the island.

"Don't you think we should discuss it first, Kurkowski?" Rockham said.

"I don't see why, Skipper." This from Mike Ferber. "It's important, we're here, and we have the skills, equipment, and manpower to do the job. Hell, it's better than some of the things we've just been ordered to do."

"Yes, Mike," Rockham said. "But this one is going to be right in the Russians' backyard. It could turn hairy fast."

"If we wanted it easy sir," Chief Monday said, "we would have joined the Air Force."

Another chuckle went through the men.

"Can't say I like the idea of going in to the Soviet Union just to scoop up some yellow snow," Pete Wilkes said.

"Hell, Pete," Kurkowski said, "it'll keep you out with the boys a bit longer."

Another laugh went around the room. All of the SEALs in the platoon knew Pete Wilkes had a family. And he had four kids, all girls.

"It looks like you've got your answer, Skipper," Chief Monday said.

"Yeah, I guess I do," Rockham said, pride in his voice. "I'll tell Captain North and Mr. Danzig that it's a go."

"Ferber can tell Sharon," Kurkowski said.

A roar of laughter went through the room at Mike

Ferber's discomfiture at the last statement. Even Rockham was surprised and amused to see the big SEAL blush.

"Okay, let's give these bubbleheads back their chow hall," Monday said to the SEALs.

CHAPTER 12

Feliks Belik had never been a patient man. As far as he was concerned, patience was for fools who could not control their world. And he controlled his world with an iron hand, which he felt was the reason he was in charge of a major part of the KGB Maritime Border Guards in the region.

But he had to wait now, and that was something he hated doing.

The Nikitich-class icebreaker *Volga* was a handful to operate. Especially since she was running short-handed. But that stuck-up naval Spetsnaz captain had wanted as few men as possible involved in the operation. That was completely understandable to Belik. Fewer men meant fewer cuts in the profits. And the profits were why he was here.

The Spetsnaz officer had been the one Belik was directed to by his black market contacts in the south. The officer had access to something big, and he needed help moving it. The plan sounded good to Belik; he was long used to shearing the sheep that traveled on the waters he controlled. And so he found himself in an undermanned boat off a point of land in the White Sea, picking up a squad of men who had landed in the middle of nowhere.

A flashing light from on shore told the KGB man that his passengers were finally available for boarding. The *Volga* moved as close to the shore as it could, but the squad of men on land still had to walk across the ice to reach her.

Eight of the silent men climbed up onto the *Volga*'s deck and waited while the last man came up. The bearing and stance of the tall officer was a recently familiar sight to Belik, and one he hated. The Spetsnaz captain obviously thought he was much better than the KGB man. But it was Belik's ship that the officer needed to move him and his men. So that should make him a bit more grateful, shouldn't it?

Captain Gregoriy Rostov turned to Vasili Rutil and Ivan Tsinev, his two lieutenants. "We shall not be on this craft long," he said quietly. "Which shall be all the better for us. Tsinev, I want you to set up your radio equipment on the upper deck. Rutil, spread out the men and check the ship."

Without a word the two Spetsnaz officers moved to do their commander's bidding. As Rostov went up to Belik, he could almost see the avarice and greed rising up above the man like a cloud. The greasy smile Belik gave him was a forced one, Rostov was sure. But the jackal can be dangerous, he thought, even when it is facing a wolf.

"Good day, Comrade Captain," Belik said in an ingratiating voice. "You men are most welcome to make themselves at home."

"Excellent, Belik," Rostov said, ignoring anything but the business at hand. "I take it that covered item on the rear deck is our vehicle?"

Only lightly rebuffed by the officer's direct manner, Belik indicated the large rectangular item. "Yes, that is a snow vehicle that matches the specifications you gave me. It was difficult to get on board, but my crew managed it. We will do the same when it comes time to be off-loaded."

"Excellent," Rostov said. "Now we should be on our way north. Here are the coordinates I want you to reach at your best speed."

Handing over a folded chart to the KGB man, Rostov turned and looked at the superstructure of the ship.

"This will do nicely," he said. "I'm sure a sturdy vessel like this will get us to our target quickly."

"Yes," Belik said with a smile. "The men are having to work very hard to do the job of twice their number. But they expect to be well paid. They have all worked with me for years and can be completely trusted."

"Oh, I'm sure I can trust them as well," Rostov said.

High Command and the politicians in Washington had decided that the chance of obtaining a sample of a Soviet biological weapon was so important that they had actually authorized a landing on Soviet soil. This operation wasn't taking place in some contested area, a no-man's-land. This was Mother Russia herself. If Lieutenant Rockham or any of his SEALs were captured, it would be a long time before they ever saw the States again.

But considering the negative possibilities was nonproductive for the mission at hand. Instead, Rockham had a very difficult set of choices to make. He had to decide which members of his Team would be going in, and who would be left behind on the sub.

SEALs train; they train constantly, to develop and hone skills. Then they practice with those skills to become even more proficient. And they did all of this—weeks, months, years, of practice, training, and rehearsal—for the chance that one day they would have a mission. A hot op. A conflict where they would learn if everything they had done, all their training, was good enough. And now Rockham had to tell his men who would and wouldn't be going to the game.

It wasn't that SEALs, or anyone in the Special Operations community, actually looked forward to war. But it was only in the arena of conflict that they could prove whether they had what it took. And for good or bad, today there were few opportunities for the men to "go there and do that."

There would be six men going in to the island, all that the SDV could take. Rockham would be one of them, and Fisher and Bryant would again have to crew the SDV. His most experienced man, Chief Monday, couldn't go in. Even if the chief didn't have the broken ribs, he knew that once you hype out, it took a long time to recover. On his next long, cold swim, the chief could hype out even faster.

No, his next most experienced petty officer was Mike Ferber, probably the most fit man in the platoon by a wide margin, due to his having been a BUD/S instructor not long ago. Besides, Mike was about as tough as an anvil, and about as solid as one to have at your back.

John Sukov would go in as the radioman; his ability to speak Russian would be a big plus for the squad. If everything went according to plan, the SEALs would never have to fire a shot. They would go in and get out without anyone ever having even known they were there. But you don't expect things to go according to plan.

If it came down to a fight, it would be a hard choice who to pick from the squad. All of the men were good. They had proven that to Rockham over and over again in the field, during training and on exercises. But he needed someone with woodcraft skills, observation ability, and camouflage knowledge.

In spite of the fact that his size would be a bitch in the back of the SDV, Rockham picked Ryan Marks as his last man. The big black man was strong, fast, and very quiet. He had also done very well at SEAL sniper school at Camp Atterbury, Indiana. Rockham knew that Marks could hide in an empty parking lot and slip up behind you while you were watching for him. The fact that he was also one of the platoon's point men meant that he could switch off with Bryant during their patrol in.

What the SEALs would have to do was get in to the island, land, and patrol in to a point where they could overlook the crossroads. There, they would have to establish an observation post. Arms would be light, each man would carry an M14. The power and range of the big rifle had proved its value during all of their winter training. Ferber would probably want to take his favored pump shotgun, which was all right with Rockham. If the SEALs got down to the point where they had a shootout, they would have already lost the game.

John Sukov also had training in Explosive Ordnance Disposal. Rockham knew that a great deal of that training involved how to handle chemical weapons. Those techniques transferred very well to the handling of biological weapons. So John would be the one to gather the samples once they had the test site located.

Having discussed the situation with both Dr. Taylor, his platoon's own two corpsmen, and the submarine's corpsman, they had come up with a kit for taking the samples. Each of the SEALs had a complete MOPP Level 4 rig, including a protective mask and enclosing protective suit they could wear while gathering the bio samples.

The actual collection of the samples would be done by Sukov with a carrying case of sterile bottles, scoops, knife, and tweezers assembled by the corpsmen. The case was held in a waterproof can, completely proof against leakage down to a hundred feet, a depth the SEAL officer did not expect to get even close to on the operation.

Everything they were going to do, all the risks they were going to take, even the serious risks to the multi-million dollar nuclear submarine itself, would be taken so the SEALs could fill those vials and containers with dirt and melted snow. It was a strange world indeed.

With his crew and their specialized gear established, it was time to work out the plan. Rockham poured over the intelligence package Lieutenant Carter had put together. He committed everything possible to memory, then wrote it down as well. In the information asked for by Danzig were maps and satellite photos from Keyhole satellites assigned to keep an eye on the Soviet Northern Fleet.

Some of the pictures from space gave a detailed view of the island. Others were of much less use. There was even a U.S. Army Corps of Engineers 1:250,000 scale tactical map included.

Map NQ 37, 38-7 showed there was a whole lot of nothing around Morzhovets Island, and for a good distance beyond as well. But the map had been prepared from information compiled in 1948! So there was a good chance some of the details had changed. But not by much, according to the satellite data.

Now Rockham had an inkling of how the war planners must have felt during the first years of WWII. Off Tarawa, the invasion planners had used charts almost a hundred years old to prepare for their invasion. But Rockham also knew of the terrible mistakes that had been made at Tarawa, and how those mistakes had led to the creation of the UDTs, and eventually the SEALs.

They would transport by submarine as close as possible to Moe. Kurkowski's off-the-cuff remark had become the code name for their target destination. The SEALs were Curly one to six, and the weapon was Larry. Who said old shows didn't have their uses?

From the sub, they would continue in to Moe by SDV. That would have to be a long, cold trip. Fisher didn't want to plan more than a ninty-minute trip either way. That meant the *Archerfish* had to close to within fourteen kilometers of Moe before launching the eight-boat. Captain North had assured Rockham that he could get the sub in, even if they only had a few feet of water over the sail and under her keel. The sub would be moving between the sea floor and the pack ice above, not a situation Rockham wanted to think about.

The trip was going to be a cold one, and getting on the island would be even colder. There was going to be so much gear going in with them, their Bergen Crusader II rucksacks would be packed full. Even then, there would be snowshoes strapped to the rucks, and cross-country skis strapped to the hull of the SDV.

All this gear meant that the SEALs wouldn't be able to take their usual breathing rigs. They would all be going off of boat air. Only Bryant and Fisher would be using their Mark 15 rigs. And even they would be having rucks and gear stuffed into their compartment.

So for the swim into and away from Moe, each member of the unit would have three bailout bottles with him. Officially called the HEED, for Helicopter Emergency Egress Device, the bailout bottle would give a man about five minutes of air from the small mouthpiece on top of the bottle. That would be enough to get the men from the SDV and up to the shore. One bottle for the trip in, one for the trip out, and a spare. All three of the bailout bottles would fit in a large ammo pouch or cargo pocket, so they saved a lot of space.

If the SEALs couldn't land on the island, or if they got lost and couldn't find the *Archerfish*, well, they had a lot of company from the men of the Teams who had gone before them. There really wasn't a way for the men to open up a hole in the sea ice if one wasn't there for them. But questions like that didn't require any consideration. They had done everything they could. Now it was time to go in and see if it all worked.

1320 ZULU
67° 22' North, 43° 7' East
USS *Archerfish*
The White Sea
Union of Soviet Socialist Republics

It had been a long, slow trip in from the Skagen to the mouth of the White Sea. For almost four days the *Archerfish* had crept through the depths, making up speed when she thought she was in safe waters. Covering almost 3,400 kilometers, they had ducked Soviet ships and any other traffic that might have detected them. Even when one of the huge Oscar-class boomers had left Polyarnny, on the northern edge of the Kola

Peninsula, the *Archerfish* had not been detected.

The monstrous submarine, over five hundred feet long and displacing 25,000 tons—compared to the *Archerfish*'s 4,762 tons, submerged—had passed very close by. But the double sonar watch Captain North had put on remained alert and warned the ship of the monster coming long before it arrived. The *Archerfish* could become a hole in the water, and the hole could move along.

Captain North had told Rockham that the *Archerfish* had undergone a complete shakedown cruise after her DDS modifications had been completed. All her new systems had been tested and wrung out. Even the crew at the Navy's Atlantic Underwater Test and Evaluation Center couldn't spot the *Archerfish* most of the time. And those technicians had known what they were looking for.

And the testing of the ship, and the captain's pride in his boat and her crew, were proving truc.

Now they were within fifty kilometers of Moe. They had been under the ice for a while, and it didn't look like the ice was going to open before they reached Moe. The SEALs were having a last good, hot meal on board the sub before their mission.

The cook had outdone himself with the meal he set before the SEALs. Steak and lobster, several desserts, fresh baked bread, vegetables, and a wide variety of spreads and condiments had been put on. Even Ken Fleming said he couldn't have done much better himself. High praise indeed, Kurkowski announced to the world at large.

The captain had come in to the crew's mess to help the men see their new shipmates off. As the meal was coming to an end, Captain North stood to say a few words to his crew and the SEALs who were sitting beside them.

"Gentlemen, and lady," North began, with a nod to Dr. Taylor, "over forty years ago our namesake, the *Archerfish* of World War Two, set a distinguished name for herself. She penetrated deep into the Japanese home waters, sinking one of their greatest ships in the process. Now we've done that memory one better. We've gone into Ivan's backyard, and we're parking next to his side door.

"The next week will be difficult at best. We will have to maintain strict noise discipline. And we will have our shipmates out in harm's way. But we have gotten these men here, and we will get them home. This mission is difficult and vital. I have every faith in each one of you and look forward to when we leave these waters with our shipmates back aboard."

That speech had been given just a few hours before. Now the *Archerfish* was on-station close to where the SDV would be launched. Each SEAL had his job to do, and was doing all of it and more. For the men who were going in to the island, each detail of their gear could mean the difference between life and death, success or failure. And their Teammates knew that everything they did could also affect the men going in. It didn't matter if they weren't going in themselves, now was not the time for disappointments. They had their

Teammates to support and that was all that mattered.

"Hey, Bryant," Kurkowski called across the compartment.

Bryant looked up from where he was checking his rucksack. "Yeah, what?"

"You know that fifty bucks you owe me from the poker game?"

"Yeah?" Bryant said slowly, expecting a cliché at any moment.

"Well, get your ass back here as soon as you can," Kurkowski said. "None of these poor bastards have any money. I want to take your mangy butt to the cleaners again."

The laugh that ran around the compartment broke up the tension that had been gradually building up.

Each SEAL was wearing a full acrylic pile undersuit. Over the acrylic suit they had the same dry suits they had worn in the Baltic only a few days before. Equipment worn under the suit had to be kept to a minimum, so their winter uniforms were going in waterproof bags in their rucks.

Each man had a pistol, a SIG P226 9mm automatic, in a holster strapped around his waist. Also in the pockets attached to this belt were the minimum items of his personal survival kit. Each man chose those items he felt would serve to best keep him alive if he were separated from his Teammates. But at a minimum, there was a space blanket, matches, fire starter, compass, gloves, a candle, and emergency high protein and sugar food packets.

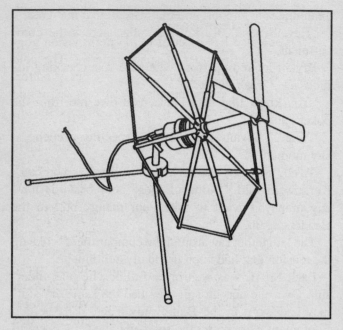

SATCOM Antenna

In the top of his rucksack or in another waterproof container went his second line equipment, including his load bearing equipment, which consisted of his web gear, pouches, and other items. There was also his weapon—the M14 with the stock folded for compactness—ammunition, magazines, grenades, a small stove or pocket stove with fuel tablets, and twenty-four hours of high density rations.

Deeper in the ruck was the third line gear, such as their overwhite camouflage suit, Gore-Tex cold weather clothing, additional clothing, sleeping gear, fuel, water, burlap camouflage netting, folding shovel, CBR gear, and other items.

Everyone also had a set of M909 night vision goggles and a large number of spare batteries. The cold could be depended on to suck the power out of batteries quickly, even when they had been kept warm and dry. Marks had a twenty-power spotting scope for observations as well as its folding tripod.

Sukov was packing the most special equipment. He had the AN/URC-110 SATCOM radio, the KY-57 encryption device, the folding umbrellalike antenna, and one of the several bio sample kits.

The contents of the rucksack were all packaged in waterproof bags or containers. Then the ruck itself was packed up in the large, German waterproof containers that resembled large squared-off black rubber rucks themselves. Once they got on shore, the black rubber containers would be used to cache their diving gear. Finally, five-foot lengths of 550-parachute cord was tied to the waterproof containers so they could be dragged in to shore behind the SEALs if necessary.

The submarine was on-station, the gear packed. And there was nothing else to say. As the SEALs gathered up their gear and began to move to the upper deck and ladder to the DDS, the normal joking and fooling about was missing. Even Kurkowski was subdued.

Alek Kondrachev, Peter Danzig, and Sharon Taylor were on the upper deck to see the men off. Of the three people, the SEALs liked seeing Sharon the best. And they had a lot of respect for Kondrachev, for what he had faced. Now they passed up their gear, climbed the ladder, and secured the DDS. They did not say good-bye.

The hour and a half trip in to Moe was a nightmare of cold and uncomfortable conditions. When the SEALs finally approached their calculated arrival point, they were just about ready to face anything they had to just to get out of the SDV and at least move around a bit. The little light that penetrated through the ice showed nothing in the water. The SDV simply cruised on through the twilight, guided by its electronics and the skill of her crew.

As the sea floor finally started sloping up, they knew they were approaching Moe. When a current started driving the eight-boat sideways, Bryant turned into it. In spite of his pain back on the *Archerfish*, Paulson had done everything he could to help the SEALs and their SDV. One of the things he had recommended was switching the speed screw they had used off Finland for the power screw. Now that Bryant was bucking a current, he was glad of Ensign Paulson's suggestion.

Both Fisher and Bryant slid back the covers over the cockpit. Now they could see the light brightening. When the SDV was in only ten feet of water, they stopped the craft and grounded it on the bottom. Over-head they could finally see the wavering light of open water.

Slipping out from the rear compartment, Rockham slipped his bailout bottle between numb lips. His face was so cold that he had a hard time holding the small air tank in place with just his mouth and lips. So he moved up very slowly to the surface with one hand held out and the other holding his air bottle.

Very slowly, Rockham broached the surface and raised his head only far enough to clear his eyes above the water. Not twenty feet in front of him was a pebble beach with windblown snow and ice buildup in shattered mounds. It was the prettiest sight he had seen in a long time. Going back down to the SDV, he gave the thumbs-up sign. The SEALs began gathering their gear and securing the SDV.

Two three-pound Danforth anchors went out, one each at the bow and stern. Bryant and Fisher went through the complicated sequence of steps needed for them to secure their Mark 15 breathing rigs in the SDV. Finally, they had their rigs strapped in place and turned off. They would have to go through an equally complex sequence to get back in the boat and breathing off the rigs.

The last thing done to the SDV was Fisher reaching in and clicking on a very small piece of special equipment. A tiny avalanche locator, the kind worn by skiers in case they were buried in the snow, had been specially waterproofed and mounted in the SDV. The weak signal put out by the locator would be almost impossible for someone to pick up accidentally, even if they were walking on the ice directly overhead. But it just might be enough to ensure that the SEALs found their means of escape when it came time to leave the island. The batteries in the locator were very long-lived. And the signal could be picked up with the special receiver the SEALs were leaving at their cache site.

Now the SEALs were lined up to go in to the shore. The men were going to do a very careful approach, but the limit on the air in their bailout bottles also meant they were going to do their approach quickly.

Marks and Bryant were the designated scout-swimmers. As such, they would be the first men in to shore. Trailing a line of 550 cord behind them, the two SEALs moved very cautiously. Their rucksacks in the waterproof containers were being dragged along on their short cord leashes.

The two swimmer-scouts slowly slipped up onto the beach, remaining hidden in the water as long as possible. Once their faces were exposed to the wind, the water would freeze quickly and they faced a very real danger of frostbite.

As they lifted up through the water, they found themselves just to the side of the mouth of a rapidly moving stream. The cold air hit their already numb faces, the pain drawing no reaction from the SEALs as they examined the sloping pebble- and ice-covered beach.

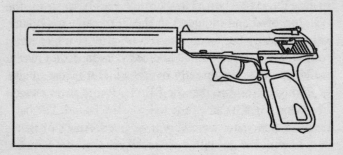

P9S with Suppressor

From long plastic bags, both men drew and prepared the pistols they had carried in. Their weapons were H&K P9S pistols with a long suppressor firmly screwed onto the extended barrels. Drawing back the slides ejected the black plastic chamber plugs into the water. The plugs had sealed the breeches of the pistols from any water leakage. Releasing the slides chambered a green-tipped live 9mm round from the already loaded magazine. The subsonic bullet of the Mark 144 ammunition would punch a hole through the white plastic disks that covered the muzzles of the suppressors. And the shot would be very quiet if the weapons were fired.

As they went up onto the beach with their weapons extended, the two swimmer-scouts could see no sign of anything amiss. Normal SOP would have them wait on the beach for a length of time before calling in the rest of their Team. But these were not normal conditions. Pulling on the thin line leading back into the water, the SEALs signaled their Teammates to come in.

The SEALs coming up on the beach were on the ragged edge of exhaustion. The cold had sapped the men badly. They were as winded as if they had run a marathon, but also stiff with cold. Hands could barely open or close, and just moving an arm or leg could take a real concentrated effort. And they still hadn't faced the worst of it.

Now the SEALs had a real ordeal in front of them. While three of the Team maintained a quick perimeter, the other three stripped out of their dry suits. Packs

SEAL in Snow Gear

were opened, bodies rubbed with a dry cloth, and uniforms quickly donned.

In spite of the speed with which they forced their bodies to move, the cold was shattering. Shivering had reached an intensity most of them hadn't faced since BUD/S. Only this time there was no bell they could ring to quit and get warm.

Chattering teeth were silenced as jaw muscles

clenched. They each put on the rest of their cold weather clothing and then moved to take their turn on the perimeter. Now it was their Teammates' turn to take off the now frozen outer dry suits and change.

It was a short while since their ordeal on the beach, and the SEALs were moving inland. The patrol formation was a standard one. The point man—at the moment it was Bryant—was the trail breaker. He had the hardest job of choosing the exact route of travel for the squad. The timing of the operation was such that the team was on the island during daylight for the landing, but the night and its concealing darkness was approaching rapidly.

Tracks in the snow were a major consideration, so the point man tried to pick a route that would help conceal those tracks as much as possible. When they could, the patrol moved under the treeline, over hard-packed snow or ice, and even the frozen tundra where it was exposed.

The number two man in the patrol was Ryan Marks. He was checking the trail as they went along. When Bryant rotated the position of trailbreaker/point, he would merely step to the side of the trail and wait. Marks would continue past and Bryant would reenter the line. They switched off every ten or fifteen minutes so the point man was always fresh.

Rockham brought up the third position, with Sukov, the radio man, right behind him. The point man chose the path the patrol followed, but it was Rockham's responsibility to see that it stayed on the correct heading.

Bringing up the second to last position was Fisher, who maintained a watch on both sides of the trail. Mike Ferber was the rear security man. He also tried to obliterate the patrol's trail as much as possible. One of the tricks he tried was dragging a brushy piece of foliage along behind him, sweeping out the slighter marks and blurring the rest.

The patrol had only a relatively short distance to cover to their preselected lay-up point. On the satellite photos and maps, Rockham had picked a point only four kilometers from the SEALs landing site. The point looked to be at the side of a small rise, centered in the inverted V of the southern part of the crossroads. The long main road ran from the southeast and the buildings some eleven kilometers away, up to the northwest and the northernmost point of the island, only three kilometers away. The short reversed-S road then ran near the lighthouse off to the southwest of the crossroads and was only some four winding kilometers long. It was up on the northwest road that Kondrachev said the test sites he knew of were located, one on either side of the road. The SEALs would have to reach their lay-up point and establish their observation post. Then it would just be a matter of waiting.

At roughly the top and bottom of the hour, Rockham called a halt to the patrol by raising his open hand. If he had his fist clenched, it would have meant an emergency halt, that something had alerted him.

But on the routine halts, the patrol just stood and listened for a few minutes. The men noticed the clean, sharp smell of the air, as well. The eyes could see movement, but the ears could detect even faint sounds. And smells carried surprising distances. A rough Russian cigarette being smoked by a soldier could be smelled for hundreds of meters in the proper conditions.

But there were no smells, sights, or sounds to break the patrol's formation. They moved on and soon found themselves overlooking the crossroads and their planned lay-up site.

Now they moved very carefully. They hooked back through the treeline they were on and overlooked their own trail for ten minutes. As darkness fell more solidly, they watched for any lights off in the distance. Nothing showed or sounded. While Ferber remained on watch overlooking the crossroads, the rest of the patrol moved far down past their lay-up site and looped back.

Camouflaging their own trail as much as possible, the patrol approached the small hillside overlooking the crossroads. On the east side of the rise the ground had been scooped away and a few boulders deposited from glaciers eons past were tumbled about. The small depression was filled in with snow and had appeared as a much larger hill in the satellite photos. It was in the side of this hill, into the depression, that the SEALs dug their observation post.

With their folding shovels and a few long snow knives, they quickly dug a short tunnel and hollowed out the first chamber. While two SEALs stood sentry, the other three set up light folding posts from their rucks. The posts went into the ground inside the hollow they had cut to support a camouflage cloth screen that would separate the observation bay from the central one and the rear sleeping bay.

The front observation bay was dug out very carefully, with the least possible amount of snow disturbance in front of the position. The bay was between two of the boulders and overlooked the crossroads as well as a good part of the main road, both north and south.

The tunnel at the rear of the OP was just long enough that a sentry at the rear of it could see the reverse slope of the small hill they had dug into the side of. From that point a sentry could cover the only blind spots to the rear and side of the SEALs' position. With the inside of the position finished, a latrine was dug as one of the last touches, and Rockham called in Ferber over the MX-300 radio. Not speaking, Rockham clicked the transmit button three times. The single return click told him that Ferber was on his way in.

Now the squad settled in to an observation post routine. A screening net had been hung over the front opening of the OP. A hanging cloth would screen the back of the OP from any light that was being used in the central portion of the position. Their gear was all sorted out and the majority remained packed for an immediate withdrawal.

Setting up his radio antenna, Sukov found he could hide it between several rocks while still pointing it back to the southern horizon and the communications satellite far out in space. For more local communications, the men ran 550 cord lines back from the mouth of the tunnel and the front OP bay. These lines would be used for a simple pull signal to get the attention of anyone in the central bay.

All the kit was packed, keeping out only what was immediately needed. The roster was assigned and the first man, Marks, went out the back tunnel for sentry duty. While a meal was being prepared over a spirit stove by Fisher, Bryant and Rockham went forward into the observation bay. There, the two SEALs set up the spotting telescope, laid out their binoculars and M909 night vision goggles, and settled in for the first watch. Ferber had the most envied job—he pulled the first stint in the sleeping bay.

At dawn the next morning, which was long hours before the sun would be showing, the SEALs began their standard OP routine. Sukov established contact over the SATCOM and sent a short message through the KY-57 encryption device. The SATCOM and encryption system condensed even the short message to a microsecond pulse, eliminating any chance of interception or radio direction finding. The message had been previously agreed upon: the team was in position and establishing their watch. There really wasn't anything else to say. The message would be further relayed by the command back in Little Creek to the Navy, and finally back to the *Archerfish* offshore.

The men all wore their first and second line equipment constantly while in the OP. Boots were kept on, after ensuring that they had dried the night before. Even while drying, only one boot at a time was taken off. The general routine in the OP was for the men not on watch to lay up and rest. Whoever was not scheduled for sleeping would sit up in the central bay and make hot drinks for the men on watch. Eat, rest, and watch was the order of the day. And the days were short with the nights very long.

CHAPTER 13

It was the middle of the afternoon on the SEALs fourth day of manning the observation post. Little more than small animals and other wildlife had been seen to break the monotonous duty. And the good weather they had been enjoying was failing fast. Thick gray clouds were moving in.

Morris Island, as the men had taken to calling it, was fifty miles north of the Arctic circle. During the early winter months the sun barely made it over the horizon during midday. Now it was hanging low, and what little light and warmth had been coming from it was blotted out by the clouds.

"Say good-bye to the sun, gentlemen," Sukov said softly to himself. That had been a favorite line of his instructors during first phase at BUD/S. It was his turn to observe the area through the binoculars while Rock-ham rested his eyes. Soon enough the light was going to be gone completely and they would have to rely on the night vision equipment in order to see. But the starlight gear wouldn't work very well under a heavy overcast. It was going to be a dark night.

Sukov suddenly froze in his rhythmic scan of the area. To the south of their position something was moving along the rough road cut through the tundra. The road led up from the beach near the lighthouse on the southwest part of the island. This was new, and it was important.

Without uttering a word, Sukov nudged his Team-mate. As Rockham looked over, Sukov held out his right hand, fist clenched and extended thumb pointing down. This thumbs-down gesture was the SEAL silent field signal for "enemy seen."

Laying aside his M14 rifle, Rock accepted the binoculars from Sukov as the man switched over to the twenty-power spotting scope set up on its compact tri-pod. All their movements were screened by the scrim net that hung down over the opening of the observation bay. Both Sukov and Rock could now make out the full-tracked snow vehicle with the enclosed cabin that was coming up the road toward them.

The two SEALs were as unmoving as the hillside they were next to as the vehicle approached. Now they could recognize it as an MT-L amphibious oversnow vehicle. It had an enclosed cabin over its rear bed and rode on two tracks like a small tank. With a clanking noise, the MT-L came to a stop near the crossroads in front of them.

As Sukov and Rockham continued to watch, two Soviets got out of the cab of the MT-L. The driver was a huge man with a large black beard. To the two SEALs, he looked more like a pirate than a soldier. The hood of the man's parka was thrown back and he moved to the back of the vehicle with a heavy, rolling walk.

The individual who got out on the far side remained almost completely out of sight to the SEALs until he appeared at the back of the vehicle. The second man was taller than the driver, and much slimmer, even in his bulky parka. He also had the hood of his parka thrown back, his head covered with one of the distinctive Russian-style black ushanka sheepskin hats. Even in the dim light, the SEALs could see the gleam of the large gold naval insignia on the brim of the man's hat.

What was interesting was that neither of the men had a rifle. They were wearing field equipment, with the larger of the two men shouldering a full combat harness with ammunition pouches. On the belts of both men there were large pistol holsters. This indicated that they were in some kind of leadership position, as sidearms were almost a badge of rank in the Soviet military.

As the two men stood at the rear of the vehicle, the taller turned and nodded to the heavyset one. The large bearded man turned and pounded on the rear of the vehicle with his fist. Immediately, both doors at the sides of the vehicle opened and men began to get out.

Six men in Russian white, hooded, winter-camouflage uniforms piled out of either side of the vehicle. The men were armed with AKS-74 folding stock assault rifles and were obviously well-trained. Without a word or order that the SEALs could hear, the six soldiers took up concealed positions in the fields on either side of the road.

Now there was a real concern that one of the Russians might move up to the area where the SEALs were concealed. As Sukov continued watching the activities by the road, Rockham moved farther back into the OP to warn the rest of his team.

Carefully moving aside the black burlap screen that separated the observation bay from the rest of the OP, Rockham motioned to Bryant, who was in the central area. Bryant had been preparing to heat some water over the spirit stove, working under the dull light of a red-filtered flashlight, when Rockham motioned to him. Placing a finger over his lips to ensure silence, Rockham held out his right hand and made a talking motion with it by opening and closing his fingers and thumb rapidly. This was the field signal for "come and listen to me." Bryant immediately went over to him and bent forward, turning his head so his right ear was facing the lieutenant.

"We have a vehicle, what looks like two officers, and six enemy riflemen in sight at the crossroads," Rockham whispered. "They have taken up positions on either side of the road. Get everything ready for a bug-out."

Bryant made an OK sign by circling his right thumb

and middle finger. Rockham slipped back past the screen to his observation position, while Bryant went back into the sleeping bay at the rear of the OP. Ferber was on sentry duty, carefully looking past a hanging screen and watching the rear approach. Fisher was taking his turn in one of the sleeping bags. He came instantly awake at Bryant's touch.

In quick whispers Bryant told the two SEALs what the lieutenant had told him. In moments all of the loose gear was packed up and being secured to the Bergen Crusader II rucksacks. The careful discipline the SEALs had maintained regarding trash and their gear had proved its worth. Within two minutes the hide could be abandoned with nothing of importance left behind. All that remained was the minimum equipment in the observation bay and the SATCOM radio. The radio would be the last thing to be broken down and packed if the men had to leave suddenly on a bug-out.

Captain Rostov stood at the side of the road and watched his men spread out and conceal themselves. Even though he had worked with these individuals for years, he cast a critical eye on their camouflage. Master Sergeant Frolik grunted his approval at the movement of the men, and Rostov could not find any fault with their actions either. Now it was time to wait at the crossroads on Morzhovets Island and watch his plans begin to bear fruit.

Within just a few minutes both men could see the gleam of oncoming headlights coming up from the road leading to the southern end of the island.

"They are a bit early, Frolik," Rostov said quietly. "But no matter. Move to the other side of the road and wait. Eliminate the guard only after I've dealt with the driver. And remember, we want this to look like an accident, so no shooting."

The hulking Soviet NCO had pulled a large P6 suppressed pistol from the holster at his belt and was locking the suppressor extension onto the muzzle of the weapon as Captain Rostov spoke. The big man secured the weapon to his belt, the long suppressor now sticking out from the open bottom of the holster. With a simple nod to his commander, Frolik moved over to the far side of the road.

Within a few minutes the approaching truck rolled up close enough to recognize. It was a normal, heavy-duty GAZ-66 truck with its back cargo compartment covered with a canvas tarp stretched over a framework. The same kind of vehicle that could be seen everywhere in the Soviet military. As he walked out into the roadway, Captain Rostov was surrounded with light from the truck's headlights.

The truck wasn't moving very quickly over the rough road, so the Spetsnaz officer was in little danger of being run over. As the truck driver stepped on his brakes, the heavy vehicle groaned to a stop. Rostov quickly walked over to the driver's side of the vehicle and stood next to the door. His parka was open enough that the first rank captain's insignia on his collar could be clearly seen.

"Driver," Rostov commanded. "Step down from your vehicle immediately!"

"Sir?" the driver, an army private, said with a puzzled look as he opened his door.

Roughly pulling the door fully open, Rostov almost caused the young soldier to tumble out of his seat. "I told you to get out!" Rostov demanded.

"But sir," the private said as he quickly climbed down from the truck's cab, "we're on a priority mission."

"What you are," Rostov said with menace heavy in his voice as he loomed over the slight young soldier, "is a prisoner of my Spetsnaz unit."

Hearing the name of the dreaded Soviet Special Forces, whose existence was just a legend to the average soldier, caused the private's face to blanch white.

"B-B-But, sir," the private stuttered, "we are on a mission—"

The rattled private wasn't given the chance to finish his sentence. The lieutenant sitting on the passenger's side of the truck leaned forward and spoke out of the open driver's door.

"I am Lieutenant Markovich, Captain. We are transporting classified materials. Would you please let us continue with our assignment?"

"What your assignment is now, Lieutenant, is to be a prisoner of my unit. We are on a field exercise and you have just been successfully ambushed." With that statement finished, Rostov put a whistle to his lips and blew a shrill blast.

To the astonished eyes of the two soldiers, the six hidden Spetsnaz troops rose up from the ground around the truck like ghostly apparitions. In their white camouflage, the men appeared to have been formed from the snow itself. Only these "snowmen" were each holding a leveled AK-74 rifle.

"Master Sergeant," Rostov shouted over to Frolik, "secure his weapon and check his papers."

As the big sergeant opened the passenger door of the truck, he reached up and grabbed the barrel of the AK-74 rifle secured muzzle-up in a bracket at the side of the cab. Climbing up on the running board of the truck, Frolik looked stolidly at the increasingly nervous officer in front of him. With one hand on the barrel of the rifle and the other on the door frame of the cab, Frolik looked as if he would tear the cab apart at a word.

"This story of yours is so much smoke," Rostov said to the thoroughly frightened private standing in front of him. "If you were transporting classified materials you would have an armed escort with you."

"No, sir," the lieutenant called down from the cab. "This is supposed to have been a secured outpost. The nature of the materials we're carrying dictates that personnel be kept at a minimum. You simply weren't supposed to be here, sir."

"My men and I have been out on this exercise for some time now," Rostov said smoothly. "We have been told nothing about a security shipment. Just what is the nature of the materials you are carrying?"

"They are six containers of classified special munitions, sir," the lieutenant stated. As he looked into the cold, expressionless eyes of Sergeant Frolik, the lieutenant couldn't help but speak the truth. The man was as mesmerized as a bird looking into the hooded eyes of a serpent.

"Six containers," Rostov said. "That's excellent."

"Sir?" the private said, puzzled.

Whatever other question the young soldier might have wondered, it would go forever unanswered. With a sudden move of his right arm, Rostov struck the unsuspecting man in the face with a heel-of-the-hand Sambo strike.

As the stunned soldier reeled back with his eyes rolling back in his head, Rostov grabbed him by his shoulders and spun him around. Pulling the young man into his chest as if embracing him from behind, Rostov reached over the soldier's head and grasped his chin. With a quick pull of his arms, Rostov broke the young soldier's neck, killing him instantly.

The lieutenant never saw the flopping, boneless form of his driver's body fall to the ground like a marionette with the strings cut. But he had seen Rostov strike the young man, and his eyes opened wide with surprise. Even as the lieutenant inhaled to speak, Frolik struck.

With a speed unexpected in such a large man, Frolik grabbed the back of the lieutenant's head with his left hand. With a heave of his shoulders, Frolik drove the man's head down onto the muzzle of the rifle. The wide steel flash hider of the AK-74 crunched through the officer's face. Driving bone splinters in front of it, the steel barrel penetrated deeply into Markovich's brain. Death came so quickly that the lieutenant had no time to even register the pain of the blow.

As Frolik stepped down from the cab of the truck, the lieutenant's body remained bent over and propped up by the barrel of the weapon grotesquely stuck into his skull. Frolik slammed the door on the twitching body and walked in front of the truck to join Rostov on the other side. Picking up the body of the driver from where he lay slumped against his truck, Frolik roughly stuffed the corpse back into the diver's seat.

"Mask and suit up," Rostov ordered his men as they approached the truck. "Then begin transferring the munitions cases from this vehicle to ours."

All of the Spetsnaz began pulling L-1 protective CBR suits from the rectangular satchels they had hanging at their sides. The suits were of butyl-rubber-covered cotton cloth and were large enough to fit over the men's bulky uniforms. They consisted of long trousers with overboots and suspenders attached, a jacket with an attached hood, gloves, and a second cap that completely covered the individual's head and neck, with only an opening for his face.

The men pulled helmetlike ShM-1 protective masks over their heads and faces before donning the L-1 coveralls. The masks had two round eyepieces that combined with the long, snoutlike corrugated rubber breathing tube to give the wearers an unhuman appearance. Suited up in the protective gear, the Spetsnaz resembled great, man-shaped insects.

After Frolik had donned his own protective gear, he climbed back up next to the cab of the truck. Grabbing the head of the dead driver with his right hand, Frolik smashed the face of the unfeeling corpse into the steering wheel. Bones crunched and blood sprayed from the dead man's flesh. Any rough postmortem examination now would appear to show that the driver had died from a broken neck received in an accident.

The Spetsnaz troopers worked at removing six metal cases from the back of the truck. The metal boxes were the shape of small cubes, almost two feet on a side. Made of stamped sheet aluminum, the dark green painted cases had no identifying letters or numbers. The only markings on them were the interlocking open circles of the international biohazard symbol. The spiderlike symbol stood out in stark red on the sides and tops of the simple metal cases.

As the rest of the men moved five of the cases to the rear of the MT-L, Master Sergeant Boris Zabotin took the last case to the side of the road. Removing the lid of the case, Zabotin picked up the steel sphere nestled inside, surrounded by protective foam. The sphere was a bright, shining steel ball about ten inches in diameter. The silver surface of the sphere was broken by a single one-inch hole, sealed with a threaded plastic plug.

The shipping plug came out easily as Zabotin unscrewed it. Placing the sphere back into its case, Zabotin then turned the ball so the open hole was facing straight up. The hole was the fuze well for the munition. Normally, a special barometric fuze would be used on a war shot, or a command-detonated fuze for a test. Either of these would simply screw into the threaded well. But Zabotin had something different in mind for this munition.

Reaching into a pouch at his waist, he removed a tan-colored paper-wrapped cylinder a little over an inch in diameter and almost three inches long. Putting the cylinder down on the open case, he pulled a silver tube about the size of a thick pen from a protective case in his shirt pocket. Carefully inserting the detonator capsule of the VZD-3M delay fuze into the seventy-five-gram cylinder of TNT, Zabotin finished preparing his explosive charge. The paper-wrapped cylinder of explosive slipped inside the fuze well of the sphere, where it rested up against the larger explosive burster charge at the center of the munition. Removing the safety pin of the fuze would now begin the mechanical delay.

To minimize problems with chemical or electrical delay systems in the cold of the Arctic, Zabotin had deliberately chosen to use the VZD-3M fuze. When the safety pin of the fuze was removed, it released a spring-loaded plunger that pulled a wire through a lead strip. When the strip was cut through, the plunger was released and it drove into a percussion cap, setting off the explosive chain.

For this mission, Zabotin had prepared his fuzes with a very short delay strip. Fifteen minutes after the safety pin was removed, the detonator would fire. The explosion of the small TNT charge would detonate the burster of the munition, spreading the anthrax spore filler over a wide area.

While Zabotin had been preparing his deadly package, Frolik had been dealing with the truck. With all of the important packages removed from the back, Frolik shoved over the body of the driver and climbed up into the cab. Starting the engine, he backed the truck up in the direction from which it had come. Gunning the engine, Frolik put the truck into gear. With a metallic grinding of the gears, the big truck started to move forward, picking up speed. As the truck approached the turn at the crossroads, Frolik jumped from the cab.

As he hit the ground and rolled to a stop, the truck sped off the road, dug its wheels into the frozen tundra, and flipped over on its side. The powerful engine roared, sputtered, and died. In the sudden silence, all that could be heard was the sighing of the wind and the squeaking of a tire as it rotated on the axle.

The tailgate on the truck had flown open on impact. The remaining supplies and crates, which hadn't been removed by the Spetsnaz, spilled out and scattered in the snow. Two of the men took several containers out of the back of the MT-L and carried the obviously heavy boxes over to where the truck lay. Reaching into the boxes, the two men started tossing the contents about the crash site.

The materials tossed about were mostly bent and twisted pieces of green-painted aluminum. There were also curved fragments of steel spheres. To anyone coming onto the site, it would look as if the truck crashed and there was a catastrophic detonation of the munitions carried in the cargo compartment. And anyone who knew what the cargo had been would be much less likely to give the area a close inspection.

Taking his rigged sphere and its carrying container over to the truck, Zabotin placed it near the back of the

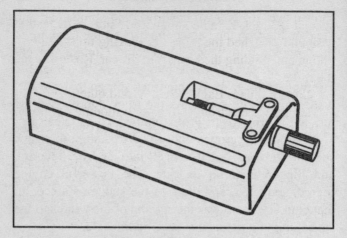

MPM Limpet with Fuze

vehicle, among the scattered debris. Walking to where the underside of the truck lay exposed, Zabotin reached into another of the pouches he carried and withdrew two black plastic boxes.

The boxes were plastic-cased MPM limpet mines, used by the Spetsnaz for all type of general demolitions and sabotage. They were both about the size of an almost two-inch-thick paperback book, and each held almost three-quarters of a pound of TNT. Leaning over the underside of the truck, Zabotin placed one of the limpet mines against each of the fuel tanks. Magnets on the bottom of the limpet mines held them securely to the steel tanks.

"Ready, sir," Zabotin called over to Rostov.

Captain Rostov extended the Kulikov antenna on the

special Severok-K radio slung at his side in its leather case and switched the radio on. Picking up the microphone and holding the headset to his ear, Rostov keyed the mike.

"Condor, this is Eagle," Rostov said quietly.

The unique electronic encryption module on the radio would make certain that anyone who overheard the transmission would receive only static. But Rostov had not reached his rank without being careful. On the KGB Nikitich-class icebreaker *Volga,* Rostov's senior lieutenant, Ivan Tsinev, had been waiting for his commander's signal. The *Volga* was only a short distance from the Morzhovskiy lighthouse on the southwestern shore of the island.

"Eagle, this is Condor," Tsinev answered.

Tsinev's voice coming out of the earphone in Rostov's hand was made mechanical and unhuman-sounding by the encryption circuits of the Severok-K. But this was something every man in the Spetsnaz unit was well used to. "Condor, prepare the nest," Rostov continued. "Eagle is returning with her eggs."

"Eagle, this is Condor. Will comply." And Tsinev clicked off.

"Boris," Rostov called out, "are your charges prepared?"

"Yes, Captain," Zabotin answered. "There are two charges on the fuel tanks. The weapon will be detonated first and then the truck will fire. The area will be thoroughly contaminated and the fire will destroy what's left."

"Excellent, arm your charges." Rostov turned to his

men and shouted, "Everyone into the vehicle."

As the rest of the men climbed aboard the MT-L, Zabotin walked over and first pulled the pin on the sphere and then the two limpet mines on the truck. The spring-loaded plungers within the VZD-3M fuzes began cutting slowly through the lead safety strips. Once started, there was no way to stop the delay.

With the last part of his job completed, Zabotin also climbed aboard the snow vehicle. With one last look around the site, Rostov climbed back into the passenger seat. With a clatter of its tracks, the MT-L moved out on the southwest road, toward the shore some four winding kilometers away.

As he settled back into his position at the observation slit, Rockham picked up the binoculars and focused on the scene at the crossroads. Very little had changed. The two Soviets were still standing at the rear of their vehicle, and the rest of the riflemen had disappeared into the snow and brush on either side of the road.

The two men just stood there at the side of the road, with the taller one leaning over to speak to the bearded man at his side. Both of them appeared to be waiting for something. It was obvious to Sukov and Rockham that the soldiers were not searching for the SEALs or scouring the area for something else. Instead, as the Soviets fanned out and concealed themselves, it looked more like an ambush setup to the professional eyes of the two SEALs.

If the Soviets were setting up a security post or roadblock, it was certainly an odd-looking one. Only two men remained on the road, and the rest were setting up what could only be interlocking fields of fire on either side. Sukov and Rockham could only watch and make note of the actions going on not more than several hundred yards in front of them. They were both certain that the observation post was secure. In the dim light of the low Arctic sun, it would be almost impossible to spot the observation post even with night vision equipment.

As the military truck arrived on the scene, it appeared to the two SEALs that the Soviets had indeed set up some kind of roadblock. The two men standing near the crossroads were talking quietly, with the head of the taller bent down to speak to the bearded one. A moment after the conversation was over the SEALs had their first clue as to just who the troops were.

"Jesus!" Rockham exclaimed in a whisper. "John, do you see the weapon the big guy just pulled out?"

"Looks like some kind of suppressed pistol, Rock," Sukov answered in a soft whisper.

"That's a P6, a silenced Makarov," Rockham said. "I think they both have them. Those aren't regular troops. Those are Spetsnaz!"

Both SEALs knew that the Soviet Spetsnaz special troops were very close to being their opposite number on the other side. It also meant that something important was going on. Spetsnaz were not troops that would be used for any kind of guard duty. These guys had to be here for a reason.

"Shit!" Sukov exclaimed. "Now what?"

"Just keep watching," Rockham said. "But break out

the camera and start snapping pictures. They're going to want a record of this back in the States."

Leaning away from his position at the spotting scope, Sukov picked up the 35mm camera the SEALs had brought with them to record intelligence information. The long telephoto lens and high speed back and white film in the camera was intended to take good pictures at a distance, even in the dim Arctic light.

Propping the camera's lens against the spotting scope's tripod, Sukov focused in on the two men in the road. With a soft click of the shutter, he began to take pictures.

The approaching truck had entered the area immediately in front of the SEALs OP. The taller of the two Spetsnaz had waved the truck to a stop and was now talking to the driver. As the driver got down from the cab, they could see that the other Spetsnaz had climbed up to the passenger door and opened it. But with the cab of the truck blocking their view, the SEALs couldn't see any details of what was going on at the passenger door.

While the SEALs looked on in astonishment, Rostov first struck and then killed the driver.

"Motherfucker!" Sukov exclaimed as he continued to snap pictures.

The entire lethal scenario played itself out in full view of the two attentive SEALs. The Soviets went through the motions Rostov had planned out and choreographed for them, without ever knowing that their every move was being witnessed and photographed.

Then the SEALs received another surprise, as all of

the Spetsnaz began putting on protective gear.

Just what the hell is going on? Rockham wondered. Was this part of the weapons test? Leaning over to Sukov, he whispered, "Whatever is in that truck, it's nasty. And I think this bunch is stealing the cargo. Try and get pictures of what they take out of the back."

Sukov nodded and continued with his pictures. Several times during the unloading of the truck, he got good shots of the boxes the men were handling. Another picture showed all of the boxes lined up at the side of the road. Then another puzzling moment came up as the SEALs watched the accident being staged.

The flipping of the truck left the SEALs almost certain that what they were witnessing was a hijack of military cargo. There was no other reason they could think of to make the site look like a simple road accident.

Sukov paid particular attention when Zabotin prepared the charge in the sphere. His own experience as a SEAL and an EOD technician allowed him to immediately recognize the sure actions of a competent demolitionist.

"Rock," Sukov whispered. "Do you see that silver ball that one Russian is playing with?"

"Yes," Rockham answered. "It looks like he's rigging a charge of some kind."

"I think that ball is one of the weapons Kondrachev described during that debriefing. These guys are stealing the damned things!"

"And that one guy is going to set one off and contaminate the area," Rockham said as he completed Sukov's thought.

"Rock," Sukov said is a quiet but intense whisper, "if we can recover that weapon—"

"Roger that, John," Rockham said. "As soon as these guys clear the area, I want us to make a try for that weapon. Do you think you can disarm it?"

"It shouldn't be a problem, Skipper," Sukov said confidently, "if we get to it fast enough. Some of these Soviet fuzes have a minimum delay of only five minutes, maybe a bit longer in this cold. And I didn't see him doing anything fancy enough to account for boobytrapping that thing."

"So we have to be ready to move as soon as they're gone," Rockham said. "Suit up now and tell the rest of the guys to have their masks handy."

Handing Rockham the camera, Sukov moved back through the cloth screen and out of the observation bay. All of the Team's bulky equipment was in the central area of the OP. Each of the SEALs wore their web gear at all times while they were operating. Even while a man was sleeping, basic survival and signaling equipment remained in his pockets. Weapons were always within close reach.

The central area of the OP was where the rucksacks were kept. Going to his ruck, Sukov lifted up the cover that held an AN-M14 TH3 thermate grenade. If the SATCOM equipment, and especially the KY-57 encryption set, had to be destroyed, every man in the squad knew they only had to pull the pin on that one grenade. When the thermate in the grenade burned for almost a full minute at 3,000 degrees, the electronic materials would quickly become just so much slag.

Moving aside the radio equipment, Sukov dug down to his CBR gear. Among the materials the SEALs had brought with them on the mission was gear from both their platoon's load-out and the *Archerfish*'s stores. Each SEAL had with him a complete CBR suit of treated cloth trousers and hooded smock as well as rubber overboots and rubber gloves. For breathing protection, they had MCU-2/P protective masks.

The new style protective masks had a single large lens for viewing that also allowed the use of binoculars or gun sights while the mask was worn. Special diaphragms called voicemitters made speech by an MCU-2/P wearer understandable by the people around him. And most important of all, the mask not only protected the wearer from chemical agents, it also filtered out known biological agents.

As Sukov suited up, Bryant and Fisher helped him in the cramped confines of the OP. Getting into his gear, Sukov gave his Teammates a quick rundown on what had been seen and what they suspected. Then, with his suit on and protective mask in hand, he went back up to the observation bay.

Taking the camera back from Rockham, Sukov settled in to observe. Now the officer went back to the central area to get on his own CBR gear and brief the rest of the squad.

In a quick but concise manner, Rockham told the other members of his team just what they had seen. It appeared that the squad might have a chance to grab one of the complete biological weapon delivery munitions. This was an opportunity that had to be taken advantage of immediately, and Sukov and Rockham were going to move on it.

The level of activity in front of the OP had ruined any value the position might have for the SEALs. Someone was going to miss the truck that had been attacked. When they showed up, Rockham intended the SEALs to be long gone. His orders were that all of the gear was to be packed up, including the radio antenna. The OP was to be abandoned almost immediately.

Mike Ferber had moved back into the observation post from his sentry position at the rear entrance. At Rockham's order, Ferber raised his hand and gave the OK signal with his thumb and forefinger. Then the men began methodically going through their routine to prepare to leave the area. And each man also made certain that his own mask and CBR gear was at the top of his pack and immediately available.

As Rockham went back into the observation bay, Sukov leaned over and whispered to him, "The man with the demolitions placed something on the bottom of the truck. He just armed the fuze on the sphere and then fiddled with the truck. Everyone is on that track now."

Just as he completed his report, the MT-L fired up and left the area. As he watched the track go, Rockham made an immediate decision to go down to the "accident" site. Returning to the central area of the OP, the two SEALs took the observation equipment and camera with them. As Sukov packed the last of their gear and broke down the radio antenna, Rockham briefed the other members of his team.

"This is it," he said softly, "we're bugging out. If

there's going to be a weapons test, we're not going to be here to see it. Everyone take their gear and get on your skis. Move out to the rendezvous point on the western ridgeline. Sukov and I will check the truck. It looks like someone placed a few charges down there, so I don't want anyone coming after us. Keep your masks handy and try to stay upwind."

Although the instructions seemed sparse, all of these men had worked and trained closely and intently with each other. Each man knew what he had to do. And what was even more important, each SEAL knew instinctively what his Teammates would do. If they were separated, they would all gather at the previously determined rendezvous point. At that moment, time was of the essence.

Rockham shouldered his rucksack and moved out of the observation point. Sukov was tracking along right behind his Team leader. Both men worked their way around the back of the ridge that the OP shouldered up against and down toward the crossroads. Though it seemed like an eternity, only a few minutes had passed since the Spetsnaz had left the area.

Even though there didn't appear to be anyone to observe them, the two SEALs made use of every bit of available cover as they moved down to the truck. And within just a few minutes of the first SEALs leaving the OP, the rest of the group abandoned the position. Since the rest of the squad wasn't wearing CBR suits, and especially the clumsy overboots, they strapped their skis on and made very good time.

As Rockham and Sukov began approaching the

truck, they moved even more carefully. One man would cover the other as he moved forward a few dozen yards. Then that man would stop and cover with his weapon as the first man caught up and passed him. Through this leapfrogging technique the two SEALs remained able to respond to a threat with immediate fire. Very quickly they were at the side of the truck.

Slinging his M14, Sukov bent down and examined the sphere resting in its open case. Rockham remained on alert, keeping an eye on the surrounding area while Sukov worked. With the light of a red-lens penlight, Sukov looked over all sides of the sphere and the box it rested in and could see no sign of a boobytrap. The sphere was snug in the foam rubber padding, and there were no marks or holes where a safety mechanism could have been removed. What was obvious was the fuze body sticking up from the open fuze well.

Sukov recognized the fuze body as the standard Soviet VZD-3M model. The only problem was that he had no way of telling what delay was in the fuze. And there was no way to stop the fuze from functioning.

Carefully reaching into the container, he gently pulled the fuze and explosive charge from the sphere. After only a momentary resistance, the metal fuze came out of the sphere, drawing the cylinder of TNT with it. That moment's resistance was enough to make Sukov feel his heart had skipped a beat. Even though he was almost certain the Russian hadn't been able to boobytrap the device, such assumptions had killed many an EOD technician over the years. It was confidence based on knowledge, coupled with extreme care, that allowed Sukov to safely disarm the sphere.

Drawing the detonator from the explosive charge was simply a matter of unscrewing the fuze and pulling it out. As the slim metal capsule of the MD-2 percussion detonator slipped out of the explosive charge, Sukov let out a breath he hadn't realized he'd been holding. Placing the TNT and the fuze down on the ground with a safe distance between them, Sukov then turned to the metal sphere.

Even in the cold arctic air, Sukov was sweating inside his CBR suit. Here was the thing they had come so far to get. Such a deadly device, and in so innocuous a form. The metal sphere had no projections or other holes except for a slotted screw head almost one inch across. That must be the filler plug for the agent, Sukov thought. Other than that, there was the open fuze well and polished metal. Seeing the plastic shipping plug for the fuze well sitting in the case in front of him, Sukov picked it up and gently screwed it back into the sphere.

"Skipper," Sukov quietly called out to Rockham.

Rockham turned and knelt down at Sukov's side. "Well?" he asked intently. "What do you think?"

"Rock," Sukov answered, "this thing fits the description Kondrachev gave us exactly. And look at the markings on the shipping can. There's no ID or lot numbers, but that biohazard symbol says everything we have to know. This is it."

"Secure it and let's get on our way," Rockham ordered.

With Rockham's help, Sukov removed his rucksack and opened it on the ground next to the shipping case.

An empty waterproof bag that had been used to hold rations was big enough to hold the sphere and still be sealed. Once the sphere was sealed in, a quick wrap with a poncho padded it and sealed it further. Then the whole package was stuffed down into the rucksack.

As Sukov stood and slung his ruck, Rockham said, "I'm going to go over and check the bodies in the truck for papers."

"Just a second, Skipper," Sukov said. "There was something that Russian did to the underside of the truck. I should check it out first."

"Okay," Rockham agreed, "but make it fast."

Sukov walked around the back of the truck and immediately saw what had been done. The two MPM limpet mines stood out plainly, even in the failing light. And each of them had the same fuze that Sukov had just pulled out of the sphere.

"Charges, sir!" Sukov said. "Attached to the fuel tanks."

Just as Rockham started to respond, the lead delay strip in the fuze on the ground was cut through. Without the lead strip to hold it back, the striker was driven forward by a spring, sending the firing pin at its tip into a percussion cap. The cap fired, setting off the detonator with a loud bang. The detonator only held a few grams of explosive, but the bang was enough to make both SEALs jump. With a shocked realization of what was about to happen, Sukov looked at the two limpet mines for just a moment and then shouted, *"Run!"*

Both SEALs were clumsy in their CBR suits and protective masks. But the realization that the mines could go off at any second compelled the men to run even in the suits and snow. Getting on the road, they quickly ran from the truck. It wasn't more than a few moments later that the limpet mines fired. The blast of over a pound and a quarter of TNT ripped open the almost full fuel tanks of the trucks, spreading the contents about and igniting them.

The flaming gasoline soaked into everything around the site of the accident. And the over fifty gallons of gasoline in the two tanks were going to burn for a long time. The fire would destroy much of the evidence, and the burned and twisted bits of metal left over would appear to be the spheres—detonated by the fire. With the apparent contamination of the entire site, any examination of the truck or bodies would probably be quick and rough. The simplicity of the Spetsnaz plan was now obvious to the two SEALs.

CHAPTER 14

As the MT-L approached the shoreline it slowed to a stop. Just a short distance away, Rostov and Frolik could see the bulk of the KGB icebreaker *Volga* waiting for them. The ship had nosed in to the shoreline, cracking its way through the relatively thin sea ice. A gangplank was let down over the side of the ship, giving the men on the ground easy access to her deck. Senior Lieutenant Ivan Tsinev was on the deck of the ship, waving to his comrades on the shore.

Quickly, the containers were taken from the cargo compartment of the MT-L and moved aboard ship. As he watched his men working, Rostov felt a grim satisfaction that his plan had gone so well. There were still several complicated stages yet to go, but the special munitions were under his control now and that's what mattered the most.

As he stood on the shoreline, the delay ran out on the limpet mines back on the truck. Even though the crossroads were almost two and a half miles behind them, Rostov recognized the sounds of the explosions. As Zabotin looked up at the officer he considered the greatest leader he had ever met, the Russian expected a smile or some sign of pleasure. Instead he saw a frown crease his leader's face, a frown that deepened quickly.

Captain Lieutenant Rutil also saw the look on Rostov's face. Moving over to where Rostov was standing, Rutil asked, "Sir, what is it?"

"Did you hear a second explosion?" Rostov asked.

"No," Rutil answered. "Just the fuel tanks going up. But this far away, we were probably lucky to hear even that."

"We have not gotten this far by depending on luck," Rostov said icily. "I only heard the one explosion. You will take the vehicle and four of the men and go check. I do not wish to remain here any longer than necessary. We will take the ship out and meet you off the northern end of the island. The vehicle is not anything we have to worry about. It can only be connected to this fool Belik. You may abandon it."

With a quick salute and a sharp, "Yes sir!" Rutil acknowledged the order. Discipline was hard in the Soviet forces, and hardest in the Spetsnaz. There was no thought of argument with Rostov in Rutil's mind. Calling for Frolik and the two youngest reconnaissance sergeants, Petr Adamenko and Viktor Nosenko, Rutil ordered his small unit into the MT-L and back along the road they had just traveled.

The heavy CBR suits worn by Rockham and Sukov caused the men to start to sweat heavily in spite of their cold surroundings. As they approached the rendezvous area where they would meet the rest of the squad, both men were reaching a point of real danger. In their sweat-soaked uniforms, the cold could do more damage to them than any exposure they might receive. And the clumsy suits made travel in the snow even harder and slower than normal. Rockham made the decision to remove the CBR gear once they reached the rest of their Team.

The situation was a calculated risk, but returning with the bioweapon had the highest priority. And they couldn't do that if they froze solid before ever getting to the *Archerfish*.

The two heavily encumbered SEALs struggled through the snow and approached the rendezvous point. The rest of the squad should have been on site for some time and waiting for them. But there was no sign of the other SEALs as Rockham and Sukov approached the windswept treeline. From the stunted bushes and scrub trees, a voice spoke quietly in the gloom.

"Who?" it said.

"Rockham," Rock said clearly, in spite of his protective mask.

"Sukov," John said in turn.

As if they were ghosts forming up from the darkness, the four SEALs waiting in concealment showed themselves. Pointing first at Ryan Marks and then Mike Bryant, Mike Ferber swept his arm out in a wide arc to either side of the SEALs position. Marks and Bryant immediately moved out to the indicated sides to maintain a secure perimeter. Only after the area was secured did Ferber move to approach his platoon leader.

"Everything okay, Skipper?" Ferber said softly, looking pointedly at the full CBR equipment both men were still wearing.

Peeling off his rubber gloves, Rockham pushed his hood back and removed his protective mask. Running his fingers through his short-cut sandy hair with obvious pleasure, Rockham said with relief in his voice, "No problem, Mike. We recovered what we think is one of the weapons. Sukov has it sealed up in his ruck. We just haven't had the chance to peel out of these suits yet. We can't be certain until it gets back to the right people, but this thing meets all the descriptions we have of the biological device that was supposed to be tested here. This is a real hot piece of intel we have to get back with intact."

Having seen his lieutenant unmask, Sukov did the same. Fisher stepped up to Sukov and helped him take off his rucksack and start to remove his CBR gear. Ferber did the same with Rockham. Both SEALs packed the CBR suits and masks back into their rucksacks.

As he packed away his suit, Rockham looked up at

Ferber and said with a wide grin, "That was a pretty miserable owl impression there, Mike."

"Well, it's not like we were expecting anyone else to wander along out here," Ferber joked back.

"Remain upwind and approach the area slowly," Rutil ordered over the roar of the MT-L's engine.

Without saying a word, the uncommunicative Frolik at the controls of the vehicle turned it off the road and into the terrain to the west of the crossroads. The road was so poor that the difference between riding across it and moving cross-country was unnoticeable at first. The blowing wind wasn't heavy, just gusting occasionally. But it was more than enough to move any loose snow. Using the drifting snow as a guide, Frolik moved upwind. The vehicle soon crested a small rise overlooking the area of the truck.

The fires had mostly burned out. But what flames there still were gave enough light to see reasonably well. Outside of the flickering flames and gusts of snow, there was no movement over the burned-out and blackened snow surrounding the truck.

"Stop just past the crest of the rise," Rutil ordered.

As the tracked vehicle rattled to a stop, Rutil reached up and unlatched the hatch over his head. Swinging the round metal hatch in the roof up and back, Rutil stood on the seat so the upper part of his body stuck out the top of the MT-L.

Standing up, the Spetsnaz officer could see the entire area around the truck, just a few hundred meters away. With the wind at his back, Rutil was not immediately worried about any possible contamination, so he refrained from putting on his ShM-1 protective mask. While the wind blew sharp-edged crystals of snow against the back of his neck, Rutil lifted a pair of BPO 7×30mm binoculars to his eyes.

As the scene in front of him came into focus, the Spetsnaz officer scanned the wreckage. What he suddenly saw there made him pause in astonishment.

Reaching back down in the cab, up toward the windscreen, Rutil turned on the outside spotlight. Mounted between the two flat front windscreens, the spotlight threw a brilliant white beam out over the snow. Blowing snowflakes sparkled in the light as Rutil moved the handle inside the vehicle and adjusted the aim of the spotlight. Sweeping the beam across the ruined tundra, Rutil stopped as he centered on the burned remains of an open shipping box.

"Chort vozmi!" Rutil cursed. Devil take it! He could see that the last open case for the special munitions was standing intact. It was obvious that the weapon it had held never detonated. And there was no sign of the metal sphere anywhere. But what could be seen in the brilliant spotlight beam concerned Rutil even more than the unexploded weapon.

Two sets of what looked like very large footprints showed up in the spotlight beam. The prints led away from the burned area, first spaced far apart and then closer together. It was as if two people had run away from the area and then slowed down to a more normal walk.

Through the binoculars, the prints looked too large

to be human and too deep and small to be from snow-shoes. But if men's feet had made these prints, the boots they were wearing must have been huge. It looked as if at least two people had found the munition and made off with it. Given that Morzhovets Island was a military site now, there were no civilians on it at all. The tracks could have been from a lost pair of hunters, or an equally lost military patrol.

Reaching down into the cab, Rutil pulled up his Severok-K radio. Placing the radio on the hull next to the hatch, Rutil extended the Kulikov antenna and switched the set on. Holding the headset to his right ear, he picked up the microphone and began to send.

"Eagle, this is Hawk," Rutil said.

"Hawk, this is Eagle," came Rostov's electronically distorted voice almost immediately. "Go ahead."

"Eagle, foxes have entered the farmyard. The egg is missing," Rutil said into his mike. "I repeat, foxes have entered the farmyard. The egg is missing."

Even with the distortion from the encryption circuitry, the menace and rage in Rostov's voice came clearly over the radio. "Hawk, this is Eagle. Foxhunt. I repeat, foxhunt. Catch them and bring me the pelts."

It was obvious to Rutil that Rostov wanted whoever they had discovered to be captured and interrogated. It would be the only sure way of learning just who it was they were chasing. It was most important to learn what they might have seen, and who they told it to.

"Understood, Eagle, Hawk out," and Rutil turned off his radio with a click.

Packing away the small special radio set, Rutil sat

back down in the cab of the MT-L. Reaching up, he pulled shut the hatch and sealed it.

"Move over to that set of tracks over there," he ordered Frolik. Moving the spotlight, Rutil stabbed the beam accusingly at the marks in the snow.

In his usual silent, almost sullen manner, Frolik drove the MT-L to where his lieutenant directed. Close up and brightly illuminated with the spotlight, the tracks could be seen clearly. The marks were still very fresh. The sharp edges of each footprint had yet to be rounded over by the blowing snow. Whoever had made the tracks was probably still very close by. Close enough to have maybe heard the MT-L moving in.

The wind was blowing in from the west, so that would help mask their engine and truck noise a bit. But speed was the weapon the Spetsnaz had to use now.

"Follow those tracks," Rutil ordered, and he pointed the way with the spotlight.

★ ★ ★
CHAPTER 15
★ ★ ★

"Sukov," Rockham called out. "Set up the radio and try to establish contact. Tell them we're extracting and to notify the sub. I expect us to make rendezvous with her in three hours."

Pulling up his rucksack, Sukov took out the folding, umbrellalike antenna and set it up in the snow. Aligning the antenna according to his compass, within a few minutes the SEAL had made contact with an orbiting satellite high over the southern horizon. With the AN/URC-110 SATCOM radio and KY-57 encryption device, he soon had made secure contact with SPECWARGRU-2 back at Little Creek, over 9,000 miles away.

Sending the short message, Sukov received acknowledgment that it had been received and understood. Command back at Little Creek would see to it that the proper communications went out by ELF transmitter to the *Archerfish*, sitting on the bottom some miles away.

Quickly refolding the antenna and packing up the gear, Sukov prepared to move out. The weapon was still sealed in its plastic cocoon in his rucksack next to the radio equipment. The deadly metal sphere looked like little more than a big wad of dirty clothes stuffed in a camper's backpack. And Sukov looked at it as though putting it back on would have the Angel of Death himself riding on his shoulders. Shaking off the macabre thought, he returned to the situation at hand.

Bryant had been watching the eastern perimeter and was the first to spot the oncoming lights. Drawing Mike Ferber's attention with a low, soft whistle, Bryant pointed off to the horizon.

"Rock," Ferber said urgently. "Look."

Both men could now see the oncoming light. As the source of the white glow wobbled and bounced, it could be easily seen that whatever it was, it was attached to a vehicle moving over the snow.

"Gear up and move out," Rockham ordered. "Guards in on me."

All of the men, Rockham and Sukov included now, could use their skis. This would let them make the best time possible. But the ground that vehicle was crossing was rough. Whatever was coming, it had to be some kind of snow machine. Rockham knew it could even be the tracked vehicle the SEALs had watched the Spetsnaz use.

There was at least three kilometers of rough snow the SEALs had to cover before they reached the cache. Even then, they would need a few minutes to dig up the gear and prepare for the dive. Once they were in the water, they knew instinctively that they would be safe. It was the rule of the Teams that had held true since the earliest days of the UDT during WWII: once you got into the water, you could be safe.

But in a race between men on cross-country skis and an oversnow vehicle, the smart money would bet on the vehicle.

Mike Ferber had called Ryan Marks over to him. As both men spoke in quiet whispers, Rockham strapped on the skis that the squad had brought with them from the OP. Standing up, he could see that Ferber and Marks had yet to put their skis on.

"What the hell are you doing, Ferber?" Rockham said. "Get your gear on."

"It will just get in the way for the moment, Skipper," Ferber said quietly.

"What in the hell are you talking about?" Rockham said. But even as he spoke, understanding was coming to him.

"You have to stay with the cargo, sir," Ferber explained patiently. "That vehicle is going to catch up with us long before we can reach the cache. Marks and I are just going to slow them up a little bit."

"Bullshit, Ferber," Sukov said vehemently. "We all go home. No one gets left behind."

"There's no time to argue," Ferber said, with the tone of a BUD/S instructor. "If you don't go now, none of us will. Get that goddamned thing back to the sub. We'll lead them off north and head out to sea on the ice. The sub can pick us up later."

All of the men knew that even in the Teams, the mission came first. The weapon they had all risked so much to get had to make it back. There wasn't anything to be said, or any time to say it in.

"It's a hard decision, sir," Ferber said quietly. "But that's why they give you the big bucks."

The logic was inescapable. And there was no time for any argument, or the sacrifice being offered by his two men would be in vain. As Rockham ordered his men away, Ferber was checking over his weapon. The breech closed on his shotgun with a snap and Ferber looked up into the eyes of his officer. The steady glance and refusal to look away spoke more than any words ever could have. Rockham knew that ordering this man away would be a useless argument. Next to him, Marks was quickly checking over his M14. The huge black man held the rifle like a light toy. And he was absolutely deadly with it.

"Move out," Rockham ordered. "Bryant, you have point. Mr. Fisher, rear security."

The squad moved out into the dark.

"Let's go, Ryan," Mike said quietly a moment later.

"Aye sir," Marks replied with a tight smile.

To pull the Spetsnaz off the trail and give their Teammates time to escape, Ferber and Marks would stage a small ambush. As the rest of the Team left, Ferber pointed to where he wanted to circle around and cover their earlier line of march. Marks nodded his agreement, and the two men moved back along their own trail.

The two SEALs moved off to the side, going at a right angle to the patrol's direction of march. After moving a few hundred feet, they began backtracking, moving parallel to the trail, in the direction they had originally come from. Marks remained close to Ferber's side as the two approached a small pile of glacial boulders sticking up from the tundra. Settling in behind the cover of the rocks, the two SEALs watched the trail.

They knew they didn't have the firepower for a protracted fight. Instead, they would have to do a fast series of hit and runs, stinging the pursuing Soviets into chasing them and giving the rest of their Team time to get to the gear cache, suit up, and escape.

With Ferber acting as his spotter and covering close in with his shotgun, Marks could snipe at the Soviets with his M14. He had trained for years for just such an occasion, and every round would find a target. As the two men settled in under cover, they planned out several different avenues of escape from their position.

"Well, this was a real good idea," Marks said quietly as he pulled the butt of his rifle tighter in to his shoulder.

"Join the Navy and see the world," Ferber said in a breathless whisper.

The Spetsnaz patrol could be clearly heard coming up the squad's trail. The Soviet's tracked vehicle moved easily through the snow but made a great deal of noise. To follow the faint tracks of the SEALs, the vehicle had to move fairly slowly, shining its lights on the snow in front of it.

Now that they could clearly see the vehicle that was approaching, Ferber had an idea. Lacking antitank weapons, they couldn't simply blast the track to pieces. But the snow machines were lightly armored at best. They had to be kept light to keep from sinking in the snow.

Ferber pulled an M67 fragmentation grenade from his harness and held it up for Marks to see. Nodding his understanding, Marks set his M14 to the side. Then he pulled out his own grenade and prepared to throw.

The paper adhesive tape the SEALs had slipped through the grenade's pull rings, to secure them to the fuze and prevent rattling, easily tore away. The metal safety clip underneath the pull ring was removed with a push of the thumb, and all that kept the grenades from arming was their pull rings and safety levers.

As the tracked vehicle approached, the SEALs could see it clearly in the gloom. And the glare of the headlights would prevent anyone inside the vehicle from seeing them until it was too late. Watching the Russians approach, Ferber pulled the pin from the grenade in his right hand. Marks armed his grenade with the same motion.

Ferber waited until the track was moving right in front of where they crouched. Releasing the safety lever made a sharp metallic ring as it snapped away from the fuze, a noise drowned out by the engine and track sounds of the Spetsnaz vehicle.

The two tennis-ball-sized dark green spheres arced through the air toward the track, thrown by strong arms that had spent childhood years on the baseball field. Smacking into the left side of the vehicle, both grenades impacted next to the track. Frolik snapped his head around at the muffled clanks of the two grenades hitting. But before the sound fully registered, the grenades detonated, bursting into orange-white blossoms of fire and steel.

The 6.5 ounces of Composition B explosive in each of the grenades was powerful enough to shatter the steel bodies into hundreds of fragments, each traveling thousands of feet per second. Normally lethal within a fifteen-meter radius of the point of explosion, neither of the SEALs' grenades managed to reach any of the men inside the MT-L. But Marks's lucky throw had gone into the track, striking the hull between two road wheels. One road wheel crunched down on the grenade, wedging it down into the track before it detonated.

The blast of the grenade tore the track and bent the wheel. Before Frolik could stop the vehicle from moving, the powerful engine had ripped the damaged track into two pieces.

The Spetsnaz squad immediately prepared to abandon the vehicle and return fire from what they thought was a full ambush. But instead of trying to fight it out, the two SEALs were already up and moving away before the Spetsnaz could react.

Piling out of the vehicle and taking up positions in the snow, the Spetsnaz quickly formed a perimeter. The crippled vehicle would do little good to them now. Looking back to where the grenades had first exploded, Rutil could see the direction they must have come from. Moving forward, he led the way, with his men quickly falling in behind him.

Covering each other as they moved forward in alternating quick rushes, the Spetsnaz held their fire as they moved ahead. Within moments the spot behind the rocks where the two men had crouched in the snow was found.

Rutil assumed these were the same two men they had been following from the truck. The only difference was that these men had skis now and could travel much faster than they had before. The Spetsnaz also had skis with them, and found them undamaged in the back of the MT-L.

The trail of the men who had ambushed them led off to the north. The Spetsnaz put on their skis and started to follow. The chase was on. The Hawk was after the foxes.

Vasili Rutil could not figure out who they were trailing. It must have been just a small unit of soldiers who had the great bad luck to see them take down the weapons transport. Captain Rostov wanted there to be no witnesses to the action, so Rutil's response was clear. But just who were they? Certainly, they didn't act like regular soldiers. They moved well and fast over bad terrain, left as few tracks as possible, and were silent in their actions. These men were not panicking.

His own men were much better, of course. He had Master Sergeant Frolik, a great Russian bear of a man, leading his team. Even while he moved his great bulk through the snow up on point, Frolik did little more than puff his breath through his short black beard. For such a large man, he moved almost silently as he broke a trail for the rest of his unit.

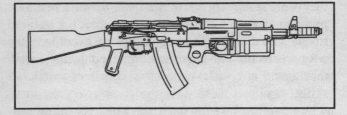

AK-74 with GP-25

Sergeants Adamenko and Nosenko were spread out on either side of Rutil. Their AK-74 rifles with GP-25 grenade launchers mounted under the barrels constantly swept the distance. All of the men maintained a firm fire discipline. They wanted to catch the unit they were chasing. It was only through a fast interrogation of the prisoners that they would be able to determine just who had seen them and if they had caught them all.

In the darkness ahead, the terrain took on a surreal aspect. The tundra was a mass of gray snow where the little available light reflected off it. The balance of the field was made up of sharp black shadows, broken only by the occasional boulder, brush, or stunted tree.

The men they were chasing were headed toward the sea, moving almost directly north, skirting the open areas of the occasional frozen lake or pond. They should have been heading to the southeast point of the island, Rutil thought. That was where the few buildings of the outpost were. Or at least directly south, where the lighthouse stood.

The path they were following helped confirm that

they were following a lost military patrol. They were probably just conscripts, Rutil decided. Confused troops who didn't even know they were heading in the wrong direction. If they were local conscripts, well, that would at least explain their excellent woodcraft skills.

As the Spetsnaz followed the trail, the snow suddenly spurted up in front of Rutil. The sound of the shot quickly followed the impact of the bullet.

As the entire squad responded to the shot as the well-drilled unit that they were, one word went through Rutil's mind: Sniper!

The shot sounded too heavy to be an AK-74, too loud to be an AK-47. It was their turn to have some bad luck, Rutil thought. They must have come across a military patrol that had the platoon's sniper with them. The SVD rifle they had would have a range advantage over the weapons of his own men. But he would have to see them in order to hit them, and the Spetsnaz did not make an easy target.

1250 ZULU
Grid Zone 38W, Coordinates LV890064
Morzhovets Island
Mezenskaya Bay
The White Sea

All of the SEALs knew that Mike Ferber had been right. There was no way all of them could get away together. At best, the troops following them would have caught them on the beach, since they had to stop and change into their underwater gear. There had been nothing else that could have been done.

Rockham and Fisher, Mike Bryant and John Sukov, had done the correct thing in leaving Mike Ferber and Ryan Marks behind them. And none of the men had ever committed an action in the Teams that had left a more bitter taste in their mouths. But even with the two SEALs staying back to cover the extraction of the rest of the crew, the situation was still very dangerous.

The remaining men of the patrol moved out very carefully, leaving as slight a trail behind them as they could. Their Teammates were making a great sacrifice to give them the chance to get away. And that sacrifice would not be allowed to go to waste. They moved out with Bryant on point. Fisher moved to the rear security position, where he could watch their back trail.

To keep their ski tracks to a minimum, Bryant guided the patrol over hard snow, where the wind had blown away the soft cover. Hard patches of ice were also used to hide their movement. The SEALs traveled carefully, quietly, and quickly.

Moving in the relatively protected position in the center of the patrol, Sukov maintained possession of the device they had recovered. With Fisher covering their rear and Bryant watching to the front, Rockham and Sukov kept an eye on either side of their route of march. Even with the care they exercised in moving through the tundra, they still covered ground fast. Within a short time they arrived at the shoreline of the bleak island.

In spite of the difficulty of following a magnetic compass in the far north, Bryant proved his skill in navigating by putting the patrol within a short distance of their original landing site. Their cache of diving gear was only a few hundred meters away. But the final approach to the site could be the most dangerous time for the SEALs.

If the cache had been discovered by the Soviets, a unit could be waiting in ambush for them to return to their equipment. But the Team also couldn't waste time in getting clear of the island. That point was brought home solidly by the grenade explosions the men had heard off in the distance. Ferber and Marks had made contact with the enemy, and no doubt successfully decoyed them off the trail of the squad.

Each man held his own counsel within himself. They all knew the dangers of the mission when they had first taken it on. You didn't get into the Team by being timid. These were men who lived on the sharp end of life. But the cost of such a life could give anyone pause.

The explosions and then, later, the few rounds of gunfire the men heard didn't mean Ferber and Marks had been taken out. The SEALs knew that their Teammates would have put up a very hard fight, paying a high cost for every minute they could buy for the rest of the Team to escape.

Nothing appeared disturbed at the cache site. The few telltales that had been left about—a branch set just so, gravel scattered so that stepping on it would drive it into the earth—were unmoved. One good piece of luck was that no new snow had fallen. And there hadn't been enough drifting of the snow already on the ground to cover the cache site.

As Sukov and Fisher stood watch, Rockham and Bryant dug up the waterproof bags their equipment had been cached in. All of the gear was in good shape, though the thin film of water that had been on the exposure suits was frozen. The suits were stiff but still very usable. A quick, thorough check of the bailout bottles showed plenty of pressure in the little tanks.

Rockham and Bryant removed their white overgarments and Gore-Tex parkas and trousers. With their warm outer clothing removed, even the mild wind cut through their clothes like razor-edged knives of ice. But they'd had to change because the immersion suits wouldn't fit over the heavy outer clothing. And only the suits would keep a man alive in the frigid arctic waters. Even then, the suits had to be worn over a dry set of acrylic pile underwear to keep the men warm during the SDV trip.

Stripping off their outer uniforms was hard enough in the arctic cold. Then on went the fresh acrylic-pile clothes and the uniforms again. Over this went the rubber dry suits.

The suits were stiff and hard to get in to, the ice crackling and snapping off as the men forced them on. Each man helped the other seal up his rig, pulling the large zipper across the back and shoulders until the immersion suit closed.

When Rockham and Bryant had finished suiting up and prepping their gear, they picked their weapons back up. Now it was Fisher's and Sukov's turn to get ready for the swim. While Rockham and Bryant stood watch, the other two SEALs prepped their gear. Finally, all of the surface equipment was packed into waterproof containers. With the area policed up and all signs of anyone having been there erased, the four men, facing the shore, backed into the water.

The sea ice was still too thick to break through. No ice had yet formed in the mouth of the swift-moving stream where the SEALs had first come up on shore just a few days earlier, but the cold water made itself known to the men as it rose along their legs. The immersion suits kept the water from flooding their clothes and quickly freezing the men to death. Still, the first clamp of the icy sea along their bodies made them gasp.

Holding their weapons with mittened hands, the SEALs ducked underneath the sea ice and moved out to where they had left their SDV.

For a moment the painful cold felt almost as if their flesh was burning. Then the pain faded, to be concentrated around their hands, mouth, and crotch. Moving through the water warmed their bodies up a bit, but each of the men had to make a concentrated effort to keep the mouthpiece of his air bottle clamped between numbing lips.

Visibility was almost impossible in the dark waters. It was only the glow of their compasses that made following any direction possible. Pulling soft plastic chem lights from their rigs, the men bent the tubes, shattering the glass capsules inside. With a quick shake, the chem lights began to glow with a soft greenish light, enabling them to see at least a short distance through the waters surrounding them.

Fisher and Bryant held small waterproof plastic boxes they had pulled from pouches on their rigs. The boxes gave out a quiet *beep-beep* as they picked up the very weak signal from the avalanche locator beacon inside the hull of the SDV. With their swim buddies at their sides, Fisher and Bryant led the way.

It was just a short swim to where the eight-boat rested on the seabed in all of ten feet of water. But even in the frigid waters, several of the SEALs felt like sweating inside their immersion suits. If the SDV couldn't be found, they would have to return to the island. Not the best prospect for their further survival.

Looming up from the black gloom around them, the hull of the SDV appeared, looking for all the world like the corpse of a small black whale. First there was nothing but indistinct wavering shadows, and then it was just there. The hull was still solidly moored in place on her two anchors. Fisher and Bryant quickly began checking over the exterior of the boat by the glow of their chem lights. With nothing appearing wrong to their searching eyes, the two men moved into the forward cockpit compartment.

Rockham and Sukov opened the rear compartment hatch and began securing the gear bags. The skis were untied from their equipment bags and again strapped to the sides of the boat. The few minutes all of the preparation was taking seemed like hours to the men. Both of them noticed the room available in the eight-boat now that two of their number weren't with them. But there was no time to dwell on their Teammates' fate. The waterproof container Sukov had packed with his rucksack, and the device it held, was carefully lashed to the forward bulkhead, where it would ride between the two men.

While Sukov secured the device, Rockham removed the Danforth anchors from the seabed. Even though the anchor points for the SDV would probably never be found, policing up even this small evidence of their visit was a detail not to be overlooked. Finally, Rockham and Sukov seated themselves in the rear compartment and switched over to breathing boat air. The regulators hissed and bubbled as the men drew in the cold air from the eight-boat's compressed air tanks.

In the front compartment, Fisher and Bryant had been busy prepping the boat and their own breathing rigs. The Mark 15s were still operational; none of the internals had frozen up. Now there would be enough boat air for the four SEALs boarding the SDV while still maintaining a safety margin. But that wasn't reflected upon as Bryant and Fisher prepped their rigs.

The heavy lead weight in the keel of the SDV was cranked along its threaded shaft to trim up the craft. Once the boat was moving, Bryant would finish trimming up the balance of the boat, making up for the missing weight of their two Teammates.

With the power eased forward, the five-bladed screw on the rear of the boat started to turn. With a short blast of compressed air, Bryant blew out a small amount of water from the ballast tank. The eight-boat rose from the bottom and began to move forward. As Bryant eased the power forward, the black hull of the SDV began picking up speed as it moved through the water.

As on the trip in, the trip away from the island was cold, dark, and long. The rear compartment of the eight-boat was not as crowded as it had been, but Rockham and Sukov had no reason to enjoy the extra space. And the environment was far too cold to hold any kind of physical comfort, no matter what their situation.

All of the men had connected to the boat's intercom system when they secured themselves into the SDV. But there was little in the way of conversation on the trip. No one had much to say to begin with. The boat still had to rendezvous and then dock with the parent submarine. Hopefully, that wouldn't be a problem. Bryant and Fisher conversed as they had to in order to drive and navigate the boat, but they both had a job to do and could concentrate on their work. Rockham and Sukov sat in the rear of the boat, in the dim light, quiet in their own thoughts.

The eight-boat continued back along the reciprocal heading of the course they had originally come in on. The reverse heading should take them exactly to the spot where they left the *Archerfish*. As the navigator, Lieutenant Fisher kept an eye on the inertial navigation system along with the other instruments that helped him determine their location. Bryant drove the boat and kept a careful watch on the magnetic compass and elapsed time clock to his lower left on the instrument bulkhead.

Being so far north, the men had little tide to contend with in the White Sea, so Bryant was able to make good headway while staying on a conservative rev count on the screw. Power had to be conserved. The silver-zinc batteries in their pressure cylinder were the best available, but the cold of the surrounding water could sap electrical power from the cells just as it drained the strength of the men.

Flexing and working their muscles helped fight the cold, but only to a degree. The long, cold trip was an ordeal that had to be endured. Just another example of why SEAL training was so hard. They had made it through worse in training, if not much worse.

Finally it was time for Fisher to contact the *Archerfish*. He sent out a call on the DV-811W UQC. For security, it had been arranged that the submarine wouldn't return the call. Instead, the *Archerfish* would activate the Burnett 512 pinger. When the men on board the SDV saw the indicators that the signal was being sent, they knew the *Archerfish* was nearby.

Captain North had been notified as soon as sonar detected the SEALs call on the UQC. After he authorized the pinger to be activated, the whole crew knew the SEALs were coming in. The level of activity on board the *Archerfish* began to rise. The DDS crew immediately moved into the hangar chamber to begin their flooding procedures. Like a sleeping leviathan of the deep, the *Archerfish* awakened.

Within minutes the big submarine had begun to stir and rise up from the seabed. With her great screw barely turning enough to give headway, the *Archerfish* moved slowly through the Arctic waters. Rising to just below the ice, the *Archerfish* maintained station and waited for the SDV to arrive.

Approaching the submarine with little difficulty, the

eight-boat came in over the stern, clearing the great screw and control fins by a safe margin. Communications between the submarine, the SDV, and the DDS crewmen inside the flooded hangar chamber were short and to the point. There was no need to put extra signals in the water for a passing Soviet ship to possibly overhear. The DDS crew had already opened the outer hatch and deployed the SDV cradle along its tracks on the hull of the submarine.

The DDS men disconnected themselves from the submarine and moved out to the approaching SDV. Catching up to the eight-boat, they attached a line to the nose of the small craft, secured it to the raised tether, and began lowering it down to the waiting cradle. The only light the divers had to see by was that from their handheld lights and the weak illumination from the open hatch of the DDS. But long hours of drill had made the men expert at their jobs. They could almost conduct a recovery operation blindfolded. And the dark, frigid water under the ice came close to duplicating being blindfolded.

The motor of the SDV was shut down and she was pulled down and secured into her cradle. With the recovered eight-boat now drawn in to the DDS hangar, the great outer hatch could be closed and sealed. Air bled from inside the submarine quickly forced the water out of the hangar, finally releasing the almost frozen SEALs from their confinement. Even with assistance from the DDS crewmen, the SEALs climbed out of the SDV with difficulty. The men were all dangerously close to hypothermia. But there was a much greater danger posed by the container Sukov kept hugged close to his chest.

Sukov finally relinquished his package, handing over the waterproof container to one of the DDS crewmen. Handling the package as if it held a live bomb, the crewman took it over to the inner hangar door leading to the access sphere, where Tinsley and Limbaugh, the two SEAL corpsmen, waited.

A large plastic bucket with a tight-fitting lid sat open on a tarp in the center of the access sphere. The package containing the sphere was passed through the hatch and immediately sealed into the bucket. Even the plastic tarp that had been placed across the deck to catch any drips from the package was folded up and sealed in the container.

Now the bucket was moved into the hyperbaric chamber on the far side of the access sphere. There, it was lowered into a plain plastic garbage can, surrounded by towels, and bleach poured in over the towels.

The garbage can itself was secured inside the hyperbaric chamber, tied in place so it couldn't move no matter how violently the submarine might maneuver. The lid of the garbage can was replaced and taped down. With the chamber door shut and sealed, the rest of the ship was as safe as it could be from the horror the SEALs had recovered from the island.

Before any of the SEALs could enter even the access sphere of the DDS, they had to be decontaminated. Procedures had been quickly established by Dr. Taylor and agreed to by both the captain and the corpsmen. The SEALs were hosed down with foul-smelling disinfectant from containers held by the DDS crew-men. Each man kept on his individual breathing equipment and simply held it up during the spraying.

Shivering from the cold that penetrated their dry suits, the SEALs were thoroughly sprayed, scrubbed with pot brushes from the galley, and then sprayed again. Now they had to face one final ordeal from the cold.

One at a time, in the tight confines of the hangar, they stripped off their dry suits and uniforms and stood naked in the cold and wet. The inner hangar door opened and the SEALs stepped through into the access sphere, again one at a time, and down into the submarine. Waiting for them in the submarine was a hot shower and fresh clothing. But now that the weapon had been secured, their first concern was for their Teammates back on the island.

CHAPTER 16

The threat of oncoming snow now appeared to be a false one to the two SEALs remaining on the island. In spite of what the average person might think, there actually was relatively little snow that came down in the Arctic regions. It was just that whatever snow did arrive stayed.

But the threatening snow clouds failed to dump their burden on the White Sea and the two SEALs crossing the small island below. The snow would have been welcome to the SEALs. It would have done a lot to help hide their tracks as they moved along.

And they could use every advantage in getting away from the men who pursued them. They still wanted to keep the Spetsnaz from going after their Teammates, but the rest of their patrol should have been in the SDV and long gone by now.

Now the SEALs would try and cut back on the odds against them. Marks was a trained sniper, and they would use that skill against the men behind them. They still did not have a solid idea as to just how many men made up the Spetsnaz unit on their trail. The vehicle they had disabled so far back had been able to carry over a dozen men, though they didn't know how many were in it or how many had escaped their ambush. But a shot from the darkness would help cut back on them no matter how many there were.

The two SEALs knew they did not have the firepower for a protracted firefight. It was a simple rule in the Teams: you didn't allow yourself to get into a position where you had to fight a much larger force without support. When attacked, a SEAL squad or platoon could put out a huge volume of fire, but only for a relatively short time. If the shock effect of the firestorm they put out didn't knock back a larger force, the platoon did what the two SEALs were doing now—it ran.

But for the moment, they were done running. They had come to an open area of little cover, a field with merely a scattering of glacial boulders and some short scrub brush. The snow cover was very thin and looked as if most of it had been blown away. It could be that they were looking at a frozen-over marsh or shallow pond, but that didn't matter. This time, instead of going around such an open area, Ferber wanted them to pass through it.

Holding up a clenched fist, he called a sudden halt to their forward movement. Turning to Marks, he crossed his arms in front of his chest, indicating an open area to their front. Then he pointed at Marks and held up his shotgun, aiming it at the clearing. Finally, he pointed at himself and then held his hand up to his eye, as if he was looking through a tube held in his fist.

The short, silent conversation consisted of Ferber

telling Marks that they had to stop because there was an open area in front of them. While Marks provided covering fire, Ferber was going to move ahead and recon the field.

Constant practice and drills had made the SEALs fluent in such silent communication. Their training together had also taught the men how each other thought in a given situation. Marks understood what Ferber wanted, and he held up his thumb and forefinger in a circled OK signal.

So Ferber quickly went out into the field while Marks crouched down, his M14 at his shoulder. It was a quick, fast ski across the field for Ferber, who gained the other side without incident. The skis had slipped across the frozen surface, the ice telling Ferber that his original thought about a pond had been the correct one. He raised his clenched fist and pumped it up and down rapidly. Marks caught the signal and got up from his position. Now he crossed the field while Ferber provided covering fire.

Once Marks was safely on the other side, Ferber looked back at the two sets of tracks they had cut across the thin snow of the clearing. Holding his hand up in front of his face, he gave the signal for a hasty ambush to Marks. Ryan nodded his understanding. Ferber pointed to the western side of the clearing, sweeping his arm in an arc that ended up pointing into the field, then he pointed at Marks and swung his thumb out in the direction of travel.

Again Marks nodded, and the two SEALs moved out. This time Marks was in the lead and he would be picking their firing position. In the treeline, really just a scattering of thicker brush and some stunted plants that could only generously be called trees, the snow was even thinner on the ground.

Marks moved along until he found a position that suited him. Holding up his hand over his shoulder, he signaled a halt. Then he held his hand out to the side, palm down, and slowly lowered it toward the ground. Then he reached down and undid the bindings on his skis.

Ferber read the message and got into position where he could cover Marks with his shotgun. He too had to remove his skis to get into a prone position to take advantage of the slight cover around the pair. The big black man settled in silently and watched their back trail with unblinking eyes.

1442 ZULU
Grid Zone 38W, Coordinates LV892084
Morzhovets Island
Mezenskaya Bay
The White Sea

Frolik was in the position he preferred most in a patrol, out front on point. Breaking the trail was no great difficulty for the powerful man. And he liked the freedom of movement being out front gave him. The men they were following were quality troops, much better than the usual cannon fodder the Spetsnaz went up against during training maneuvers. And their skill in trying to conceal their tracks was fair, but certainly no difficulty for the experienced master sergeant to follow.

But it would not do to underestimate his opposition. That mistake had been made when they faced the twice-damned mujahideen down in that mountainous dry hell of a country, Afghanistan. So when Frolik came up to the open field, he called a halt to the patrol.

The Spetsnaz had been moving in a normal diamond formation. Frolik was on point, while Rutil brought up the rear. Adamenko and Nosenko were out on either flank. When Frolik lifted his arm, bent at the elbow, with an open palm forward, Rutil immediately stopped. The two men flanking also stopped when they saw the signal.

Moving forward carefully, Rutil came up alongside Frolik. Silently, the sergeant pointed out the faint trail of two skis going out across the field. Then he pointed to the side where the marks in the snow indicated someone had stopped and crouched. The sniper in Frolik suspected a trap. That's what he would have done if he was in the place of their quarry. Rutil nodded.

Frolik pointed to Nosenko and Adamenko and swept his arm out in a wide arc, indicating the east side of the clearing. Then he pointed to Rutil and swept his arm out along the west side. Without waiting for an acknowledgment, the big Spetsnaz sergeant moved forward silently on his skis.

Vasili Rutil had long been used to the sullen attitude of the big master sergeant. That was just Frolik's way, and he always got the job done. But it had proved to be an easy attitude to misunderstand for a new officer coming into the unit. Once they had operated in the field with the very competent sergeant, they soon got over any resentment they might have felt at his attitude.

Actually, Rutil could not have felt more confident in the operation. The big sergeant was skilled and loyal, though most of that loyalty was reserved for Captain Rostov. The two Spetsnaz moved out around the clearing, silent and alert for any signs.

The Spetsnaz had only been a few hundred meters behind the SEALs during most of the chase. The SEALs knew they should have entered the clearing by now, unless they had turned off or lost the trail. Ferber was going to give the ambush another five minutes and then signal a pullout to Marks.

Marks lay still in the snow. His thoughts were almost neutral. Instead, he allowed his senses free range out into the surrounding environment. Any stimulus caused the sniper to bring cold concentration on whatever had caught his attention. Nothing else mattered. He had entered his bubble, that zone of concentration where he was just another part of the surrounding area. His self had been suspended, and no matter how uncomfortable he was, he wouldn't move or give any indication of being alive except for the slow lifting and lowering of his back as he breathed.

In his bubble, Marks could shoot very accurately in all kinds of environments. But he was not isolated from what went on around him. If anything, his sense of awareness had been increased. And that was what caused him to hear the sound.

There was a very faint crunching-swish approaching from the south. It was slight, enough noise for maybe two pairs of skis slipping through the snow. But it was a loud alarm bell to the SEAL.

Turning his head toward Ferber, Marks let go of his weapon's grip and pointed to his ear. Then he pointed his thumb off to the south. His hand had only moved inches, but it was enough to draw Ferber's attention. Seeing the "I hear something" signal, followed by the direction indication, Ferber concentrated on what Marks might have heard. Then he too heard the sounds of someone moving, very quietly, through the snow.

The Spetsnaz had suspected or sensed the SEALs' trap. Now the Team men had become the hunted again. Slowly, Ferber reached down to his web gear and removed another fragmentation grenade. Marks noted his partner's action and did the same.

As Ferber slowly pulled the grenade up to his face, he slipped his finger through the ring and pulled it free of the securing paper tape. Pulling the safety pin, he flipped the safety clip free with his thumb. Now the only thing keeping the fuze from igniting was the pressure of his hand on the safety spoon.

Marks had gone through the same procedure, arming his grenade and waiting for Ferber's signal. Ferber was facing toward the sound, and the slight noise had grown louder. Suddenly, the SEAL raised up and let fly with his grenade.

Rolling over on his back, Marks tossed his grenade

hard in the same direction his partner had. As the grenades left their hands, the safety spoons flew off with a slight metallic clang. The fuzes had ignited and the delays were burning down to an explosion.

With his senses tuned to almost the level of a hunting wolf, Frolik heard a metallic *ting* from the distance in front of them as if it had been a church bell ringing. The big Spetsnaz hadn't been to church ever in his life, but his response to the sound was immediate. He dove into the ground, flattening himself down against the frozen surface.

Rutil saw Frolik hit the ground in a sudden flat dive. Without thinking, he immediately followed the sergeant's example. The bindings of the skis the Spetsnaz had been traveling on popped free, releasing their feet.

In the dark Arctic night, two red flowers of flame once again bloomed.

If you were to ask which SEAL had thrown the grenade, neither man could have told you it was his. As soon as the explosive spheres had left their hands, the SEALs ducked down to cover themselves from the blast. One of the grenades went wide, but with the weird kind of luck that just happens in combat, the other grenade would have landed directly between the two Spetsnaz. The blast and fragmentation could have shredded the two men. But that never happened.

That wasn't the cosmic moment for the two Russians. The grenade hit what was one of the very few exposed slim tree trunks in the area and bounced away into the clearing. There, it exploded harmlessly, expending its deadly fragmentation in an expanding dome.

The two SEALs jumped to their feet immediately and withdrew from the area. Crouching, they ran to the north. What was far worse than the fact that they had missed nailing any of the Spetsnaz in the simple ambush was lying in the snow at their abandoned positions. The fastest way of moving through the snow was now lost to the two SEALs since their skis had been left behind.

Following the grenade explosions, Frolik and Rutil quickly raised their heads and pointed their weapons forward. If the men they were chasing initiated an ambush, they would find the Spetsnaz were ready to break through. But no fire came. Instead their ears were ringing from the sound of the two blasts.

Now Nosenko and Adamenko were leapfrogging across the clearing to come to the aid of their sergeant and officer. But there was no aid needed. Rushing forward, Frolik intended overwhelming any soldiers who were in front of them. But no one was there, only two sets of skis that lay in the snow.

Now the Spetsnaz had a real advantage. They could move much faster than whoever had abandoned their equipment. Tracks in the snow led off to the north. Whoever they were following was headed back in the direction they had originally been traveling.

Ignoring Rutil, who had been trying to follow the reflex actions of the big sergeant, Frolik went back to their own skis. Quickly slipping his boots into the bindings, he started back after his prey. The other members of his squad had to scramble to keep up with the silently moving sergeant.

Both SEALs were now in trouble, and they knew it. As they ran through the snow, it dragged against their legs. Each step drained at their reserves of strength. To slow up any pursuit a bit more, Ferber pulled out a gray-painted canister grenade from his harness. The single red band around the body of the grenade indicated that it was a gas canister; the red letters CS said its contents were tear gas.

Ferber pulled the pin and tossed the M7A2 upwind and to the side of their direction of march. Marks quickly did the same with an AN-M8 smoke grenade from his own harness. As the two grenades burned, billowing out their contents into the cold air, the SEALs moved forward. Now, when the Spetsnaz came up behind them, the smoke would help obscure their trail, and the tear gas would prevent their easy use of night vision devices.

On through the snow the SEALs ran.

Within an hour of escaping the Spetsnaz, the SEALs were moving under very different skies. A high altitude northern wind had blown away the cloud cover. Now there was an incredibly clear Arctic panorama above. No cities were within hundreds of kilometers to put their sky-shine up into the night air. The brilliance of the stars shone down like a dusting of diamonds scattered across a black velvet cloth. The view was almost too beautiful to be real.

Farther north, overhead, a natural light began to bloom. Ribbons of ionized air began to ebb and flow. The northern lights, the aurora borealis, began to build its sun-pumped pyrotechnic show. Blue and green flames of light rippled and flexed. Like living neon signs, they crept across the sky, moving south. And far below the glows, two figures moved across the ice.

Even for men in as great physical condition as the SEALs, the run across the ice was heartbreaking. The two warriors knew that if they kept up their present pace, they would soon be too exhausted to fight. The chase had been going on for several hours now. Allowing the Spetsnaz following them the occasional glimpse of their quarry, or a snap shot fired by the SEALs at a momentary target, had proved enough to keep the chase on.

The two SEALs had moved out onto the ice pack, and cover was sparse. They were only a relatively short distance from the island, and the only real cover that they had was the enveloping darkness all around them. The M909 night vision goggles they wore were all that kept them from slipping on a crack in the ice, possibly breaking a leg and certainly ending the chase. And they were already exhausting their last set of batteries.

Their pursuers would catch them in the open now, no matter how hard they ran. Their only chance was to turn and fight. There were no tricks left. The men behind them were sharp professionals and wouldn't fall for anything.

No SEAL had ever been taken prisoner. And neither Marks or Ferber intended to be the first.

A ridge of ice was nearby, and the two men scrambled to it and the cover it provided. The small Spetsnaz squad had spread out to make themselves a harder target, but the irregular line of men continued along the SEALs' trail like a pack of wolves. As the Soviets drew closer, the two SEALs made ready for their last stand.

Marks had a full twenty-round magazine in his M14, and a reload close at hand. Ferber was holding his Remington 870 shotgun at the ready. In his left hand, Ferber had several loose twelve-gauge rounds held between his fingers for a quick reload. As the first Spetsnaz crouched low and approached the ice ridge looming in the darkness, his boots crunched down on a piece of ice.

Sergeant Petr Adamenko never recognized the shadow that moved up from around the ice ridge in front of him. As his lips were forming a curse at the noise he'd made, a sudden flower of red-gold flame bloomed with a roar in front of him. The tube of his NVT-22 night vision goggles bloomed out from the muzzle flash and all Petr saw was a field of bright green, and then darkness. The heavy load of buckshot smashed into Adamenko's chest, the lead pellets narrowly missing several of the VOG-25 40mm grenades in his pockets. The man flew backward, his unseeing eyes wide with shock.

As Ferber blasted the Spetsnaz, he saw the man throw his arms wide, sending the AK-74 rifle he was holding flying. In the muzzle flash from his shotgun, Ferber registered that the rifle had a GP-25 grenade launcher under the barrel. As Ferber instinctively pumped his shotgun's action, racking another round into the chamber, Marks stood up and opened fire on the other Spetsnaz.

The *clack-chunk* of Ferber's shotgun being racked was drowned out by the roar of Marks's M14 firing on full automatic in short controlled bursts. Normally, the sniper only fired his weapon on semiautomatic with a single round per target. But there were times when full automatic fire definitely had its place. For the average shooter, firing a powerful rifle like the M14 on full automatic was simply a waste of ammunition. Marks's immense strength held the rifle steady and made the difficult action appear easy.

The heavy blasts of fire from the rifle were intended to hit as many of the Soviets as possible in the opening fusillade. In the dark, the spread of bullets would have the greatest chance of hitting a dimly seen target. But the Spetsnaz had each dropped or dove for cover at the sound of the first round.

The Spetsnaz were also disciplined warriors. Fire was immediately returned in the direction of the SEALs' position. The deep boom of the shotgun and loud roar of the M14 were matched with the staccato cracks of AK-74s. Only for a moment did the SEALs hold the advantage of surprise. But that instant quickly passed, and there wasn't anywhere to run to anymore.

1632 ZULU
66° 51' North, 42° 36' East
Off Morzhovets Island
Mezenskaya Bay
The White Sea

In the cold sea below, the *Archerfish* moved under the ice. With the SEALs and their SDV securely on board, the submarine was cruising slowly and preparing to move out.

"Sir," sonarman Peters called from his position at the BQQ-5. "I have a contact on the surface."

"Where and what, Peters?" Weapons Officer Tullerbee asked as he moved behind the sonarman.

"Distance about four thousand meters sir, bearing two-ten-zero degrees," Peters answered promptly. "It sounds like gunfire on the surface. It's coming through the ice muffled, but I'd swear I heard a shotgun."

With the microphone to the overhead MC-1 already in his hand, Tullerbee put it to his mouth and said, "Captain, this is Sonar."

"Go ahead, Sonar," North answered only a moment later.

"We have a surface contact on the ice," Tullerbee responded. "Peters says it sounds like gunfire sir, claims he can make out a shotgun firing. Bearing 210 degrees, distance four thousand meters."

In the control room, Captain North looked at Peter Danzig and Lieutenant Greg Rockham, standing near him. Rockham was covered in a blanket and had a hot cup of coffee in his hands, but he was still suffering from the exposure to the sea. Senior Chief Monday was also nearby.

"That can only be one thing, sir," Rockham stated firmly. "Ferber had a shotgun with him, and the Soviets don't use that weapon in combat. Unless you have some kind of lost hunter up there and a really bad-ass game warden, that's my LPO and sniper fighting it out."

"There's very little we can do from this position, Lieutenant," North said.

Standing at a firm position of attention, Senior Chief Monday asked formally, "Permission to take some of my platoon out of the lock, sir."

"Permission denied, Senior Chief," North replied crisply. "By the time you and your SEALs were geared up and got to them, it would all be over up there. Besides, we have no idea how close they are to open water. That's solid pack ice on the surface."

"That's correct, Captain," Danzig interjected sharply. "We have what we came for and more. Our mission now is to get the sample back with as little risk to this ship and crew as possible."

The Arctic waters surrounding the submarine were balmy and warm compared to the chill in Captain North's voice as he turned to Danzig.

"Do not presume to tell me how to operate my boat, Mr. Danzig," North said as he looked the CIA man straight in the eye.

Everyone in the control room sat or stood straight at their stations, attention riveted on their work displays in front of them. They had never heard such menace in their skipper's voice before. In the frozen tableau of the CIA officer and the Navy captain, the CIA man broke eye contact first.

Looking away, Danzig said apologetically, "Captain, of course I didn't mean to—"

"Of course you didn't," North said, contempt heavy in his tone. The rising fear in Danzig's voice had been obvious to all in the control room, even in the few words he had spoken.

"I have the lives of 130 people on board this boat in my hands," North continued. "And that includes yourself and Dr. Taylor as well. In addition, there's the not inconsiderable cost of this craft and the investment she represents to the people of the United States. I would have to weigh that, and the international incident it would cause if we were captured in these waters, against the lives of two brave men."

As North turned his back on Danzig, he locked eyes with the SEAL lieutenant. "Helm," North called out. "Bring her around to 210 degrees."

"Two-one-zero degrees, aye sir," Hackett answered from his position at the controls.

"Sonar, this is the captain," North said into the intercom.

"Sonar," Tullerbee responded immediately.

"Weps, I want an ear kept out for that surface contact. Give me range updates every five hundred meters and let me know when they are directly overhead. Keep an eye on the BQS-14 and sing out when we have thin ice."

"Aye, Captain," Tullerbee answered.

"COB," North called out to his chief of the boat. "Please go with Senior Chief Monday."

"Aye sir," Master Chief Richards responded.

"Senior Chief," North said to Monday. "Get me an armed gun crew from those SEALs of yours. Have them ready to go up to the bridge as soon as the sail breaks the ice. I want our radar signature to be as small as possible so we will not fully surface. You'll have to bring your people in through the bridge hatch, and it's going to be crowded up there. We will be out of here as soon as we recover your men."

"Aye sir," Monday replied.

As the SEAL chief left the control room, Captain North turned to Lieutenant Rockham. In a low voice, North spoke so just Rockham could hear. "I've been surrounded by the Soviets before, Mr. Rockham."

★ ★ ★
CHAPTER 17
★ ★ ★

The Spetsnaz were regrouping, organizing their approach to the SEALs' position on the ice. Though Marks and Ferber had been moving along the ridge, ducking from cover to cover, their room to maneuver had run out. The Spetsnaz were becoming more certain of the location of the two SEALs and were moving in accordingly. The next rush by the Spetsnaz would probably be their last, as they would overrun the SEALs' position.

"Well, looks like the Indians are going to win this one, Ryan," Ferber said.

"Yup," Marks said. "At least one of those rifles had a grenade launcher under the barrel. They'll probably drop a few rounds in here before they come in to mop up. Rotten bastards won't even give us a chance."

"Well," Ferber said, "it's not like we'd give one to them if the positions were reversed."

"You've got that one right."

"Doesn't look like we're going to have much of a chance of finding the sub," Ferber continued.

"Find the sub?" Marks said sarcastically. "You mean

you actually meant that bull back there? We're going to get to the North Pole and find Santa Claus before we find that sub."

"Well, if we do," Ferber continued quietly, "I'll put in a good word for you with the jolly guy. You can be his first black elf."

"He tries to make me wear one of those pointy hats and I'll eat his reindeer," Marks said with finality.

They heard a muffled pop nearby. Trailing sparks and hissing, a small dot of light climbed into the sky over the SEALs. With a pop and hiss, the magnesium flare ignited. Dangling from its parachute, the burning flare cast a blue-white light across the ice.

The two SEALs ducked into the shadow cast by the ice ridge and made ready for what would be their final stand. Ammunition was running low; their last reloads were in their weapons. But before a single shot rang out, a deep rumble and groan sounded through the area. Twenty meters from the SEALs' position the ice heaved up like a sleeper rolling underneath a bedsheet.

With a great cracking sound, the ice lifted up and broke in half, revealing the sail of the *Archerfish*. As the black sail lifted into the air, it resembled the growth of some gigantic malformed tree rising up from the soil. Chunks of ice rolled away from the metal as it moved. The huge fairwater planes on the sail, each the size of a garage door, were rotated so they pointed straight up and down to clear the ice. When the sail finally stopped its majestic rise, big chunks of ice were still balanced across the bridge on its crest.

Slowly, one of the large blocks shifted and then fell

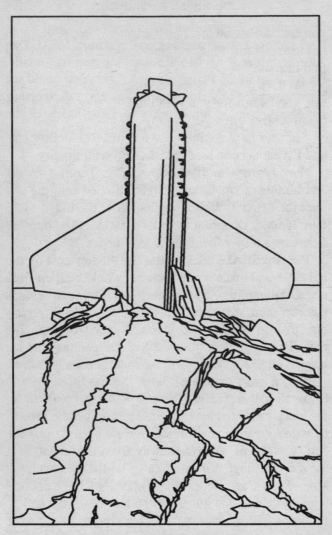

Sturgeon Sail through Ice

to the side. A deep-voiced *"Hoo Yah!"* bellowed out as the ice moved. Now standing on the bridge, SEAL Dan Able shouldered his M60E3 machine gun like a rifle. By the light of the Russian's own flare, Able could see his Teammates crouching on the ice and the Spetsnaz soldiers beyond them. Aiming over the heads of the SEALs at the ice ridge, Able poured out a blasting hail of fire toward the Spetsnaz positions.

Popping up on the opposite side of the bridge, Wayne Alexander had dusted off his hands from when he had heaved the big block of ice over the side. Picking up a matching M60E3 machine gun to the one Able was firing, Alexander added his firepower to that which was roaring out from the submarine.

As the two SEALs were firing, Senior Chief Monday stood up between them with a foot-long silver cylinder in his hand. He smacked the base of the cylinder with his other hand, the pop flare fired and threw a sizzling rocket high into the air.

The rocket soared four hundred feet up, arched over, and out popped another burning magnesium flare, dangling from a small white parachute. Now, with two burning flares in the air, the wavering shadows on the ice crisscrossed each other in dizzying patterns.

Still holding the empty tube of the PG 431 illuminating rocket in his hand, Captain Lieutenant Vasili Rutil watched the huge sail of the submarine rise up from the ice. Americans! But how? Why? They were his last thoughts before he was smashed down by the first burst of machine gun fire. Four of the 150-grain 7.62mm slugs stitched across the Spetsnaz officer's chest. Moving through the air at 2,300 feet per second, the pointed full-jacketed bullets scarcely slowed as they continued through Rutil's body to spend the last of their energy in the ice beyond.

Master Sergeant Frolik dove for cover as the next blast of slugs ripped through Viktor Nosenko, who had aimed his grenade launcher at the intruders. As his trigger finger convulsed in his death spasm, Nosenko fired his GP-25 Kastyor for the last time. The high explosive VOG-25 grenade sped out of the barrel and flew past the sail of the submarine. Arching high into the air, the grenade exploded unnoticed against the ice far off in the distance.

Frolik scrambled under some chunks of ice as the heavy fire of the machine guns, each spewing out ten rounds a second in short bursts, tore up the landscape around him.

"This bus is leaving," Monday shouted over the roar of the weapons on either side of him. "Would you two care to join us?"

The two SEALs on the ice had gaped openmouthed for a second or two as the huge black apparition had first appeared. Then adrenaline surged through their bodies as they realized they wouldn't be dying that day. They both scrambled up and ran for the sail under the cover of the machine guns.

The two M60E3 machine guns kept up a constant stream of fire, alternating from one gun to another as Ferber and Marks reached the base of the sail. Climbing up on the mounded ice, the two men took hold of the ladder grabs welded to each side of the structure.

As they climbed to the bridge, each man was grabbed and pulled unceremoniously aboard. Shoved toward the open hatch, the two men heard Monday's shouted, "Get below!"

When the two SEALs were safely climbing down the ladder inside of the sail, Monday shouted at his two machine gunners still on the bridge. With empty brass and steel belt links skipping across the metal deck, Monday bellowed, "Clear the bridge! We're getting the hell out of here!"

Able fired away the last of his ammunition belt and moved down the hatch. Keeping the Soviets' heads down until the last minute, Alexander blasted out one long last burst that emptied his weapon and left the barrel smoking hot. Then it was his turn to go down the hatch, being urged on by his chief, who would be the last one off the small bridge.

Monday slid down the ladder to the interior trunk of the sail and pulled down the hatch to the bridge, securing it in place with a spin of its central wheel. As he went through the second hatch into the hull of the sub, Master Chief Richards reached up and secured the hatch. "Hatch secured, sir," Richards announced. "All personnel aboard."

"Dive the boat," Captain North ordered in a quiet voice.

The sail of the submarine began to disappear back into the sea as the one, lone Spetsnaz survivor raised himself up from the ice. Frolik scrambled to where Nosenko's body lay and grabbed up the grenade launcher from the dead man's fingers. Before he could fumble a 40mm grenade from Nosenko's ammunition pouches, the huge sail was almost out of sight. As it disappeared, the broken ice settled back down over the water.

Frolik screamed with impotent rage at the escaping submarine. His English was functional, but he was anything but proficient. He had heard one word clearly, and that word kept ringing through his mind. It made no sense, focusing on one word, but it wasn't his native language. The sound of that voice was now a center for his hate and rage. He knew he would hear that SEAL's voice for the rest of his days.

"Bus!" he shouted. *"Bus!"* he screamed. And as he ran to the spot where the sub had gone down, he emptied his weapon in a long futile burst against the uncaring ice.

1632 ZULU
66° 35' North, 41° 38' East
Icebreaker *Volga*
Gorlo Strait
The White Sea

"Hawk Two, wait for pickup. Eagle out," Rostov said into the microphone.

Handing the headset and microphone back to Lieutenant Tsinev, Rostov was enveloped in an icy calm.

"Ivan," Rostov said, more gently than Tsinev had ever heard him speak. "It seems there has been a development on the island, or more exactly, on the ice to the north of the island. Some new and unexpected players have entered the game. They seem to have won this match.

"Our transportation from here will be arriving within minutes. I want us to be prepared to meet it. We shall have to carry on and make do with the men on board. See to it, please."

"Yes sir," Tsinev said smartly. The use of his first name had startled the officer at first. But the icy control and exaggerated courtesy in Rostov's tone had actually frightened the Spetsnaz lieutenant. In all of the years he had served with Captain Rostov, Lieutenant Ivan Tsinev had never heard him speak in such a way.

There was a white-hot rage flaming through his commander, seething just under the surface like magma waiting to blow out of a volcano. Whatever had caused that anger, he was glad it had nothing directly to do with him. Instant and unquestioning obedience seemed the safest course.

While Tsinev went off to talk to the Spetsnaz on board, Rostov went forward to the bridge of the ice-breaker. There, he found Feliks Belik playing at being a sea captain. The KGB man was a thug and completely without honor. But he had demonstrated his uses.

As Rostov further dampened the rage he felt inside at the loss of his men, he was calmed a bit by the thought that he wouldn't have to deal with Belik much longer.

Playing the part of the captain of a ship a little too much, Belik turned to Rostov as he came into the bridge.

"Welcome to my bridge, Comrade Rostov," Belik said, intentionally leaving off the honorific of the officer's rank. There could only be one captain aboard a ship, and Belik reveled in the thought.

Looking up at the KGB buffoon with dead, glacial eyes, Rostov ignored the slight and simply said, "Could you please meet me on the stern deck in a few minutes . . . Captain."

The pause before the rank was almost an unconscious one for the Spetsnaz officer.

Even the brutish KGB man had a certain amount of animal cunning. Without it, he wouldn't have lasted as long as he had before being torn apart and discarded by those stronger than him. And at that moment, the animal in Belik recognized the pale death raging in front of him. Like a lesser dog lowering his head and cowering before a great wolf, Belik grunted assent and turned away.

Later, on the stern deck, Belik faced Rostov and wondered just what the Spetsnaz officer could possibly want with him out there. The vehicle that had filled the deck was gone, and now there was simply a large clear space where it had stood. Someone had even stowed the tarp that had covered the vehicle, and all the loose lines were put away.

But before he could say anything, a growing noise in the sky drew his attention. It was not something particularly unusual, but it was certainly unexpected so far away from any bases.

"A helicopter!" Belik said with surprise. "But where could one have come from?"

"It's not here from a local base, my dear Feliks," Rostov said. "It came from an icebreaker out of Penchenga."

"A second icebreaker, but why? Your base at Penchenga is over six hundred kilometers from here."

As Feliks spoke, two men from Rostov's Spetsnaz squad came up, both men wearing their gas masks. Ignoring Belik, other than to cover him with their weapons, they snapped to attention. "The ship is secure, sir," one of them stated in a dull voice, muffled by his gas mask.

"Secure? Just what is going on here, Rostov?" the KGB officer shouted.

"Excellent timing, Ivan," Rostov said to his second in command, Tsinev. As he turned to the KGB officer standing red-faced and angry on the deck, Rostov casually rested his left hand on his belt through his open coat, his right hand now coming out of his coat pocket.

"Feliks," Rostov continued in an easy tone, "you could not have truly believed that I would trust my future and that of my men to a neoculturny buffoon such as yourself, do you? Your ship and crew of thugs are going to suffer an accident at sea, apparently due to some stolen munitions that were badly mishandled. Too bad the weapons will never be recovered from the wreck, if it's ever located."

Staring openmouthed and stunned, the KGB officer stuttered, "Accident?"

"Why yes. My men have secured your crew below. And I'm afraid they have all been exposed to the weapon, just as you have. But do not fear, they will not suffer. In fact, they'll never live to reach shore. A number of small scuttling charges will see to that."

His shock having worn off, the viciousness of a cornered animal rose up in Belik. "I haven't been exposed in any accident," he snarled. "And anything you do will take you with me."

As the heavy KGB man made a desperate lunge toward Rostov, his hand scrabbled for the Makarov pistol under his coat. The two Spetsnaz grabbed his arms, pinning them to his side. Feliks was as secure in the strong men's grip as if tied with a rope.

As the KGB man struggled, in a single smooth motion Rostov pulled his own gas mask from under his coat and pressed it over his face. His right hand came up with an odd, rectangular object hidden in his palm. Pointing the weapon at the struggling KGB man's face, Rostov pulled the trigger on his Piroliquid pistol. A slight pop and puff of vapor was all that came from the weapon, but the KGB man reacted instantly to the chemicals in the gas.

An involuntary gasp from Belik drew the deadly contents of the pistol shot deep into his lungs. Eyes bulging and face grimacing with pain, the heavy man suddenly hung slack in the arms of the Spetsnaz men.

"I do believe he's had a heart attack," Rostov said lightly.

His voice hardening into a commanding tone, Rostov addressed his men. "Now throw this garbage into the hold with the rest of the refuse. We have a helicopter to catch. Nemec, make certain that the charges are armed on the hatches, deck, and hull. I want us to be on our way in three minutes."

1710 ZULU
68° 12' North, 42° 27' East
Officer's Wardroom
USS *Archerfish*
The mouth of the White Sea

In the wardroom of the *Archerfish*, Chief Monday and Lieutenant Rockham were enjoying a short moment of peace. His excellent physical condition had helped Rockham quickly recover from the cold and exposure.

Lieutenant Fisher, Bryant, Marks, and Sukov were each reveling in a "Hollywood" shower, compliments of Captain North. Even on a nuclear submarine, fresh water was something not to be wasted. Normally, a shower on a submarine was a fast wetting down, soaping up, and then rinsing off. A shower much longer than a few minutes was considered a luxury, one Captain North felt the SEALs well deserved.

For Chief Monday and Lieutenant Rockham, their luxury for the moment was a hot cup of coffee. The coffee was especially good since it had been fortified with a liberal dose of brandy, prescribed for medicinal purposes by their own corpsmen. As the two men sat, Dr. Taylor entered the compartment.

"Congratulations, Lieutenant," Taylor said, "I understand you brought us back considerably more than just a sample."

"I just hope it turns out to be what you wanted, ma'am," Rockham answered as the chief sipped his coffee. "I don't see us being able to go back for any more for quite some time," the SEAL added with a quiet smile.

"From what I've heard so far, it certainly seems to be what Mr. Kondrachev described," Taylor said as she sat down at the table. "Not only getting us the sample of the weapon but also the means by which it is employed will mean a great deal to the analysts back home. I only wish I could have a chance to examine it now."

"You haven't seen it?" Rockham asked with a puzzled expression.

"No," she said, emphatically shaking her head. "Captain North refuses to allow the weapon aboard his ship. Or anyone to go in and out of the chamber it's locked in."

"Just as long as it's safe for the time being," Rockham said.

"Oh, I'm certain the device is safe, Lieutenant," Dr. Taylor said. "It's well strapped down in the decompression chamber. Your corpsmen, Tinsley and Limbaugh, sealed it in plastic and then covered it with towels soaked in several gallons of bleach."

"Now the whole mess is sealed inside another can," Chief Monday interjected. "If that shit can leak out, it'll be dead. The whites may not be the cleanest they could be on this boat for a while, but it is safe."

"Outstanding, Chief," Rockham said with a grin.

"That'll take care of it for now. Tell all the men to stand down except those on watch."

"Aye sir, it'll be a pleasure," Monday said with a wide grin of his own.

"Oh, and Chief," Rockham said as he reached into his pocket and drew out an aluminum tube with a screw cap and Spanish writing on the side. "It seems I managed to find this in my gear. I know you normally prefer your own, but I wonder if you'll do me the honor of accepting this?" And he held out the tube that could now be seen to be a quality cigar.

"Sir," the chief said, drawing himself up to attention, "it would be a pleasure."

As he accepted the proffered tube, the chief's eyebrows went up a notch in surprise. "A Havana, no less," he said with a very pleased smile. Withdrawing the thick, brown cylinder from the aluminum tube, the chief rolled it between his fingers and passed it underneath his nose. He drew in the aroma with obvious pleasure.

Slicing off the end of the cigar with his razor-sharp pocket knife, the chief clamped the cut end between strong white teeth. "If you will excuse me, sir," he said, "I will be getting back to the men. Hanging out here in officers' country just doesn't seem proper for a lowly chief."

"Excellent, Chief," Rockham said with a wide smile. "Carry on."

With a nod to Dr. Taylor, accompanied by a pleasant "ma'am," Chief Monday moved out of the compartment, taking his coffee with him.

"I've noticed just how much the submarine's crew defers to you SEALs," Dr. Taylor commented, "But I do hope that man doesn't intend breaking any regulation by actually smoking that thing on board. The air can be quite thick enough aboard this ship."

"It's called a boat, Dr. Taylor," Rockham said in an exasperated tone, "and there's not going to be any problem with smoke bothering your delicate sensibilities. The senior chief has no intention of smoking that cigar."

"Not smoke it," Taylor said incredulously, "an expensive and, as I noticed, illegal cigar?"

"No, ma'am," Rockham said, "he won't be smoking it. Chewing a cigar after an op is over is an old tradition of the senior chief's dating from the end of his Vietnam days. After the chief's last operation, he shared a cigar with a wounded friend of his at a field hospital in Hue City. Since it was a hospital, they never lit up. That's become kind of a tradition with the senior chief since then. He always has a cigar after an operation's over, but he never lights them. And by the way, I bought that cigar for the chief back during our deployment in Norway."

"That sounds like a waste of money to me," Dr. Taylor said in an irritated voice.

"Yes, ma'am. Well, I guess we sailors are a superstitious lot, and we do love our little traditions."